Breeze Spells and Bridegrooms

Breeze Spells and Bridegrooms

A Historical MM Romance

Fae & Human
Relations
Book 1

Sarah Wallace & S.O. Callahan

For those who are bold enough to look for magic in unexpected places, we hope you find it.

For Anna - Ruth

Sal Walk

CONTENTS

CONTENT WARNING

Breeze Spells and Bridegrooms is a cozy historical fantasy set in a queer normative world. As such, we hope our readers will find it a soft and light read.

But please note that this book will contain some on-page sex scenes and prejudice between human and fae communities.

TORQUIL'S TRIBUNE

Greetings fair folk and haphazard humans,

For those just now returning to London, welcome back.

Did you miss me?

The summer months are always horrifically dull for this humble writer. So little gossip to share. So little havoc to wreak. We are excessively relieved to see people return to the city. Whose lives shall be changed this Season? Who will fall in love? Who will flirt with scandal? We are, as ever, eager to find out.

It would appear that the Council for Fae & Human Magical Relations is preparing to convene soon, a whole month before the Season begins. To what do we owe the pleasure of a group of blustery and generally useless politicians to our fair city?

Well, the trend of human children receiving low scores on their Hastings Exam has started to reach a crisis point. Low scores have always been a potential result of the magical testing process, but high scores are becoming increasingly rare. As more and more humans with low Hastings scores reach adulthood, we are seeing the strain on society.

This strain is not caused by those with low scores but rather the way the world treats them. We are seeing more humans rejected for employment opportunities, or reaching the age of majority without a single marriage proposal. As human children are increasingly less likely to receive the desired score, this presents a troublesome insight into our future.

Will the Council find a solution? This writer considers it unlikely. But who knows? Perhaps a hero will emerge from the midst. It hasn't happened since King Arthur's reign but, as they say, nothing is impossible where magic is concerned.

Your esteemed editor,

Torquil Pimpernel-Smith

CHAPTER 1

ROGER

ROGER BARNES ATTEMPTED to surreptitiously dab at the beads of sweat gathering on his forehead. The Council's chambers were notoriously hot, even in the waiting area. Some blamed it on the heated debates between councilmembers, but Roger privately believed it had more to do with the placement of the wing. It really did get the most atrocious amount of sunlight. Convening in late summer did not help. Roger had a brief wistfulness for his family's country estate, wind gliding over the pond as he read by a tree. He shook his head and reined in his thoughts. Now was not the time for wistfulness.

He took his notes out of his pocket, reading them for what felt like the hundredth time. The paper was crumpled from so much handling. He didn't need to read the notes; they were memorized already. But he tended to get flustered when he was nervous, agitated, or generally upset. Quite frankly, flustered was practically Roger's natural state. He folded the paper, his hands shaking. He put it back in his pocket, decided he ought to have it handy just in case, and pulled it out again. He tapped the paper against his thigh, decided that wasn't doing the crumpled state any favors, put it back in his pocket, and clenched his hands together.

He could hardly believe he was doing this *again*. Was he really foolish enough to approach the Council for a third time? When an aide appeared at the door and beckoned him in, he concluded that, apparently, he was foolish enough to do just that.

He felt six pairs of eyes follow his progress into the room. He had always believed that an even number of members was an absurd way to assemble a council responsible for big decisions, but no one cared much about his opinions on the subject. In this case, his reasons for approaching were so important that Roger felt overwhelmed by it all. He walked up to the little stand and placed his wrinkled notes down, smoothing out the edges. He looked up and found his father sitting at the end of the table, the lowest-ranking human councilmember, and the only person in the group that did not thoroughly intimidate Roger.

"Well, Mr. Barnes," Councilmember Williams said, his gruff voice making Roger feel even smaller, "to what do we owe the pleasure this time?"

He tried to hide his wince. He glanced at his father, who gave him an encouraging smile. He cleared his throat, "Thank you, sir. I am grateful for the opportunity to approach this august company again." He could tell his voice sounded monotone as he read out the words, but monotone was preferable to stuttering, so he kept going. "I understand that the Council is working to find a solution to the…Hastings score…situation and I-I would like to offer a suggestion."

Councilmember Cricket glanced at Roger's father. "Yes," she mused. "I suppose you would have opinions about that."

"I hope it is different from your last suggestion," Councilmember Gibbs sniffed. "Your last one left much to be desired."

His last suggestion—to raise the testing age to eighteen—had been squashed in record time. It was a pity. He'd really believed in that one. However, he had been significantly less prepared when he'd approached the Council before. His reasoning behind changing the testing age had not been well argued. Perhaps now that the situation was more dire, the Council would be more willing to hear his solution—particularly when his notes were better organized.

"To be fair," Councilmember Applewood put in, "the previous suggestion was not a bad one. But I'm still concerned about keeping families in suspense about inheritance for so long. It would be very taxing, particularly for the children involved."

"Not to mention, valuable time would be wasted that could be spent training heirs in what they need to know," Councilmember Williams added.

"There is little need to go over the subject again," Councilmember Wrenwhistle said coolly. "I take it Mr. Barnes has a different solution in mind this time."

"Y-yes," he stammered. "My proposal is to move away from the Hastings Examination rubric altogether."

There was, predictably, a small clamor at that, mostly from the human side, although there were a couple of fae members who were chattering too. He thought they seemed approving. Councilmember Applewood was looking at him pensively, a smile playing upon her lips. Roger felt a small bit of hope at that expression.

Councilmember Wrenwhistle raised her hand to silence the rest. "That is certainly a bold suggestion. I am curious to hear your reasons and what you suggest as an alternative."

"Well," he said. "My reasons are fairly simple, I think. As you know, the success rate for the Hastings Exams are extremely low. Some families see children with no passing rates at all, even from powerful bloodlines. My belief is that the exam is too narrow in its observations to be properly conclusive. My proposal…" he shifted his notes so the second page was on top, "is to have a more nuanced approach to testing. We only test human children on one spell. If we were to broaden the scope of the examination, we could test multiple strengths at once. I do not have a new model fully drafted yet, but I believe testing for…er…spell force, as we currently do, but also control, attention to detail, and…creativity, would be beneficial."

Councilmember Williams scoffed. "Creativity? What, are we going to have students offer up poems to their examiners?"

"N-no, sir. But it would be good to see students apply principles of basic theory to multiple spells. Sort of a theoretical examination on top of a practical one."

"Roger," his father said, his tone mild, "what do you propose for the fae examinations? I agree that the Hastings Exam may be out of date, but it is the most standard form of testing we have and has the benefit of being the most closely aligned to the fae test, the Sciurus Exam. Both rubrics must be comparable."

"I admit, sir, that I do not have sufficient expertise on fae magic," Roger said. "I would cede to the Council on that part, although I do agree that it is an important part of the issue."

"It hardly matters what the testing rubrics are," Councilmember Cricket sneered. "*We* do not treat our children like outcasts when they don't do well. I think that is the most critical issue at hand."

His father looked like he wanted to agree but Gibbs was quick to say that the fae had issues of their own, thank you very much. Then Cricket argued that whatever issues the fae had, they at least protected their own, which could not be said for humankind.

Roger felt himself wilt a little. This was more or less what happened the first time. He had made a proposal that started a debate, then he had been unceremoniously sent out. It wasn't quite as bad as the second time, when he suggested the testing age be altered. That time he had practically been laughed out of the room. He supposed if he had to choose, watching the Council descend into its usual chaos was somewhat preferable.

Wrenwhistle raised her hand again. The arguing died down, primarily because the fae were pointedly respectful to their Head of Council and the humans couldn't very well argue against silence. When the bickering stopped, she was silent for a long moment before saying, "Your proposal has merit, Mr. Barnes." Roger felt hope kindle in his chest. "But," she went on, quickly extinguishing that brief feeling, "a vague idea is not sufficient. We will give you a fortnight to come up with a detailed proposal, a workable testing rubric. I agree that a comparable model for testing fae magic is necessary, although I appreciate your restraint in overstepping beyond your expertise." Roger thought this was said with some sarcasm but he tried to pretend it wasn't. "So for now we will give you an opportunity to present to us a real solution. Something we can act upon. If your rubric is accepted, we will assign a fae to work with you on a comparable rubric for fae magic. Are we in agreement, Councilmember Williams?"

Williams gave Roger a long look. Finally, he nodded. "I believe that will suffice."

"Thank you, Mr. Barnes."

Roger knew a dismissal when he heard one and wasted no time in leaving. Once outside the room, he allowed himself to process his warring emotions. On one hand, they actually listened to him and hadn't laughed at him outright! That was certainly progress. On the other hand…he had not figured on developing the testing rubric himself. He had ideas, but with his Hastings score, he didn't have much hope that those ideas would be taken seriously. However, his mind was already starting to churn. He strode down the hall, lost in thought.

CHAPTER 2

WYN

AT ONE POINT IN TIME, Wyn supposed, the grandeur of the Parliament buildings along the Thames had been quite impressive. Countless spires stretched from the rooftops, tall enough to pierce the dreary, unwelcoming clouds that often collected overhead. Inside, the ogive arches helped to draw attention to the stained-glass windows and intricate stonework on the walls and high ceilings. It was easy to let your jaw go slack at such a spectacle if you were not accustomed to it.

Wyn had been visiting his grandmother in the Council's chambers his entire life, effectively numbing him to the beauty of the architecture. Even the meticulously manicured grounds that surrounded him on his brisk walk along the cobbled path had long since faded into familiarity.

He followed his older brother Emrys up the steps, who touched his fingers to the brim of his hat as he greeted the doorkeepers by name.

"*Ugh*," Emrys moaned as they passed through the vestibule, quick to voice what both men were thinking. "Could it possibly be any hotter?" Even the echoing of their footsteps in the long hallway seemed muffled by the stifling air inside the building.

Wyn struggled to ignore the way the damp fabric of his cravat was sticking to his neck. His discomfort wasn't enough to make him regret wearing his thick, wavy hair long enough to reach his shoulders, though. It was a decision he'd made just recently, opting to let it grow out of the more fashionable cut that most men were wearing. His mother could protest many of his decisions, but this would not be one of them.

He took a deep breath and let it out in an impatient sigh.

"I just hope Grandmother makes this quick," he muttered, still trailing behind Emrys toward the chambers. There was an invitation to the first event of the Season with his name on it sitting atop his dressing table. He would wear something far less stuffy than his high boots and heavy coat. With any luck, the evening would dissolve into a more private situation that required no clothing at all.

"When has she ever been known to do that?" Emrys asked with a faint chuckle. "Although, maybe if I show her the way my new clothes are being ruined with sweat stains, she'll take pity and grant us leave."

As they approached the final corner in the maze of window-lit hallways, someone called Emrys' name. Both men turned to look over their shoulders and discovered the familiar smile of Keelan Cricket, one of Emrys' closest friends and the son of another councilmember.

"Go ahead, I'll catch up with you in a moment." Emrys left no room for argument as he pivoted and took off in the direction they'd just come. Wyn rolled his eyes, knowing that was the exact opposite of the truth, and turned the corner—directly into someone else.

"Watch it," Wyn hissed, taking a steadying step backward, trying his best to maintain appearances in case his brother or anyone else had seen. Upon realizing who had run into him, his annoyance flared. Of *course* it would be Barnes getting in his way.

"Apologies," the shorter man mumbled, his hands doing a ridiculous little dance, as though he couldn't decide between reaching for the scraps of paper he'd dropped on the floor or fixing his spectacles that had fallen askew after crashing into Wyn's chest.

Wyn crossed his arms and watched as Roger bent to pick up the papers from where they had fluttered to their feet. His mouth curled into a faint smirk.

"Had to draw yourself a map to find the exit, did you?"

Roger righted himself with a puff of an exhale and quickly folded his papers away into a pocket, fixing his spectacles with an indignant glare. Wyn's gaze slid down to the man's shoes and back up again. Barnes had never known how to dress for his plump figure, nor find a suitable color palette to match the light brown of his skin. Such a pity.

"I've been here just as many times as you, Wyndham," Roger said. Wyn bristled instantly at the casual use of his name. "I know my way around—"

"You will call me Mr. Wrenwhistle," Wyn ground out with a slow emphasis on each word, his jaw tight. The man was a year older than he was, but the fact remained that he wouldn't tolerate the disrespect of being addressed by his first name in public, especially by the likes of Roger Barnes. They might've known each other since they were children, but that did not make them friends.

He felt it then, the familiar tingling, and Wyn knew his magic was seconds away from begging to be set free. It was an issue he'd dealt with for as long as he could remember. Returning to London was most stressful for a fae who struggled with being surrounded by disorder. For Wyn, his melancholy was exacerbated by the stress, resulting in his magic demanding to be felt as his emotions flared.

Wyn drew in a deep, silent breath and held it, eyes sliding shut. He focused on what he could feel. The growing ache in his chest from holding the sweltering air in his lungs. The perspiration clinging in some unmentionable places. The cool, smooth metal of the rings on his fingers. He exhaled as these thoughts filtered through his mind, quelling the surge of emotion that had dared to unwind him right there in the hall.

"Are you…feeling quite the thing?"

The sound of Roger's voice, laced with just enough concern to sound sarcastic, washed away every speck of control Wyn had just regained.

"Do get out of my way," he said brusquely, stepping around Roger and continuing down the corridor.

The heels of Wyn's boots clacked harder than necessary all the way to the final door that separated him from the Council's chambers. He slammed through it with a flourish, coat whipping about his hips as he went. Without needing to read the nameplates hanging outside the offices, Wyn approached his grandmother's and let himself in.

Iris Wrenwhistle lifted her gaze from the papers on her desk, a pleasant look of surprise on her face despite the fact that she'd been the one to request his presence. This was the way she always regarded her grandchildren. She treated every interaction with them like a small gift.

"There you are, darling," she said with a warmth that helped wash away the last of Wyn's twist of frustration. "Where is your brother?"

"Chatting up a friend," he replied. The chair by the window had always been his favorite. He plunked into it like a sullen teenager and crossed his arms over his chest, eyes cast to the floor.

"Ah, yes. It's good to be back in London with everyone, is it not? A little early, but we've got important work to do."

I hate it here, he wanted to tell her. *I hate it more than anything.*

Wyn wanted to be back in the country where he could enjoy the fresh air and sunshine and nights under the stars without the constant bustling and noise of high society. Somewhere he was not continually reminded that, despite his magical aptitude, he was inferior in the eyes of others thanks to the score he'd been given when he was just a child.

"It's good to be back," he agreed, though the lie burned hot on his tongue.

CHAPTER 3

ROGER

ROGER MADE it back to his rooms in one piece, although it seemed rather a near thing. The collision with Wyndham Wrenwhistle unsettled him, and he had already been unsettled enough as it was. "*Mr.* Wrenwhistle," he whispered under his breath. He was almost relieved he could expend his energy on an emotion other than anxiety or the dread of letting people down. Irritation with Wyndham and his particularly aggravating flavor of contempt won out in the forefront of his mind. He slammed his notes down on his desk and tried to ignore the way a pile of papers toppled to the floor. It didn't matter anyway.

He collapsed into a chair and let out a long breath. At least he hadn't made a complete cake of himself that morning. At least the Council had heard him. At least—well, he tried not to think of the last thing on his mind: the prospect that generations of humans were depending on him. He took off his spectacles and rubbed the bridge of his nose. The prejudice against those who had scored low on the Hastings Exam was not a new phenomenon, but it had steadily grown into a normal social attitude. He had been one of the lucky ones.

Many humans, once they reached the age of thirty and came into their majority, had been kicked out of their homes, deemed burdens by their own families. The poverty rate was steadily increasing as more and more low-scoring humans were left with few choices for their futures.

Roger's scores had not been high, but his parents continued to support him, even though he had no career and no marriage prospects. He was grateful for that—of course he was—but he never liked how often people reminded him how grateful he *ought* to be. As if treating a child like a person rather than a tool was so very laudable. It was good, it was kind, it was decent, he *knew* this. But it also shouldn't have been considered rare. And parents like his were becoming more and more rare. As such, he was determined to help others who were less fortunate than he, and hopefully resolve the situation before it became even more of a crisis.

His manservant Notley—an impressive combination of valet, cook, and butler—knocked on the door and brought in a note as well as the one society paper Roger bothered to subscribe to.

"A reply is expected, sir," he said, handing over the note first.

The note was from his mother. He heaved a sigh and opened it: a reminder that she had accepted an invitation to a dinner party on his behalf for that evening. He would have vastly preferred to stay at home and get started on his project—his new *Council-assigned* project—but he knew better than to go against his mother's social plans. His father would likely want to talk to him about the proposal anyway.

"Be so good as to inform her that I will be there," he directed.

Notley nodded and left the room.

The society paper, *Torquil's Tribune*, was mostly a small rant about the ongoing Hastings score issue. It wasn't terribly surprising; Pimpernel-Smith was well known to be progressively minded. Though they were careful to avoid siding with fae or humans on any topic, it made sense that they would take up the cause of those facing prejudice in this case. Roger imagined briefly that he might be the potential hero in the situation. The thought made him feel warm. He attempted to squash it. He stared at the paper for a long time. Perhaps it would help to have the public on his side? The Council wouldn't care if he shared the news; after all, if he failed, he was the one who would look like an idiot. That thought gave him pause. He hated looking like an idiot. It seemed to happen all too often.

He thought of Wyndham Wrenwhistle again. How he'd love to wipe that smug expression off the fae's insufferable face. *All right*, he reasoned, *it* *was a beautiful face, what with his aristocratic nose, his flawless fair complexion, those fae green eyes...*He'd love to wipe that expression off the fae's impossibly beautiful, annoyingly smug face. He nodded. There, that was a fair assessment. With that in mind, he went to his desk and wrote out a letter to Torquil Pimpernel-Smith. Before he could talk himself out of it, he rang for Notley, had the note sent out, and requested an outfit be picked out for dinner. Then he sat down at his desk and began writing down ideas.

The afternoon went by in a blur. Before he knew it, Notley was knocking on his door to tell him it was time to get ready. He was dressed in his best suit—which was, unfortunately, in last Season's style. He tried his utmost not to need his parents' money too much. They were generous, but he knew himself to be a burden, and he didn't like to push that generosity too far.

When he finally arrived at the St. Clairs' party, he sought out his parents immediately. His mother tutted and gave his cravat a tweak.

"I do wish you'd let us take you shopping, dear," she chided.

"Good evening, Mother."

She smiled and kissed his cheek. "Your father says you did very well today at the Council."

"I think Iris was impressed," his father chuckled. "It's very hard to impress that woman."

"She could have fooled me," Roger muttered.

His mother fussed at his cravat a bit more and then shooed him off.

He wandered the room until he found his best friend in the crowd: Anthea St. Clair. She smiled when she saw him approaching and then kissed his cheek.

"If I'd known you were coming, I'd have worn my green dress."

"Don't be daft," he said. "You look perfectly fetching and you know it."

She laughed.

"Anyone of note tonight?"

"The Prince of Petulant Beauty is in attendance."

He frowned in confusion. She indicated with her head to the center of the room. He looked at where she had discreetly pointed and groaned. Wyndham was there, because of course he was. And he looked outrageously beautiful in an embroidered satin waistcoat in robin's egg blue, because of course he did. His light brown hair was combed back to show his pointed ears and the colorful waistcoat brought out the green in his eyes. He always looked infuriatingly perfect. Roger had always found the gentleman attractive, even if that attraction was merely of the aesthetic variety. He tried to look away but couldn't bring himself to ignore the way Wyndham's cravat made his jaw look particularly sharp, or the way his smile was half-mocking, half as if he was keeping some sort of secret.

Then Wyndham turned and met his gaze. He cocked an eyebrow and Roger, blushing, looked away hastily.

"It would be so convenient," Anthea sighed, "if these fae looked less hauntingly beautiful. I could hate them all so much more."

While he agreed with her, he knew it wasn't wise to voice such opinions, even to a friend like Anthea. "To be fair," he said, "they have their virtues, like anybody."

"Yes," she said, "and they're actually correct about the whole Hastings scores situation. Perish the thought."

"You know sometimes you sound like *Torquil's Tribune.*"

"Sometimes Torquil is the smartest person in town."

Roger nodded his agreement and then looked around the room. "Quite a crush for this time of year, isn't it?"

"Yes, Mama was quite pleased with herself for getting so many acceptances to her invitation. I suppose it helps that she invited half the Council. I told her two dozen was a rather obscene amount for a dinner party and that ten is a far more respectable number, but she would have none of it."

Two dozen meant he was unlikely to be paired up with Anthea for dinner. He thought longingly of his quiet rooms, his messy desk, and all of the work he had to do.

He was snapped out of his thoughts when people began trickling into the dining room. Anthea was collected by Lady Fitzhugh. Roger waited impatiently for his own escort. His parents strolled past him and he looked to see who else was left. To his horror, Wyndham strode up to him.

The fae's expression was one of absolute disgust as he held out an arm. "I can only assume I have angered our hostess tonight. Be so good as to not make this any more painful than it has to be."

Roger took the offered arm. "And how do you propose I do that?"

"Preferably, keep your mouth shut."

Roger braved a glance at his companion. "Are you always such a scintillating dinner partner?"

Wyndham helped him into his seat and then leaned over to murmur in his ear, "Think I'm scintillating, do you?"

Roger couldn't help the blush that crept over his cheeks. He quickly distracted himself by unfolding his serviette. "Decidedly not."

Wyndham's smile was mocking as he sat next to him. "So you always stare at people with your mouth open? You must be invited to all the best parties."

Roger glared at him. "My mouth was not open. And besides—" He broke off as he didn't know what he had planned to say.

Wyndham's smile widened. "Besides?"

"Besides, I was looking at your waistcoat, and not you at all. What sort of person gets their clothing made in that particular shade of blue?"

"One with taste," Wyndham replied, taking a sip of his wine. Roger tried not to notice the other man's lips on the glass. They were so well-shaped. It was a pity they so rarely said anything worth hearing. As if to prove Roger's thoughts, Wyndham went on, "and I am hardly interested in your opinions on fashion, Barnes." He looked Roger slowly up and down, and the corner of his lip curled slightly. "Just how old is that suit?"

"Some of us," Roger said, trying to calm his temper, "understand the value of frugality."

"I suppose you'd have to with prospects like yours. Remind me again of your Hastings score?"

Roger's hand shook as he reached for his own glass of wine. Much to his annoyance, he could think of nothing to say in reply.

CHAPTER 4

WYN

THERE WERE NOT ENOUGH FERMENTED grapes in all of London to make for a pleasant evening dealing with Roger Barnes. Wyn knew because he had lost count of how many glasses he'd consumed before they'd even reached the meat and vegetables course. By the time the meal was over, Wyn had accepted his fate of being completely useless come morning. He had a sneaking suspicion that his evening would wrap up quite the same if he continued on the way he had been. He decided to make the most of it while he still could.

"Dance with me, sister," he purred, extending a hand to Aveline as the excessively large party made its way into the great hall for the second half of the festivities. This would be more tolerable than sitting around forcing conversation with nowhere to escape.

"Why, of course," Aveline smiled, accepting her brother's invitation as they took the floor. Both of them were eligible, but she was the only one who had ever truly been interested in looking for a partner that lasted for more than one night. The least he could do was show her off and support her romantic endeavors.

"I couldn't help but notice your grimace throughout dinner," she said with a shimmer of delight in her voice. Wyn suppressed a groan as they performed the steps of the dance with ease, as simple as breathing. The music was bright and elegant, filling the room with energy all the way to the ceiling. He pointedly ignored the weight of everyone's eyes on them.

"I'll be sending Mrs. St. Clair a token of my appreciation in the morning for her deliberate assistance in my misery," he assured her.

"Some wine, perhaps? It appeared as though there was a leak in your glass. Certainly you'd do well to replace a small portion of the reserves you've drained this evening."

Wyn laughed dryly. "I was thinking more along the lines of something hot and fresh in a bag from yours truly." Aveline's delicate brows pinched, and then an expression of horror crossed her face as Wyn gave her a wink and let her go, strolling toward one of many sets of double doors along the far wall that had mercifully been thrown open to allow for a breeze.

As much as he enjoyed the banter he and his sister always shared, running into Barnes twice in the span of a few days had well and truly done him in. He needed some air. The man was exhaustingly boring, always falling back to his same old spiel about the welfare of the poor talentless humans that nobody wanted to hire or marry. What did Wyn care about either of those things? His family was one of the wealthiest and most formidable in all of London and had generations of magically powerful children to prove it, himself included.

He paused with his hands on the railing of the low balcony. Throughout their schooling, Barnes had an answer to every question, eager to share what he'd absorbed from whichever book his nose had been stuck in. When it came to application, however, his magic was average at best. His nervousness in front of the other children left him clumsy and forgetful, making him far too easy to mock and ridicule.

Much to his chagrin, Wyn realized that he and Roger Barnes had ended up in a very similar place in life. Neither of them had scored well enough to inherit. Both of them remained bachelors, though he did not know if Barnes remained so by choice. The difference was that Barnes had yet to accept his fate.

Wyn let out a huff and made for the stairs. It took only one lap around the gardens to find what he'd been searching for.

After a deep breath, the tingling of his magic stretched from his core to the tips of his fingers and the soles of his feet. The curtain of soft lavender wisteria hanging from the pergola overhead swayed and stretched on a gentle breeze, thickening and growing to cover the open sides and enclosing Wyn in his own private sanctuary. It was the first time all evening he was able to relax.

At the snap of his fingers, a collection of fairy lights burst to life, casting a soft glow across the space. It was just enough for Wyn to find the garden pillows piled decoratively in one corner. After pulling off his boots and removing his stockings, he ran a hand through his hair and reclined on his makeshift pillow bed with his toes in the lush grass and waited.

When a hand swiped roughly through the hanging vines, Wyn gazed up at his visitor with a mild grin. Sage Ravenwing was rather pettish, and Wyn was prepared for his whingeing before it began.

"Show me to the tasteless fool who puts *seven* pergolas in their back garden," the man complained as he forced his way through the purple petals. "You might've been more clear in your note on which one you meant to use."

"You found me regardless," Wyn mused. "And the paper was very small. How did you expect me to fit directions on a scrap such as that?" He watched as Sage removed his shoes and set them aside before he sank to his knees between Wyn's and leaned over him to press their mouths together.

By the time they broke apart, several articles of clothing had been untied, unbuttoned, unwrapped. Wyn let his head fall back against the pillows with a soft moan as a trail of kisses were pressed down his freshly exposed neck and chest.

He'd missed this. Not necessarily with Sage, although he usually enjoyed the man's company, and he was a competent enough lover. But he'd missed the spontaneity and excitement of a late night fling. It always brought a delicious, honey-sweet surge to his magic that was difficult to find elsewhere, and was depressingly impossible to recreate solo, though he'd spent years trying valiantly to prove otherwise.

When Sage's hands started to wander beneath Wyn's clothes, the fairy lights dancing lazily above them began to glow brighter, flickering with the steady uptick in Wyn's pulse.

"Those damned lights are so distracting," Sage muttered as he kissed beneath Wyn's ear, one forearm supporting his weight while the other hand disappeared into the front of Wyn's trousers.

"You're just jealous you can't call them as I can," Wyn whispered back.

He removed his hands from where they were tangled into Sage's silky black hair and snapped with both this time. The air around them lit up like a cloudless night, with twinkling stars speckled as if they'd been placed by an artist. And hadn't they?

"Showoff." Sage kissed him deeply then, and just as Wyn was starting to lose himself to the pleasure, there was a rustling from beyond the temporary walls of their sanctuary, and in tumbled Wyn's hapless dinner partner.

Roger looked around at the small space in a panic, his eyes wide behind the rims of his spectacles. He panted as though he'd sprinted from wherever he'd come from.

"Do you mind?" Wyn asked flatly, some of the fairy lights blinking out or drifting away as his magic settled a bit. When Roger finally looked at him, a new wave of emotion crossed his features, and even in the low light Wyn could see the way he flushed. There went his jaw falling slack again, just as it had earlier when Wyn had caught him staring from across the room.

"I-I…I thought there was a fire of some sort," Roger managed.

"You've well extinguished that," Wyn replied, glowering now at the fact that Barnes was still standing there. When Sage finally removed his hand from Wyn's trousers, there was a squeak from their intruder and he left without another word.

Wyn sighed heavily and collapsed back against the pillows, a hand coming up to press several fingertips to his forehead. There was the headache he'd been expecting. When Sage went in for another kiss on his neck, Wyn slapped him away halfheartedly with the back of his hand. Sage made a sulky sound and gave one last feeble attempt to rekindle what they'd had going. Wyn scoffed and shoved him aside. Maybe he hadn't missed this as much as he'd thought.

TORQUIL'S TRIBUNE

Greetings faint folk and hopeful humans,

The Council for Fae & Human Magical Relations (which should really consider changing their name, if only for my sake—ink isn't cheap!) is apparently entertaining a proposed solution for the Hastings score issue. A source close to the Council has reported that the proposal involves a complete change in the examination rubric, which would likely be a welcome solution to many. We cannot pretend high hopes for its success, but we are glad someone is thinking creatively. And we're not a bit surprised that the someone in question is not on the Council.

With the Council back in London, events are beginning to trickle in, with the first event last night at the St. Clairs' residence. This is a gossip column after all, and our refined readers come here for all the latest news, so:

According to sources, the event was a success with over two dozen guests. Personally, we'd attribute that more to Mrs. St. Clair's savvy timing and less about her hostessing skills, but we'll see if this social success was a flash in the pan or if Mrs. St. Clair is on the verge of a rise in popularity.

Miss Anthea St. Clair reportedly looked fetching in a rose hued gown. Those of us who have seen Miss St. Clair are not surprised to learn that she was one of the most beautiful people at the event. She was seated next to Lady Fitzhugh and rumors are already circulating about how well the two ladies seemed to get on. Could this be the spark of romance?

Sparks did not fly, however, on the opposite end of the table. Mr. Wyndham Wrenwhistle, arguably the most attractive and irrefutably the least endearing of the Wrenwhistle siblings, was seated next to Mr. Roger Barnes, a gentleman who can best be described as aggressively average. One might suppose they'd be a match made in heaven, particularly with mutual ties to the Council for Fae & Human Magical Relations. However, sources say that the gentlemen spoke briefly before the fish course and then did not exchange words the rest of the meal. We're sure many would like to lodge a complaint for the insufferable lack of drama.

Mr. Sage Ravenwing was notably absent for the later half of the evening, although where he disappeared to and, more importantly, who he disappeared with has yet to be discovered.

This writer wishes there was more exciting information to impart but, alas, the first social event was not particularly thrilling.

Your esteemed editor,

Torquil Pimpernel-Smith

CHAPTER 5

ROGER

ROGER HAD A HEADACHE. At least, that was the best term he could think of for the painful memory of crashing into the glowing flowers to find Wyndham Wrenwhistle half naked and hair mussed. Someone was kneeling between his legs and Roger found it embarrassing that he had paid so little attention as to not even know who the person was. He hadn't been able to take his eyes off Wyndham. And then he couldn't take his mind off the incident as he attempted to work on his proposal.

Roger gave up and rang for tea, even though he had barely been working for an hour. Halfway through the teapot, the latest Torquil column was delivered. Roger winced at the description of himself as "aggressively average" although he supposed there were worse descriptions. He didn't quite know what to make of the comment that he and Wyndham should be "a match made in heaven." He was mildly amused to have Pimpernel-Smith fill in the blank as to who had been between Wyndham's legs. Roger half-considered telling the writer just that, but then dismissed the idea. After all, Wyndham would know who had leaked that little detail.

He reread over the paragraph that mentioned his proposal, pleased that his prediction was correct and that Pimpernel-Smith was more or less on his side in the matter. Although the lack of optimism was hardly encouraging. He sighed, drained his teacup, and got back to work.

Roger worked all through lunch and was prepared to work until dinner when another note from his mother was delivered, inviting him to come to tea as soon as he received the note. He glanced at the gossip column, the likely culprit behind the summons.

The Barneses resided in Mayfair, as most respectable people did. Their house was not on one of the most fashionable streets, but it was close enough to evade censure. The butler took his hat and coat and led him into the sitting room, where Roger froze on the threshold.

His mother had invited the Wrenwhistles to tea as well. Mrs. Wrenwhistle was sitting next to Roger's mother with a carefully polite expression. Aveline was sitting in the second best seat, cheerfully accepting a slice of cake. And there was Wyndham, sitting on a sofa that was conspicuously half-empty. Wyndham's eyes narrowed. Roger wished he hadn't left his rooms.

Roger's mother sprang forward and ushered him over to the sofa. "We were just talking about your proposal to the Council, dear."

"Yes, your mother says that you have a solution to save all those poor humans," Mrs. Wrenwhistle said in a somewhat affected tone, suggesting she wasn't all that interested but wanted to sound invested.

Roger took the offered cup of tea from his mother and glanced at Wyndham, who was pointedly examining his own fingernails. "Well," he said, returning his attention to Mrs. Wrenwhistle, "I'm afraid it isn't fully… um, that is...the Council wants a detailed plan, but I only have a vague notion in my head. So I expect to be very busy preparing everything."

"It is good to see young people with a passion for such things," Mrs. Wrenwhistle murmured, her eyes flicking to her son. "I understand this is a topic of particular interest to you."

"Yes, ma'am."

"Seeing that you received a low score, yourself."

He felt his face flush but he nodded.

She smiled at his mother. "It does bring me a sense of peace to know that there are some human parents who take proper care of their children."

Her expression suggested she expected him to reply. "Yes," he agreed hastily. "I was certainly most fortunate."

Mrs. Wrenwhistle smiled beneficently at him and then returned to conversation with Aveline and Roger's mother, leaving Roger alone to entertain Wyndham.

To his surprise, his companion spoke first, his voice low. "I think '*aggressively average*' might be my new favorite description of you."

"Better that than '*least endearing.*'"

"Speak for yourself. I have no interest in endearing myself to fae-humans like Pimpernel-Smith."

"Oh, you're a snob. How shocking. I daresay you'd rather endear yourself to people like Mr. Ravenwing."

Wyndham's lip curled. "Funny. I hadn't thought you'd even noticed him."

"I couldn't help but notice him."

He sighed. "My word, you're even a boring liar. I do not know what I have done to keep being punished by your presence, but I find your silence somewhat more compelling than your chatter. So why don't we trudge through this social obligation in dignified quiet?"

Roger did not point out that Wyndham had been the one to start the conversation. He drank his tea and watched the clock drag its way through the visit. Finally, the guests left.

His mother turned to him and smiled. "I've always liked Aveline Wrenwhistle. If you were more attracted to feminine beauty, I'd suggest a match."

He gave his mother a weary look. "May I ask what makes you think her brother would be a better match?"

"Well," she said, dragging out the word, "you two were the subject of gossip this morning. I was curious to see you together. His mother was inclined to agree."

"You spoke to his mother about it?"

"Yes, dear."

"You do realize that humans and fae are not encouraged to marry each other? Their children are always outcasts. Think of Pimpernel-Smith. Their mother was disinherited and Pimpernel-Smith was barred from practically every institution. Even the university we went to, which included fae and human students, reportedly rejected them."

She tutted. "Don't be so old-fashioned, darling. The Pimpernel-Smith scandal was simply ages ago. Sometimes society changes for the better over time. Besides, your father works with Iris Wrenwhistle. It isn't at all objectionable for our families to be better acquainted."

"I think Wy—I think Mr. Wrenwhistle would disagree. He *detests* me, Mother."

"Silly boy. Who could possibly detest you?" She stood and kissed the top of his head. "Although I would like to give that young writer a piece of my mind. I didn't like the way they spoke about you."

"I've heard worse. I wouldn't worry about it."

She tilted his face up and frowned at him. "I cannot understand why you remain unmarried, Roger. You are intelligent, kind, you have a beautiful face and a beautiful soul." She ran a hand through his hair affectionately.

"I…do not think most of society would agree with that assessment," he said carefully.

He thought back to the day of his own Hasting's Exam. He had been twelve, of course, and the school had deemed it more convenient to conduct one Hastings Exam and one Sciurus Exam each year, rather than at every child's birthday. The fae students in his class had been enjoying what essentially resulted in a free period with most of their human classmates getting tested. Roger had been distracted by Wyndham as he entertained his fae friends at the back of the classroom by making a bundle of torn up paper swirl in a funnel over their heads. Even at eleven, Wyndham had been a distracting creature, all sharp angles, witty remarks, and an easy confidence in his own abilities—so unlike Roger in every possible way. Roger had been staring, as fascinated by the boy as he was by the show of magic, when his name was called. He had jolted in his seat and scurried after the examiner into the testing room. He remembered how much he fiddled with his spectacles. He remembered stuttering over the incantation and the way the pencil slipped in his sweaty palms. But, most of all, he remembered the utter devastation he felt when he received his score. It had been as though the floor had dropped out from beneath him. And it had gotten worse as each of his friends reported their own scores throughout the day.

As young as he was, Roger had known what lay ahead. He knew he had one of the lowest scores in his age group. He knew that he was essentially cut off from any of his dream jobs—councilmember, professor, examiner, researcher—with a score so low. Unless he grew up to be a great beauty or a great wit, his chances for marriage were similarly hopeless. He remembered how much he had cried in his room afterwards. And he remembered how his parents had comforted him when they learned about it. They had assured him that everything would turn out all right. But then, they had always seen the best in him.

Even now, his mother was looking at him with a tender expression that suggested she didn't see his point. He added, "My Hastings score was quite…embarrassing. No one would want their child to marry a—"

"Your qualities amount to a great deal more than your magical abilities," she chided. She gave him a long look. "I think I've given you more than enough time to find someone on your own. This Season, I will be handling your social calendar."

Roger felt dread coat his stomach. "Oh, dear. Must you?"

"Yes," she said crisply. "And I intend to see you married before the end of the Season." Her expression turned sympathetic. "I want to see you safely settled, dear. I won't deny I'm worried about you."

He sighed a little and gave up that particular battle for lost. He had always been susceptible to sympathy and his mother wielded it very well.

CHAPTER 6

WYN

"I suppose we can all be glad that Pimpernel-Smith's column made no mention of how much—or little—clothing you'd managed to keep on by the end of the evening this time," Emrys chided, sending a glance in Wyn's direction from the sofa. He reclined in the large family sitting room, which had been done up in the latest fashion a scant few days before they'd arrived. The stench of wallpaper adhesive had been strong enough to make Wyn's eyes water. "There's nothing more disconcerting than learning through a public gossip paper who your youngest sibling has been tumbling with."

"You know as well as I do that Torquil's column is rubbish," Wyn argued, casually glazing over the fact that his treat of the evening had, in fact, been mentioned by name in the *Tribune* once again. In his defense, they hadn't done much of anything.

"I quite enjoy it," Aveline said with a grin, her eyes never lifting from the pages of her book. "Torquil has a way of making me laugh, even when something isn't particularly funny."

Wyn snorted and uncrossed his legs to cross them again in the opposite direction, one knee bent neatly over the other. "It's easy to laugh when you're not constantly the topic of conversation."

"Something else you and Roger Barnes have in common, dear brother," Aveline cooed. "*A match made in heaven.*' Now that one had me rolling!"

Wyn sneered at her even though she wasn't looking in his direction.

"Mother would do well to reassess her plans if she thinks I'll be roped into any more parties or social gatherings where he is in attendance. We've been here less than a week and I've already had my fill."

The footman passing through the doorway drew their attention. It was rather late in the day for visitors. "Mrs. Iris Wrenwhistle," he announced, stepping aside to allow her into the room.

"Good evening, my darlings," she greeted warmly, before wasting no time in sharing her intentions. "If I might have a word with Wyndham alone?"

Aveline and Emrys kissed her cheek on their way out. Wyn was only slightly curious as to what he'd done as he followed his grandmother to the low sofa by the open windows. She took a breath and fixed him with a look, her lips pressed together in a thin line. *Ah*, Wyn thought, *here it comes*.

They'd had this conversation before. Many times, in fact.

Wyn felt himself growing defensive. "Grandmother, I cannot believe that you deign to read that ridiculous gossip paper. It's cheap entertainment for the humans who have little better to do with their time, nothing more." He read the column as often as anyone else, but it was beyond uncomfortable knowing that his grandmother's eyes were scanning the same salacious bits of news over her breakfast plum cakes.

Iris took a moment of pause, carefully collecting her thoughts before she spoke again. "Your mother informed me today that you're still at odds with young Mr. Barnes."

"That's putting it lightly," Wyn said under his breath. Iris put her hand on top of his.

"You realize that Roger's father is someone I work with very closely. As the Head of the Fae Council, I feel it's my responsibility to maintain a professional but friendly relationship with all of my colleagues. And I do mean all of them."

Wyn's forehead wrinkled. "What does that have to do with me?"

"The Council is finally beginning to make real progress in proving that fae and human magic can exist congruously. When the entire city is reading about a tense relationship between the son and grandson of two councilmembers at a time such as this, who do you suppose that reflects poorly on?"

Wyn shoved himself off the sofa and paced away, arms crossed tightly over his chest. It wasn't his fault their names were in the paper together. If it had been up to him, Barnes would've remained on his side of the room where he belonged.

"I'd thought perhaps having the two of you partnered at dinner last night would've provided the perfect opportunity for some casual chatter. It appears I was wrong."

Wyn's eyes went wide as he spun back around.

"*You* were the one who paired us?"

"Indeed. I asked Mrs. St. Clair to seat you together as a favor."

Wyn's magic flared bright in his chest as his arms flew out wide in mock surrender. It was strong enough to flutter the sheer curtains framing the windows and rustle loose pages of music scattered atop the piano.

"What am I to do? Befriend him to appease the rest of society?" A strained whimper of a laugh forced itself out of his throat. He'd sooner give up wine, or raffish men, or just about anything else than become *friends* with Roger Barnes.

"It's not the worst idea," Iris said with a simple, elegant shrug.

Wyn pushed the fingers of both hands into his hair, fingernails digging painfully into his scalp. This was absurd. The notion—

"I'm sorry, Grandmother," he managed, his voice shaking a bit. He swallowed thickly. "I'm suddenly feeling unwell. I bid you good evening."

Wyn escaped to his room upstairs as quickly as he could. The air responded to his fit as it was sucked in through the open windows hard enough to rattle the glass; his magic lashed out like a whip to slam the door shut in his wake.

In his nearly thirty years of life, Wyn had never felt so alone.

His eldest brother, Auberon, had finally gotten married to a lovely young woman over the summer and started his life away from the family, effectively abandoning Wyn to the rest of the Wrenwhistles without so much as a reassuring letter. Auberon was the one Wyn always turned to when he needed advice, someone to sooth his temper, or to simply sit and listen to him rant until he felt better about whatever had been troubling him.

Wyn sat heavily onto the edge of his mattress and put his head in his hands. He had no friends in the city. He had no friends at all, really, but especially not in the confines of London. All anyone talked about here was the hows and whys and whens of merging the divided societies. Wyn couldn't stand to listen to one more "bright idea" or "thought-provoking theory" on what might bring about positive change.

Wyn closed his eyes and thought of their estate in the country. He imagined he was back there, away from everything that felt heavy enough to crush him flat. Away from the people who never saw things from his perspective. Away from the words of people like Torquil Pimpernel-Smith, who wanted nothing more than to stir drama and make their readers feel better about themselves at the expense of others.

At the expense of Wyn, more often than not.

Wyn lifted his head and stared at the latest gossip pamphlet sitting on his writing desk where he'd tossed it earlier that morning. Ink and paper, nothing more, but it held so much power. Even his own grandmother took the words at more than face value, and she was one of the most intelligent people he'd ever known.

Was that really the only way to be seen in the city? To be heard?

Wyn stood and walked to his desk, pulling his chair out with one hand as he picked the pamphlet up in the other.

Just ink and paper.

Words that made people listen.

Perhaps it was time for Torquil to write something that Wyn wanted to read for a change.

TORQUIL'S TRIBUNE

MONDAY 20 SEPTEMBER, 1813

Greetings, frank folk and hesitant humans,

This writer is delighted to share some gossip with you gentle readers, particularly in regards to the proposal currently being considered by the Council for Fae & Human Magical Relations.

According to one source, the person who has submitted the proposal is not the hero we need right now. We received information that the would-be hero has not fully thought through the details of the proposal and does not seem entirely confident in his own success. While this writer was aware that the person in question received a low Hastings score himself, our source pointed out that this closeness will mar the objectivity of the proposal, and expressed concerns that the Council was considering input from such a person. It would appear that this source is of the opinion that anyone else would be more fit to take on this challenge. Quite frankly, this source's views smack of the very same prejudice the Council is seeking to correct.

Our source also congratulated our description of Roger Barnes as aggressively average, adding that the gentleman lacks the imagination necessary to be truly eligible. There was a very long description of Mr. Barnes' dreadful fashion choices, his dull conversational skills, his inability to even tell interesting falsehoods, and that any person who resorts to squeaking when alarmed would make for a terrible companion.

The report did go on to clarify that the Barnes family is generally respectable but that Mr. Barnes is arguably the least endearing of the lot. Considering the similarity in that particular description to this writer's recent description of the youngest Mr. Wrenwhistle, one might wonder who is truly lacking in imagination.

This writer might also suggest that the sender of the note received this morning might, in fact, be a little too enthusiastic in his dislike for Mr. Barnes, unremarkable though he may be.

Your esteemed editor,

Torquil Pimpernel-Smith

CHAPTER 7

ROGER

ROGER PACED the length of his study, shaking with fury. Who did that self-centered, toffee-nosed, spoiled little prat think he was?

Roger was upset about the attempted character assassination, of course he was. But he was also filled with a righteous anger that Wyndham (because there was no doubt it had been Wyndham who had sent a letter) was attempting to undermine his work. This didn't just affect him; it affected an untold number of humans who were being discarded like apple cores, learning that they were useless, and then struggling to find any footing in society. It made him want to retch.

The worst part was that he was so upset he couldn't think, which meant he couldn't work. Being unable to work just felt like he was proving Wyndham right, *damn him*.

A very silly part of him wanted to go to his parents. He wanted his mother to admit she was wrong about Wyndham and that he wasn't worth their time. He wanted his father to offer to help fix this problem, volunteer to talk to Wyndham's grandmother, do *something*. He sagged into his easy chair. He knew he wouldn't go to his parents. Baring his soul always made him feel like a burden. Besides, his parents had already done their part by providing for him. That's what anyone else would tell him. So now it was his turn to do his part.

He approached his desk, glaring at the gossip column. He picked it up and scanned the list of insults again: his fashion choices? Why the devil did Wyndham care how Roger dressed? What did his clothes have to do with his ability to carry out the task at hand? Why did such a silly thing matter? It was almost laughable that Wyndham criticized his conversational skills, considering the fact that Wyndham kept goading him into conversation in the first place. And his ability to lie—well, he rolled his eyes at that one. It was true that he *had* been lying about Mr. Ravenwing, but it was just like Wyndham to take his own vices and twist them to be Roger's fault instead. The squeak bit was particularly infuriating. Roger had practiced restraint, for God's sake! He could have easily told everyone who had disappeared with Ravenwing. But he was above such antics. It was as if Wyndham was trying to trick Roger into retaliating. He slammed the paper back down.

Then he considered. Perhaps his parents weren't the ones who could help him. Perhaps he needed to return to the source. Wasn't there some saying about an eye for an eye? Perhaps he should take the bait. After all, Wyndham was guilty of far more scandalous misdeeds. At the very least, it would help him get the unspoken rage out of his mind.

He sat down at his desk and wrote another letter to Torquil Pimpernel-Smith. He read it over three times, had it sent out, and then buried himself in his work.

CHAPTER 8

WYN

WYN MADE a point to stay away from the Park when it was crowded. Unfortunately, that was almost all of the time. Both sides of society enjoyed appearing outdoorsy while strolling and riding their horses along the wide gravel paths, greeting each other demurely and having the same, short conversation over and over again: good morning, good morning, how are you, quite well and yourself, oh just fine thank you, and so on. Wyn found it amusing when he wasn't directly involved.

In an effort to avoid the swarm, he would pack up his travel case of colors and brushes, tuck a fresh canvas under his arm, and arrive when the gates opened at six o'clock sharp—a horrific, albeit necessary, solution for someone who valued sleep as much as he did. He'd set up under a stand of trees close enough to the water that he could watch the swans gliding by without disturbing them.

With a name like Wrenwhistle, he felt an odd sort of obligation toward appreciating all sorts of birds. But something about the swans had always drawn him in. Perhaps it was how they stood out effortlessly among the other waterfowl, their long necks towering over the common ducks and geese. Or maybe it was the quietly romantic way that they mated for life, taking equal responsibility in caring for their gawky cygnets year after year.

Wyn huffed out a short laugh through his nose as he peered at them over his canvas. No, it was the way they would hiss and peck if you got too close. He could relate to that most of all.

He returned a critical eye to the morning's work. He'd stood in that exact spot many times before, but somehow he always ended up painting something entirely different. Everchanging seasons and weather made for wonderful muses when the subject matter was so susceptible to both.

With a delicate touch, Wyn swirled his brush in the small jar of water, tapped it against the lip twice with a faint *tink-tink*, and then dabbed the bristles into the pot of cerulean paint before lifting it to add long, purposeful strokes to the horizon of his scene.

Distractions such as this had been the only way he'd made it through the last several days. Writing to the gossip column had been impetuous on his part, and though he was no stranger to making rash decisions thanks to his admitted volatility, he'd found that he hadn't felt better in the slightest after his letter had been sent out. If anything, it had added yet another layer to the thick stack of emotions he was already shouldering.

Reading his own words through Pimpernel-Smith's heavy-handed editing had been something else altogether. To make matters worse, Torquil *still* managed to throw a jab at Wyn in the end. A little too enthusiastic? Of course he had been; why else would someone write such a letter to begin with, if not to share something worth whispering about?

Wyn set his paintbrush into the jar of brownish water and closed his eyes. He shuffled his toes against the grass beneath his bare feet. A lock of hair tickled the pointed tip of his ear as a light breeze picked up around him, nevermind that he'd stirred the air up for his own purposes. The bubbling of magic simmered in his chest and he let out a slow exhale.

Roger Barnes was not going to ruin this morning for him.

After another hour or so had passed, Wyn was no longer alone in the Park, which was his cue to leave. He'd put on his boots and collected his things, savored one last glance at the swans, then started for the crushed stone pathway that would take him to the gate nearest to home.

The tall stretch of decorative iron had just barely come into view when a sharp whistle came from somewhere to his left. Wyn's brow arched as he turned toward the source. He wasn't a stranger to catcalls, and while they didn't usually come so early in the morning, he was not opposed to a quick romp behind the neatly trimmed hedgerow.

On second thought, he rather liked the fit of the beige trousers he had on. It would be a shame to ruin them with grass stains.

"Mr. Wrenwhistle," came a familiar voice.

"Mr. Ravenwing," Wyn greeted in return, shifting the folded easel to a more comfortable position in his grip. The fae looked particularly put together, which could only mean one thing. "A fine morning to promenade with a potential suitor. Or so I would imagine."

Sage offered a coquettish grin in reply. "Wouldn't you, though."

"I haven't the time to be bothered with such things," Wyn said flippantly. "My social calendar is already overflowing with hobbies and engagements that actually interest me."

"Is that so?" Sage took a step closer and lowered his voice a bit. "Speaking of engagements, my mother fully expects this to be the Season I find a spouse, so I'd appreciate it if you kept my name out of your business moving forward."

It took no time at all for Wyn to follow his implication.

"What is that supposed to mean? I'll dare to remind you that it was your name listed in the pamphlet, not mine."

Ravenwing's eyes narrowed slightly. "I take it you haven't read this morning's *Tribune*?" Without waiting for an answer, Sage dug into his breast pocket and pulled out his own copy.

Wyn set down his art supplies, canvas propped against his shin, and took the paper without hesitation. He scanned the words faster than he could absorb at first, only slowing when he read his own name once, twice, three times in the span of a few sentences. An icy shock of emotion splashed low in Wyn's gut. He swallowed hard, jaw muscles working.

Sage's lips curved into a small, mocking frown. "I expect you'll be receiving some rescinded invitations after this."

TORQUIL'S TRIBUNE

Greetings, foul folk and hackneyed humans,

It would appear that this modest little gossip column has turned into a small battleground. This writer isn't complaining as drama is the stuff of life.

The subject referred to in the most recent column has, understandably, taken offense to some of the things printed about him by yours truly. The surprising part is that he is actually doing something about it. We did not think he was capable of retaliation. Nevertheless, here we are. We almost admire him for it.

Our new source would like it to be known that Mr. Wyndham Wrenwhistle is a cad. That, in and of itself, is not news. However, a recent report does suggest that Mr. Wrenwhistle was the mysterious companion of Mr. Ravenwing at the St. Clairs' party. Which is news, albeit unsurprising. Furthermore, our source has their own list of grievances against Mr. Wrenwhistle. He is: a vainglorious, feckless, arrogant, shallow fool, who disgraces the respectable family he was born to (*Entre nous*, the insult faded a bit at the end there. Still, it enjoyed a solid start). The report goes on to state that Mr. Wrenwhistle's virtues are few and entirely superficial at that. This writer thinks the source in question might consider why he is so interested in Mr. Wrenwhistle's virtues at all.

The Council will hear the new proposal soon. We are all eager to hear how it goes and are already preparing ourselves for disappointment.

Your esteemed editor,

Torquil Pimpernel-Smith

CHAPTER 9

ROGER

IT DID NOT TAKE LONG for Roger to regret his impulsive decision. He liked to consider himself a person of good judgment, sound reason, and compassion. His message to Pimpernel-Smith exhibited none of these; it had been petty and vindictive. He was fairly confident that such news would do little to Wyndham's social standing, and his reputation as a rake was already pretty well known. All the same, Roger knew he had acted poorly and rashly.

But he couldn't quite bring himself to submit a retraction to the paper, or to send an apology to Wyndham himself. After all, no apology had been sent to him. That particular thought was the only thing that kept him from losing himself in his own regrets. It was unlikely that Wyndham had any of the remorse that he was currently experiencing. If anything, the cad had probably been extremely proud of his own letter—Roger could just imagine Wyndham's smug expression.

He let that thought buoy him all the way to his next appearance before the Council. He was a bit of a wreck as he sat in the waiting room. He had all of his notes organized and even copied out his plan six times to give a copy to each councilmember. His hand ached by the end of that particular exercise. He had practiced his speech so often, he'd fallen asleep thinking about it and awoke picking up where he had left off. He'd even had dreams about the proposal and what the Council would say.

When he was finally called in, he clenched the papers and walked to the little stand. He smoothed the papers, took a deep breath, and began: "Thank you again for the opportunity to present this proposal. I have prepared a rubric I think will provide better scope and nuance to the testing process. I have copies for each of you."

"Excellent," Councilmember Wrenwhistle said. "Please bring them forward."

He didn't dare look her in the eye as he approached and passed the papers out. Did she know about his foolish act? He glanced at his father, wondering if he knew. His father gave him an encouraging smile, which made him feel a little better.

"As you can see," he said, returning to the stand, "I have composed a list of different aspects of magic I think should be tested: power, focus, control, understanding, and intuition. I have also outlined some sample spells for each that I think would exhibit these traits."

"What is the difference between focus and control?" Councilmember Gibbs asked.

"Excellent question," Roger said in what he'd hoped was a chipper tone, but he was fairly sure it came out like a squeak instead. *Damn Wyndham for getting that thought into my head.* "Focus will be about the scope of the spell and control will be about the ability for the caster to adjust power."

Gibbs nodded, still frowning in concentration. "I see."

"And understanding and intuition?" Roger's father asked. Roger was fairly sure his father was simply asking to give Roger an opportunity to prove his hard work. "Understanding would be about the caster's knowledge of spells and magical theory. As the exams are done at the age of twelve, a thorough knowledge of magic shouldn't be expected, but the basics should be covered. Intuition would be the ability to apply known principles to a new spell. I realize that this might sound the same as understanding, but I think it would be important to see that theoretical knowledge and practical application are both examined."

Roger's father gave him a smile. "Thank you, Mr. Barnes. That makes sense."

"Five qualities," Councilmember Wrenwhistle said slowly. "I think that is a good amount of skills to be tested. Don't you agree, Williams?"

Councilmember Williams nodded. "May I ask, Mr. Barnes, if this new rubric would have any impact on your own Hastings score?"

Roger swallowed. He had anticipated this question. "It would impact my score, sir, but it would not impact my standing within the family. You will understand, of course, that I have not applied this rubric to anyone in a practical sense. But my brother would still likely inherit, as he has all of these qualities in abundance. My sister would probably score closer to Bernard, as she has excellent control—probably the best control out of anyone in our family—but does not have the same amount of power. At this point, Bernard has spent years studying magic and would likely excel in the last two scores."

Williams nodded. "Thank you, Mr. Barnes. I am relieved to see that this is not merely for personal gain. That clears up the majority of my own doubts." He looked around at the rest of the Council. "I believe that Mr. Barnes' proposal is well thought out. I would like to see these lists of potential spells to be reduced to one spell for each rubric."

"Agreed," Councilmember Wrenwhistle said. "However, the root of the solution is sound. I think that a five quality rubric will be a better standard moving forward. Does anyone have any other concerns?"

"I would like to have a better understanding of how this will solve the current problem," Councilmember Gibbs said.

"My hope is that it will create more nuance in the conversation around scores," Roger answered. "Currently, there is a very clear indication of what is considered a low score versus what is considered a high score. With this new rubric, most children would achieve high scores in at least one aspect of the test, if not more. By identifying what skills need improvement, it will be easier for them to enhance whatever skills are most lacking."

Councilmember Applewood smiled. "Magic imitating life then, Mr. Barnes."

"Yes, ma'am," he replied.

"Then we are in agreement?" Councilmember Wrenwhistle asked, looking around at the other councilmembers and apparently taking stock of the answering nods. "Well done, Mr. Barnes. We accept your proposal."

Roger let out a deep breath and even let himself smile a little.

She gave him a small smile in return. "I concur with Williams that more specificity would be helpful. Before sending Mr. Barnes with the task to hone his proposal further, I suggest it might behoove us to make sure we are aligned between both magic systems first. I appreciate that his work has been done by a layman in this case, so I would recommend we use that same tactic for the alignment portion of this proposal."

"Am I correct in assuming you already have someone in mind, Iris?" Roger's father said, in a tone that sounded like he already knew the answer.

"You are," she replied. She turned to motion to one of the attendants at the back of the room. "Be so good as to send him in."

When the door opened, Roger's good mood promptly evaporated. "I would like to recommend my grandson work with Mr. Barnes on bringing our testing formats into alignment. As both have a solid grounding in their respective magics and are similarly in a position to want a better scoring rubric, I believe this will be a productive partnership." Strolling into the room, looking a little confused, was Wyndham Wrenwhistle.

CHAPTER 10

WYN

SHIRKING responsibilities was something Wyn had come close to perfecting. He could avoid just about anything with a clever smile or well-timed excuse. By the same token, he could usually get his way if he knew how to play whomever he was dealing with.

The only exception was his grandmother.

When he received the urgent message to meet her in the Council's chambers on Monday morning, he'd had no choice but to go.

Wyn stepped out of the family carriage and into the steady rain, the first he'd seen since arriving in the city. While he would've preferred to feel more of it falling on his skin, he took what he could get and lifted his face to the sky as he climbed the steps. The doorman greeted him as always, but Wyn was too distracted to offer anything in return.

Once inside he removed his greatcoat, a rather warm but necessary choice to protect the delicate silk of his honey-yellow waistcoat embroidered with swirls of green vines and petite pink flowers. He trudged through the endless hallways to an empty office. The only person around was Iris' personal aide. She looked as though she'd been waiting for him.

"Mr. Wrenwhistle, if you'll follow me."

The woman was ancient, so following her was a painfully slow process.

When they eventually reached the door to the Council's chambers, Wyn gave the aide a questioning look.

"I'm supposed to meet with my grandmother," he explained. Why had she requested him specifically at this time if she'd known she would be in a meeting?

"As you say, love," she croaked affectionately, gesturing with her arthritic fingers toward the door just as it opened.

"I would like to recommend my grandson to work with Mr. Barnes on bringing our testing formats into alignment. As both have a solid grounding in their respective magics, and are similarly in a position to want a better scoring rubric, I believe this will be a productive partnership."

There was absolutely, positively, unquestionably *no* chance he'd heard that correctly.

Wyn blinked at his grandmother, who was smiling at him from behind the massive mahogany desk that spanned the front of the room. The rest of the councilmembers were staring down at him from their perches with varied expressions of curiosity and mild amusement.

Roger was gaping at him like a codfish pulled freshly from the lake.

Councilmember Williams broke the silence. "An interesting choice."

Murmurs and nods of agreement spread amongst the other councilmembers. Wyn took the opportunity to tear his feet from where they'd temporarily frozen to the floor so he could approach them, surging past Barnes as though he wasn't even there.

"I beg pardon, Grandmother, did you say *partnership?*" he queried, emphasizing the first letter of the word so hard he saw his own spittle fly.

"Good morning, darling," she greeted him warmly. "Thank you for coming on such short notice. I had a very good feeling about this meeting, so I took the liberty of sending for you without being certain of the Council's decision. Now that we have our answer for Mr. Barnes, it's time for me to provide an answer to the question you had the last time we met."

Wyn's vexation washed away instantly at her words.

What am I to do, he'd asked. *Befriend him?*

Could his own grandmother be so cruel?

Wyn's magic gasped deep in his chest. It strained mightily to be felt, to respond, but it had nothing to draw on in the chambers; the windows were shut tight because of the rain. Beneath his feet were several stories of building, not grass and dirt. The only trees within reach had long since been destroyed to create the furniture in the room. He was trapped.

"The Council will grant a fortnight for the two of you to work together on testing Mr. Barnes' new rubric. I would like to see full, detailed reports to go along with whatever results you produce during this time, no matter if the outcomes are favorable or not."

"With all due respect, ma'am—" Roger had apparently found his voice somewhere in the background, but Iris raising her hand was all it took to silence him again.

"I trust the two of you are capable of working out the details of when and where you will be conducting your testing. Please do let a member of the Council know if you need any assistance with materials, locations, and so on. I'm certain a stipend could be arranged if necessary."

A heavy silence settled in the room. Wyn wondered how it was possible to feel so supported and yet so betrayed all at once.

Neither of them were in a position to argue with the Council's decision. It was one thing to turn up in the gossip column week after week, but refusing a direct order from the Council for Fae & Human Magical Relations would most definitely reflect badly on both of their families.

The moment they were dismissed, Wyn spun around and whisked toward the exit, grabbing his coat off the chair where he'd dropped it. He managed to evade what was coming until he made it to the cobblestones outside.

"Mr. Wrenwhistle!" Roger's exclamation was mostly a puff of fatigue after running to keep up with Wyn's long stride. He tried again as he hurried down the steps. "Mr. Wrenwhistle, if you'll wait just a moment!"

The length of Wyn's greatcoat twirled dramatically around his legs as he turned to face the man. Despite the rain, there were still plenty of people walking by, and most of them were staring thanks to Barnes' shouting. Wyn closed the distance between them and stopped so that their faces were only inches apart, his own chest still heaving as he struggled to breathe through his exasperation.

"If you think for one *bloody* second that I'm going to help you with this task for any reason other than to make my grandmother happy, you are sadly mistaken," he seethed. The way Barnes' eyes doubled in size was deliciously satisfying. It was lucky that Wyn's hands were fisted tightly into his coat as he held it closed against the weather, otherwise they might've found their way to violence. "Come 'round my house this time tomorrow and we'll begin."

With that, Wyn left Roger standing in the rain as he boarded his waiting carriage and sped off.

TORQUIL'S TRIBUNE

Greetings, formidable folk and holistic humans,

This column is reaching you later than usual because this writer received a request to delay publication until the Council for Fae & Human Magical Relations had heard the proposal scheduled for today. We are pleased to report that the proposal was approved. Everyone can go home feeling satisfied that they actually did something useful for once.

The architect of this new rubric provided us with some of the details. The approach will be more nuanced and have wider scope so as to provide a better understanding of individual talents. This will keep children out of severely low scores, thereby reducing the prejudice around one specific test result. Rather than testing children on a single spell during the Hastings Exam, children will instead be asked to perform multiple spells in order to display a variety of skills. The skills that will be measured are: *power, focus, control, understanding, and intuition.* Mr. Barnes, the gentleman who submitted this proposal, will be identifying which spells are best to test these skills.

This writer's opinion is that the rubric is a clever idea, but does not solve the issue of people being horrid. The problem runs deeper than test scores. With fae integrating into human society barely a century ago, repairing the rift between the two groups is well overdue. How much longer will humans be distrustful of the wildness of fae magic? How much longer will fae be disdainful of the resourcefulness of human magic? And how much longer before we find the similarities between ourselves rather than the differences? Are we doomed to forever be at odds? We can, however, admit that the test is an easier solution than a cultural shift.

The Council accepted the proposal, but has determined that the Sciurus Exam will also be changed to keep the two systems in alignment. Thus, they have assigned a partnership between the original source for the proposal, Mr. Roger Barnes, and Mr. Wyndham Wrenwhistle. Readers who have read between the lines in recent letters (and this writer can admit that the lines were not very difficult to decipher) may well be curious as to how this partnership will fare. However, this humble writer is hopeful that this young pair will surprise us.

There have been precious few social gatherings to report and a shocking absence of spiteful correspondence, so this sadly concludes today's column.

Your esteemed editor,
Torquil Pimpernel-Smith

CHAPTER 11

ROGER

ROGER BARELY REMEMBERED anything after Councilmember Wrenwhistle's final speech. He vaguely recalled staring at Wyndham in shock. He remembered Wyndham's general agitation—and, for once, he couldn't entirely blame him. He was embarrassed by the memory of chasing the gentleman out of the building, that Wyndham had gotten remarkably close to his face, that Wyndham had looked ready to murder him, and that he mentioned something about coming to the Wrenwhistle townhouse the following day. He had been distracted by the sight of the yellow embroidered waistcoat Wyndham had been wearing—*silk? On such a rainy day? Was he mad?*

As Roger compiled these memories in his mind, he concluded that maybe he remembered more than he thought he did. He would have liked to ask Councilmember Wrenwhistle what she had been thinking. He would have liked to ask his father for advice. But he barely had the wherewithal to snatch his notes from the stand before scurrying after Wyndham.

So he did the only thing he could under the circumstances: he went home and bounced between celebrating the success and sulking about the outcome. Sometime before he went to bed, he pulled himself together enough to write down a copy of his plan to give to Wyndham. He stared at the writing, wondering how it would be received. Would Wyndham toss it in the fire, tear it into pieces, throw it in his face, or merely curl his lip and insult all of Roger's hard work?

The idea that such an important task now depended on the one person in London who hated him most made him ill. He went to bed and lay awake for hours, fretting about how he would survive the next fortnight.

He woke up early the following morning, his stomach thick with anxiety. He spent far more time than he would ever admit trying to pick a suitable outfit, finally concluding that Wyndham would likely say something contemptuous regardless. He rang for breakfast, found he couldn't eat, collected his notes, and walked across town to Mayfair.

Once he arrived at the Wrenwhistles' home, he was led to a sunny sitting room. Every fabric in the room was expensive, paired with intricately embellished furniture. Roger immediately felt out of place and yearned a little for his own dark and messy rooms.

Wyndham took his time, showing up nearly a full hour late. Roger decided not to comment on it, although Wyndham's arched eyebrow was clearly daring him to do so.

"Good morning, Mr. Wrenwhistle," Roger greeted, in his politest tone.

Wyndham snorted and lounged on the closest sofa.

Roger handed him the notes he'd copied out, holding his breath.

Wyndham took the papers and glanced over them with obvious disinterest. "Five aspects of magic will be tested?"

"Yes," Roger responded.

Wyndham yawned. "This took you a fortnight to come up with?"

Roger rolled his eyes. "Well, it should be even easier for you to come up with a similar format since you already have something to model it after."

"Oh, I see. You expect me to thank you for paving the way so beautifully."

Roger willed himself to have patience. "Not at all," he said slowly. "I am well aware of your regard for me."

"I have no interest in pretending otherwise."

"Clearly."

"Your handwriting is atrocious."

"Well, I'm sure your proposal will be far superior then."

"Are you attempting to mollify me with this attitude?" Wyndham snapped.

Roger took a deep breath. "I am attempting to establish a good part-nership."

"We both know that is impossible. I refuse to give you the satisfaction of moral superiority. Did you bring anything other than these notes? Any texts I can read about human magic?"

"I…er…well, to be honest, I wasn't sure what you might need. I wanted to ask you yesterday but—"

"Oh, you mean when you shouted at me like some sort of fishmonger?"

Roger sighed and sank into a chair. "Please, Wy—Mr. Wrenwhistle. I know you hate me, and I daresay you have good reason to at this point. Is there not some way we can work together…amicably? This…this project is so very important."

"To you."

"Yes, to me. But also to hundreds, if not thousands of children. They are depending on this. People are already struggling to find jobs. There were many people last year who didn't find a match before they reached their majority." He was included in that number, but decided not to point that out.

Even though he'd dutifully attended years of social Seasons, he had yet to be asked for his hand. He took a deep breath and continued on, trying to keep the issue from being personal. "Until we can reduce the stigma of low scores, we can at least reduce the number of low scores that are given. That would mean reducing the number of people who are without means, without jobs, without spouses, and without…without hope. We can help the next generation of children if we act now."

"I don't see how the fate of human children is my problem."

Roger stared at him in horror. "You mean you don't care what happens to them?"

"I mean that my people take care of their own. Why do the fae have to clean up human messes? It would serve you all right if we let you destroy yourselves. You are already doing it so efficiently. It wouldn't take long for your race to dwindle into nothing."

"They're children!"

"If you care so much, why don't you start a school? Start a petition? Do something about it?"

"I *am* doing something," Roger shouted, jumping to his feet. "You are the only reason my work is being stalled. What the bloody hell is your problem?"

Wyndham scoffed and stood as well. "My problem is that I have been saddled with an idiotic human who sees fit to peddle my personal information to whoever happens to be listening. My problem is that I have been tasked to help you with this absurd project that does not benefit me or my people. Yet we have to step up to help your people as we always do."

"You're right," Roger said. "No one asked you what you wanted. But no one asked me for input on my partner either. I feel bound to point out that you were the first to peddle personal information. Did you really expect me to take your abuse lying down? You jeer at me for being a coward and then get angry when I react. What the hell would you have me do?"

"Get out," Wyndham said, his voice low and dangerous.

Roger rocked back a little in surprise. "I beg your pardon?"

"You heard me, you little ingrate. Get the fuck out of my home."

Roger pinched his lips together. "You know what? Fine. I'll leave. You can go back to sulking about how everyone has wronged you. When we appear before the Council again, I will have done my part. I don't give a damn if you've done yours." He stomped to the doors and paused, turning on his heel. "I'll leave my address with your footman. If you change your mind and decide to be something other than a spoiled prat and actually do something for others, you will know where to find me. I'm not your lackey and I will not come here again to cool my heels while you lounge about and then deign to grace me with your presence. If you decide you want to work, you will come to my study and we will work."

With that, he left. He handed his calling card to the footman as promised, and then strode out. As angry as he was, it felt uniquely good to finally have the last word in a conversation with Wyndham.

CHAPTER 12

WYN

ROGER LIVED on a street that Wyn had never visited before. If he'd ever heard it by name, he had since forgotten, or had simply lacked enough interest to remember it in the first place. The carriage dropped him off in front of a building that was altogether unimpressive, aside from its height. Wyn left specific instructions for the coachman to wait outside and be ready to depart at a moment's notice.

Barnes' rooms were several floors up. Wyn took the stairs at a gradual pace, the stench of humans making it nearly impossible for him to breathe. He'd never been in such a place; he was able to hear snippets of conversation as he passed one door, music as he passed another. It was all very unsettling and hardly conducive to focusing on an important task.

The valet opened the door to Roger's rooms and escorted Wyn into his worst nightmare. Dark, dreary, and dreadfully sad were the first words that came to mind.

Even at the late morning hour, candles were the main light source, as heavy drapes were drawn over almost all the windows. One candle burned dangerously low on a small table in the entryway and another several were dotted along tables and bookcases, of which there were at least half a dozen.

Wyn wasn't sure where to look. It seemed as though someone had picked up the entire room, shaken it, and set it back down again. The multiple bookshelves held enough reading materials to rival any home library he'd seen, including his own, but they were distressingly askew. Some were standing, while others were tilted or wedged into spaces they clearly did not belong, and that didn't include the open ones lying about.

Then there were the papers: papers on the shelves, papers on the desk, papers crumpled on the floor.

In the midst of the chaos stood Roger, who only looked up from his reading when the valet announced Wyn's arrival.

"Oh," Barnes said cautiously, adjusting his spectacles. "You're here."

"You'll do well to remember your manners with guests, Mr. Barnes," the valet chided as he exited the room. Roger fully straightened himself from where he was stooped over his desk and cleared his throat.

"Good morning, Mr. Wrenwhistle," he tried again, a perfect echo of himself from the previous day.

Wyn rolled his eyes and came farther into the room, hands clasped behind his back as he stepped toward a series of shelves that held glass jars of various sizes, some more full of mysterious powders and liquids than others.

"What is all this?" Wyn asked sharply, unable to mask his curiosity. He needed something to distract him from the mayhem.

"Those are some of the items I use for spells," Roger started, taking one careful step around his desk. "Herb blends. Dried flowers. Extracts and oils."

Wyn bit the inside of his cheek. No wonder he couldn't tell what they were. The petals and leaves and bark had all been muddled beyond recognition. Human magic, much like humans themselves, relied on destroying the gifts of nature rather than working with them organically. There was a twinge in his chest as his magic reached out, mourning the sight.

It was no small mercy that fae and humans were separated for magical studies during their academic years. Subjects such as literature, maths, and even history were taught collectively, but anything to do with magic was done entirely apart. As a result, outside of a general awareness, Wyn knew little of what to expect with human magic. He had only ever seen it done on a handful of occasions; a number of times by household staff, and once by a human tailor who was new to London and eager for a chance to serve and impress wealthy fae patrons. His shop closed within the year.

Wyn turned away from the shelves and considered the room instead.

"I'm quite surprised at the state of your study. Normally having a valet prevents a man from living in squalor, does it not?"

"Notley knows to leave my study alone." Despite his confident answer, Wyn watched Roger's gaze flit around at the mess as though he hadn't realized it was as bad as it was until that moment. "I assure you he does a marvelous job of keeping my other rooms in perfect order."

An awkward moment passed as the two men stood without speaking.

"Are you going to offer me a seat?" Wyn finally asked impatiently.

Roger jumped into action, apologizing as he stepped over a pile of indeterminable rubbish and reached for the stack of papers preventing Wyn from sitting in one of the few chairs in the room. Rather than picking them up to move them somewhere else, Roger hastily pushed them onto the floor and retreated to the other side of his desk.

"I could've done *that*," Wyn muttered as he sat down, crossing one knee over the other.

"Sorry, it's just—" Roger blurted, before he paused to compose himself. "It's just that you're being…well, that is, you're acting quite civil at the moment, and I can't help but wonder if I'm being pranked?" His voice went high and thin at the end, which satisfied Wyn greatly.

Wyn's fingers tapped a slow, four-beat rhythm against the armrests of his newly acquired seat as he considered his response, as though it hadn't been the only thing occupying his mind for the last twenty-four hours.

He could've refused. Iris Wrenwhistle was a powerful woman, both on the Council and within his family, but Wyn didn't stand to inherit anyway. Emrys held that position. So what did it really matter if he told her no? Sooner or later, he would have to accept that he was more like those damned humans than he cared to admit. His magic was incredible, but it still wasn't good enough. *He* wasn't good enough.

"As you're well aware, thanks to a certain bi-weekly publication, the entirety of London now thinks I'm feckless and proud. What better way to prove them all wrong than to help you with this proposal out of the kindness of my heart?" A sly, calculated smirk tugged at the corner of his mouth.

The color drained from Roger's face.

"Furthermore, I have conditions I'll need satisfied if we're to do this. First, we will meet when it is most convenient for me. My social calendar is excessively full and I will not be adjusting it for any reason. Second, I'll need your valet to learn how I take my tea. And third, I expect you to make at least a minimal effort with your wardrobe moving forward. Pimpernel-Smith has so graciously linked our names publicly now, so if you're to be seen, it'll be in a tasteful outfit."

Wyn didn't bother asking Roger if he would agree to his terms or not. It was already decided.

"I also want you to provide me with some reading materials so I can better understand human magic. I've witnessed it on rare occasion, but I would prefer to have a more solid grasp on the subject if I'm to be dragged into helping you perform it."

Wyn stood gracefully from his chair and maneuvered toward one of the windows. He yanked the thick curtain aside, looped it behind the holdback, and opened the window far enough to let in some fresh air. His lungs were desperate for it as he breathed in deeply, his eyes closing for a moment on the exhale. It would have to do.

"Finally, you will keep this window open at all times throughout the duration of our project. Curtain tied back, as well. I don't know how you could possibly stand to keep this shut, what with the smell."

When Wyn turned around to gauge how closely Roger had been paying attention, he found the man hunched over his desk once again, scribbling something onto parchment like it was the most important thing he'd ever written.

"Did you hear what I said?" Wyn challenged. When there was no response, Wyn's hands came up to rest impatiently on his hips. "Barnes!"

"What? Yes! Yes, I heard you," Roger said, his focus still on his paper. "How do you take your tea?"

CHAPTER 13

ROGER

ROGER WAITED, pen poised, but Wyndham didn't speak. He glanced up at him.

Wyndham sighed. "I think it would be simpler to have him come in now and hear it himself."

"Oh," Roger said. "Would you...er...would you like some tea now?"

"I am certainly in need of it under the circumstances," he replied, eyes darting again at Roger's messy desk.

Ah. Well. That was somewhat understandable. Roger wasn't accustomed to having guests in his study and it hadn't occurred to him that Wyndham might actually show, so he hadn't bothered to tidy up. As Wyndham continued to stare at him expectantly, he pulled himself together and rang for Notley.

When Notley came in, Roger said, "Some tea, if you please. And Notley, Mr. Wrenwhistle will be working with me for the next fortnight. Kindly take note of his preferences."

Notley looked at Wyndham for instruction.

"I would like one splash of milk," Wyndham said, "and a sprig of lavender. If you do not have fresh lavender on hand, lavender buds will do but make sure they are taken out before the tea is brought to me. If you have no lavender at all, I will accept a single drop of rose water, but decidedly no more than a single drop. Is that understood?"

Roger thought he might get a headache from the effort of not rolling his eyes at the ridiculous request, but Notley replied, "Certainly, sir." He glanced at Roger.

Understanding what the look was meant to ask, Roger waved his hand, "Yes, by all means, the whole pot. Thank you, Notley."

Wyndham raised an eyebrow.

"I only have one teapot nice enough to use for company," Roger admitted. "Unless you wish to look at the chipped piece, I am afraid I will have to share your preferences for the time being."

"How fortunate for you. My preferences are impeccable."

Roger gestured at the chair. "Would you care to sit?"

Wyndham gave the window a long look and then moved back to the seat without a word.

"Right," Roger said as Wyndham sat. "I think all of your terms are reasonable. Although I confess to some uncertainty about the fashion one. I cannot exactly go buy new outfits simply for the next fortnight of work."

"Whyever not?"

"My funds are not that—besides clothing takes—that is, could you not simply choose which of my pieces are the least objectionable?"

Wyndham was silent for a moment. "I suppose I will allow that concession, provided you have pieces that are, in fact, unobjectionable."

"Thank you," Roger said, managing to sound only slightly sarcastic. "I think the next thing to determine is your social calendar. Should I make a list of your obligations or would you prefer to take it one day at a time?"

"The latter. My parents are hosting a party tonight, so I will not be here until late afternoon tomorrow."

"Right. Well, I can give you some books now but...er...unless you wish to read the entirety of the books, it might be preferable if I mark the sections that are most applicable?"

"Decidedly preferable."

"I can do that," Roger said, a little too hastily. He still couldn't quite believe Wyndham was being so cooperative. "Perhaps today we can simply talk through the proposal and I can answer any questions you might have? And then I will have the texts ready for you tomorrow."

Wyndham's lips pinched together for a moment. "Very well."

Roger took his own seat and waited for Wyndham to speak. When he didn't, they sat in awkward silence until Notley returned with the tea.

"Lavender buds, sir," he explained to Wyndham, before pouring out. He put a splash of milk in Wyndham's cup, and then milk and two sugars in Roger's cup.

Wyndham gave a small snort as the valet left the room. "That can barely be described as tea, Barnes."

Roger took a tentative sip and it took everything in him not to grimace. The tea tasted like he was drinking a bouquet. "How is it?" he asked nervously.

Wyndham took a sip. "A little heavier on the lavender than I'd like," he pronounced. "I shall have to request that he only put in a few buds next time."

Roger was secretly relieved to hear that. "So," he said, putting down his cup. "Did you have any questions we could discuss now?"

"I understand you intend to come up with some spells that would be used for testing purposes?"

"Yes."

"What are they?"

"I…er…haven't gotten that far yet," Roger admitted. Wyndham's eyes narrowed. "I am working on it," he added quickly. "I have about twenty spells I'm considering. I feel as though I ought to try each one first and I'm short a few ingredients."

"I see," Wyndham said. "Don't work through the spells without me here. I believe being present will help me determine appropriate fae spells."

"I can do that," Roger said. Then, because Wyndham was still drinking his tea in a leisurely way, Roger added, "If you'd like, I can try to mark one of my books for you while you are here. That way you do not have to leave empty-handed."

Wyndham nodded. "That would be acceptable."

Roger forced a smile and then went to his bookshelf. He pulled out Knopp's *Fundamentals of Magic* and sat down again. He tore a sheet of paper into strips of different lengths. "Long strips will indicate the beginning of a section and the short strips will indicate the end. Will that do?"

"Yes."

He got to work, relieved that he had something to do other than sit and watch Wyndham drink tea and pleased that he had an excuse to forget about his own cup. By the time he finished marking all of the relevant sections, Wyndham had finished the teapot. Wyndham took the book and stood, placing it on his chair.

"I will look at your wardrobe now."

Roger led him into the bedroom, feeling a little self-conscious about having the gentleman in such a space.

Wyndham did not seem to notice his discomfiture. If he did, he clearly didn't care. He opened the wardrobe and began flicking through the suits, muttering to himself. He reached the end of the selection and sighed, sounding very put upon, then started over again. He pulled out a formal suit and held it up to Roger.

"This is…almost bearable," he pronounced. "You will wear it to any evening functions you attend."

Roger took the suit and nodded.

Wyndham returned to his perusal. "My word, man," he murmured. "What do you have against decent fabric?"

"The expense," Roger muttered.

"You don't spend money on teapots or clothing. What the devil do you spend it on?"

"Well, there isn't all that much of it to be dallying with," Roger explained. "But food, rent, and magical supplies are the main priorities for me."

Wyndham hmphed in response. He finally pulled out another suit with a disgruntled expression on his face. "I suppose this will have to do. You can wear this during the day and that one at night. Where are your cravats?"

Roger pointed at a chest of drawers.

Wyndham pulled open the first drawer and took out one of Roger's oldest cravats. "You ought to repurpose this into a rag," he murmured. "But it will suit my purposes." He shoved all of Roger's clothes to one side of the wardrobe and tied the cravat to the rail. Then he held out a hand for the suits Roger was holding. "There," he said, hanging them up. "Now you will have no excuse not to forget. See to it that Notley does not rearrange this until we're done."

Before Roger had a chance to respond, Wyndham walked out of the room. Roger scurried to follow. Wyndham scooped the book off the seat and walked to the door. Roger thought he might actually leave without a word until Wyndham turned. "Use the teapot with the crack next time. I'd rather look at you using a cracked teapot than see perfectly good tea go to waste. For a man so concerned about finances, you are a shockingly wasteful creature."

Roger thought this a tad unfair, but he didn't say so. Without another word, Wyndham left. Roger collapsed onto his seat in relief. Wyndham had been in his rooms, rifled through his clothes, and drunk his tea. In a short space of time, he'd even managed to leave his mark on the place, with the curtain pulled back and the breeze fluttering through the open window. While Wyndham had hardly been kind or friendly, he had been mostly civil. It was the closest they'd ever had to friendship. Roger was unsettled by it. He took a cautious sip of his cold cup of tea. Now that he no longer had to disguise his dislike of it, he winced at the floral flavor.

There was a small part of him that wondered if he ought to inform his parents that he and Wyndham were working alone in his rooms. They would most certainly require a chaperone. But the fragile nature of their relationship felt too important to ruin with an additional party, so he dismissed it as quickly as he had considered it.

Then he got up and got to work, pulling books off of his shelves and leafing through them for the most relevant information. The project now had a greater element of pressure to it, as he not only had to prove himself to the Council, to all of London, and effectively help the children depending on this work, he also had to prove himself to Wyndham Wrenwhistle.

CHAPTER 14

WYN

UNSURPRISINGLY, the Wrenwhistles were gracious hosts to both sides of society throughout every Season, inviting whomever was most appropriate for the occasion. Wyn thought they tended to overdo it with their lenient guest lists and had told his parents as much countless times, but they refused to listen.

He often wondered if things would be the same if his grandmother wasn't Head of Council.

This evening, however, was another party to celebrate his eldest brother Auberon's recent wedding. He and his new wife, Rose, had come in special for the occasion so their parents could show them off at the London house. Somehow three separate events at their country estate hadn't been enough.

It suited Wyn well enough that humans typically seemed to have little interest in lavish wedding festivities that went on for weeks. As such, the guest list for the evening was strictly fae.

Wyn descended the stairs to the first floor, fashionably late and even more fashionably dressed in his soft green tailcoat trimmed with intricate swirls of gold thread and matching metallic buttons. He was met with a few sideways glances and little more. Most everyone was already engaged in conversation, drinks in hand. Wyn had little interest in what any of them were saying, so he didn't mind that they kept it to themselves.

After securing his own glass of wine, he wandered through the open doorway separating the two large rooms and found it was Rose gracing them with her skill on the pianoforte. He stopped at a distance to watch the way she had captivated her small audience, smiling politely all the while.

"I cannot deny that her musical aptitude is one of the things I find most endearing," came Auberon's voice to his right. Wyn turned his head slightly to look at him, eyes trailing to his shoes and back up again, before his focus returned to the corner of the room.

"Glad to see marriage hasn't killed you yet, brother," he said.

Auberon laughed. "It's scarcely been a month, Wyn. There has been little time to find displeasure in it."

Hearing his brother's casual use of his nickname caused a bit of a pang behind Wyn's ribs.

"I should imagine this is the part when you tell me that it was well worth the wait?" Auberon was nearly forty, and as the first of the four siblings to get married, he was setting an easy standard for the rest of them.

"Don't be daft. I wasn't waiting for anything, just as you haven't been, if your reputation is any indication."

Wyn took a purposefully slow pull of his wine.

"However, I must admit it's been nice to settle down with someone. I never realized how much I would enjoy sharing a quiet breakfast with the person I'd gone to bed with the night before." Auberon let out a soft chuckle. "Sometimes, I can hardly look at her across the table without abandoning my meal to take her again——"

"Oh, *all right*," Wyn's face pinched with distaste as he cut him off. "That's all very well and good. I'm endlessly happy for you both."

Without the pressure of carrying on the family inheritance, they had been free to marry with love and affection in mind, rather than duty. Emrys was the heir, but the rest of the Wrenwhistle children also benefited from the family wealth and station. It seemed his eldest sibling was wasting his fortune on discarded dressing gowns and uneaten breakfasts.

Auberon reached up to clap a hand on Wyn's shoulder, squeezing lightly.

"Has Mother said anything about making a match for you this Season?"

Wyn dipped discreetly away from his brother's touch, adjusting his shoulders and tilting his chin up a bit higher.

"She has not, and will not, if she knows what's good for her. Besides, Aveline and Emrys are next in line. It would be a bad look for me to be courted before they have any serious prospects, at the very least."

Wyn hoped that his voice hadn't betrayed him as he struggled to speak through a wave of nausea at the thought. He drained the last of his wine and instinctively scanned the room for another tray of drinks being carried around.

"And we all know how much Wyndham Wrenwhistle cares about the way things look," Auberon said, patting Wyn's upper back affectionately before winding his way through the crowd toward his blushing bride, who had started to sing along with her playing.

SOME HOURS LATER, Wyn was entranced with the flame of a candle on his mantlepiece as it danced seductively on the breeze from the open window. He idly swirled the last few sips of wine in his glass, the bowl of it cradled in his hand.

"What do you know of human magic?" he asked, his voice distant.

Sage offered a slightly hurt noise as an answer, shifting lazily beneath the rumpled bedclothes. "The one time you break your rule and talk to me after, and *that's* what you wish to discuss?"

Wyn finally blinked his way back into focus. He brought the wine glass to his mouth for a sip, carefully avoiding looking at the item in the room that had held his attention ever since it had been given to him earlier that day.

On his relatively short ride home, Wyn had flipped through the pages of the book Barnes had lent him. To his surprise, the margins had been completely filled with scribbles of notes and indecipherable sigils that made no sense to him whatsoever. Roger's handwriting really did leave much to be desired, but on the few lines Wyn could make out, it was evident that Barnes actually knew a great deal about human magic.

Wyn hadn't realized how long he'd spent looking at Roger's handiwork until he was late to a party in his own house.

Sage sighed heavily at Wyn's lack of response and sat up some, removing himself from Wyn's side, though their legs remained a bit tangled.

"Only what everyone else knows, I'm sure," he ceded, albeit bitterly. "They use all of those little lines and squiggles to write out their spells and then burn the papers after."

"I heard that if they don't burn them, the magic could eventually eat through the paper and seep into whatever surface it had been resting on, effectively giving the magic to that item."

Wyn and Sage both looked down at the man whose head was resting on Sage's hip.

"Nobody *actually* believes that to be true, Brooks," Sage said tersely, though his hand had moved from Wyn's chest to smooth over the man's short, dark hair in a fond manner. To Wyn's understanding, this was the potential suitor Sage had been waiting for in the Park. They'd apparently hit it off.

"How comparable do you think it can be to fae magic, given the right circumstances?" Wyn allowed himself a glance at the book where it sat on his desk.

"I would imagine it's quite similar, actually, if you're making an effort." Sage looked up at Wyn. "We all know that's a bit out of your reach, though."

"Oh, that's right," Brooks said with a laugh, shifting up onto his elbow. "I read that you've been paired with that tottering moron. Barnes, was it?"

"He and Wyndham have been at odds since they were children," Sage offered. Wyn felt a lick of annoyance at his words. Ravenwing didn't know the first thing about his relationship with Barnes. Admittedly, he wasn't wrong in what he'd said, but the fact remained that Sage had no room to speak on the subject. Neither of them did.

"How unfortunate for you," Brooks said, almost sounding sincere. "Perhaps you could use a bit more distracting?"

Brooks' hand snaked its way over the mussed sheets, his touch gentle on Wyn's lower stomach. Brooks hooked a finger in the edge of the sheet there, pulling it down as he got to his knees and crawled over Sage's legs.

"Make no mistake about it, Roger Barnes is the unfortunate one in this situation." Sage sat up, taking Wyn's wine glass from his hand and drinking the last of it himself before he leaned over to set it on the bedside table. He moved from doing this directly into kissing Wyn on the jaw. "Wyndham might be an insufferable jackass, but Barnes is altogether a waste of a human."

Wyn's mind flew to something Barnes had said upon their first official meeting just downstairs, and the gentle intensity with which he said it.

I know you hate me, he'd said, *and I daresay you have good reason to at this point. Is there not some way we can work together amicably? This...this project is so very important.*

It was important to Barnes because he was one of the children who had grown up to face so many prejudices, Wyn realized.

He wasn't good enough, either.

But he was willing to work with someone who disfavored him—and, arguably, someone he disfavored right back—in order to make a difference.

Wyn pushed both men off him and got out of the bed. He bent to pick up the first piece of discarded clothing he came to, and then the next, until he'd collected everything from the floor that didn't belong to him. With the flick of his wrist, he tossed it all into his sleeping hearth.

"As it so happens, I think his passion for the proposal is quite intriguing." Wyn picked up the candle he'd been watching before, getting lost in it again for a moment. His magic stirred within him at the presentation of an opportunity to play. "Moving forward, Mr. Ravenwing, I'd appreciate if you kept your own self out of my business."

Wyn dropped the candle unceremoniously onto the pile of clothes before him. His magic sprang to life, tingling wildly as Wyn called upon it. A gust of oxygen-rich air rushed into the room, feeding the little flame until it was a fully formed fire burning there on the hearthstones in a matter of seconds.

"Wyndham!" Sage cried sharply behind him, followed by a gasp. He knew the reaction held no connection to the loss of the clothes. Sage had a wardrobe that outshined even his own. The real price was his pride, which is what Wyn was after, for his lover had plenty to spare. "You hateful man," Sage added with a fretful whimper.

He listened to them shuffling around, followed by the sound of bare feet on the floor. Wyn stared at the guttering shades of orange and yellow until the door closed behind them and he was alone. He turned and walked pointedly to his desk, retrieved *Fundamentals of Magic*, and slid into his bed to continue where he'd left off.

TORQUIL'S TRIBUNE

THURSDAY 30 SEPTEMBER, 1813

Greetings, frivolous folk and home-loving humans,

It might be reasonably supposed that the Season has all but begun for our fae brethren. Last evening's party at the Wrenwhistle home was, by all accounts, vastly successful, even considering the time of year. Some reports suggest that noteworthy fae families returned to London specifically for this event. Human readers may well be surprised by the turnout for a party that has technically been going on for a month.

The recently married Auberon and Rose Wrenwhistle were exactly as beautiful and glamorous as society remembers them. There were a number of broken hearts when these two announced their engagement. Reports suggest that the couple appear to be very much in love. So any readers harboring hopes of scandalous affairs might as well give up now.

Even with the couple in attendance, Miss Aveline Wrenwhistle was considered the beauty of the evening, looking ethereal in cerulean. Perhaps this Season will be the one in which she finds romance as well?

This writer has saved the most delicious tidbit for last. Our sources say that Mr. Ravenwing and Mr. Brooks left while the party was still ongoing and with different clothes than they came in. It has been suggested that they left in cloaks that looked suspiciously like ones belonging to the Wren-whistle family. It would appear Mr. Ravenwing cannot control himself in the presence of Wrenwhistles. As this event was exclusive to fae guests, this exit did not have the uproar it might have had with a human audience. The gentlemen can most certainly be grateful for small mercies.

Your esteemed editor,

Torquil Pimpernel-Smith

CHAPTER 15

ROGER

As much as Roger strove to not need his parents' assistance, he did enjoy their company. Knowing he would not see Wyndham until the late afternoon, he walked to his parents' house to join them for breakfast. He was wearing the suit that Wyndham had grudgingly approved. It made him feel strange to obey the man's wishes even when he wasn't around.

His parents greeted him warmly as he walked into the breakfast room. Not wishing to appear as if he had merely come for the food, he sat down at the table without getting a plate first.

"How are things going with young Wyndham?" his father asked.

"Well enough," Roger answered cautiously. "Father, did you know he was going to be suggested?"

His father chuckled. "Yes, Iris told me her plan that morning."

"And you *approved* it?"

"Obviously. He was an excellent choice."

"You do realize the gentleman hates me, don't you?"

His father raised an eyebrow. "Does he?"

"Yes!"

His father hummed. "No, I did not realize that. I have, however, noticed that you can never seem to take your eyes off him when he's in the room."

Roger groaned.

His father laughed. "There were other reasons."

"Such as?"

"Fix yourself a plate, son."

Roger obeyed, secretly relieved that he had been invited to do so. His parents employed an excellent cook. When he sat back down, his father continued.

"We agreed that he was one of the best options for the task. We knew we wanted another person connected to the Council. That narrowed our options significantly. Keelan Cricket was considered, but between you and me, Keelan is not the cleverest of fae. Cricket's other child is not in London at the moment. Applewood has a daughter who is quite intelligent, but as she is the heir to her family's fortune, we quickly rejected that option."

"Why?"

His father gave him a long look. "This matters to you. And it matters to you because you have a kind heart. But it also evidently matters because you can relate to what these children are going through. It was important that whoever was assigned to work with you would have similar motivation. We are looking at changing the way we quantify magical talent. This will have a direct impact on which children inherit. It was obvious, therefore, that we could not select an heir to work with you; it would have been at odds with what they stand to benefit.

"Young Wyndham is quite like you, you know. He is remarkably intelligent and he is fiercely talented in his own magic. From what I understand, he very nearly inherited, but was just short of the mark. I confess, I would like to see you make more friends from the fae set. And I think Wyndham could probably do with a friend like you."

"I don't think he's interested in friendship, Father."

"Oh, I don't know," his mother mused. "I saw the way you two were at the St. Clairs' dinner party."

Roger stared at her. "Yes, he spoke to me for about three minutes and then pointedly ignored me for the rest of the meal. It was even in the *Tribune*."

She took a sip of tea. "He spoke to you," she pointed out. "He seems to speak to you often. I rather think he enjoys your company more than you realize."

His father smiled. "Perhaps more than both of you realize."

Roger rubbed his forehead. "I love you both, but you're rather impossible sometimes."

"Your mother wants to see you get married," his father said.

"To Wyndham Wrenwhistle?" Roger asked, his voice louder than he liked.

"He wouldn't be a bad choice."

His mother laid a hand on his arm. "Darling, I don't like to see you living alone in that dreadful little set of rooms. Particularly when we would be happy to have you stay here with us. Don't argue," she said as he opened his mouth. "But if you insist on being so independent, the least you could do is look to your own happiness."

Roger was past the point of regretting his visit. "I understand. But could you not wait on the matchmaking plots until the Season has begun? I'm really quite busy at the moment."

"According to the *Tribune*, the Season has practically begun already."

"When did they say that?"

"In this morning's column."

"Oh, I haven't read it yet."

"I'll get it for you," she said, getting up and leaving the room.

"It's going well then," his father asked in the quiet, "with you and Wyndham?"

"It's going as well as can be expected." Roger immediately felt guilty for the assessment. "Actually, it's going better than I had expected. He…er…he seems to be willing to help, which is a surprise."

"I'm glad," his father said, smiling into his tea.

His mother bustled back into the room and handed him the paper. Roger read it quickly and then read it over again with more care. Wyndham hadn't been mentioned at all, despite the fact that his family had hosted. Roger felt a sudden and inexplicable feeling of relief. Then, just as suddenly, he tried to squash that feeling, uncomfortable with having felt it in the first place.

He handed the paper back to his mother. "Thank you," he said. "And thank you both for breakfast. I'd probably better get back home and prepare for the project."

"Why don't you go to the Park with me?" his mother asked. "It's early yet. The Wrenwhistles had a party last night. He won't be up for hours. I'll even have our carriage take you back home."

Roger agreed. His mother had the carriage readied and they rode to Hyde Park together. He couldn't deny that it was nice to see some of his friends. He got to see Anthea, Cyril Thompson, and Harriet Thackery. Each of them wrangled a promise from him to come visit for tea later in the week. It was, he had to admit, nice to be wanted after his recent interactions with Wyndham. He was quite sure his mother was observing his conversations closely to look for any promising suitors. After they'd completed a circuit of the Park, she drove him back to his flat as promised.

Stepping inside his study, he stared at the mess for a long time. He tried to imagine it through Wyndham's perspective. Wyndham, who lived in luxury, whose home was filled with windows, and who took his tea with flowers in it. Wyndham, who was helping him even though he didn't like him (whatever his parents said on the matter). He took a deep breath and began doing something he hadn't done in months: tidying his study. He knew he would never be truly tidy, but he could at least attempt to keep the look of horror off Wyndham's face.

First, he put together a little fire spell. He wrote out the sigils and diagrams on a small paper and placed it in the hearth. Carefully, he sprinkled the powders on top. Once he'd cast the spell and the paper caught on fire, he added a few logs to the hearth. Fire spells had long been among his favorites to cast. He appreciated the way they destroyed themselves, thereby taking that step out of the process, and he rather loved the way the magic spread into something tangible and real. The magic-initiated flames caught onto the wood and he stepped away, satisfied.

He began collecting his discarded papers, putting them into the fire. When his floor was clear of debris, he picked up all of his notes and set them in tall, tottering piles on the floor by the window. After a long moment of consideration, he added books to the top of each pile to keep them from blowing away in the wind coming through the window.

He was just stacking up the books he had marked for Wyndham when Notley knocked on the door to announce Wyndham's arrival.

CHAPTER 16

WYN

WYN COULDN'T HELP but notice the obvious difference in his surroundings as he entered the study. Though it appeared Roger had attempted to recreate the London skyline out of books and loose papers along the far wall, the rest was a pronounced improvement. He hardly had to step over anything on his way toward the window for a quick breath of fresh air.

"That book you marked for me was nearly useless with all of your illegible scratch in the blank spaces. I believe I managed to glean some useful information from it, however." He'd forgotten it on his bedside table. He would have to return it another day.

"That's…good to hear," Roger tried, sounding uncertain.

Wyn turned from the window to look at him.

"While I understand the importance of documentation when it comes to matters such as this, I am largely a visual learner. I'll ask that you make haste in showing me what you're actually capable of."

Barnes stared at him for a moment before he looked away, seemingly flustered, which was disconcerting for Wyn. The last thing anyone wanted to see before a show of magic, be it fae or human, was confusion.

Before they could start, Notley entered with tea.

Wyn took his respective seat when it was offered and noted the way the valet had used the teapot from the previous day for his lavender brew, while a significantly more ordinary one had been brought out with Roger's blend of choice inside. From the smell of it, there was a hint of citrus. How predictable.

The two sat in silence long enough for Wyn to finish his first cup. When he moved to stand for a refill, Roger reached for the fancier of the two pots first and held it out.

"Allow me," he said. While he poured, Roger continued. "I read that your family's party last evening was a success. How wonderful to still be celebrating your brother's marriage."

"I find it quite tedious," Wyn drawled. There was nothing he wanted to think of less than the previous night's happenings.

"Ah, well, I suppose it's better to end up worn out from the festivities rather than wishing they'd gone on longer." Roger made a little shrug as he sat back down. "Both of my siblings got married early in the morning, and the whole thing was over by lunch."

"All the better," Wyn said as he lifted his fresh cup for a sip. Barnes had nearly drowned the flavor entirely with his heavy-handed pour of milk, but Wyn made no mention of it.

Another pause in conversation lingered.

"Everyone seems to think your sister will find her match this Season—"

"Are you quite finished?" Wyn snapped, glaring from his seat.

"Oh," Roger muttered, looking down into his cup with a small frown. "Yes, quite." He set the cup onto his desk and took a deep breath before putting on a smile. "What is it that you'd like to see first?"

"Perhaps something you're comfortable with," Wyn offered. "I have no interest in watching you struggle."

At that, Roger made a strangled sort of noise as he stood from his chair and began rifling around in the endless stacks of paper, crowded drawers, and jars of powders cluttering his desk. Wyn stood slowly and set aside his cup, his focus zeroing in on the small area Barnes had cleared as he stepped closer.

Roger's splayed fingers paused over the workspace briefly, before his hands curled into fists. He hummed with uncertainty until he seemed to have an idea, index fingers flicking out with a quiet *aha!* Barnes reached for the tray on which their teapots had been served. With a dramatic clatter, the man cleared them away and placed the tray down in front of him.

"I…er…typically use this spell on the hearth," he explained. Wyn's eyes shifted to the low flames already burning there. A fire spell, then. He tried to recall what he'd read about them. Easy to cast; even easier to lose control of.

His attention returned to the old desk, which was made of solid wood and still covered with books and unbalanced papers that would ignite instantaneously, given the opportunity. Roger seemed oblivious to all of this as he set up to spark a fire directly in the middle of it all upon the silver tray.

In a tick of horror, Wyn gasped and called to his magic. The gust blew in from the window strong enough to billow the heavy drapes as it sought out the hearth, effectively blowing the fire out at once. Unfortunately, it also scattered the papers all around them, ruining much of the work Roger had done to tidy up.

Roger's mouth fell open as their eyes met across the desk.

"I—" Roger started, but Wyn held up a hand to stop him, his eyes squeezing shut as he worked to settle his magic after such a wild burst.

"Have you absolutely no concern for safety? I should love to see the look on the headmaster's face if he knew how little you've retained from all our years of schooling." Wyn's eyes snapped open when Roger tried to speak again. "I do not want your explanation," he said coolly. "Just move the demonstration."

Roger was able to take his piece of paper covered in seemingly random marks and place it on the hearthstones, which were still warm but safe to touch. Wyn stood aside and watched as Roger poured ingredients from the jars into several small piles. When he cast his spell, a tiny flame flickered to life before their eyes. Wyn crouched smoothly by the hearth to get a closer look, temporarily losing himself with interest.

"What were the ingredients?" he asked mildly.

"I use powdered rosemary, dried ash wood pulp, and peppercorns," Roger explained, adding new cuts of wood to feed the flames before he sat back on his heels.

Wyn's tongue slid out to wet his lips as he stood, his teeth catching the corner of his bottom lip as he contemplated what he'd just watched.

He'd never seen anything like it up close before. His mind whirled. How could they possibly find a compatible match of fae magic for this? He could give fire life once it was already burning, of course. But to create it from nothing?

"Show me something else," he demanded.

Under Wyn's direction, the pair worked into the evening, with Roger showcasing what he could do until Notley interrupted with an inquiry as to whether or not Mr. Wrenwhistle would be staying for a late supper.

"Certainly not," Wyn said, smoothing his hands down the front of his raspberry waistcoat as he peered outside. The sun had nearly set. He cleared his throat in mild surprise and averted his gaze from the mess they'd made of the study. It was entirely unsurprising that the man did not pick up after himself as he went. Anyone looking to solve a mystery would be lucky to follow a trail left behind by Roger Barnes.

For the briefest moment, Wyn considered offering his assistance in cleaning up a bit before he departed. He'd been the one forcing spell after spell out of him, after all.

"You'd do well to clean this up before our next meeting," is what came out instead as he made his way toward the door, where the valet was waiting with his things. He shrugged on his coat and tucked his hat under his arm as he took his leave in silence.

CHAPTER 17

ROGER

ROGER WAS sure he ought to be upset that Wyndham had left him with a mess to clean up. But after such a productive day, after seeing Wyndham's expression of interest, his probing curiosity, and his eagerness to learn more, Roger couldn't drum up the usual outrage.

He went to bed feeling satisfied, but without being able to put a finger on why. He woke the following day feeling vaguely excited. When he realized he was looking forward to working with Wyndham again, he struggled to decide if this was a good thing or not. He finally decided not to worry about defining it and got up, ate breakfast, and began putting the room back to rights.

When he was done, he read over the notes he'd been jotting down throughout the day and after Wyndham had left. He'd shown Wyndham the fire spell, a shrinking spell, a glowing spell, a spell for balance, a spell for shade, and a finding spell. In between these, they'd discussed Roger's ideas for how each spell would be useful for measuring different skills, his concerns about certain spells, and he even discussed the ones he'd been considering but required ingredients he didn't currently have in stock.

Roger was so accustomed to thinking of his magic as ordinary or unexceptional. He knew that compared to the rest of his family, he was lacking in skill. Part of him worried about this a little, thinking that Wyndham had received a poor introduction to human magic with him as the guide. Wouldn't it have been better if Frederica had shown him how she worked, or Bernard, or even one of their parents? His father, in particular, was a very patient and thorough teacher of magic. Bernard was less patient, but had been sent to school for the purpose of studying the science and was regarded as an expert in some circles. Quite frankly, when his brother and father were in the room, Roger usually *felt* his low scores as they talked in technical detail. Bernard was always quick to tell Roger that his own study in magic lacked the necessary organization. Surely Roger was the least qualified person he knew for such an undertaking?

But he thought about what his father had told him the previous morning. If his father was right, Wyndham's skill was comparable to his own. Roger knew he had skill, but he was inclined to think of it as average. Perhaps that was the key: two average people coming up with an appropriately average gauge for magic.

This thought brought upon further ruminating. The first was that while Wyndham could be described as many things, Roger didn't think *average* could possibly be one of them. Wyndham was far from ordinary. Whatever the fae's skill, Roger struggled to see it as similar. The second rumination was that Wyndham's reaction to Roger's magic had suggested it was anything but ordinary or unexceptional. They had worked without noting the time, without realizing how many hours had passed. Wyndham had been so fully absorbed watching Roger's magic as to lose himself in the experience. And Roger found, most terrifyingly, that he *liked* that. Perhaps a little too much.

He also deeply wanted to be the center of Wyndham's focus again, so he set about composing a list of possible spells they could work on that day and what questions Wyndham might ask and, further, what questions Roger could ask to draw more information from Wyndham about fae magic.

When Wyndham arrived in the early afternoon, Roger felt prepared. As it turned out, he wasn't prepared enough because Wyndham set a few packages on the desk and explained, "I believe these were the ingredients you said you required," and Roger had found himself incapable of appropriate response.

Finally, after a long moment of staring at the purchases (some were rather pricey, which was why he hadn't yet replenished his stock), he stammered, "That was very kind of you. Thank you. I…er…I suppose I'd forgotten that the Council offered us a stipend for this work. Clever of you to remember it."

Wyndham's expression was unreadable before he replied, "Yes, well, I prefer to be prepared when I begin a project. Your dwindling supplies were hardly a promising start."

Roger allowed himself a small smile. "How fortunate that I have your help."

Wyndham's eyebrow lifted. "Indeed. Shall we begin?"

"Wouldn't you like tea first?"

Wyndham blinked. "Ah, yes. Tea. Of course."

Roger rang for Notley, wondering idly if he'd missed something crucial. As they sat down in their usual seats, Roger put a stack of books on the table. "You forgot these yesterday," he said. "I daresay neither of us expected to work so late. Would you still like to read them?"

Wyndham took the stack and leafed through the book on top. "Do you scribble in all of your books?"

"Writing out my thoughts helps me to think," Roger admitted.

Wyndham gave a small snort. "Going by the number of papers you use, it would seem you require a great deal of mental assistance." He clapped the book shut and set the stack aside. "Yes, I'll take these home with me. Assuming I can decipher them amongst your chaotic writing, I might be able to glean something useful."

The tea arrived and they drank in silence. Roger would have almost described it as companionable, though that term seemed incongruous with Wyndham's prickly personality.

It was Wyndham who prompted them to begin. He seemed to have continued thinking about their project after he'd left the previous day, as he launched into a great deal of questions. He wanted to know how Roger acquired his materials, if he ever prepared any ingredients himself, if he ever used raw ingredients, whether there was rhyme or reason to what was dried, what was powdered, and what was liquefied. He wanted to know if the different forms of materials changed the way they were used in spells. He wanted to know how much of the written part of magic had to be memorized or whether it was expected for a human to refer to their books as often as Roger did when casting spells.

Roger found he liked Wyndham's questions. They were unusual and unexpected. He answered them all: he got all of his materials from experts, preparing ingredients was dangerous so he never did it himself; raw ingredients were too potent for practical use; different forms of ingredients brought out different strengths from each item so there was intention behind each material item and how they were employed in each spell; and it was common to need books for spells that were not cast daily although Roger's collection was probably greater than average. Once he answered, Wyndham asked further questions. The back-and-forth turned more into the realm of a discussion, and Roger realized he was gaining an understanding of Wyndham's mind for the first time. He found he liked the way the man's mind worked. Then he promptly pushed that thought away.

Roger performed more spells for Wyndham, showing him a cleaning spell, using his chipped teapot as the focus, and a dicing spell for a piece of produce that Notley procured for their experimentation.

He even showed Wyndham a scrying spell his family had established in the country estate. "These are fiddly," he explained, "and need a great deal of preparation. You see, they have to be set up on one end first. My parents set this up when we were all learning magic. When we went off to university, they put it back up at our request so we could look at it whenever we got homesick. It has stayed ever since. Whenever one of us is at home, we like to put little messages on that table there, so that anyone who scries into the room can read the message." He heard the wistfulness in his own voice.

Embarrassed, he cleared his throat. "Anyway, they have to be established on one end and part of the setup is including who else can cast the other half of the spell. That way you don't get thieves or strangers poking around in your house, visually-speaking. So each member of the family is included in the initial process when the spell is cast."

Wyndham stared at the empty sitting room for a long moment. "Has this spell been sitting there for years then?" he asked at last.

"In a manner of speaking," Roger replied. "It is refreshed several times a week."

"With the same paper?"

"No, a different paper. Each time it is cleaned up, the previous spell is usually burned up. My brother, Bernard, is living at home right now with his spouse. Neither of them like London very much, and Bernard will be inheriting the house. So he's usually at home even if my parents are not. He maintains the spell regularly. It's probably silly," he added, "keeping a spell to view an empty room just in case someone in the family gets homesick."

Wyndham pursed his lips. "No," he said slowly. "It's not silly."

Roger waited for him to continue speaking, but he didn't, so Roger moved the conversation along to the next spell on their list.

When Notley came in to ask again if their guest was staying to dinner, Wyndham reacted as he had the previous night. He glanced out the window, then at the clock, and hastily gathered his things.

Roger handed him the stack of books. "Don't want you to forget these again," he teased with a smile.

"No," Wyndham said, taking them. "It would indeed be dreadful if I had to hear you attempt to explain it all."

Roger thought he heard a bit of sarcasm in the insult. Was that wishful thinking?

Wyndham looked at the books in his hands. "These might keep me busy for most of the day. I'm not sure I shall be able to come over tomorrow. I have a garden party the following day, so I doubt I'll be able to work on this again until Monday."

"That's all right," Roger said, trying to repress his sudden disappointment. "You did warn me that you had many social engagements. At least you'll have the books during that time. I'm sure that will help expedite our discussion on Monday."

"Yes." As he had on the night before, Wyndham gave the study a thoughtful look.

"I'll clean it up before you return," Roger offered.

Wyndham's gaze flicked to his. "Good," he murmured quietly.

CHAPTER 18

WYN

WITH THE BORROWED books on his desk burning a hole into his mind, Wyn was unable to sleep in as he preferred. He requested that his breakfast be brought up to his room.

He donned his navy silk dressing robe over his bare shoulders and cinched the sash loosely at his waist. He set up to study on the low sofa situated by the double doors that led to his balcony. His view was nothing worth mentioning, but it let ample air into the room so he could think more clearly.

Wyn crossed one ankle over the other and opened the first book, *Basic Spellwork* by Alistair Comden, on his lap. He was careful to keep one hand free to turn the pages, as his other hand was occupied by a piece of toast slathered generously with orange marmalade. No matter how badly Barnes decided to ruin his own books with pencil marks and dog-eared corners, Wyn had no interest in adding his own sticky, citrusy contribution.

He was pleased to find that much of what Roger had shown him was described with more detail on the pages, from ingredient options to tips on what to do if something wasn't working. *How curious*, he thought, *to provide alternatives for magic.*

By the time Wyn finished several cups of tea, he'd moved on to the thickest book in the stack, *Principles of Magic Theory*. He crossed his legs and bent forward over the pages as he skimmed through; this one was far too detailed to read cover to cover.

He found multiple sections that caught his attention. After skipping over the pages covering fire, he came to a part that discussed levitation. Barnes had shown him a neat little spell that encouraged a piece of paper to float several inches above the desk. Wyn had waved his hand underneath to test the air and found that it wasn't like his own ability to make things float, but more of a suspension within the air itself. Though in both instances, it was possible to grab the item from the air and move it—

"But could that alter the...yes, certainly it would disturb the spell..." Wyn mumbled to himself as he turned the page, brows furrowed in thought.

An Introduction to Magical Ingredients turned out to be his favorite of the three. It was overflowing with colorful illustrations of flowers, fruits, seeds, leaves, and more. A tickle in his chest told him that his magic felt his excitement, too.

In the bottom left corner of a page toward the back of the book, there was an explosion of cupped, purple petals delicately displaying their prized stigmas. He was reminded of how elated Barnes had looked when he'd found the tiny jar of saffron he'd brought with the rest of the ingredients the day before. Wyn took the time to read the description next to the flower in an attempt to forget this memory.

It would've been wise to ask his grandmother for the Council's stipend before wandering into one of London's finest magic shops. Barnes had been correct that some of the ingredients were surprisingly expensive, but Wyn was no stranger to expense, so he'd simply asked the shop owner for what he needed and left.

Unwilling to mark up the pages, Wyn got up from the sofa to procure some paper for notes of his own. A thousand questions had crossed his mind already and he was certain there were more to come. If he wasn't going to see Barnes for a few days, he would need to write them down so he wouldn't forget.

A soft knock on Wyn's door was the only thing to tear his focus from his research. He'd ended up sitting on the floor with all of his notes and the four borrowed books spread around him. He looked up to find his mother standing in the doorway with a look of surprise on her face.

"Wynnie, dear, is this where you've been all morning? I was starting to think you'd spent the night somewhere."

Wyn blinked hard and brought his hand up to rub at the spot between his eyebrows. "What time is it?"

"Nearly time for lunch," she said, wandering closer. "What's all this?"

"Ah, just some research for the project with Barnes. You know I find it difficult to work on something without having as much information as possible." Wyn started to collect the notes, stacking them into piles, suddenly feeling a touch embarrassed under his mother's inquisitive eye.

"Just like your father," she cooed. "I'm so proud of you for taking this project to heart as you have. It's wonderful to see you committing yourself to something."

Wyn bristled, stepping over his mess as he stood and attempted to herd his mother out of his room. He'd never liked her propensity for lingering.

"Yes, well, I wasn't given much of a choice, was I?" he asked with a tight grin, placing his hand on her back and steering her toward the door. She laughed sweetly and went without a fight. Wyn nearly had the door closed when she turned around and pushed her way back in just a little, so that her face was poking through the crack. He clenched his jaw tight.

"You really should give yourself a break after all this hard work, though," she said. "It's not healthy to stare at those books for so long. Your eyes will cross."

Wyn sighed and brought his hand up again, rubbing a small circle against his temple with his fingertips. His head did ache a bit, now that she mentioned it.

"I'll see to it that I take a break when I reach a good point to stop. I was right in the middle of something." He glanced over his shoulder at the paper he'd been writing on. It was another question for Barnes about illumination. The spells he'd seen in one of the texts were much different than the glowing spell Roger had performed; he wanted to know if either of them was more closely connected to his fairy light magic, if at all.

"Oh, oh, yes," his mother said apologetically, removing her hand from the door where she'd been pushing to keep it open. The latch clicked loudly as the door shut in her face. Wyn couldn't bring himself to feel bad about it. He listened for a moment to make sure she walked away, and then returned to his nest of human magic research.

He'd barely sat down when the door swung open again.

"Mother!" he wailed.

"Wyndham!" she mocked lovingly, offering him her brightest smile. "Remember that we're going to the opera tonight. I expect you to be ready to leave on time."

"Yes, *all right*," he said, agreeing to anything so she would leave him alone.

When she finally shut the door for good, Wyn leaned his head back onto the sofa with a heavy sigh. Maybe she was right. He had a bad habit of becoming rather consumed with things if he wasn't careful. He lifted his chin to look over the back of the sofa, out the double doors. It would be a nice evening and he wouldn't mind the walk to stretch his legs after sitting for so many hours. Although, his mother would likely force them to ride in the carriage; shuffling in with the rest of society was unbecoming.

Wyn sat up and found where he'd left off. Pausing for a moment to remember what he'd been writing, he continued in a sweeping, elegant script that he was quite proud of.

Without realizing, he'd come away with nearly a dozen pages of questions on which he wanted Roger's input. Wyn frowned at the stack of papers. It seemed ridiculous to save them all for when they met again, as it would probably take an hour or more to go through. He decided the best option would be to send them out so Roger could read over everything and have answers ready when they reconvened.

Wyn hopped up to get the papers ready to be sent. He chose his nicer stationery to serve as a cover letter explaining himself. He blotted his pen and began to address the letter to Barnes, but paused.

Perhaps it would make more sense to ask the questions in person. After all, it was highly likely he would have follow up questions for Roger, and by the time they were able to speak, he probably would have forgotten what he asked in the first place.

Wyn turned in his chair to look at the items still scattered across the floor. He thought of Roger's study and how it looked that way all the time. If Roger was feeling the way Wyn was at the moment—determined but a bit overwhelmed—then maybe he could also use a break. The last thing Wyn needed was for Roger to become too exhausted and embarrass them both in front of the Council.

Pen to paper, he wrote out a short letter to Barnes and had it sent at once. The rest of his notes remained on his desk as he went downstairs for lunch.

CHAPTER 19

ROGER

ROGER WAS FEELING unsure of what to do with himself for the day. As promised, he had tidied up the study. But with Wyndham reading through the borrowed texts, Roger didn't know how to prepare for the inevitable questions. He wasn't sure if Wyndham would want to see more spells so he didn't know what he ought to set aside in advance. It felt odd to be waiting on someone else. At the same time, it felt a little exciting because he knew Wyndham would have thoughts and questions.

He was in the midst of doing a second circuit of rifling the piles of notes into tidier stacks, when he received a note from Wyndham. Opening it, he read one of the last things he would have expected to hear from the gentleman, short of a declaration of love: it was an invitation to join the Wrenwhistle family in their opera box that evening.

Roger sat down with a thump. There was no question of whether or not he intended to accept the invitation; the question was when had Wyndham changed from despising him to voluntarily choosing to spend time with him? The note stated that Wyndham had questions about the books he'd read and the questions were better suited to an in-person conversation. Still, Roger wasn't sure that the opera was going to be a night filled with academic discussion. Perhaps he was reading too much into it? He finally decided that must be the case, quickly penned an acceptance of the invitation, had Notley send it out, and explained that he would be going out for the evening.

When it finally came time to get dressed, he was strangely relieved to have Wyndham's reluctant approval of his formal wear. He found he hated the idea of embarrassing the Wrenwhistles at their opera box.

At the appointed time, the Wrenwhistle carriage arrived to collect him. When the door to the carriage was opened, he found Wyndham, Emrys, Aveline, and Mrs. Wrenwhistle all politely greeting him. He was struck by the strangeness of the situation. He had never spent much time with Wyndham's family. Emrys helped him into the carriage and before he knew it, he was seated next to Wyndham and the carriage was on its way back to the nicer part of town.

"I'm so glad you were able to join us," Mrs. Wrenwhistle said.

"It was very kind of you to invite me," Roger replied.

She smiled. "I was delighted when Wyndham told me he'd extended the invitation."

"Why do you live all the way out here?" Emrys asked.

"Well, I reached majority last Season," Roger explained.

"Your parents didn't want you to stay with them?" Aveline asked, her expression puzzled.

"N-no, they did," he replied. "They frequently tell me they'd prefer it if I moved back with them. But, well, I can't live on their generosity forever, you know. I thought it best to get accustomed to it sooner."

"I'm surprised," Mrs. Wrenwhistle said, "I would have thought your mother would be keen to see you married."

Roger felt he was on dangerous ground with this conversation, but he responded, "She is. In fact, she's mentioned that she would like to see me matched by the end of the Season, but considering my age and...and everything, I'm not sure—"

"I am determined to see these three married soon as well," Mrs. Wrenwhistle said. "So I daresay we will see a great deal more of each other when the Season begins."

Wyndham shifted restlessly next to him and Roger turned to give him an inquiring look. Wyndham didn't meet his eyes.

"How is your little project going?" Emrys asked.

Roger tore his gaze from Wyndham's face and turned back to his brother. "It's going well, I think."

"I hope you're telling Wyn where he can go anytime he's nasty to you," Aveline said.

"Er...there's no need. Mr. Wrenwhistle has been...he's been a very... courteous and engaging partner in this task." This statement was met with varied amused expressions from the rest of the Wrenwhistle family. Roger quickly attempted to redirect the topic. He turned again to Wyndham. "You said you had questions for me?"

"Yes," Wyndham replied in a clipped tone. "But I don't think the carriage is the right place to discuss it. Perhaps when we go to dinner afterwards."

"Oh." Roger hadn't realized there was more to the evening than the opera.

"The Crickets are having a little soiree at their home after the opera. Nothing too formal," Mrs. Wrenwhistle explained. "Just a few friends for dinner and cards. Possibly some dancing. Do you like to dance, Roger?"

"I-I do, but—"

"Excellent," she said. "I'm sure we'll be able to find you a dance partner."

"You might be the only human present," Emrys said. "I'm sure that will be new for you."

"Will they mind my being there?" Roger asked, nervous. "I wasn't invited, after all."

"Nonsense," Mrs. Wrenwhistle replied. "You're with us. They won't mind at all."

Roger was relieved when they pulled up to the opera house and the conversation came to an end. Emrys helped everyone down from the carriage, but it was Wyndham who offered Roger his arm as they walked into the building. Roger had been to the opera several times over the course of his adulthood, but never in the company of people as elegant as the Wrenwhistles. They greeted others with little nods and smiles as they ascended the stairs. Roger caught some hopeful glances at each of the siblings and several incredulous looks at himself.

When they were seated in the box, Mrs. Wrenwhistle insisted Roger take the centermost seat, with Wyndham on his side. Wyndham rested his elbow on the arm rest and drummed his fingers rhythmically.

Roger leaned over and murmured, "It was very kind of you to invite me."

The drumming paused for a moment before picking up again. "It was nothing. I was more concerned about forgetting my questions. We are likely to stay out late, and then we have the garden party tomorrow. Far too long to go on trying to remember a few questions."

"Ah," Roger said. "I can understand that. Did…did you like the books?"

"Some more than others."

"Which?"

Wyndham gave a little sigh. "I don't wish to get into a discussion, only to have it cut short by the performance. Why don't you relax for once, Barnes, and enjoy the evening for a bit? We'll discuss the project at dinner."

"Oh. Sorry." Roger sat back in his seat and straightened his cravat. Then he adjusted his cuffs. Pushed his spectacles up his nose. Crossed and uncrossed his ankles. He was just about to straighten his cravat again when Wyndham reached over and placed light fingers on his wrist.

"Are you always this nervous around others?" he asked, his tone sounding amused.

"No," Roger answered.

Wyndham gently guided Roger's hand away from his cravat. Roger dropped his hand into his lap and clenched his hands together.

"Far be it from me to discourage you from paying attention to your cravat, but it isn't going anywhere." He paused. "And frankly it's far too plain and boring to require that much attention anyway." He leaned over to Roger and said in a low voice, "Relax, Barnes. The project will keep. You've been working yourself to the bone for the past few days—in fact, I imagine you've been working yourself ragged for weeks, or even months now. It would hardly do either of us any good for you to run yourself into the ground. As difficult as you are sometimes, I don't think your corpse would be much of an improvement in terms of a work partner. It would certainly answer fewer of my questions." The lights began to dim. "You do know how to relax, don't you?"

Roger nodded.

"Good. Do make the attempt."

Perhaps it was because Wyndham had invited Roger to spend the time with his family, or perhaps because Wyndham spoke in a soft voice in Roger's ear, or perhaps because he had *almost* complimented him—Roger followed the man's advice and relaxed beside him.

CHAPTER 20

WYN

ROGER BARNES WAS the most distracting person Wyn had ever attended the opera with. When he wasn't fidgeting with his clothes or shuffling in his chair, he was watching with his mouth wide open, breathing loud enough in his intense focus that Wyn could hear it over the performers at times. On top of all that, the lights of the opera house reflected in Roger's spectacles, catching Wyn's attention in his peripheral every time the man moved his head.

Was this what it was like spending leisure hours with humans?

One of the times Wyn had been drawn by the reflection, he glanced for long enough to see Roger smile at something that happened on stage. It was a faint little thing, but it was there. Wyn's gaze was still lingering on the corner of his mouth when Roger turned his head to look at him. His smile faded in an instant, and Wyn looked away.

The carriage ride to the Cricket residence was full of chatter from Wyn's family. They gushed about the performances, the performers themselves, and commented at length about who had been seen with whom in the audience.

Wyn watched out the window, itching to pull out the pages of notes tucked into his breast pocket as soon as they could escape the loud company they found themselves in.

What he really needed was a glass of wine.

Predictably, Wyn and Roger were seated together at dinner, but it still felt like poor timing to discuss his notes. He knew his mother would've scolded him endlessly for pulling them out during a meal at someone else's home. Instead, Wyn tried to pick up where they'd left off, since it was something Roger had sounded interested in.

"*An Introduction to Magical Ingredients* was most beautifully illustrated," he started after setting his drink down by his plate.

Roger turned to look at him, his chewing slowed for a moment before he swallowed and reached for his own glass to wash it down.

"Er, yes, I agree. That book was a gift from my parents, actually. I had mentioned once that I felt most of my reference books were sadly lacking in examples of what the ingredients look like, before they're…well, before they're ground up, you know."

Wyn hummed his understanding.

"I have a theory about that," he said, using his fork to push around some of the food he wasn't planning on eating.

Roger turned more in his chair to face Wyn. "Oh?"

"It's something we'll need to experiment with," Wyn explained softly, knowing that Emrys, Aveline, and the other guests could likely hear everything he was saying. "I'm not sure I could explain it without showing you."

The rest of the meal dragged on for entirely too long, which was something Wyn always disliked about these smaller dinners. The fewer the guests, the more there was to talk about, it seemed.

When dessert was finally over, Wyn all but leapt from his chair and helped Roger out of his own, showing off his best manners in case his mother was watching, which she always was. Wyn led Roger through the connecting room out onto a small balcony overlooking the street, closing the doors behind them.

His notes were in his hands in seconds. He split the stack to give half to Roger. A gentle breeze rustled the pages as Wyn leaned his hip against the metal railing, crossing one ankle over the other.

"Your glowing spell. It creates a light, similar to some of the other illumination spells I read about. But what is the ingredient you used to create the heat to go along with it? Is there some kind of a reaction between the materials used, or does it simply become light and heat because that's what you've asked it to do?"

Roger paused in his reading of the notes to consider the question. His mouth opened slightly, but no words came out, and Wyn's patience had run too thin for that kind of a reaction. He rolled his eyes and brought his hand up to snap his fingers. Between them, a small cluster of fairy lights bloomed into life, buzzing around a bit at first before they settled.

"I want to know if this is something we can use comparatively between the two rubrics, but—" Wyn stopped to reach out for one of the fairy lights. It floated away from his fingers as they got closer. He tried again with the same result. "You cannot touch them to know if they're warm or not."

When Roger only gaped at the lights, Wyn sighed and waved them away, sending them floating into the night air. He returned to his notes, trying to find some of the more pressing questions.

"Oh," he said, pushing away from the railing to stand next to Roger so he could point to what he'd written. "The shrinking spell. Is it something that's easily reversible?" Wyn looked around them on the balcony, searching for something he could work with. A window box full of flowers would have to do.

Wyn breathed in deeply and called to his magic, seeking out the little red and yellow blooms. Wyn gestured to them to make sure Roger could see as they grew and thickened, as though they'd been served the finest mix of soil and manure that ever existed.

"I cannot make them shrink, but I can make them grow. They'll stay like that as long as they're properly looked after. That's the only way the magic will remain. Otherwise, they'll die as they would have anyway." Wyn looked down at Roger to try and gain some kind of response from the man.

"*Oh*," Roger breathed. Wyn's notes were crumpled in his hands.

Wyn's brow furrowed. He looked at the flowers again and then at Roger. He chuckled dryly and crossed his arms. "New to fae magic, are we?"

"I—" Roger began.

"Take my notes home, then. Read them at a pace that won't make your little human brain ache. Then we'll discuss them." Wyn wrestled the notes out of Roger's hand and smoothed them against his thigh, before adding them to the rest. When Roger didn't move to take them fast enough, Wyn pulled Roger's coat open and stuck them in his breast pocket. "They'll be expecting us inside," he said shortly.

When they returned, it wasn't a moment too soon—or too late, rather—as they were swept up into the first dance of the evening. Wyn groaned internally, knowing that the Crickets were very fond of their bouncy country dances rather than the slower dances that were most popular in the city.

As the last two to join, they were paired together at the end of the double lines. The music began and the room erupted into fits of tipsy giggles and flirtatious smiles as everyone worked to move together through the fast footwork. After an awkward start, Wyn and Roger fell into stride as best they could, learning as they went how to move with one another.

It became obvious quite fast that while Wyn was a natural dancer, Roger actually *enjoyed* dancing, as he'd said earlier in the evening. The lines shifted and partners shuffled around their neighbors. Roger began to smile and laugh with the rest of them. His steps were a bit clumsy at times, and he stepped on Wyn's foot more than once, but Wyn couldn't find it in him to mind much.

By the time the music ended, everyone was out of breath but deliriously happy, as they clapped and thanked the leading couple.

Despite himself, Wyn wore a small grin.

"You're an excellent dancer," Roger said, and Wyn looked down to find him standing closer than he'd been before.

"My mother would've allowed for nothing less," Wyn told him.

"I suppose I'll have to thank her." Roger began to look around the room as though he was actually seeking her out to do just that, and Wyn felt a twinge of panic.

"You can thank her later," Wyn started, leaning down a bit. "Right now I want to know more about why your reaction to my magic was that of a man witnessing a miracle. You're aware that you can also do magic, yes?"

Roger's shoulders came up toward his ears and he shook his head a bit as he laughed, indicating that he didn't have a good answer at that moment. The smile on Wyn's mouth, which had never left, grew a little bit more. The music started up again, indicating it was time for a second round.

"Do you want to share another dance?" Roger asked breathlessly.

Wyn's grin vanished. His gaze swept around the room to the couples who were lining up together, to his mother watching him from across the room as she spoke to their host, to every other pair of eyes on him.

Two dances in one evening. They all knew what that meant. Wyn knew what that meant. Certainly Roger had to know, as well?

Wyn took a step back, then another, and then he turned and walked away.

CHAPTER 21

ROGER

ROGER REALIZED IMMEDIATELY that he had made an error. He'd only wanted to keep dancing. He'd also wanted to keep that small smile on Wyndham's face. But when the smile transformed into a look of horror, Roger wished he could take back his words.

Part of him wanted to follow Wyndham, to explain, to apologize. But he felt fairly sure that such a strategy would only make things worse. So he left the dance floor and made his way to a chair.

Mrs. Wrenwhistle asked where Wyndham had gone and he answered that the gentleman needed to step away from the crowded dance floor. She did not seem to believe his response, tsked disapprovingly at her son's behavior, then strode off.

Roger pulled Wyndham's notes out of his breast pocket and looked over them. He supposed there had been a part of him that had forgotten Wyndham's role in the project. He'd never seen fae magic before. His father said that his and Wyndham's skill levels were comparable. But after seeing Wyndham snap lights out of thin air, make a plant *grow*—and all without any formulas, ingredients, or calculations—Roger was in awe. And he wasn't entirely sure fae magic was as comparable to human magic as everyone said. He could never do something like that. Then again,

Wyndham seemed to disagree. His chest warmed at the memory of the other man's words.

He turned his attention to the papers in his hand, deciding that the very least he owed Wyndham was a consideration of his questions. He read until Wyndham informed him that they were ready to leave. He wanted to explain his foolhardiness earlier, or talk about Wyndham's questions, but one look at the gentleman's face told him it wasn't the right time. They didn't speak as they left the Crickets' home and the carriage ride was awkward as Wyndham sat stiff and unspeaking beside him.

He thanked them all for the invitation and went up to his rooms. He stayed up late into the night, writing out answers to every one of Wyndham's questions.

The following morning he was awoken by Notley, who promptly handed him a note from Roger's mother, explaining that a response was expected. Blearily, he read the note, a short reminder that there was a garden party that afternoon and she expected him to attend. Hadn't Wyndham mentioned a garden party? Could it be the same one? He wasn't sure if he hoped it would be or not, but at the very least he could give the gentleman his responses.

When the time came, he dressed in the Wyndham-approved day suit, tucked both sets of notes into his breast pocket, and went downstairs to meet his parents in their carriage.

"How is the project going, dear?" his mother asked as he took his seat.

"It's going well, I think," he answered. "Mr. Wrenwhistle has been asking some very insightful questions and he even started discussing some ideas he had for fae spells that were somewhat comparable..." He paused and turned to his father. "Have you ever seen fae magic performed?"

"I have."

"Then how—that is, do you really think the two systems are all that comparable?"

"Why not?"

"Well, Wyn—Mr. Wrenwhistle made a flower grow right in front of me! And he did it without any tools or preparation. I-I rather think fae magic is considerably more impressive."

His father smiled. "That is probably because you understand your own magic. Anything can lose its wonder once the mysteries are revealed."

Though Roger saw his father's point, he didn't entirely agree. He wanted to mention the fairy lights, but that felt too special to speak about. Instead he said, "But our magic requires so much more."

His father looked thoughtful. "Not exactly. Let's examine the two more critically, shall we?" His tone took on a distinctly instructional note. "We know that magic is in all things, yes? And we know that to perform magic, we are essentially pulling from our own magical resources, yes?"

"Well, yes, but...all right, for example, the flower that Wy—Mr. Wren-whistle helped grow yesterday. As a living object, a flower has a great deal of magic in it. Our magic could not accomplish such a thing. He was offering it as a similar spell to a shrinking spell. The difference is that while one could make a living thing shrink, it would take a great deal of our own magical resources."

His father smiled. "And why is that?"

Roger sighed. "Magical Balance Theory. But that's just my point—"

"Precisely," his father said, leaning forward. "In order to make anything shrink, you need to counterbalance the magic you need with power of your own. So to make a flower shrink, you would need a massive reserve of your own magic—so massive, you would probably drain your own power to a dangerous amount."

"That's just my point!" Roger said. "He did that and then he *danced* afterward. He was anything but drained."

"You are mistaking comparable with identical," his father replied. "Our magic systems are comparable, but they are not the same. Human magic functions through Magical Balance Theory. Fae magic still requires balance, but of a different kind."

Roger frowned. "What do you mean?"

His father considered. "Let us imagine you are lifting a heavy item off the ground—no magic, just through your own personal strength—to lift the item, you need an equal but opposite force. For example, you are unlikely to be able to lift this entire carriage off the ground as it weighs significantly more than you. However, if you were to put a plank under the carriage and use something to leverage the plank, you would be able to lift it. Why is that? The carriage still weighs the same."

"I suppose...because the plank is taking that weight and distributing it in a way that I could not do alone."

"Exactly! Now, fae magic still requires balance and still taps into the caster's own magical resources. But instead of trying to lift the magic up by themselves, they are tapping into the living thing's magic to encourage it to do something within its nature. There is an innate balance to that. Rather than brute force, they leverage the magic. Do you see?"

Roger wasn't sure he did.

"Let me explain it differently. The flower that Wyndham grew. He didn't grow it out of his hand, did he?"

"No, the flower already existed; he made it grow larger."

"So he tapped into the flower's magic *directly* and encouraged it in the direction he wanted. Humans transfer magical power from other items and ingredients in order to infuse the item they are working with, thereby creating a balance between the caster and the spell so the caster doesn't siphon off their own magic in the act. Fae don't necessarily transfer any magical power at all; they simply use their magic to interact with the innate magic of whatever they're working with. It's almost like a different form of communication, if you will."

"But that's so much more remarkable," Roger protested.

His father chuckled. "It is remarkable. But I would argue that our own magic is something to be proud of, too. If Wyndham is asking questions, he must be curious. If he is curious, it is because he is intrigued. That's no small thing."

"I suppose," Roger muttered, finally ceding the point.

"Did you say he danced afterwards?" his mother asked in a too-casual tone.

"Er…y-yes. We were at the Crickets' home. He…er…well the Wren-whistles invited me to join them in their opera box last night and then to the Crickets' dinner party after."

She beamed. "How lovely. Did you have a good time?"

He weighed the discomforts of the evening—his anxiety at the opera, the look of horror on Wyndham's face, the awkwardness of the carriage—against the pleasures—watching fae magic on the balcony, dancing with Wyndham, hearing the gentleman compliment him, and his small smile before Roger ruined everything. "Yes," he said at last. "I did."

"We shall have to have them all over for dinner after your proposal is accepted."

Roger glanced between his parents and their far-too-obvious smiles. "Yes, I think that would be nice," he responded cautiously.

When they arrived at the Grenvilles' garden party, Roger was surprised by how large the crowd was. "Isn't it a bit early for this sort of turnout?" he asked.

"The Council convened early," his father explained as he helped Roger's mother out of the carriage. "We've been seeing more people trickle back to town as a result."

"Besides," his mother added, "the Season is just around the corner. Oh! I think I see the Wrenwhistles. Why don't you go greet them, dear?"

As much as he disliked the idea of talking to Wyndham under his mother's watchful eye, Roger did as she suggested. He had notes to give Wyndham anyway. And he was rather desperate to find out if Wyndham would still look at him in horror.

Thankfully, instead, Wyndham curled his lip at Roger's suit. "If I shove you into the lake, would you consider that a sufficient inducement to buy a better outfit?"

Roger had never been so relieved to hear an insult. "How do you know it hasn't already been waterlogged?"

Wyndham rolled his eyes. "I wouldn't be in the least bit surprised, considering the state of it."

"I read through your notes," Roger said.

"Already? I only gave them to you last night."

"Well, I read them at the dinner party and then I continued reading them after I got home."

Wyndham frowned. "Don't you have better things to do than stay up all night reading about magic?"

Roger waved that question aside. "I wrote out some responses to your questions. I wasn't sure if you'd like to read them before we meet tomorrow or—"

Wyndham heaved a sigh. "You seem to think I have nothing better to do with my time either."

"We can wait and just discuss them tomorrow if you'd—"

"No, no, give them here." He snatched them out of Roger's hand.

"Of course I'll explain whatever questions you have. And, er, if you have any difficulty reading my handwriting."

"So basically all of it," Wyndham said, glancing over the first page. Then he folded the bundle and tucked it into his own breast pocket.

"Ah, Roger," Mrs. Wrenwhistle greeted, just noticing him. "I'm so glad you're here. Wynnie, why don't you take him to get some lemonade? It really is rather warm for a garden party."

Wyndham nodded and offered Roger his arm.

"I've explained it in my notes, but I never answered your questions from last night," Roger began.

"Yes, I recall," Wyndham said. "I believe all I got in response from you was an open mouth, a few blinks, and some crumpled up notes."

"Yes, well, I was rather amazed."

"Clearly."

Roger glanced up and was delighted to see there was a small smile on Wyndham's lips.

"Have you given any thought to what I said after the balcony?"

"Yes," Roger answered slowly. "I even…er…sort of discussed it with my father on the way here. That is," he added hastily, "we discussed the differences between fae and human magic. I am of the opinion that your magic system is significantly more impressive. He argued that I was confusing comparable with identical. And then it got very technical."

Wyndham hummed thoughtfully. "I'm rather sad I missed that. I'd be curious to hear a technical discussion of your magic."

Before Roger could respond, he heard someone shout his name and then Harriet Thackery was running over, her skirt kicking up around her heels in a thoroughly unladylike manner. She pulled him into a hug and then smacked him on the shoulder as she pulled back.

"You beast!" she shouted. "You promised to come visit."

"It's only been a few days since I saw you."

"It was last week and I require a rigid acknowledgement of the calendar, thank you very much."

"Oh, for God's sake, Harriet," Cyril Thompson moaned as he approached. Despite being out of breath from racing after Harriet, Cyril looked impeccably put together, his dark hair combed becomingly and his collar points sharp. There had been a brief period of time where Roger had fancied himself in love with his friend, although he had eventually admitted to himself that it was merely another aesthetic fascination. "You sound plebeian when you talk about calendars. Mr. Wrenwhistle is going to think all of Roger's friends are common. Good afternoon, Mr. Wrenwhistle. And may I say that your waistcoat is lovely."

Wyndham opened his mouth to respond but Harriet cut in, "Of course his waistcoat is lovely. Everyone knows he dresses well. Quite frankly, we'd appreciate it if you taught Roger some of your tricks."

"It might interest you to know, Harriet," Anthea St. Clair said, having materialized at the side of the group, "that I had to tell your mother you saw a bee and that was why you took off running. She was about to faint, I swear she was." Without waiting for a reply, she reached between them all and picked up a cup of lemonade. "Oh, Mr. Wrenwhistle," she said, smiling at him and executing a short curtsy. "Are you joining us now that you're chummy with Roger? That's lovely. We could all use more elegance in our lives."

"Especially Harriet," Cyril added. "Pray don't blame all of us for her outrageous behavior. We have been doing our best with her."

Roger laughed and turned to Wyndham. "Cyril's only saying that because he wishes he had Harriet's gumption."

Harriet crowed.

"You're one to talk!" Cyril said.

Roger held up his hands. "I never said I had gumption."

"That's right," Harriet said, sandwiching herself between Roger and Wyndham as if they were some sort of protectors. "Roger understands me. You do too, don't you, Mr. Wrenwhistle?" Then she looped her hands around both of their arms. "Did you know that they have the boats out on the lake today? I've been saying we simply *must* go out on the boats but Anthea is trying to spoil my fun."

Anthea rolled her eyes. "I'm only trying to keep you from falling in the water. *Again.*"

"How funny," Wyndham said dryly. "I was just saying I hoped getting Barnes in the water would result in a new suit. I'm so glad the hosts are sympathetic to my needs."

Cyril barked a laugh. "Oh, good. I was sure you'd be on our side. You simply had to be. But don't let Harriet bully you into anything, Mr. Wrenwhistle."

"Yes," Anthea said. "Once she's decided you're her friend, she becomes a bit of a tyrant."

"Oh, nonsense. You all love me," Harriet said.

Roger hadn't realized how much he'd missed his friends until he was completely surrounded by them again. He was pleased that they liked Wyndham. He looked up to see how Wyndham was faring with the onslaught of enthusiasm. To his dismay, Wyndham gave a terse smile and then promptly excused himself.

CHAPTER 22

WYN

In theory, Wyn knew a garden party should've been the one social event he could tolerate. It was the perfect excuse to stay outside, enjoy the flowers and greenery that were always so lovingly tended by the gardeners, and consume lighter refreshments than were typical at a dinner party.

Instead, he often found that they were the hardest for him to get through. Garden parties were usually attended by both sides of society, which made it imperative for him to control his magic. Being surrounded by so much fresh air, sunshine, and flourishing life made that nearly impossible. It sat in his core like an itch on the bottom of his foot that he could not remove his shoe to scratch, no matter how badly he wanted to.

After excusing himself from Roger's boisterous group, Wyn sought shelter under one of the large shades designed to offer respite from the warm setting sun. He looked longingly at the glasses of lemonade he'd left behind, having failed to get one for himself.

"I couldn't help but notice Roger Barnes running toward you the moment his family's carriage arrived," Aveline said from somewhere nearby, her voice laced with delight. The skirts of her soft pink dress swished against Wyn's boots as she came to stand at his side.

"He had notes to give me in response to the ones I'd previously given him," he explained.

"What sort of *notes?*" she asked, her eyes twinkling.

"*Research,*" he emphasized.

"Oh, you're such a bore." Aveline visibly deflated, her shoulders drooping before she tilted her head and regarded the crowd with a wistful sigh. "At least you have someone who is interested in you. I fear I'll be forgotten about entirely if I'm unable to find a match this Season."

Wyn was instantly thankful he'd not taken a lemonade, for fear that he would've choked on it over her words. "Aveline, what is it you're trying to imply, exactly?"

His sister regarded him with a pitying look. "For someone so smart, you really can be foolish sometimes. Did you know that?" In the next breath, she was waving to one of her friends and left him to his own thoughts.

Wyn's gaze swept the crowd, pausing on the faces he knew. His own parents and siblings, members of the Council and their respective spouses, people he'd known since he was in school. Not too far away, Sage Raven-wing was standing with that fellow Brooks on his arm. Wyn had overheard his mother saying that an engagement between them was all but secured; the only thing left was the announcement in the papers to make it official.

A shriek of laughter made Wyn turn his attention in the direction of the lake. Barnes and his friends had apparently made up their minds to give the boats a go. Wyn watched them, carefree in their antics as they rowed out to where the water was deeper and the carpet of flowering lilies thinned considerably.

Roger was sharing a vessel with Harriet, whose name he remembered only because they'd all said it so many times as they attempted to…warn him about her, perhaps? He wasn't quite sure. The other two were paddling steadily away in their own small boat, seemingly to escape Harriet's targeted splashing in their direction.

The longer Wyn looked at the lake, the more he felt a desire to paint the scene before him. The leaves were starting to change with the season, peeks of red and yellow and gold mixed in with the green. The water reflected the colors, mixing with the peaceful blue of the sky overhead.

And yet, it was more than the landscape he wished to capture with his watercolors. It was the way the boats were gliding on the water as his swans would, remaining mostly steady despite the raucous happening on their backs. It was the uninhibited joy of the friends as they flicked water into each others' laps, mussing their clothes and hair, carrying on without a single worry about what anyone else might think.

That was something Wyn had never experienced before.

All at once, Roger's boat listed to one side as Harriet leaned too far. Both of them screamed, and Roger reached out for Harriet to bring her safely back onto her bench seat. Wyn's magic swelled at his own surprise of the near-capsizing, eyes widening as he took an involuntary step forward. They managed to save their balance, but one of the oars had slipped free from its mount, floating away faster than either of them could reach.

With a slow exhale, Wyn's magic reached out across the garden to the surface of the lake. Gentle ripples formed on a new breeze, hardly noticeable in the aftermath of their commotion, but were enough to slow the oar to a stop and encourage it back toward the boat. Such an extension of his power caused a tantalizing shiver to run down Wyn's spine.

Before anyone could realize what he'd done, he turned and slipped back into the crowd.

THE FESTIVITIES CONTINUED WELL into the evening, as none of the partygoers wanted the first big event of the Season to end. Wyn had lost count of how many finger sandwiches and two-bite cakes he'd consumed, many of which had been delivered by his sister and mother when they swept by to divulge gossip.

Wyn had found a heavy stone bench tucked into the high, squared hedgerow toward the back of the garden. With a glass of wine by his hip and one knee crossed neatly over the other, he'd become absorbed with the notes Barnes had given to him. Page after page contained answers to each and every question Wyn had asked.

"I daresay I've never seen you with such poor posture."

Wyn looked up to find Sage approaching slowly, hands clasped behind his back and a familiar look on his face. Wyn straightened and arched his brow. Apparently the man was not in the mood to hold a grudge.

"Good evening, Mr. Ravenwing. You seem to have lost your new appendage."

Sage laughed a little too hard. "You are the expert on my appendages, after all." He picked up Wyn's glass, finished the wine, and sat heavily on the bench beside him. He leaned over Wyn's shoulder to look at the pages. "Whatever are you reading out here alone in the dark?"

Wyn folded the pages and tucked them away.

"What do you want?" he asked flatly.

"I want you to come back to the party," Sage encouraged with a bit of a whinge, his hand coming to rest on Wyn's thigh. Wyn brushed him off.

"I've nothing left in me to give this evening," Wyn admitted. The words felt more raw coming out than they'd felt when he was holding them in, and he regretted saying them to his present company. "Aveline knows to come find me when our carriage is brought around."

"Poor luck," Sage tutted. "I saw your sister thoroughly engaged in conversation with a rather dashing young man just as I was coming this way. It seems she's not going to come and rescue you any time soon." Sage leaned close to Wyn's ear and tried again. "Come back to the party with me?"

Wyn bit the inside of his cheek and got to his feet. He allowed Sage to escort him back through the maze of hedges toward the music and chatter and lights that he'd been glad to escape. Wyn grasped his elbow with the opposite hand behind his back to avoid slouching.

Humans and fae were mingled together, talking and laughing, bumping into Wyn and stepping into his path no matter which way he tried to go. The air was thick with too many smells and emotions. It seemed everyone in attendance had converged into one small area of the garden to experience a collective sense of jubilation and he was trapped in the middle of it all.

Wyn turned away from the hand Sage had on his lower back and started for the gravel path that led to the carriages. Waiting there with the horses and coachman would be preferable to enduring one more moment of the party.

"Mr. Wrenwhistle!" Roger's voice cut through the noise, but even the newly-familiar sound of it wasn't enough to make Wyn stop. "Mr. Wrenwhistle, I wanted to thank you—" There was a sound like a bag of marbles spilling, and Wyn could only assume it was Barnes tripping over his own feet on the crushed stones.

"I cannot imagine what for," Wyn said, his stride lengthening.

"The—on the lake, of course. I saw you there, by the water, watching us—"

Wyn whirled around. Roger nearly crashed into him, his shoes unsettling the gravel once again. "I was not *watching* you," Wyn spat. Had he been watching them? He felt his face go warm.

"Oh," Roger said, his hands coming up with his shoulders in an uncertain shrug. "But I thought it was you who helped to push the oar—"

"Why would you need my help when you've so many others to provide all the support and companionship you could ever wish for?"

Wyn felt his stomach drop. Even in that moment, he knew it was a terrible thing to say, but it had come out before he could think to stop it. For the second night in a row, Wyn turned and left Roger standing alone.

CHAPTER 23

ROGER

As ROGER WATCHED Wyndham walk away, he couldn't determine what he had done wrong. Was it because he had shouted Wyndham's name? Was it because he had thanked him for his help? Had he done something earlier and not realized it?

Then again, Wyndham's eyes had been wider than normal and there had been a paleness to his skin that did not look altogether healthy. He had been walking towards the carriages—perhaps he didn't feel well and needed to go home? Roger thought back to the rest of the party; he had barely seen Wyndham after he'd walked away from the lemonade table. Anytime he'd spotted the gentleman, he had been alone by the trees or on the edge of the lake.

He stood on the gravel, uncertain if he ought to do something. Should he bring Wyndham a lemonade or a glass of wine? Should he leave him alone? Did the Wrenwhistles know their youngest might not be feeling well? He weighed his options, ultimately deciding that Wyndham would never forgive him if he kicked up a fuss for nothing. For all he knew, the man had simply vanished to rendezvous with a lover. It certainly wouldn't be the first time. Oddly enough, this thought did not make Roger feel any better.

He was about to turn back to the party when he heard someone say, "You really ought to stop pestering him, you know."

Mr. Sage Ravenwing stepped out of the shadows, almost as if he had been summoned by Roger's memory of the garden incident.

"I'm sorry?" Roger said.

Mr. Ravenwing rolled his eyes. While Roger often saw him at the same parties he attended, he scarcely had reason to interact with him. He was an attractive person with jet-black hair, green eyes, and an olive complexion. Although Roger thought the typical fae beauty settled ill on Ravenwing's features. He always looked sulky and peevish. Right now he looked smug, which made Roger even more suspicious.

"I said that you ought to stop pestering Wyndham. It's bad enough that he has to deal with your nonsense for this ridiculous project you've roped him into."

Roger took a moment to process the words. "I didn't rope him into the project; he was assigned the task by the Council."

"Oh, come now, Barnes. You've been pining after him for years. Everyone knows that."

Roger felt his face get hot. "I have not been pining after him. I'm not apt to pine after anyone." He wasn't sure why he was arguing the point so he deviated the topic. "I had no intention of pestering him either. I was simply concerned."

Ravenwing scoffed. "Concerned? You? After all the work you're putting him through these days. He's barely any fun anymore. His head's full of human magic."

"It sounds as if you're more concerned about your loss of fun than you are about Mr. Wrenwhistle."

"I know him far better than you will ever hope to," the other man spat. "I know what he looks like when he's in the thrall of pleasure, I saw his devastation when he received his magic scores, I know his favorite wine, how it feels to be surrounded by his magic. And you?" He looked Roger up and down with evident distaste. "You spend half a week with him and consider yourself his friend?" He leaned closer. "Wyndham Wrenwhistle doesn't make friends. And he certainly wouldn't stoop to befriending a halfwitted human like yourself. He's only humoring you. He's been talking my ear off about what he really thinks of you. Trust me, he won't even acknowledge your existence once this little project of yours is over. You will go back to being just as insignificant as you were a month ago."

Roger knew better than to ask but, despite his good judgment, he found himself saying, "What do you mean, what he thinks of me?"

Ravenwing shrugged. "Nothing particularly surprising, I suppose. He thinks you're dull and stupid. But you know as well as I do that Wyndham has a way with words. Let me think, what were the exact ones he used?" His smile broadened as he remembered. "Ah yes, I believe 'that tottering moron' was said more than once and he described you as 'a complete waste of a human.'" He gave another delicate shrug. "So you'd only be proving him right if you went after him now. No one wants someone useless trundling after them. I should think you're at least smart enough to realize that."

Roger felt cold at the words. It wasn't possible, was it? Wyndham, who invited him to the opera, who had danced with him, who saved the oar, who asked question after question as if Roger's knowledge mattered? Ravenwing was clearly speaking from a place of jealousy, wasn't he? Then again, he had been escorting Wyndham when Roger found them. Perhaps he did know the gentleman better than Roger thought. He remembered Wyndham's look of horror when Roger suggested a second dance. He remembered how Wyndham left shortly after meeting all of Roger's friends. He thought of the way Wyndham was always making cutting remarks about his clothes or his handwriting or his intelligence. Those always seemed to simply be Wyndham's particular brand of teasing. But perhaps Roger had been foolish and ought to be taking those cutting words at face value.

He realized Ravenwing was still standing next to him. "I see," he said at last.

Ravenwing chuckled. "Don't take it too hard. You were never meant for him anyway. Come on, I'll escort you back to the party, just to prove there's no hard feelings. I'll even dance with you, if you'd like."

Roger shook his head. "No, I don't think I'm up to a dance at present." He sighed. "But I daresay I could use a glass of wine."

"Yes, you certainly look like you need one." Ravenwing held out an arm and Roger took it, feeling a little numb as he walked back to the party.

TORQUIL'S TRIBUNE

Greetings, fashionable folk and happy humans,

The London Season has officially begun, as evidenced by the Grenvilles' Garden Party yesterday.

But that was not the only social gathering in the past few days, so let us be orderly:

For the fae set, the Cricket family hosted an elegant little soiree at their home. A notable addition was Mr. Roger Barnes, the only human present, and a guest of the Wrenwhistle family. Sources say that Mr. Barnes also joined the Wrenwhistles in their opera box. It might be reasonably assumed that Mr. Barnes and Mr. Wrenwhistle are coming to an affable working relationship. The two gentlemen were seen speaking together on the balcony, were seated together at dinner, and even danced together at one point in the evening. Tongues are wagging about the budding friendship.

At the garden party the following day, the two men greeted each other upon arrival. However, they were not the only pair to enjoy the festivities together.

Mr. Ravenwing and Mr. Brooks have been seen together on a number of occasions lately, from walking in Hyde Park, to sitting together at dinner parties. The two were practically inseparable for the course of the event.

Although sources say Mr. Ravenwing was seen chatting with Mr. Wren-whistle—an unsurprising exchange—and escorting Mr. Barnes to the refreshment table—a very surprising exchange. It would seem Mr. Barnes is expanding his social circle this Season. Hopefully such moves signal better relations between the fae and human communities.

Other pairs to watch include Mr. Thompson and Miss Thackery, who are well known to be friends. But after some particularly animated encounters, some sources are beginning to wonder if there is more to the friendship.

Miss St. Clair and Lady Fitzhugh took a turn around the dance floor last evening, adding to the rumors of a possible romance.

Now that the Season is underway, this writer will add the usual commentary on attire: Miss Wrenwhistle was arguably the best dressed at the party, wearing a light pink gown that made her appear, sources say, as if plucked from a rose garden. Other noteworthy attendees were Mr. Wyndham Wrenwhistle, who looked dashing as ever in a peach paisley waistcoat, and Mr. Archibald Turner, the only human to make the list, who was sporting a very fashionable cravat knot that many appeared to be envious of.

Your esteemed editor,

Torquil Pimpernel-Smith

CHAPTER 24

WYN

Wyn was up nearly the entire night after his encounter with Roger. Though he'd only had a few glasses of wine, it churned in his stomach with the overindulgence of small treats and his guilt over the way he'd reacted. It was enough to make him ill. If he hadn't been wearing one of his nicer pairs of boots, he would've walked home instead of taking the carriage.

After giving up on sleep, he'd paced across his room until he'd nearly worn a hole through the rug.

Why had he been so bloody angry? Sage's insistence on him rejoining the party had been frustrating and certainly he'd told the man as much. Though Sage never seemed to care what Wyn was feeling unless he was busy bringing him to climax. Wyn scoffed. It's likely he didn't even care then; the man was quite selfish in bed, truth be told.

After collapsing onto his sofa, Wyn stared at the ceiling for a long time, his hands resting gingerly on his fitful stomach.

He was jealous of Roger Barnes. There was no other explanation for the gnawing feeling in his gut. No other logical reason why he'd said what he did about Roger's friends. The way they'd made Barnes laugh and forget himself entirely was indication enough that they were trustworthy and supportive, just as Wyn had accused them of being in the most hurtful way possible.

Wyn brought an arm up over his face with a groan, the crook of his elbow resting over his nose.

"How callous must you be to feel jealous toward someone else's happiness?" he asked aloud in the quiet of his room.

Perhaps that was just it. He knew well and good he hadn't been watching all of them out on the water. He'd been watching Barnes.

Barnes, who had smiled next to him at the opera.

Barnes, who had laughed while they danced together.

Barnes, who had seen his magic and been amazed.

Wyn felt his entire body go hot as he sat up on his sofa, hands coming down to support his weight as his feet touched the floor.

He hadn't been jealous of Roger at all. He'd been jealous of Roger's friends.

It had, admittedly, been a bit thrilling to see Roger coming over to greet him before anyone else at the party, and not just because he hoped Roger had more information about human magic for him. Usually, the only time men came up to him at a party was to ask him if he'd like to meet somewhere more private. But Roger was only after a conversation, and it had been rather refreshing.

Wyn shoved his fingers back into his hair as he considered if this was what it felt like to go absolutely mad.

THE FOLLOWING MORNING, Wyn arrived outside Roger's building far earlier than any other time they'd met. He wasn't even certain if Roger would be home. But with their deadline creeping ever closer and the positive progress they'd made with their correspondence, Wyn was anxious to continue.

Notley answered the door and let Wyn inside, leading him to the study where he discovered Barnes slumped over a plate at his desk, the food appearing largely untouched. When his arrival was announced, Roger looked up in surprise that quickly faded to something more serious.

"Barnes," Wyn said in greeting.

Roger got to his feet slowly, looking nearly as tired as Wyn felt.

"Mr. Wrenwhistle," he said quietly, and nothing else.

Wyn had spent the morning reciting his apology over and over in his head. He'd even managed to speak the words over the breakfast he'd taken in his room, testing how they felt coming out of his mouth. It wasn't pretty, but he knew it was important. Wyn swallowed and drew in a breath.

"You look dreadful," he managed, wincing afterward. *Fuck.*

Roger sighed and removed his spectacles to rub his eyes with a thumb and forefinger. Wyn realized that he'd never seen the man without them before.

"My apologies. I was unaware I would be having company at this hour."

"I thought you might be eager to return to our work after several days of being preoccupied with various social engagements."

"You did warn me that would be the case." Roger's expression became even more sullen as he called for the valet to take away his uneaten meal. When the space was cleared, Wyn took the opportunity to set down the box he'd brought with him. Roger looked at it blankly.

Wyn was unsure how to explain what was inside after bungling his apology.

In practice, he'd said he was deeply sorry for his outburst the night before; that he was feeling overwhelmed with the crowd and needed to step away. He'd explained that he often felt this way at parties, and to not take it personally. He'd even gone as far as thanking Roger for his understanding, which he hoped he would receive, and then he would've offered the box as a small token of appreciation for said understanding. It had all gone so smoothly in practice.

"I have too many as it is," Wyn said, tilting his chin up at the box.

With considerable hesitation, Roger untied the silky red ribbon that was still wrapped around the box from when Wyn had received it as a gift; he could not recall from whom. After lifting the top away, both men peered inside at the thick folds of parchment cushioning the full set of fine porcelain teaware.

Roger carefully lifted one of the cups out of the paper and turned it around, showing off the intricate, flowery pattern of dark blue and gold.

"Why would you give me this?" Roger asked finally, looking up at Wyn.

"Because you need it," Wyn said, as though it was obvious. "I would imagine you'll find this set more worthy of being used with guests moving forward, so you can get rid of that broken old thing altogether."

Roger returned the cup to the box and replaced the lid.

"I cannot accept it."

Wyn's brows furrowed. "Do you not like it? Would you prefer a different pattern? I have others—"

"I don't want your charity!" Roger blurted. His face was flushed. Wyn glanced down at the way Roger's hands wrung together in front of him. He was still upset, then. Rightfully so.

"Listen, Barnes," Wyn began, willing himself to try apologizing again, but he was cut off once more.

"No, *you* listen," Roger urged. "I'm fully aware of how little you think of me. Of how little you've always thought of me. I know the way you talk about me behind my back. But I refuse to allow you to act as though you are better than me in my own home."

Wyn's defenses flew as high as they'd ever been, coming to the rescue after being caught off guard in a rare moment of vulnerability. His magic shuddered within him, desperate to respond to the sudden twist of emotion.

"I cannot possibly speak ill of you behind your back, for I do not speak of you at all. I do not think of you unless I absolutely must," he lied bitterly.

"I have evidence to prove otherwise," Roger challenged.

Wyn's eyes narrowed. "And what evidence is that?"

"A little bird told me everything you've been saying."

Wyn's heart was pounding. A little bird? Who could he be speaking of? Aveline, maybe, with her endless meddling. Or perhaps it was one of Roger's friends from the party, spreading falsities as so many on both sides of society tended to do.

"Do indulge me with the bird's name, if you'd be so kind."

Roger huffed out a laugh. "Of course you would care more about who tattled on you than what truths they revealed."

Wyn's hands curled into fists as his sides, jaw muscles working. "As I already said, there's no reason for me to waste my breath speaking about you, be it truths or lies. Who would even care to listen?"

Roger's mouth fell open, and Wyn had the sudden urge to step forward and knock it shut with the flick of his fingers under his chin, the same way Wyn's mother had always done to him as a child.

"Ugh, is that *all* you know how to do? Drop your jaw like a trout when you've nothing to say?"

Roger shut his mouth as his face scrunched up. "Go away," he demanded.

"Gladly." Wyn turned on his heel and collected his own coat and hat from the stand in the entryway. He raised his voice to continue. "Keep the set. Sell it if you must. Donate the money to a fund for other talentless humans. Goodness knows they'll need it when your proposal is rejected once again." He yanked the door open. "Or better yet, go and buy yourself some decent fucking clothes!"

WYN'S EMOTIONS burned like a flame all the way back across town.

If he had been at their country estate, he would've known exactly what to do. His private solace came in the form of a babbling stream tucked into the trees. Wyn couldn't begin to count the number of times he'd escaped there alone and stripped out of his clothes to sit in the gentle water, allowing it to wash away whatever was bothering him. The closest he could get in the city was having a bath drawn.

This was his demand the moment he made it inside. He rushed to his room to change, his attention drawn immediately to all of the books and papers on his desk.

"You're a lucky devil that I cannot make my own fire, Roger Barnes, or else your books would be as good as dust!" he shouted helplessly as he went to collect them all into a haphazard pile, before dumping them into the empty bottom drawer so he would not have to look at them for one more second.

Out of breath, he straightened to survey the desktop in case he'd missed something. His pile of the most recent copies of the *Tribune* were there in a neat stack. He picked them up and was ready to throw them on top of the books to be shut away, but paused.

If Roger *really* wanted to know what he thought of him, Wyn knew exactly how to deliver the message.

CHAPTER 25

ROGER

ROGER FUMED about his conversation with Wyndham. He kept revisiting past conversations, feeling progressively more foolish. He thought of all the times Wyndham demeaned his intelligence, his taste, his abilities. Even the interactions that had felt positive at the time—that evening at the Crickets' when Wyndham said things that made Roger feel as if his own magic was remarkable—were now tainted with the question of whether or not it had been condescension rather than a compliment.

The porcelain tea set would have ordinarily seemed like a touching gift, but now felt insulting. As if Wyndham was only comfortable when surrounded by things he deemed worthy. Roger knew he ought to donate the entire dratted thing, but couldn't find it in himself to do so. He handed it to Notley with strict instructions that it was not to be used.

Only days ago he'd been happy, optimistic, on the cusp of what felt like a bright new friendship. Now he was back to feeling like a failure. A breeze fluttered the papers on his desk. Roger strode to the window, slammed it shut, and let the curtains fall back. He tried to take solace in the familiar dark, but now he knew what the room felt like with a light breeze drifting through and rustling the pages. He knew what Wyndham's profile looked like partially in shadow and partially bathed in sunlight. The darkness now felt heavy rather than safe. Again he began to question the practicality of his choice to live on his own.

Maybe he wasn't fit to take care of his own affairs. Maybe if he gave up, moved back in with his parents, married a nice old gentleman who thought him a sufficient spouse, it would be enough. Maybe then he'd be worthy of respect.

He folded his arms on the desk and buried his face in the crook of his elbow. He knew that no matter what he did, he'd never be worthy of Wyndham's respect. Why was that so devastating?

He wanted to ring for tea to boost his spirits, but knew it would feel strange now to drink tea without the scent of lavender wafting out of a teapot. He was being ridiculous, acting as if a passionate love affair had ended, rather than an amicable partnership. Acting as if he'd lost years of camaraderie, rather than barely a week of civility.

He mulled over the argument, trying to find something to be angry about. Anger was easier than desolation. What was it Wyndham had said? *There's no reason for me to waste my breath speaking about you, be it truths or lies. Who would even care to listen?* The same fury that burned in his chest when he'd heard the words blazed anew. People did care about him, damn it. Even strangers did, if his frequent mention in the *Tribune* was anything to go by. Though he wasn't sure why.

That thought made him sit up straight. His project was ruined, thanks to Wyndham Wrenwhistle. His hope for fixing the testing rubric was in tatters thanks to the man's arrogance. But Roger need not be destroyed, too. He had some defenses left. He had resources. Goodness knew he still had some remaining pride.

Wyndham had been sneering when Roger had no adequate response to his insults. *Is that all you know how to do? Drop your jaw like a trout when you've nothing to say?* Roger would show him what he had to say. He would prove that he still had plenty to say, and what's more, he intended to be heard.

Before he could talk himself out of it, he pulled out a fresh sheet of paper and wrote a letter to Torquil Pimpernel-Smith.

CHAPTER 26

WYN

Wyn's horrid mood carried into the rest of the afternoon. He had all but begged his mother to leave him at home and allow him one missed social event, but she refused. They had been specially invited to a private concert. Wyn supposed of all the places he could be dragged to in such a state, an evening of music wasn't the worst possible scenario.

That is, until he realized the Thompsons were hosting the event. Cyril Thompson, as he had recently learned, was one of Roger's close friends.

As they entered the great room where the concert was to be held, Wyn's stomach soured at the sight of the Barnes family sitting only two rows from where the piano was positioned. To Wyn's relief, their seats were several rows farther back and on the other side of the middle aisle that split the rows in half.

He attempted to look at anything else in the room that could hold his attention. There were swags of flowers decorating the windows. The chairs were rather uncomfortable, but not altogether unpleasant to look at. Wyn made sure to take a glass of whatever was being handed out. To his delight, it was a beautifully strong wine that tasted expensive. Wyn drained the glass and wondered idly if the evening had been set up to celebrate some sort of special occasion, given the money that had clearly been spent.

When he grew weary of staring at nothing, Wyn's gaze shifted slowly to where Roger sat between his parents. His jaw worked as he realized the familiarity he felt staring at the back of his head.

It was the same view he'd had of the man since they were boys in school. Their seats were assigned by last name, always giving Barnes a spot at the front of the room compared to Wyn's inevitable back row vantage point. But it was evident that they both would've ended up in those chairs if given the choice.

The trouble hadn't been Barnes' interest in learning, nor his willingness to answer questions when called upon. It had been the way his hand shot up at nearly every opportunity, always ready with *something* to say. Not only that, but his propensity for stuttering and stumbling over his words was nothing new. Wyn was certain he had spent several years of his life listening to Roger Barnes attempt to form coherent sentences to share his thoughts.

His gaze fell to the floor as he remembered the way the rest of the boys had made fun of Roger for it, himself included. Mocking stammers and whispered insults had been the majority of it, but Wyn could remember one incident when he and Barnes had been set to debate an assigned topic.

The room was set up in a way similar to the arrangement for the concert, chairs split down the middle into two dueling sides. He'd been perhaps sixteen, Roger a year older, and he could scarcely recall the topic— he'd given little thought to the assignment and had planned to argue however he saw fit, as he was apt to do with just about anything. When it was their turn to speak, Roger had approached his podium with so many papers that he may as well have written a book on the subject. Wyn had rolled his eyes dramatically, earning a laugh from everyone before they'd even begun. A smirk had spread across his lips as he watched Barnes shuffle awkwardly through his notes, all crumpled and covered with ink blotches, his cheeks growing progressively more flushed until finally the teacher snapped at him to hurry up.

The moment Barnes had settled on the page he wanted to open with, Wyn had called to his magic and sent the entire stack flying to the ground. Laughter erupted from the class, and though Roger was usually able to recover enough to continue, that time he had quietly asked to be excused.

Wyn earned a week of detention for using his magic unbidden in school, but it had mattered little to him. He justified his actions by watching Roger go about his life as normal. He was always surrounded by a large number of friends, and a family that always supported him no matter how poorly he'd done on his Hastings Examination or any other assignment.

The truth was that Wyn's jealousy after the garden party was nothing new. It was something that had been festering for decades. An old wound had been ripped open at the sight of Roger laughing and enjoying himself with his friends, despite the fact that he was *aggressively average*, as the *Tribune* had put it.

Wyn was never allowed that luxury. His shortcomings had been picked apart and scrutinized since childhood. His mother was always there to remind him how he could do better, *be* better.

He had taken it all out on the one person who seemed to have everything he wished for.

Wyn's attention was drawn back to the room as everyone started to clap. The pianist had settled on the bench, arranging their sheet music, and Wyn took a deep breath to clear his mind so he could try to enjoy the concert.

CHAPTER 27

ROGER

After impulsively sending the letter to Torquil Pimpernel-Smith, Roger attempted to distract himself with work. But now every aspect of his task reminded him of Wyndham. His sloppy handwriting, his chaotic organization, even his magic were now associated with whatever Wyndham might have said about them. It was dreadful.

He was rather horrified when his parents showed up to take him to a concert at Cyril's family home. Couldn't they leave him to mope in peace? His project was ruined, he was going to be the laughing stock of London, he was already beginning to regret his hasty decision to write to Pimpernel-Smith *again*, and now he had to pretend everything was going swimmingly in front of his best friends.

Anthea would know something was wrong. She always did. Cyril likely would too, though he tended to be less inquisitive about such things. When the Wrenwhistles entered the room, Roger could practically feel Wyndham's glare. When he turned to sneak a glance, Wyndham wasn't looking at him at all. Which was almost more depressing.

He slumped in his seat, feeling thoroughly dejected. Ravenwing had been right. Wyndham didn't think of Roger at all. He was probably only thinking about how tedious the evening was or criticizing the soprano's range. Roger normally enjoyed such music—he'd been enthralled at the opera—but now the arias were grating on his nerves. He wanted to be at home. He wanted to be in bed. He wanted to be anywhere but in the same room as the man who hated him and who had single-handedly destroyed his hopes and dreams. He had given himself a headache with the tears that followed after Wyndham's departure.

After the performance was finally over, Anthea hauled Roger over to a corner, plied him with wine and demanded to be told why he looked so glum. Before Roger had managed to pretend this wasn't at all the case, Cyril had popped up to ask Roger when he started hating music so much. Then Harriet scuttled in to ask what they were all chattering about and did Roger know his eyes were puffy?

He was finally able to tell them that he was simply exhausted from working on the project, although he was pretty sure that Anthea didn't believe him.

"I'm surprised you didn't sit with the Wrenwhistles," Harriet commented. "They're here tonight, you know."

"I'm aware," Roger muttered.

Anthea narrowed her eyes. "Did something happen between you two?"

"What?" Roger squeaked. "What could possibly have happened?"

"Hm," Cyril hummed. "Very convincing. What did he do? Did he say something cutting?"

"No," Roger lied.

"If it makes you feel better," Anthea responded, "he looks just as miserable."

That caught Roger's attention. "He does?"

She smirked. "Whatever spat you had must be irking him too."

Harriet clapped her hands. "We should reunite them!"

Roger groaned. "I beg you to do no such thing."

"Well, it's only for the good of humanity," she said.

"I think humanity will be much better off if we never—if we don't interact just now."

"I don't know," Cyril mused. "According to the *Tribune*—"

"Oh, hang the *Tribune*!" Roger sputtered. "And hang Pimpernel-Smith. Half the things they print are false anyway."

"Which parts?" Anthea asked, leaning forward.

"Half of them," Roger said. "I don't know. I haven't exactly run inventory."

Anthea gave him a long look, sighed, and turned to Cyril. "I'm not convinced."

Cyril pursed his lips. "*You* said they'd be inseparable tonight. I think you should pay up."

"It's just a lover's spat, obviously," Anthea said. "They'll be back at it tomorrow, I'm sure of it."

"*Lover's*—" Roger sputtered.

"Remember how he smiled at Roger at the lemonade table?" Harriet asked, poking Cyril in the shoulder and completely ignoring Roger.

"He was insulting Roger's clothing," Cyril reminded her.

"Everyone does that!" Harriet said.

"Exactly," Anthea said. "It's still on. Give them…" She cast a beady eye at Roger. "A week. At most."

Cyril sighed. "Oh, all right. But then the bet's off."

"*Bet?*" Roger repeated. "Were you all wagering on—"

"Oh, do catch up, Roger," Harriet huffed impatiently. "All of London is wagering at this point."

"Mm," Anthea hummed. "And most of them are on my side." She arched an eyebrow at Cyril.

He hunched and crossed his arms. "I just think it would take a lot to capture Roger's attention, that's all."

Roger didn't like to mention that Cyril had once captured his attention, although admittedly that had only been for a few months. He quickly resolved to *not* mention it. "I wish you'd all stay out of my business," he muttered instead. "And that goes for the rest of London."

"You should put in an advertisement with the *Tribune*," Anthea suggested. "That is, if you can stop squabbling with Wyndham Wrenwhistle through it."

Roger opened his mouth, but had no proper response. He closed his mouth with a snap, realizing with horror that his letter to the *Tribune* would likely not be the cut-down he'd hoped. Would it really only add more fuel to the gossip? Could he never win? He buried his face in his hands. "I hate everything," he groaned.

Harriet patted him on the shoulder. "No, you don't!" she chirped. "You love us. And you love Wyndham Wrenwhistle. You just don't know it yet."

"I'm not at all sure about the first part right now," he mumbled. "And the second part is decidedly not true."

"I'll believe that," Anthea said, "when I see either of you being less obsessed with the other."

Cyril sighed. "Quite frankly, I'm not sure Anthea's wrong, old boy. I only bet against her because it was more interesting that way." He paused. "And Harriet made me. She said it would add some flavor to the proceedings."

"Disloyal, the lot of you."

Harriet kissed his cheek. "You love it."

Any other day, he might have agreed with her. He did love their nonsense. But right now, the very idea of him with Wyndham made his stomach turn. If they knew the horrid things Wyndham said about him, they wouldn't be placing bets on some made-up romance.

Hopefully after his failure with the project, he could bury himself in his rooms and never talk to anyone ever again.

TORQUIL'S TRIBUNE

Greetings, felicitous folk and harmonious humans,

You may be surprised to receive an edition of this humble column on a Wednesday. This writer typically releases on the same days every week. However, yesterday afternoon letters were sent to this press containing information regarding two figures who have graced this column's pages frequently of late. This information was of such import, that this writer could not wait another day to share it.

We are delighted—nay, honored—to announce the engagement between Mr. Wyndham Wrenwhistle and Mr. Roger Barnes.

Many readers will see this news and smile knowingly. After all, brief and unique though this pair's courtship has been, it has certainly been a thrilling one filled with high emotions and, evidently, true passion. Being thrown together in such a way, it was practically inevitable. After long days of working together, late evenings dancing together, sunny afternoons sipping lemonade together, it is no wonder that romance was to follow. Sources say Mr. Wrenwhistle's most recent visit to Mr. Barnes involved an elegantly wrapped package. It has not yet been reported to this writer what was in the package, but there is little doubt it was an engagement gift.

This news is welcome indeed amidst recent tensions between the human and fae sets. Many hope this marriage will result in better understanding and empathy throughout society. Perhaps this pair will usher in a brighter day for everyone who chooses love over prejudice.

In any case, this writer offers Mr. Wrenwhistle and Mr. Barnes heartfelt congratulations and well-wishes for their union.

Your esteemed editor,

Torquil Pimpernel-Smith

CHAPTER 28

WYN

A FAINT KNOCKING STIRRED Wyn out of his sleep the following day. He breathed in slowly and turned his face from one side to the other against his pillow, arms tucked safely underneath. He'd requested a special concoction the night before to help him sleep after so many restless attempts. One peek at the windows told him it had done the trick; judging by the light, it was early afternoon.

More soft thumps against his door made him groan.

"Do go away," he complained, his voice muffled against the pillowcase. Wyn always locked his door at night. He had no interest in being woken up before he was ready.

There was commotion in the hallway, and then the knocking turned into pounding. He feared the fist might come clean through.

"Wyndham Nolan Wrenwhistle, you get yourself dressed and come downstairs this *instant!*" his mother's voice shrilled.

Wyn pulled the pillow over his head and tried to pretend he hadn't heard her. It was quiet for long enough that he thought maybe she'd left him alone, but what came next made his eyes snap open.

"Wyndham, darling. I need to speak with you at once."

It was his grandmother.

Grudgingly, Wyn dragged himself from bed and got dressed after washing the sleep from his face. Whatever he'd done this time, it was a bad sign that his grandmother had been called in.

His first thought was that it had something to do with Barnes. He'd likely complained to his parents about the fight and Roger's father said something to Wyn's grandmother, and now he was in all sorts of trouble. Wyn glared at nothing as he fixed the line of buttons on his waistcoat. *Perhaps I should wear my favorite one instead*, he thought absently, *if I'm about to step into my own funeral.*

Wyn had barely started down the steps when the chattering in the sitting room died to whispers and then to silence. His mother and grandmother were there, along with Emrys and Aveline, who both wore amused expressions that told him quite a bit before anyone said a word to him. Wyn's brow furrowed as he came to a stop before them all, feeling that taking a seat wasn't appropriate, all things considered.

"What have I done this time?" he asked finally.

"More like what *haven't* you done," Emrys said.

"Emrys," his mother warned sharply. Had she been crying?

A spark of real concern tingled in Wyn's chest. He couldn't take any more of the silence. He decided to start with trying to explain himself.

"If this is about what happened between Barnes and me, I—"

"When were you going to tell us?" Aveline asked in a rush. She looked practically giddy in her chair. Wyn knew she thrived on gossip, but it was a new low for her to take so much joy from their misery.

"I hadn't realized it would be so surprising," Wyn muttered, which caused his mother to choke out an incredulous laugh. The handkerchief she pressed delicately beneath her eyes confirmed his suspicions.

"Surprising?" she blubbered. "Not only do you keep it a secret, but your own mother has to find out from the *Tribune* of all places!"

Wyn's stomach plummeted. So Torquil had published his words. Perhaps they'd twisted them in an especially terrible way this time? Wyn started to speak again, but then realized it was a day early for the column to come out. Emrys must've seen the confusion on his face. He leaned forward and dropped the latest copy onto the table between them.

"Special early release," he explained as he settled back against the sofa, his smirk growing. "On account of the big announcement."

Wyn stepped forward and picked up the pamphlet, opening it to where it did, in fact, have that day's date printed.

Greetings, felicitous folk and harmonious humans, he read, thoroughly unprepared for what came after. Words he never imagined would appear next to his name were there in fresh ink. Delighted. Honored. *Engaged.*

At some point, Aveline had come over to wrap her arms around him in a tight hug. "Congratulations, little brother. I knew from the start that you and Mr. Barnes would make a perfect match!"

Wyn temporarily forgot how to speak. His eyes darted to Emrys, then to his mother who was now openly weeping, and finally to his grandmother who had been oddly silent during the whole ordeal. When she finally offered him a gentle, knowing grin, his words came back to him in a rush.

"We are not engaged!" he said, louder than he meant to.

"It's in the paper, Wyndham," his mother sighed. "Of course you are."

"There's been a mistake." Wyn looked down at the column he was still holding, before he threw it down onto the table as though it were covered with spiders. "I would never ask him to marry me!"

Emrys chuckled, clearly enjoying every second of Wyn's panic. "Funny, I would've thought Mr. Barnes would be the one doing the asking. What was your gift to him? It must've been terribly romantic if it was enough for him to overlook your awful personality."

"It was a—" Wyn replied, his voice falling to barely above a whisper at the end. "A tea set." He brought a hand up to cover his mouth as realization of what he'd done rained down on him. *An engagement gift.*

Someone had seen him bringing Roger the box, wrapped up special with a bow, with no explanation. Two eligible men did *not* go around giving each other gifts for no good reason, unless—

Wyn's eyes went wide as he looked at his grandmother again.

Iris got up slowly and approached Wyn to rest a gentle hand on his arm.

"It's in the paper," she said, with a sense of finality that made Wyn's blood run cold. "With it being midday, certainly the whole town has read the news, or heard it from someone who has." Iris studied Wyn's face for a moment. "Was it truly a mistake?"

"Yes," he said, without hesitation. But why did something sharp twist inside him at the word?

Iris' lips pressed together in a thin line as she moved her hand down to cuff her fingers lovingly around his wrist. Wyn was certain her touch was the only thing keeping him from falling apart.

"You'd best go and collect young Mr. Barnes. We have much to discuss."

CHAPTER 29

ROGER

ROGER WAS STILL MOPING. He wasn't proud of it, but he couldn't make himself stop either. He'd hidden away in his bed and instructed his valet not to bring him any messages or deliveries, and that he was not at home to callers. Notley did not approve of this behavior and made it quite clear.

"You should talk to him, sir. I'm sure it was just a misunderstanding."

But Roger merely shooed the valet out of the room and continued to feel sorry for himself.

In the afternoon, he heard murmurings in the other room that suggested a visitor. He grumbled to himself and turned away from the door. To his irritation, the door opened and Notley said, "I'm very sorry, Mr. Barnes. He insisted it was urgent."

"Oh, for God's sake, Notley, what part of—" Roger started, sitting up in annoyance. He stopped mid-complaint to stare open-mouthed at the visitor.

Wyndham Wrenwhistle was standing in his bedroom doorway with a pained expression.

Roger's anger spiked. "There's no call for you to look at me like that," he snapped. "I didn't invite you."

To his surprise, Wyndham didn't snap back. Instead, he sighed, "I know you didn't. Trust me, I wish myself away from here too." But then, he closed the door behind him and sat on the edge of Roger's bed.

Roger scooted back a little. "Er...what are you doing?"

"I take it you haven't heard then?"

"Heard what?"

Wyndham wordlessly passed Roger a paper. As he took it, he recognized that it was *Torquil's Tribune*. His stomach tightened with anxiety about what the writer had said about his letter. But Wyndham didn't look angry so Roger opened the paper and read it. He felt his mouth opening in shock.

"Well," Wyndham said in a dry tone. "At least we won't have to worry about flies in our house. I can just say things to you and wait for you to catch them with your mouth."

Roger snapped his mouth shut. Then he bolted to his knees on the bed. "What is this?"

"What does it look like?" Wyndham asked wearily. "It's our engagement announcement."

"But we're not engaged."

"I know."

"But—"

"But now we are." Wyndham sighed and ran a hand over his face. "I think someone saw me bringing the box here and...misunderstood my intentions."

"What, so they were inquisitive enough to watch you come in but not inquisitive enough to watch you storm out?"

"I don't know. It's a mistake. But it's all over town by now. I've come here to bring you back to my house so we can discuss—"

"We'll talk to Pimpernel-Smith. If it's truly a mistake then they will print a retraction."

Wyndham frowned at him. "If?"

Roger leaned forward and pointed to a line on paper. "It says here that they received letters of import." He paused and bit his lip. "I might as well confess to you that I...well I was angry and I sent them a letter. About you. Again. But it certainly didn't say this."

Wyndham got up. "I wrote one as well," he murmured slowly. "You think this was done with malice?"

"I'm not sure," Roger admitted, studying the paper again. "But something doesn't add up. It wouldn't make any sense for them to receive two messages from us, saying how much we—how angry we were with each other, and then hear from someone else that you brought me a box, and draw *this* conclusion."

"Damn," Wyndham whispered. Then he opened Roger's wardrobe. "Get dressed. We're going to talk to them."

Roger shuffled off the bed and picked up the trousers Wyndham had tossed at him. "Are you…er…going to stay here while I change?"

Wyndham rolled his eyes. "I have seen the naked form before. And if we can't get them to retract, we'll be getting married anyway. So it hardly matters."

"You haven't seen *my* naked form," Roger muttered.

Wyndham made an impatient sound and left the room, sending Notley to help Roger change.

Once he was dressed, Roger tucked the *Tribune* into his pocket, and went to his study. Wyndham was standing by the window, which was opened again with the curtain pulled back. For a brief moment, it felt as if nothing had changed between them. When Wyndham turned to look at him, his expression wasn't mocking or hateful.

"Ready?"

Roger nodded.

Without a word, they left the room and got into the Wrenwhistle family carriage. Wyndham gave the driver the address to Torquil's press and they sat in silence as the carriage trundled down the road, stopping at a narrow alleyway.

Roger had never been to the building where the *Tribune* was printed. Wyndham gave the structure a curious look as he helped Roger out of the carriage, and led him to the door.

"There's magic being used on the building," he commented.

Roger didn't know how Wyndham could tell but he trusted his word. They walked into the short, dark building that had small windows letting in tiny shafts of light. A large printing press took over the bulk of the space and they could see a skinny person bending over it.

Roger cleared his throat awkwardly.

The person straightened and turned, then gave a slow, wide smile. "Ah," they said, "how nice. The lovebirds themselves decided to grace me with their presence. I did wonder if that might happen."

Torquil Pimpernel-Smith was of middling height and scrawny physique.

They had dark wavy hair that was tousled and messy, and a beauty that suggested fae blood. But their movements were just gawky enough to suggest their human nature as well. They stuffed their hands in their pockets and strolled forward.

"What can I do for you today, gentlemen?"

"We're here to find out why you printed that announcement," Wyndham said.

"And request that you retract it," Roger put in.

"Retract it?" Torquil repeated. "Why would I do that?"

"Because it's incorrect," Roger explained.

"Is it?"

"Yes!" they both replied in unison.

Torquil chuckled. "Well, I suppose it might have been incorrect this morning, but it certainly isn't now."

Roger wasn't sure what he'd expected from the writer, perhaps an apology, perhaps embarrassment, but this casual amusement was certainly not it. "Did you do it intentionally?"

"Of course."

Roger's mouth went dry.

"Why?" Wyndham asked, as if the word had been wrenched out of him. "Why would you do such a thing? You, of all people, ought to know how difficult it is for fae and human couples to be married. For goodness' sake, your parents—" He cut off his own words and glared. "Is that it? Was this some sort of malicious trick to punish us or something?"

Torquil cocked their head at the question. "Malicious? No, no, certainly not."

Roger pulled out his copy of the *Tribune* and reread a part that had stuck out upon first reading. *Many hope this marriage will result in better understanding and empathy throughout society.* "Oh," he murmured softly.

Torquil smiled. "Yes, I thought *you* might understand."

"Understand what?" Wyndham asked.

Roger glanced between them. "They want our marriage to change the way society views relationships between fae and humans. Have you been planning this?" he demanded of Torquil.

Torquil shrugged and walked back to the press. "I've had the idea for a little while now, but I hadn't made up my mind to act on it or not. I honestly hoped you two might fall in love a little faster and save me the trouble."

"Fall in love?" Wyndham asked. "Are you mad?"

Torquil plucked some letters out of the press and began putting them away.

"We are *not* in love," Wyndham said, a little louder.

"Not yet. Although I've suspected for some time that neither of you were…" They glanced over their shoulder, "shall we say, as impartial in your opinions as you let on."

"What do you mean?" Roger asked.

They went back to tidying up. "Your letters were very entertaining. I didn't get a chance to thank you for that. I burned them, of course. Wouldn't do to start a marriage off on that footing."

"And you think *this* is a better footing?" Roger asked.

"You'll work it out. You were nearly there last week. Whatever happened?" they asked, looking up.

"That is not your concern," Wyndham said.

Torquil turned back to the press. "You'd be surprised by how many messages I've received in the past fortnight asking about you two. Do you know that three different people told me about that little present you brought over?"

Wyndham shifted his weight, looking uncomfortable.

"That is one thing I sort of regret. Calling you the least appealing member of your family, I mean. You really are quite adorable when you put your mind to it. I cannot wait to see how you are in the engagement phase and I am certain you will make a very endearing husband." They smiled at Wyndham as if they had delivered a genuine compliment. "And as for you," they went on, turning to Roger. "Well, I'm very eager to see what your future holds. You have a great deal of potential, you know."

"I…thank you?" Roger replied.

Wyndham rubbed the bridge of his nose. "This was a waste of time."

"Yes," Torquil laughed. "But I did enjoy the visit. Next time you come, I'll try to be a better host." Roger and Wyn turned to the door. "I know you aren't thinking it yet," they shouted to their retreating backs, "but you'll thank me eventually. And you're welcome."

Wyndham slammed the door shut behind him and helped Roger into the carriage before telling the driver to take them to the Wrenwhistle home. Then he sat in the seat opposite Roger and glared out the window.

"I'm sorry," Roger offered. "I thought they might—"

"I know," Wyndham murmured. "I did too." He heaved a sigh. "What a mess."

With those words, Roger allowed himself to finally dwell on the situation they were both in. They were going to be married. He was going to marry a man who hated him, who thought he was foolish and worthless. He had long since given up the idea that marriage might promise bliss, but he had never anticipated such misery.

CHAPTER 30

WYN

W YN HADN'T the faintest idea what to say to Roger on the ride back to his home. After two stolen glances, he decided that he'd never seen the man— perhaps *any* man—look so sad. Typically, he would've still been caught up on his own concerns over the situation. But there was something about the way Barnes had his hands pressed together between his thighs and his eyes cast down that made it impossible to think of himself.

Did Roger even prefer the company of other gentlemen?

Wyn's own history in that regard had been public knowledge for some time. Not that he made a point of speaking about it with anyone, but it was still far from a secret on both sides of society.

Barnes was another story. Wyn knew nothing of his inclinations, if he had any at all. The only thing he could say for sure was that humans had a ridiculously strict code of conduct to follow when courtship was concerned. Barnes hardly seemed like the type to go against it.

Wyn helped Roger from the carriage when they arrived, and the two of them made their way inside with silence still hanging between them. When they stepped into the sitting room, it was as though royalty had walked through the door.

"Oh, Mr. Barnes!" Wyn's mother cried, hurrying over to offer her congratulations in a way that only she could; both smothering and respectful all at once. "We are so excited to welcome you into our family. Please, do come sit. We were just about to start afternoon tea."

Roger was ushered into the room without a choice. Emrys gave Wyn a sly look after rising from his chair.

"That took longer than expected."

"We took a bit of a detour on the way back," Wyn explained. He had little interest in sharing details of their failed attempt at the press across town.

Emrys snorted. "I'll bet you did," he purred, before he poked his tongue hard into his cheek in a suggestive way and quirked his eyebrows.

Wyn rolled his eyes dramatically and stepped around his brother to join everyone else for tea, but Iris slid her arm into the bend of his elbow before he could make it far. She led him into the hallway where they couldn't be easily overheard.

"Wyndham, darling. I'm sure it goes without saying that I am limited in what I can do to help this situation." She sounded sympathetic, but he couldn't help noticing the faintest twinkle in her eye. "You understand how difficult it would be to retract such a statement, especially because it concerns not one, but two families of the Council."

"Yes, I'm aware that it would be nearly impossible," Wyn said, wishing still to forget the experience with Torquil Pimpernel-Smith.

It was well known that Torquil was half-human and half-fae, the result of a passionate love affair that miraculously did not end in complete disaster. Though it was not until recent years that their union and others like it had become more accepted by society.

A lump formed in the back of Wyn's throat as he realized the weight of his own newfound reality. He swallowed it away.

Wyn wondered absently if that was why the building where the press was located had felt so odd to him. His own magic had stirred upon arrival as it recognized the strength of another fae. But there was also something inherently human about the way the entire place felt like it was warding off anything that might cause harm to those inside, or even the building itself. Whatever it was, the combination had been rather intoxicating. He'd been more than happy to leave when they did.

"So you'll also understand that we will need to discuss formalities moving forward. Expectations. All of society will be watching the both of you until the day of your wedding, and likely for a long time after that."

"I understand," he said quietly.

This was never supposed to be his role in the family. Emrys was set to inherit, and with that came the burden of carrying the attention of the town. *His* engagement was supposed to be the one everyone swooned over. *His* wedding was supposed to be the one the papers named the most anticipated social event of the Season. *His* marriage was supposed to set an example of what a formidable union looked like for the rest of society to emulate.

Now Wyn feared all of this responsibility would fall to him for reasons he never dared to imagine.

Iris raised her age-weathered fingers to his chin, lifting his face from where it had fallen. She held his gaze in a purposeful way and gave him another of her gentle, knowing grins.

"Not to worry, darling. There are far worse people to become engaged to." Her hand moved to offer a loving pat to his cheek. "The Barneses have hearts of gold, each and every one. Hear me when I say you'd be wise to soften your heart toward that young man. He just might surprise you."

"Thank you, Grandmother," Wyn said without emotion.

The pair returned to the sitting room. Wyn's eyes went directly to where Roger was seated on the sofa between his mother and Aveline, wearing a polite, closed-mouth smile as they chattered on. Certainly he would be glad that they both took their tea as he did, with a hint of citrus and copious amounts of milk and sugar.

"Mr. and Mrs. Barnes," their footman announced suddenly. Wyn turned toward the second entrance of the room where Roger's parents sidled in. Wyn tried not to notice the familiar way the elder Mr. Barnes' jaw went slack as the two of them peered around the room.

"Mother. Father." Roger stood from the sofa and went to them without hesitation. They embraced him at the same time and Roger disappeared into the warmest family moment Wyn had ever seen. He looked away.

"Imagine our surprise when we read the news this morning," his mother said with a smile when they finally broke apart. "Darling, we are so happy for you." Her eyes found Wyn's across the room. "For both of you."

Roger looked at him for the first time since they'd left the press. A spark of emotion crossed his features, almost pleading.

Wyn took a slow breath and stepped toward them, offering a small bow.

"Your congratulations are much appreciated," Wyn said, grinning when he lifted his face to Roger's mother again. He offered his arm to guide her toward the far end of the room where the rest of his family was waiting to greet them.

Only after everyone's excitement had been tamed with tea and biscuits did the conversation pick back up in a significant way. It was Wyn's mother who broached the subject.

"Well, I suppose we have much planning to do! Of course, we will be hosting the first engagement party this weekend. Mrs. Barnes, do draw up a list of guests and I'll send the invitations out at once. It is rather short notice, I know, but anyone who cannot attend is more than welcome to reserve their invitations for any and all subsequent celebrations."

"Oh yes," Mrs. Barnes said with a polite but genuine laugh. "In all of the excitement, I'd forgotten about lengthy fae weddings. Human weddings are very simple, you know. Reading of the banns, small ceremony, breakfast after." She gave a content hum before returning to the topic at hand. "I will have the list drawn up and sent to you by tomorrow morning." She exchanged a look with her husband. "Naturally, we would also like to host everyone at some point before the wedding."

Engagement. Guest list. Celebration. Wedding. The words were already whirling around in Wyn's head, making him dizzy despite the chair supporting him. His gaze darted to the open window that wasn't nearly close enough.

"Another very important matter to consider: we would be overjoyed to hold the wedding at our country estate. My eldest son was married there just this past summer. Wynnie, would that make you happy?" His mother's dreaded nickname for him pulled his attention back to the conversation.

"Pardon?" he asked mildly, sitting up a bit in his seat. His mother offered him an understanding smile.

"We do not have to decide everything today," she said.

"I feel there are some things that need to be discussed at present," Mr. Barnes started then, leaning forward to set his empty teacup down. "First and foremost: Roger has already reached majority, but my understanding is that Wyndham has not?"

"That is correct," Iris answered, the tone of her voice dipping as she seemed to catch on to what Mr. Barnes was getting at. She gave Wyn a pointed look. He returned it with a look of mild indignation. Certainly he wasn't trying to imply…

Mr. Barnes turned his attention to Roger. "These meetings you've been having to work on the proposal have been unchaperoned. I do not think any of us realized we should be worrying about any, er…*untoward* behavior going on in your rooms."

Emrys let out a burst of laughter. Wyn wasn't sure if that or Mr. Barnes' words alone were what made Roger startle so badly he nearly spilled his tea. Wyn's mother scolded her older son under her breath and shooed him out of the room.

"I can assure you that nothing untoward has occurred, Mr. Barnes," Wyn said smoothly. "But if it would be preferable, we can start meeting with a chaperone present."

"Very good," Mr. Barnes said with a slight nod, satisfied.

Mrs. Barnes reached out to rest her hand atop Roger's. Wyn noticed that she had that watery shine in her eyes that indicated she was holding back tears. Combined with her smile, she looked sincerely happy.

Wyn looked down into the last sip of tea in his cup. He swirled it once before he brought it to his lips, wishing it was a bit stronger of a drink.

"Oh!" Wyn's mother clapped her hands excitedly before she buried them in the skirts of her dress. "And of course, we will need to set aside time for them to work on their wedding spell."

Wyn lowered his cup and immediately locked eyes with Roger.

The wedding spell.

CHAPTER 31

ROGER

"Wedding spell?" Roger's mother asked. "What's that?"

Roger was relieved she had asked the question. He didn't entirely trust himself to speak. Everything was happening too quickly. Wyndham had barely said a word to him since they'd left Pimpernel-Smith and Roger couldn't determine the emotion behind their exchanged looks.

"It's part of the fae wedding tradition," Wyndham's grandmother explained. "The couple always performs a spell together on their wedding day, before all of their friends and family. It is meant to symbolize their harmony and compatibility. And love, of course," she added with a fond smile.

Roger swallowed and finally spoke, "Has this tradition ever been performed with a fae and a human?"

"You aren't the first fae and human to get married," his father said in a mild tone. "Don't think of it as two separate magic systems, but as a way to work in tandem with each other."

"Rather like your current project," Wyndham's grandmother added.

"We'll think of something," Wyndham said, his gaze on Roger with that same infuriatingly undecipherable expression. Was he angry? Was he miserable? Annoyed? Pitying? Roger almost would have preferred outright disdain. Although he couldn't deny it had been a relief that Wyndham had put on a courteous front in front of Roger's parents. It was a kindness he hadn't expected. "Of course," he went on, "it will be challenging to find the time. What with the project and my social engagements. I'm already concerned about our completing the project at the appointed deadline."

"I imagine if you ask the Council for an extension, they will understand," Wyndham's grandmother said.

Roger's father chuckled. "Indeed. If anything, we'll all be relieved. The Council's purpose is to create better understanding and collaboration between the fae and human sets. Your marriage will be a great boon in that regard."

Roger squirmed a little at his father's forthrightness. After their conversation with Pimpernel-Smith, Roger felt little more than a pawn in someone else's game. To hear his father applaud the maneuver was disconcerting.

Wyndham surprised him by saying, "Perhaps, by your leave, Roger and I can take a turn about the garden? We've had precious little time to discuss these matters between ourselves. And I'm sure you will want to start planning events."

"Of course," Wyndham's mother said. "Be so good as to stay in view of the house."

Wyndham nodded his understanding and then turned to Roger, offering his arm. Roger took it, unsure of the other man's intentions. Wyndham led them both through the house and into the garden at the back. It was a nice garden for a townhouse, moderate in size and very well tended.

"I don't think I've ever met anyone who wears their emotions so plainly on their face as you do," Wyndham commented as soon as the door shut behind them.

Roger sighed. "I'm sorry. I'm still a bit overwhelmed."

Wyndham was quiet for a moment. "I know," he said at last. "I am too."

"You're certainly keeping that hidden better than I am," Roger commented.

The corner of Wyndam's mouth lifted. "Practice."

Roger studied his face. Wyndham's lips were pressed together and there was a paleness to his skin, not unlike how he had been at the garden party. It pained him to see such indications of distress, but it was strangely comforting to know he wasn't alone.

Then Wyndham asked, "Your parents are unaware of the nature of this engagement, I take it?"

"Correct. Although, I'm a little surprised that they're accepting it at face value."

"Hm. My family did too. At first."

Roger cut him a glance. "But they know the truth now?"

Wyndham nodded. "Yes."

Roger considered this. "That was very kind of them then, to be so welcoming."

"Why wouldn't they be?"

Roger hesitated. "I'm well aware I'm not your first choice."

Wyndham huffed. "*Marriage* was not my first choice."

"Oh."

He deposited Roger on a bench and then leaned against a nearby stone wall. "We both know I was not your first choice either. I'm sure you expected a love match, rather than…"

"This strange arranged marriage for the benefit of society?"

Wyndham cracked a smile. "Well I was going to say marrying someone you hate, but that works too."

Roger stared at him in surprise. "I don't hate you."

Wyndham's expression turned unreadable. "Don't you?"

"Of course not. I…I rather thought you hated me."

Wyndham rolled his eyes. "You idiot. I brought you a tea set, for goodness' sake. And in such a way that it was mistaken for an engagement present."

Roger shrugged. "I assumed that was pity or something."

"We've known each other for years. When have you ever seen me give someone a gift out of pity?"

Roger sat with that realization for a moment. "Oh."

Wyndham heaved a sigh and then sat down on the bench beside him. "Look. I don't know who that little bird was or what they told you. But all of London thinks we're in the midst of some whirlwind romance. We're going to have to get over our…*argument*, and pretend we're in love."

Roger hadn't made it that far in his planning. The door to the house opened and footsteps could be heard on the gravel. He looked up to see who it was. But then Wyndham curled a finger under Roger's chin and turned his head back to face him. Roger's breath caught, much to his annoyance.

"Consider this a practice round," Wyndham murmured. "No matter where we go, everyone will be watching us. They will be examining every look, every gesture, every move we make."

His eyes raked slowly over Roger's face and Roger felt as though his skin was on fire from the glance. "Right," he whispered. "I understand. I-I can pretend. I know what's at stake here."

"Good." Wyndham said. "I was sure you would."

A laugh sounded around the corner. "Stars above. We leave you two alone for barely a quarter of an hour and this is how I find you?" They both turned to see Wyndham's mother standing nearby, looking amused.

Wyndham pulled away slowly and dropped his hand to rest on top of Roger's. "I'm sorry, Mother. Did you need us?"

"The Barneses are preparing to leave. They wanted to know if Roger would like to be taken home."

"Oh," Roger said, standing. "Yes, th—that would be nice. Thank you."

"We'll be right in," Wyndham added, laying a hand on his arm.

She laughed again and walked back inside.

"I'll try to call on you tomorrow, so we can continue our project and I can give you a proper list of my—*our* upcoming social obligations."

"To be honest," Roger said, taking Wyndham's arm. "I'm very bad at remembering those. You might as well just send me a message each day with where I'm expected to be and when. It's what my mother does."

Wyndham chuckled. "Duly noted."

They went back inside and everyone politely said their goodbyes. Roger discovered that apparently the Wrenwhistles had invited him and his parents over to dinner the following evening.

Once inside the carriage, his parents both turned to him with broad smiles.

"I'm so happy for you, darling," his mother said.

"Indeed," his father said. "I've long thought you two would suit each other."

His mother laughed. "It is so nice to be right, isn't it?"

"And it's a very advantageous match, all things considered. The Wrenwhistles are a powerful family in society."

Roger frowned. "We're not too bad, ourselves."

His father chuckled. "We're perfectly respectable. But one of the many reasons the fae integrated into human society at all was the economical boost they added. Fae hold more land than humans do and, as such, their wealth is much more significant. They might have integrated into human society, but they fundamentally changed it. As such, the Wrenwhistles *are* society."

His mother looked thoughtful. "Perhaps I ought to teach you some aspects of running a household."

Since receiving his low scores at twelve, Roger had long anticipated that any potential marriage would likely result in being his spouse's dependent. But to suddenly realize he would be *Wyndham's* dependent, that he would be taking his arm when they entered a room together, and expected to obey him, was a harrowing thought. His expression must have shown his anxiety because his mother patted his arm.

"Don't fret, darling. My father showed me how to run a household when I got engaged. And although I didn't teach such things to either of your siblings, as they are heads of their own households, I'm confident I will be able to teach you everything I know. Besides, I'm sure young Wyndham will take good care of you. You won't have anything to worry about."

"Yes," his father agreed. "I'll be discussing the matter in more detail with them soon, but I imagine you will be set up very comfortably."

Roger wanted to argue the point but knew that impulse to be ridiculous. So he simply thanked them with as much sincerity as he could.

"And tomorrow morning, I'll collect you to go shopping," his father announced.

"What? Why?"

"I know you take pride in your economy, but you really do need new clothes. Now is the perfect opportunity."

"Is it really necessary?"

"Yes," his mother replied. "You are officially engaged and we will be joining with a prominent fae family; it will be important to dress accordingly."

He could see her reasoning, even if he didn't like it. At least he would no longer have to wear the same two suits every day. He had to admit he was relieved by that.

"I think we also need to talk about your rooms," his father continued. "We will obviously be ending the lease on them. It might be wise to start moving you back into our home. That way all of your things will be packed and ready to move after your wedding."

"And then we can offer chaperonage when you and young Wyndham work on your project together."

"Oh," Roger said quietly. "Yes, I can see how that would be practical."

He didn't know why but the sudden and complete loss of his relative independence felt like the worst part of an already shabby situation. He knew it to be silly, as he'd never truly been independent; his parents paid for his rooms and gave him money for his food and living expenses. Still, he'd enjoyed being on his own. It hadn't occurred to him how temporary that was. Then again, he'd always expected to get married someday, he'd just always vaguely assumed he'd marry someone who could afford to give Roger his own study to work in. Would such a thing be possible with Wyndham?

"I'll tell Notley to start packing things tomorrow," he said.

"Excellent," his father said, smiling at him warmly. "And we'll send one of the servants with supplies to help."

"It will be good to have you in the house again," his mother said, giving him a fond look.

The following morning, Roger instructed Notley to start packing. To his surprise, the valet looked pleased.

"I've missed Cook's lemon cakes," he explained.

"That's loyalty for you," Roger muttered.

His father arrived soon after, with a pair of servants in tow, armed with packing crates. "Shall we?" he asked.

"Wyn—Mr. Wrenwhistle said he was going to come by and work on the project," Roger said.

His father looked amused. "I imagine you can call him by his first name now, son. But in any case, we can leave a message with Notley to inform him of your errands."

Roger realized that Wyndham would probably be relieved to hear he was getting new clothes, so he took his father's advice in giving Notley more instructions. He gave one final lingering look at his study, feeling wistful about the stage in his life coming to such an abrupt end. Even the single open window made him feel oddly raw.

He brushed off the feelings and followed his father out the door.

The shopping trip was, in a word, chaotic. People stopped them to congratulate him everywhere they went. People walking down the street, people shopping, people riding by in carriages. Some people were enthusiastic, telling him how exciting and romantic it all was, others congratulated him with a hint of incredulity (and a touch of envy, Roger suspected), informing him what a catch Mr. Wrenwhistle was. Several seemed intent on explaining what an important change this match made for society as a whole.

Roger wanted to run back to his study and hide away from all the attention, but his father engaged in every conversation, dragging Roger into it. Besides, his study was currently being packed up; there was nothing to run back to.

Other than the constant interruptions, the shopping itself went smoothly. Roger's father had always been very matter-of-fact about clothes, attending to a list of items with sharp efficiency. Roger was uncomfortable with the expense put forth. Not only was he given several ready-made suits to wear that week, but he was fitted for more outfits than he currently owned.

When he attempted to protest, his father held up a hand. "A new trousseau is perfectly commonplace, Roger."

Roger sighed and ran a thumb over the new fabric. "It hardly seems worth it."

His father put a hand on his shoulder. "I want you to listen to me very carefully."

Roger looked up at him, surprised by the sternness in his voice.

"I'm well aware that you have been fighting this Hastings score battle as hard as you have because your own score caused you so much distress. I'm also aware that you insisted on living alone, wearing old clothes, employing only one servant, to avoid being a burden. But you must know that we love you. You have never once been a burden. You have always been wanted, always been cherished. You are most certainly worth the expense and fuss of a fine wedding. Do you understand?"

Roger looked away, embarrassed, and nodded.

"Good," his father said on an exhale. He kissed Roger's forehead. "Besides," he continued, "just think how nice you'll look for your betrothed, hm?"

Roger's face flushed and he gave up the argument for lost.

CHAPTER 32

WYN

Wyn was unable to keep his word about calling on Roger the next morning. From the second his eyes opened, his mother caught him in a whirlwind of engagement party planning questions. The worst part was that he knew she already had opinions and answers for everything she was asking him, she just didn't feel it was right to leave him out.

After giving a half-hearted glance at the three versions of the invitation she'd somehow had printed and delivered to their home in less than twenty-four hours, Wyn groaned and collapsed against the back of the sofa.

"Mother, can you *please* just make these decisions for yourself? I do not care if it has flower embellishments, nor if the paper is white or cream."

"Sit up, Wynnie, it's a bad look to slouch." He could tell by her clipped tone that she was getting annoyed with him. He wanted to assure her that the feeling was mutual, but he sat up anyway. "Now, certainly you have an opinion on if the edges should be plain or if you'd like them to be lined decoratively in silver or gold?"

Wyn swallowed down the scream of frustration sitting at the back of his tongue just begging to be set free. "I should think something like that would be reserved for the actual wedding invitations, would it not?"

"Whatever you'd like, my love," his mother said, her smile brightening.

This horrible game went on for several hours, until Wyn was certain his ability to make decisions had been broken entirely. His only respite was when Aveline joined them and offered her own thoughts, at which point his mother decided to start over from the beginning and review all of Wyn's choices with her.

"May I be excused now?" Wyn asked, trying not to beg.

"Yes, but do not go far. I've invited the Barneses to dinner this evening. Since your father was working when all of the excitement happened yesterday, I thought it appropriate to have a more formal gathering so he can officially welcome them into our family."

"Yes, Mother," Wyn said hastily as he finally escaped his confinement in the sitting room.

BY THE TIME Wyn was summoned for dinner, he had only slightly recovered from his mother's morning of torture. Truth be told, his head was pounding. He hadn't enough time to request a salve or concoction be brought up to him between being roused from his nap and dressing for company.

He'd decided to wear one of his favorite waistcoats to lift his spirits; deep purple velvet, double-breasted with two lines of fashionably sized silver buttons down the front. As he tied his cravat in the mirror, he hoped the darker color would subtly indicate to his mother that she'd nearly sent him to his death with all of her nonsense earlier.

Wyn was the last to arrive downstairs, though it seemed nobody felt the need to wait before engaging in some pre-dinner mingling and drinking, which was even better. Wyn slipped into the room and found himself compelled to rescue Roger from the middle of the crowd, where everyone had their eyes on him like a dancing bear in the street.

After weaseling his way between his mother and sister, he paused to greet Roger's parents with a polite grin. "Councilmember Barnes, Mrs. Barnes, good evening. Pleased you could join us again so soon."

They greeted him in return, and then Wyn's attention shifted to where Roger was standing, looking a bit like his nerves were already shot. Or perhaps it was still lingering from the day before. He stepped closer to the man and arched an eyebrow.

"Barnes," he said, eyes trailing down to Roger's shoes and back up again. Without thinking, he started to raise a hand to touch the fine fabric of the coat Roger was wearing. He caught himself and clasped his hands behind his back instead, tilting his chin up to indicate what he was referencing. "I daresay you must be the only man in London who could look so miserable while wearing a new suit of this quality."

"Mr. Wrenwhistle," Roger returned, before glancing down at himself. "Father thought it was appropriate that I should add some new pieces to my wardrobe, considering the…recent events."

"Your father is a smart man," Wyn said with a small smirk. "I see my family has already driven you to the bottom of your drink."

Roger held up his empty wine glass and gave a nervous sort of chuckle as he inspected it. "I hadn't realized." Then his eyes went a little wide. "N-not to say that your family was the reason for—"

"Trust me," Wyn cut in, "I will also need my share of wine to make it through this evening. Shall we?" He offered Roger his arm and the pair trailed behind the rest of the party as they migrated to the dining room.

After helping Roger into his seat, Wyn took his own beside him.

"I do apologize for this morning," he started, his voice soft so only Roger could hear. "I had every intention of coming 'round, but I was captured by the teeth and claws of the biggest party planning beast in London."

"Oh dear," Roger murmured. "That sounds dreadful."

"It was."

"Well I hardly think it was any more enjoyable being paraded around town as I went shopping for new clothes. Humans and fae alike were practically popping out of thin air to offer their most heartfelt congratulations."

Wyn's face pinched in a grimace as he reached for his wine. "Hm. Perhaps that does sound worse. But only slightly."

Before dinner was served, Wyn's father stood at the head of the table and cleared his throat, drawing everyone's attention. If he had been a man of many words, Wyn might've felt the heat of embarrassment creeping up his neck, but he knew better.

"I wanted to thank the Barneses for joining us this evening. There is nothing that brings more joy into our home than a celebration to plan, for it is the only time Mrs. Wrenwhistle leaves me in peace." Laughter bubbled around the table, and Wyn's parents shared a look of pure affection.

After forty years of marriage, their relationship had grown to be a strong one. Wyn often wondered if the time they spent apart was the secret to their happiness. Even with the comforts of wealth to support them, his father kept busy with work he enjoyed and was gone more than he was home. And though she wanted for nothing, his mother treated every gift he gave her upon his return like it was something she'd dreamed about since she was a girl simply because it was from him.

Wyn and his siblings had always benefited from the circumstance, as well. Along with the trinkets and sweets, he also brought a sense of tranquility to their home, his satisfaction with the other parts of his life fortifying his soft and supportive personality. They were fortunate to have at least one calm parent.

"Let us enjoy this meal and all those to follow in recognition of our families uniting." Mr. Wrenwhistle raised his glass, and everyone else did the same before taking a sip to seal the toast.

Wyn listened as the conversations around the table picked up where they'd left off. It seemed both of their families had only positive things to say, sharing their own personal excitements over the impending nuptials, reflecting fondly on their own courtships, and so on.

Before long, the emotions swirling in the room made Wyn's headache turn from a dull pain to something sharper and less easy to ignore. He closed his eyes for a moment and felt his magic reaching out toward the open windows as he breathed in slowly.

"Are you quite well?" Roger's voice beside him was gentle, and he opened his eyes to offer a reassuring smile, but it felt a little too small to convey what he'd meant it to.

"Yes, fine. Just a small headache." Wyn set his fork down on his plate and reached for his wine again. He realized this would be a perfect opportunity to send Roger home with his books. Wyn leaned slightly closer to Roger and said, "If you've no objections, we'll retire to my room when dinner is over."

CHAPTER 33

ROGER

ROGER KNEW the invitation must be an innocent one, but he couldn't help the swell of panic that rose in his chest at Wyndham's words. They were going up to Wyndham's room? Alone? He weakly hoped the gentleman had some sort of sitting room; Roger wasn't entirely sure he could countenance seeing the state of Wyndham's bed—he was quite sure it would cause him to imagine it later and he was equally sure he didn't want to do that. He still remembered how unnerving it had been to have Wyndham sitting on the end of *his* bed. He had taken a seat as if it was the most natural thing in the world, rather than an indication of intimacy. He was vaguely aware that he was being absurd. He took another sip of wine to try and hide his nerves.

After dinner, as promised, Wyndham took him upstairs after assuring his parents he would keep the door open. Wyndham's bedroom was immaculate, which was not the least bit surprising. It was done up in shades of green, with white accents not limited to the cornice boards and detailed chair rail that stretched along the walls. Lively potted plants sprouted from every available corner and surface; plush rugs were scattered about the space, supporting various islands of seating options, including a spot before the hearth that seemed designed to be particularly inviting, if one was so inclined.

Wyndham seemed entirely unfazed by Roger's presence in his private space. He strode to a desk and opened up a bottom drawer. He pulled out a pile of books and placed them on the desk.

"Here," he said. "I wanted to be sure and return your books to you."

"Oh," Roger said. "Thank you." In all the flurry of emotions over the past week, he'd completely forgotten about the books he'd loaned to Wyndham. "Did you...did you like them?"

Wyndham nodded. "They were most informative. I still have your notes from the other day. I shall have to revisit them before we go back to work tomorrow."

Roger felt as though he was supposed to go to the desk and collect the books himself, but he felt rather glued to the floor, unwilling to step further into the room than he had to.

Wyndham raised an eyebrow. "Never been inside another gentleman's bedroom, I take it?"

Roger shifted his weight awkwardly. "N-no."

"I'm not going to seduce you."

Roger felt his face get hot. "I know."

"Not yet anyway," Wyndham teased with a grin.

Roger startled. "Er...I suppose that is good."

Wyndham cocked his head slightly. "Do you want to be seduced, Mr. Barnes?"

"What? No! My parents are downstairs."

He laughed. "I didn't mean *now*. I mean..." He hesitated and then stepped a little closer to Roger. "Would such attentions be welcome to you?"

Roger blinked, at a loss.

"From another man," Wyndham clarified.

"Oh," he mumbled. "It didn't occur to me that you wouldn't know that. Yes. I do find other men attractive."

Wyndham looked curious. "Women?"

"Some women. More often men though. And also those who identify as both, or neither. But mostly men. I haven't...that is, I haven't done any... er...well, I find them nice to look at. That's all."

Wyndham looked amused by his flustered state. "Well, that is a relief," he said softly. "I would hate to have a husband who didn't find me attractive."

Roger rolled his eyes. "I think that would be rather impossible."

Wyndham's gaze sharpened. "Oh?"

Roger stepped around him, more uncomfortable with Wyndham's curious expression than with being in the room. "Yes," he replied, once the other man's face was out of view. "You do realize you're a very attractive person."

"Oh, I do. I'm just pleased to learn that you know it too."

Now that he was a little further into the room, Roger found himself intrigued by it. He glanced up at the artwork on the walls, wondering if Wyndham had picked the pieces himself or if they had been selected for him. He carefully didn't look at the bed, turning his attention to the little sofa by the open doors leading out to a small balcony.

"You prefer open windows, I take it," he observed.

"That's a rather fascinating change of subject," Wyndham commented. "And, yes. I like to have the outside world around me as much as possible. It's a nice view—for London."

Roger took that as an invitation and stepped boldly towards the balcony. To his surprise, Wyndham followed, standing close behind him.

Roger cast about for an appropriate topic of conversation. "Your room is lovely."

"Thank you. It's something of a refuge when I'm in town."

Roger felt a pang of sorrow. "I can appreciate that. My rooms were the same."

"Were?"

Roger nodded. "My parents informed me I ought to move back in with them until the wedding. Notley began packing this morning."

Wyndham was silent for a long moment. "I'm sorry," he said softly. "Will you get your own study?"

"I'm not sure."

"You should ask for one."

Roger sighed and turned back to the room. "I don't feel entirely comfortable doing that."

"Why not?"

Roger didn't know how to explain it to Wyndham. He gestured vaguely by way of an answer.

"You could simply explain that you need space to work on the project. I'm sure they'd understand."

"Yes, perhaps I'll do that," Roger said, already trying to think of a new topic. His eyes caught on an easel with a partially finished painting on it. He stepped closer. "Did you do this?"

"You really are a mass of topic changes right now, aren't you? And yes. I did all the paintings in this room."

Roger stared at him. "All of them?"

Wyndham raised an eyebrow. "Is that a problem?"

"That's marvelous!" He turned back to the easel. "This is…this is incredible. I could never do something like this," he added quietly.

"Thank you," Wyndham said, matching his tone. Then he straightened. "We'd better go back downstairs before anyone comes looking for us."

Roger quickly snapped back to the present. He scooped up his pile of books and followed Wyndham out the door. But through the rest of the evening, he couldn't stop thinking about the paintings in Wyndham's room. They had been so full of life and feeling, so exquisitely beautiful. He felt as if he'd seen a part of the other man's soul and it was unlike anything he would have imagined.

CHAPTER 34

WYN

AFTER HAVING HIS EGO—AND decidedly nothing else—stroked so thoroughly by Roger's compliments, Wyn bid everyone a good night, requested the strongest tonic that could be made in-house, and promptly went to bed. He'd fallen asleep ruminating over how pleasurable it had been to see Roger's jittery reactions to his questions. And, ultimately, he'd gotten some answers that felt quite pertinent to their situation.

Wyn had agreed to meet Roger at his parents' home the next day, seeing as his rooms were in a state of disassembly that would've made it difficult to get any meaningful work done.

The Barnes residence was within a fair walking distance, so Wyn decided to stretch his legs after being cooped up the day before. Almost immediately, he was surrounded with the same type of behavior Roger had described, both familiar and unfamiliar faces offering their congratulations at every turn. Fortunately, Wyn was well-versed in the art of evading such situations, and he was only truly held up once or twice by someone he knew it would reflect poorly on him to avoid, including Roger's father as he set off toward the Council's chambers.

"We received our invitation for the engagement party not but an hour ago," Mr. Barnes said with a smile. "Such finery will certainly set the tone for the event before it has even begun."

"Yes, my mother has a way with details," he offered diplomatically.

Mr. Barnes looked over his shoulder at the house. "We've just finished with breakfast, so I expect Roger is ready for you." The man turned back and held his gaze. "As much as he would deny my saying so, I believe he's struggling a bit with moving back home temporarily. Am I too bold in requesting that perhaps you could offer him some reassurance about what the future holds?"

"Not too bold, sir," Wyn confirmed.

He knew that Roger's father and his father had retired to the study after dinner to discuss the business matters of their union. As such, Mr. Barnes knew well enough about the modest property Wyn was set to take owner-ship of when he reached majority or got married, whichever came first.

It appeared as though he was going to fall just short of turning thirty and moving to his humble country estate in solitude as he'd always planned.

Mr. Barnes' smile grew as he reached out to offer a solid, almost affec-tionate pat to Wyn's shoulder. It took him a bit by surprise, though he didn't think it had shown on his face.

"I'd best be off. Good luck with your work on the project." Wyn watched as he climbed into the waiting carriage and then it eased down the street.

Wyn was welcomed inside the townhouse and led to a sitting room that was reserved for the family. It felt cozy compared to what he was accus-tomed to at home, or in most of the homes he'd visited before. The furni-ture was in fine condition and everything was in respectable order, but something about the room said *come and stay a while, make yourself comfortable.* He rather liked it.

The view from the windows left something to be desired, but it wasn't much of a concern, as Wyn could see where Roger had picked up his love for heavy window coverings. He wandered over to one and peered out, resisting the urge to crack it open and let in some air.

"Mr. Wrenwhistle," Roger said behind him after a short time. Wyn turned to find him standing in the middle of the room, hands by his sides. He was wearing another new set of clothes. They didn't fit him quite as perfectly as custom pieces would, but they were still a vast improvement.

"Barnes," Wyn said, closing some of the distance between them. He waited for Roger to say something else. When he didn't, Wyn cleared his throat a bit and sent a vague look about the space, reaching for something pleasant to say. "This room is inviting in a very unassuming way."

"Oh, y-yes," Roger fumbled, looking around as though he was becoming reacquainted with the space himself. "Mother has kept it this way since we were children."

Wyn hummed. "What a novelty. My mother changes almost everything about our townhouse before we come in for the Season each year. The only room she's not allowed to touch is mine."

"Why is that?" Roger asked, finally seeming to relax a bit. He even remembered to offer Wyn a seat as he gestured toward the cluster of chairs nearby.

"I enjoy my privacy," Wyn explained as he sat, his knee crossed over the other in one fluid motion. He allowed a small grin to tug at the corners of his mouth. "My door remains locked at all times, and only the most *privileged* of guests are allowed inside."

Roger's eyes narrowed slightly. "What…what do you mean?"

Wyn offered him a bland look, though the implication behind it was quite the opposite. Roger's mouth fell open before he sputtered and looked away, his hands gripping his knees tightly. Wyn chuckled before he shifted to reach into the inside pocket of his coat.

"I regrettably did not get a chance to go over your notes last night. I drank my tonic and fell asleep before my head touched the pillow. Shall we review them again together?" Wyn began unfolding the papers he'd brought with him, scanning Roger's messy handwriting to find something that stood out as a good starting point. "I'll admit that I can hardly remember where we left off."

"Yes," Roger said mildly. "Quite a lot has happened since the last time we were able to speak about our research." The melancholy in his voice was enough to draw Wyn's attention away from the notes in his hands.

"Barnes." Their eyes met, and Wyn bit the inside of his cheek as he considered his next words. What could he possibly say to comfort Roger the way his father had asked him to do? It hardly seemed like the appropriate time to divulge the future that had been plotted out for him in one late-night meeting, effectively tearing him away from the things that brought him joy in life.

"Yes?" Roger asked finally.

A shuffling in the hallway caught Wyn's attention.

"We have company," he murmured.

Roger turned around in his chair to look toward the doorway just as his mother peeked around the corner.

"How long have you been standing there?" Roger yelped.

"Whatever do you mean?" Mrs. Barnes entered the room then, walking pointedly to the windows so she could pull back the drapes and allow more light in. "I was only coming to ask if you needed anything. Are you thirsty, Mr. Wrenwhistle? Shall I have some lemonade brought up for you?"

"Mother, we are here to work, not laze about," Roger protested.

"I would gladly take a glass of lemonade," Wyn said with a smile.

"Wonderful," Mrs. Barnes said, bustling out of the room.

Wyn waited until he couldn't hear her footsteps anymore.

"Come on," he urged under his breath, standing up. "Show me your room."

To his relief, Roger indulged his request, and the man led him upstairs to his bedroom without protest or delay. The moment Wyn shut the door and turned the lock, he felt the wash of upturned magic. All of Roger's belongings were crammed into one corner of the room. Furniture was shoved together at awkward angles; books were spilling out of crates.

"This feels like your shrinking spell," Wyn said carefully.

"It makes moving much easier," Roger explained with a shrug.

Wyn turned to eye him warily. "You're able to shrink items as large as bookshelves?"

"Yes?" Roger blinked at the mess of his belongings. "Yes."

Wyn's eyebrows went up in surprise. Then he let out a sigh and moved to stand in front of Barnes, willing himself to say what he really meant for once in his life. No skirting around the topic, no sarcasm, no insults. He could do this.

"The stench in here is absolutely nauseating. Did you pack a small dead creature with your things?" *Fuck.*

"Oh," Roger said, cringing a bit.

"Ugh. That's not what I meant to say," Wyn added quickly. He swallowed hard and stared over Roger's head at the window. "What I meant to say," he tried again, looking down through Roger's spectacles and settling on his brown eyes, "is that I...I want you to know that everything will be all right. I know there's very little that we have in common, but one thing we do share is our respect for our families. I do not think either of us wishes to disappoint them or tarnish our family names."

"No," Roger agreed, barely above a whisper.

"We will have a place to live. You will be provided for." Wyn looked at Roger's piles again. "You will have space to keep all of your things the way you wish to keep them."

Roger laughed half-heartedly at that, breaking the tension that had built between them. "You mean I'll be allowed to keep my mess behind closed doors, is that it?"

"Precisely."

CHAPTER 35

ROGER

ROGER WAS a tangled mess of nerves. Spending the night back under his parents' roof had felt like a regression in ways he hadn't anticipated. He had tossed and turned all night, thinking about the inevitable extension on their project and what that meant for all of the humans currently being deemed unworthy. He felt as though he was letting them down by taking longer. He was annoyed that the delay was due to a marriage that neither he nor his future husband had asked for or wanted. And he fretted that he was being selfish in thinking about himself at all, which had sent him down a spiral of self flagellation. He was very much afraid that these messy emotions were spilling out in an obvious way, if Wyndham's gentleness was anything to go by.

He hadn't wanted to be so obvious. He had tried so hard to pretend cheerfulness during breakfast. He had even remembered to inform his mother of Wyndham's tea preferences. Of course, when he'd found Wyndham in the sitting room, he realized he had forgotten to open the window. Then he'd felt a rush of frustration all over again, frustration with his own shortcomings, frustration with the delay in their work, and over-whelmed by all of this upcoming marriage business. It was all too much and he didn't know if he had it in him to rise to the challenge.

Now Wyndham was looking at him with such intensity, as if he could see right through him. It was dashed unsettling. Roger did not feel as though he deserved Wyndham's kindness. Then again, he rarely felt as though he deserved the gentleman's insults either. He sniffed a little.

"I am sorry about the smell," he said. "Sometimes things get upturned and certain ingredients have a particularly unsavory scent when treated. I'll have to—"

"Barnes," Wyndham said. "Don't worry about the smell. It wasn't what I meant to say."

"You can't pretend it isn't true," Roger responded, feeling doleful.

"Well, all right, it does not smell particularly nice right now but I can appreciate that being the result of your magical ingredients. I hadn't meant to say anything though." He sighed. "Sometimes I open my mouth and the wrong thing comes out, no matter how hard I try."

Roger blinked up at him. "Really? That surprises me. I don't think I've ever heard you described as tactless. I would have remembered."

Wyndham pursed his lips briefly. "Yes, well. It seems to primarily happen around you. I will try to be better about that."

Roger felt his mouth open in surprise.

Wyndham lifted one hand to Roger's chin to close his mouth. "Yes, yes," he said. "You heard me correctly. Don't make me repeat it." He looked around the room again in his critical way. "Come on. Let's go back downstairs before your mother comes to check on us."

Roger led him back to the drawing room. His mother was in the room, waiting for them with a glass of lemonade. "I was just going to go up and check on you," she said.

"We were discussing the shrinking spell used on his study," Wyndham explained, accepting the offered glass. "Thank you very much, Mrs. Barnes."

She beamed at him. "Well, I'll leave you to it," she said, before bustling out.

Roger gestured for Wyndham to take a seat and then he opened the windows and sat down, turning to Wyndham apologetically. "I meant to have them opened before you arrived. I've been a bit distracted today."

"Understandable," Wyndham said slowly. He took a sip of lemonade and then set it aside. "I can't imagine how I'd feel if my bedroom was packed away and upended before I was ready."

Roger gave him a grateful smile. "Well, I should have known it would happen eventually." He felt himself over-gesturing with his hands and he tucked them behind his back. "Did—did you say you wanted to go through the notes?"

Wyndham's gaze was still focused on him. "Perhaps we ought to wait until after the engagement party to resume our work? I'm not sure either of us are focused right now."

Roger flapped his hands in frustration, despite himself. "See? That's the problem! The whole point of this exercise was to help solve the Hastings score situation. Instead of doing that, we're having to worry about all of *this*. But I know you're right because I am completely incapable of concentrating right now. I've been trying and I just feel—I just feel so *useless*." He whispered this last bit as he sank onto the sofa and covered his face with his hands, embarrassed. "I'm sorry," he mumbled. "I daresay you didn't come all the way over here just to see me act like—"

"Stop," Wyndham cut in. "It's going to be all right," he said in a low voice. "I know how much this means to you. It's no surprise at all that you're feeling agitated. But we both know that a fortnight was not sufficient time to begin with. We were trying to cram learning about each other's magic systems while acting as experts in our magic at the same time. The extension may not be an entirely bad thing. It will give us time to be more intentional and thorough. You wouldn't want to submit a slapdash proposal. Neither of us would."

Roger let out a deep breath. "You're right. Sorry. And...er...thank you."

"Once the engagement party is done, we should be able to find some sort of rhythm again."

Roger nodded.

Wyndham paused. "And thank you for opening more windows. It helps." He reached for his lemonade again.

"Of course," Roger replied. He glanced at Wyndham. Perhaps because Wyndham was being so gentle with him, or perhaps because he'd already made something of a fool of himself already, he decided to be bold. "Can I ask you a...*personal* question?"

Wyndham paused with his lemonade raised to his lips, his expression becoming immediately guarded. "If you must."

"I've noticed that there are times, at social gatherings, when you are… paler than usual, or you seem generally uncomfortable. Will…will all of these upcoming events be difficult for you?"

"I'll be fine. I'm used to it."

"But, is there anything I can do to make it more…I don't know, comfortable for you?"

"I doubt it. Being in mixed company is uncomfortable for me because of my magic. You can't really help that."

"What do you mean?"

Wyndham frowned, but it seemed more in concentration than irritation. He set his glass aside. "Fae magic is still not generally accepted in society. I can let my magic loose when I'm in the country, but in the city I have to keep a tight rein on it. With people around—particularly humans—I have to be especially careful. I frequently have to withdraw in order to keep control of my magic, and because keeping control makes me irritable."

Roger felt his eyes widen. "Your magic is already so remarkable. Do you mean to say that *that* is your magic under control?"

"Very strict control."

"So it is even *more* powerful?"

"Yes," he replied on an exhale.

"I should like to see that sometime," Roger said quietly.

The corner of Wyndham's mouth ticked up. "Well, we'll be seeing a lot of each other in the future. I imagine that can be arranged."

Roger thought back to when he'd witnessed Wyndham in such situations. He was always leaving a room, isolating himself in some way. "So when this happens in town, you try to be alone? And it helps?"

"Yes, it helps. At least to a degree."

"So if I notice that you're uncomfortable, perhaps I could help you get that space you need?" He didn't entirely know why he was pushing this matter. Wyndham was clearly not enjoying the topic. But he hated the idea of seeing Wyndham looking that way, knowing the cause, and being unable to do anything.

Wyndham seemed to consider the question. "That might help. People don't usually notice though. There's no need to strain yourself trying to catch it."

"Your skin gets paler, your eyes get wider, you press your lips tighter, a- and sometimes there's a bit of whiteness around your mouth."

Wyndham gave him a long look. "You have been paying attention."

Roger felt himself flush. "Well, you're usually so...collected. It's noticeable."

"Don't fret about keeping watch over me," Wyndham demanded. "As I said, I'm accustomed to it."

Roger privately resolved to do so anyway.

"Now," Wyndham said, elegantly crossing one leg over the other, "why don't we discuss what we have left to work on? Then when we get back to work next week, we will have a better starting point."

Roger straightened, relieved to have a clear direction.

CHAPTER 36

WYN

THE ONLY THING Wyn disliked more than attending a party was being at the center of one. His preferred method of getting through such gatherings was to blend in, go as unnoticed as possible, drink plenty of wine, and quietly disappear at the end. Accomplishing this at his own soiree would be impossible, so he'd started with the wine earlier to help compensate.

He hadn't even been allowed to arrive late, as his mother demanded that he and Roger be present when the first guests started to show up. Wyn supposed it made sense, but that didn't make him any less miserable. He'd been busy wallowing when the Barnes family was announced.

Wyn turned from where he was practically hanging out of the window to see Roger standing uncomfortably with his parents and two other vaguely familiar people he knew to be Roger's siblings, along with someone else. There was no mistaking them. The whole Barnes family shared similar attractive faces and fat figures.

As Wyn stepped forward to greet them, he couldn't deny the relief he felt in knowing that he would at least be able to share the burden of the evening. After the usual pleasantries, Roger gestured to his sister and brother.

"You may remember Frederica and Bernard," he said. "And this is

Bernard's spouse, Darby." Wyn offered a polite nod to each of them, one hand gripping his opposite elbow behind his back.

"I'm very glad you were all able to make it," Wyn said.

"Mary so wished she could attend," Frederica offered apologetically. "She's home with the children, but sends all her love to you both."

"That's very kind." Wyn wasn't sure how to feel about wishes of love coming from someone he'd never even met before, but he decided it was appropriate enough for the occasion. "My eldest brother Auberon and his wife are also unable to attend this evening, considering the short notice."

Bernard laughed and nudged Roger with his elbow. "Yes, we were all quite surprised to hear the news. We were starting to think Roger might never join us in settling down with someone special."

Wyn and Roger met eyes at his brother's words, and then Roger looked away, a slight flush forming across his cheeks. Wyn was no stranger to wishing for respite from the jabs of siblings. He reached out and curled his fingers around the crook of Roger's elbow, guiding him away.

"We'd best prepare for the other guests to arrive soon," he explained with an added flourish to keep them from continuing the conversation. Wyn held the act until they had safely disappeared into the adjoining room, coming to a stop near the piano.

"Much appreciated," Roger mumbled quietly, looking back to make sure nobody had followed before he said anything else. "It's been like that since the moment they arrived today."

"You're lucky they do not live in the same house," Wyn ground out. "This morning I woke up to my sister's handiwork: an entire curtain of flowers hanging up from my bedroom door that I was forced to walk through like some sort of mythical fairytale creature in a storybook." Roger's mouth opened, and Wyn cut him a look. "Don't."

The shorter man chuckled at that, and Wyn couldn't help but grin.

"I do like all of the flowers," Roger mused as he looked around the room.

It appeared as though Wyn's mother had personally requested every bouquet of cut flowers in the entire city.

"I would've much preferred they were still in the soil," Wyn said softly, his magic squeezing in his chest.

"Oh," Roger said, realization evident in his voice.

"Mother says the blooms will die eventually either way, but I like to think they would hardly agree with that sentiment. Regardless, here they are, so we might as well enjoy them."

Wyn reached out toward the vase of deep red roses sitting on the piano and plucked one out, bringing it to his nose. He twirled the long stem between his fingers and drew in a deep breath, exhaling slowly as the petals unfurled themselves to perfection, twice as magnificent as they had been just moments before.

The sound of new voices carried from the next room, announcing the arrival of more guests they would be expected to greet. Wyn glanced toward the doorway and then looked down at his rose. He leaned forward a bit and carefully guided the stem back into the vase with the other flowers.

"Shall we?" he asked, offering his arm to Roger.

BY THE TIME the last guests arrived, Wyn's face was sore from putting on his brave smile and repeating the same few sentences over and over again. He and Roger started the evening as a united front, but they'd been pulled in different directions as more people arrived. Wyn couldn't even say the last time he'd seen him.

Wyn took a sip of wine and continued his path at the edge of the room, ducking into the hallway. He really wanted to escape to the back garden or his bedroom, but he knew his mother would throw a fit if he disappeared for too long, so he settled for taking a seat on the stairs instead.

He'd barely been off his feet for five seconds when an arm snaked around his neck, pulling him close. Wyn didn't have to guess who it was as they sat beside him.

"When were you going to tell me your happy news?" Sage asked sweetly, pressing a kiss to Wyn's cheek. Wyn shifted his shoulders and pushed Sage away weakly.

"I suppose you found out the same way everyone else did," Wyn said. "Try not to feel too left out."

"I feel many things, but that is not one of them."

"Where's Brooks? Did you bring him along?"

Sage smirked. "Why? Did you want him to join us again?" When there was no response from Wyn, Sage sighed haughtily and leaned back against his elbows. "It's not going to work out for us, I'm afraid. He was much too boring."

"I'm sorry to hear that," Wyn offered, finally turning his head to look over at where Sage was reclined next to him. "I'm sure there will be others to come along and catch your eye."

With a scoff, Sage sat up. "That's easy for you to say. Somehow I think *Roger Barnes* snagged the last decent man in London." The negative emphasis he'd put on Roger's name made Wyn's brow furrow. When Sage went for his glass of wine like he always did, Wyn held it out of his reach and stood up.

"I'll not hear you speak of Mr. Barnes that way. We are formally engaged, and as such, you'll offer him the same amount of respect you offer to me, little as it may be. Is that clear?"

Sage's expression went from surprise to something a bit more scandalized, but Wyn decided he didn't have time for any of it. He left Sage sitting on the stairs and went to rejoin the party.

Wyn made a point to never be the first to approach anyone else in a social setting, knowing it would make him responsible for creating and continuing the conversation. Oftentimes, he struggled enough just to contain his magic, let alone think of interesting topics of discussion.

When he finally spotted Roger speaking to Councilmember Williams, he got the strangest feeling. Roger wouldn't make him speak if he didn't want to. He would understand his desire to quietly observe.

Wyn drank the last of his wine and set the empty glass down on a table before he carefully maneuvered through the crowd toward Barnes.

CHAPTER 37

ROGER

ROGER WAS surprised how unsettled he felt when Wyndham wasn't in view. Occasionally he'd see the gentleman in the midst of a small crowd or smiling politely at a well-wisher. Even more surprising was how frequently Roger wished they were able to stand near each other. It had been comforting to have someone at his side, knowing he wasn't alone. But the crowd gradually tugged them farther apart, until Roger was seeking out glimpses of his fiancé.

At one point, he even circled the entire room trying to find him. He couldn't determine if his inability to do so was due to his own short stature or if Wyndham had disappeared to be alone as he was apt to do. Roger found himself wishing he knew for certain.

As he began his second circuit, he was pulled into a conversation with Councilmember Williams. The gentleman was in a cheerful mood, helped by the Wrenwhistles' fine wine. Roger reached for a glass of his own from a passing tray and saw Wyndham out of the corner of his eye, approaching with a sort of single-minded intensity. Roger shivered a little. He was growing accustomed to Wyndham's focus but he usually saw it directed toward spells or magic. As Wyndham approached, he noticed that the other man's jaw was tight, but his usual tells were not yet present. Wyndham gave him a small smile.

Roger took Wyndham's arm, feeling a little silly for the possessive gesture. Williams, however, seemed to think it normal and chuckled at them goodnaturedly.

"I was just telling young Barnes here that the Council feels particularly responsible for this little romance."

Wyndham's returning smile was thin—another small tell. Roger squeezed his arm in what he hoped was an encouraging way and said, "Yes, I'm sure nobody expected such a result from our project. I knew I had hoped to improve the lives of other people. It has been quite a surprise to find my own life changing so drastically as well."

Williams laughed again. "Ah, young love. Seeing you two together, it was no surprise to anybody else."

Before Roger could try and determine what that meant, Williams gave them both a big wink and strolled off. Roger leaned close to Wyndham. "Are you all right?" he murmured.

"Just…exhausted."

Roger gave him a long, searching look. "Do you need to be alone?"

"Not yet."

Roger felt as though he'd accomplished something important with the confidence. The tension in Wyndham's jaw and thinness of his smile appeared to be indications that he was working to control his magic. Roger found himself wondering why Wyndham had sought him out so particularly. Was it because he trusted Roger to notice when he needed to be alone? Did he find Roger an easier person to be around when he needed to keep his magic under control? Considering he had sought Roger out but did not seem inclined to talk made Roger feel as though he had been given care of the final reserves of Wyndham's energy.

To his shock, this brought a unique sense of protectiveness. As they wound their way slowly through the room, Roger took over in the role of receiving the assorted congratulations. It was strangely easier to be responsible for conversation and social niceties when it was done for someone else. Having Wyndham at his side made it even easier, giving him a little boldness he didn't usually have.

After an hour, Roger noticed that Wyndham's skin was pale and the tension in his body was more prevalent. Roger squeezed his arm lightly. "Do you need to step away?"

Wyndham glanced around the room. "My mother will never forgive me if I disappear during my own engagement party."

Roger considered. "Would half an hour be sufficient respite?"

"It would, but——"

"Then why don't you lead me towards a library or study or drawing room. I'll stand outside the doors while you sit down. If your mother asks, I'll tell her that I'm feeling a headache coming on and didn't feel comfortable asking any of the household staff to assist me. You will disappear long enough to graciously fetch me some tonic or other." He paused. "But of course, you don't need to actually get me a tonic. I don't really have the headache."

"Yes, yes, I understand." Wyndham rubbed the space between his eyebrows. "The library will suit our purposes. You will still be in the center of the party and I'll be able to find you later." He walked in a purposeful way to one side of the room. "And thank you," he added in a low voice.

Roger fought the smile that threatened to spread over his face. "Don't mention it."

Wyndham slipped through a pair of double doors and Roger stationed himself outside them, feeling important and still processing that feeling of protectiveness. Was this what married life would be like? Going to parties escorted by a tall and quiet husband and then making up reasons for said husband's disappearance? He found he didn't mind the notion. He had always liked helping people. He also decided he'd need to start coming up with better excuses.

Roger sipped his wine and continued to greet people who approached him. Wyndham's mother did ask him where her son had gone and Roger duly told her the agreed-upon fabrication. She gave a fond smile, patted his cheek, and left. Roger allowed himself a small swell of pride at his success.

Thankfully, no one tried to access the library until the half hour was nearly up. When there were just under ten minutes left of Wyndham's allotted time, Mr. Sage Ravenwing approached the doors and, without even glancing at Roger, reached for a door knob.

Roger slid in front of the door. "Having a pleasant time, Mr. Ravenwing?"

Ravenwing rolled his eyes. "You can save your little watchdog act. I'm just going to talk to Wyndham."

Roger pasted on a smile. "Ah, then you'll understand that he wanted to be left alone."

"Don't be stupid. I don't count."

"Well, I did promise him I'd see to it he wasn't disturbed. I'm not one to go back on my word, especially to my betrothed. I'm afraid you'll have to wait."

Ravenwing gave a little hiss of displeasure. "What did you do to steal his affections? You must have done something. No one has managed to capture his heart in all the years I've known him. What the hell is so special about you?"

Roger gave him a bland look. "I'm sure I don't know, Mr. Ravenwing. When last we spoke, you were very clear in what Mr. Wrenwhistle thought of me. Although," he went on with a little smile, "I should almost thank you. If it weren't for our little conversation, I'm not sure I'd even be engaged right now."

The other man glared at him.

"I've heard you and Mr. Brooks are something of an item," Roger continued. "The *Tribune* has linked your names together a couple of times. Perhaps we'll be coming to your engagement party soon."

"Oh, go away. I have no interest in making small talk with you."

"Gladly, just as soon as my fiancé has returned." He gave an embarrassed chuckle. "I'm afraid I'm still getting accustomed to saying that."

The other man stormed off.

Roger let out a breath, adjusted his cuffs and spectacles, tweaked his cravat, and then glanced at the clock, wondering if Wyndham was feeling any better.

CHAPTER 38

WYN

DURING THE DAY, the bay window in their library served its purpose well, providing a seat with a thick cushion and a lovely view of the garden. Sometimes it even became a battle of focus, splitting attention between the flowers and the words in whichever book had been plucked from the shelves.

Wyn sat with his cheek against the frame of the open window, allowing the cool night air to whisper across his face. He wished so badly to untangle the fabric tied decoratively around his neck. It wasn't exactly tight, but it was snug enough to bother, especially as he tried to calm himself with slow breaths.

He had been right about Roger. Somehow he'd known what Wyn needed more readily than he'd even known himself, and he usually took a bit of pride in knowing when his body was trying to tell him something. Then, Barnes had taken Wyn's confession and jumped into action, seemingly without a second thought.

Upon opening his eyes, Wyn let his focus wander over the garden in the scant moonlight. He had been unable to control himself any longer when he'd landed on the bench seat and thrown open the window. The blooms were now wide and wanting. The greenery had thickened and stretched, reaching nearly double its previous height.

His magic had settled significantly after such a powerful outburst. He couldn't recall the last time he'd allowed it out with such little restraint. It had felt incredible at the time, as it always did, but it left him drained and ready to sleep.

Voices coming from outside the door pulled Wyn's attention from the garden. If he'd been more alert, it might've concerned him to know that his hideaway was about to be discovered, but he simply leaned against the corner where the windows were joined and rolled the back of his head against the pane to look at the doors.

Barnes was speaking to someone. Maybe he was returning from the party to check on him? Wyn's brows came together. Certainly he hadn't been standing there the whole time? Wyn listened closer, trying to make out more of what was being said.

"Well, I did promise him I'd see to it he wasn't disturbed. I'm not one to go back on my word, especially to my betrothed. I'm afraid you'll have to wait." Roger's voice was calm but firm, though Wyn thought he could hear a slight waver on the word *betrothed*.

The resulting sound of frustration was all too familiar.

"What did you do to steal his affections? You must have done something. No one has managed to capture his heart in all the years I've known him. What the hell is so special about you?"

Wyn sat up and turned toward the closed doors. That was Sage giving him such an attitude. Sage, spitting venomous words toward Roger. The last few lingered like a fog: *what the hell is so special about you?*

He sat in silence, barely breathing so he could hear the rest of the exchange more clearly. What other conversation was Barnes referencing? What could Sage have possibly said about Wyn's opinion of him? It'd been years since the rivalry of their youth turned to mutual avoidance, markedly absent of any and all discussions regarding the man, up until their project on the proposal had begun.

Realization swirled uneasily in Wyn's gut.

When the voices stopped, Wyn got to his feet, striding to the doors and pulling one open just a crack. A line of light cut across the dark room.

"Barnes," Wyn said sternly, instantly regretting it when Roger jumped.

"Mr. Wrenwhistle," he responded as he turned around, peering through the opening. His voice shrank to a conspiratorial whisper. "How are you feeling?"

Wyn didn't have a response. Instead, he opened the door wider and grabbed the front of Roger's waistcoat, dragging him into the room. He shut the door without a sound and whirled around to find him still standing rather close. He didn't step away, and neither did Roger.

"It was him, wasn't it?" Wyn demanded, though his voice was devoid of the emotions he was feeling, still empty from his exertion on the garden.

"What?" Roger's voice went high and breathy at the accusation as though it was directed at him.

"Your *little bird*," Wyn said bitterly, trying not to sneer. "Sage is the one who spoke to you. What did he say?"

Roger looked down and took a small, retreating step. "It hardly matters," he said with a shrug. Wyn knew it mattered quite a lot. It had been enough to spur the argument between them. Enough to hurt Roger in a very real way.

"I need to know the truth. If we are to be married, then you must be able to tell me things with complete honesty." Roger kept his face turned away. Wyn pressed his lips together and stepped forward to close the gap that had formed between them. "I need you to trust me," he added.

Roger's face turned up at that. Even in the low light, Wyn could see the way his emotions passed over his features, each one battling for victory.

"He—" Roger stopped, swallowing thickly. "He said that you believe me to be dull and stupid." Barnes' facade faltered with a tiny wobble of his chin. "A waste of a human."

Wyn's lungs may as well have collapsed inside his chest with the difficulty he had drawing his next breath. He gasped to fight the struggle.

"I never—" he started numbly. "I *never* said—"

"Please," Roger cut him off, adjusting his spectacles as he looked away again. "What's done is done. I cannot blame you for something you might've said when we were still at odds."

Wyn's hands found the sides of Roger's face all on their own, guiding him back again. The way his attention flicked to Roger's mouth was purely to see if his chin was still quivering with emotion. How could he possibly make him believe that he was telling the truth, especially considering their history?

"Roger," he said faintly. Barnes had gone rigid, frozen in place. "You would do well to blame me nonetheless. The words may not have come from my own mouth, but my allowance of them was equally as unacceptable. Ravenwing is a hateful, jealous man, and I am truly sorry he spoke to you this way."

A long silence stretched between them, and Wyn only became more and more aware of the way he was cupping Roger's cheeks in his hands. Eventually, he let go, his arms falling to his sides. He knew Barnes did not have to forgive him, or even accept his apology, but Wyn found himself wishing that he would.

"We should go back," Wyn said finally. There was a hint of defeat in his voice. "I would hate for your family to get the wrong impression of me, stealing you away to a dark, empty room for too long."

CHAPTER 39

ROGER

ROGER SPENT the rest of the evening in a daze. With the two subjects of the party being stretched to their limit, the party wound up ending early, so it was probably just as well that he didn't feel up to socializing; it meant Wyndham got to escape even sooner.

Roger needed to escape too, although for entirely different reasons. He couldn't shake the memory of Wyndham's hands cupping his cheeks, the way Wyndham's gaze flicked briefly over his lips, the way he'd said Roger's name so very softly. Roger decided it wasn't a bad thing that Wyndham hadn't seduced him; he'd be powerless in the face of such charms, considering the fact that he was weak in the knees from Wyndham not even trying.

He managed some idle chatter with his family on the way home, agreeing with their assessments of the success of the party, how nicely everyone was dressed, how well he and Wyndham looked together. He was too distracted to put up a fuss when his mother informed him that she and Mrs. Wrenwhistle had arranged for both families to meet in the Park the following afternoon. He ought to have been irritated about the change in the schedule, the delay in getting back to work. But all he could think about was what he would say to Wyndham when he saw him again.

He went to bed, still trying to sort out that particular puzzle. After they returned to the party, they had been swept up in the congratulations and the chatter and there had been no time to tell Wyndham that he did trust him, that he accepted his apology…that he'd really enjoyed hearing his name on Wyndham's lips.

He had worried Wyndham was angry with him when he'd been pulled into the room. When he realized the anger was directed toward Ravenwing, his relief was palpable. The intensity of Wyndham's reaction had also helped remove the remaining doubts in Roger's mind that Ravenwing knew Wyndham better than Roger did.

He thought back to the day after the garden party and the teapot Wyndham had given him. He sat up in bed. The gift really *hadn't* been pity. He chewed idly on a fingernail. Now that he had a better idea of what Wyndham was going through during parties, he realized that the gentleman's escape to the carriages had nothing to do with him. He probably would have appreciated someone making sure he was all right and bringing him a glass of lemonade. *Damn.* He laid back down. What a mess he'd made of things. He burrowed under his blanket and promised himself he'd make things right.

AT BREAKFAST THE NEXT MORNING, Roger was a little more equipped to field the multitude of questions his family saw fit to ask. Bernard was keen to know more about Roger's project and what he'd learned about fae magic. Frederica commented that Wyndham was very attractive but seemed to be of a pale complexion and was full of advice on what Roger ought to offer to improve his fiancé's health. Darby was mostly irritated that the engaged couple had not danced, so no one else had danced the whole evening.

"If I'm going to be in London," they remarked, "I'd like to dance, thank you very much."

Roger was struck with the realization that he no longer had to worry about how many dances were appropriate to share with Wyndham. He assured Darby he would attempt to rectify the dancing situation at the next event.

"Goodness knows there will be plenty," his mother said with a laugh.

"Mrs. Wrenwhistle has given me a list of what we can expect. We shall all be very busy until you two are married."

After breakfast, Roger retreated to his room where he attempted to compile notes of where he and Wyndham left off and what work remained. By the time his mother informed him it was time to leave, he was tolerably satisfied with what he had come up with.

They met up with the Wrenwhistles so seamlessly, Roger was a little alarmed by their mothers' machinations. Wyndham looked weary, but less drawn than he had at the party. Roger was relieved when their families gave them some space to walk together and carry on a somewhat private conversation, even if that conversation was constantly interrupted by wellwishers.

Roger took Wyndham's arm. "I feel as if I have a great deal to tell you," he began, before he could think better of the words.

Wyndham's eyebrows raised. "Good gracious, that sounds ominous. The *Tribune* hasn't even released yet."

"No, no nothing bad. I…well, first I need to give you this." He fished his notes out of his breast pocket. "I compiled a list of everything we have left to work on and where we left off."

Wyndham took the paper and smoothed it out as he greeted a passing couple. Then he read over it quickly. "Is your handwriting getting better or am I just getting better at deciphering it?"

"The latter."

"Perish the thought." He folded the paper and pocketed it. "This will help when we are finally permitted to work again."

"Good," Roger said. Then he fell silent, trying to be more intentional with his next words.

Wyndham glanced at him. "I take it there was more on your mind."

"Er, yes." Roger looked up and then away. "I wanted to say…well, I wanted to tell you that…I do. Trust you. And…and I accept your apology, but that you don't really need to make it because it is I who should be apologizing. I mean to say, the things I said…I was up half the night thinking about it and—"

"Roger," Wyndham interrupted softly. "It's all right. You don't owe me an apology."

"I didn't even thank you for the teapot," Roger muttered, his tone annoyingly plaintive. "It is lovely, by the way. It might be one of the nicest things I've ever owned. Although I'm afraid I was a little too upset to use it. I'll have to tell Notley to bring it downstairs."

The corner of Wyndham's mouth ticked up and Roger thought that, maybe, everything was going to be all right after all.

CHAPTER 40

WYN

As much as Wyn enjoyed being in the Park, an afternoon promenade was far from his idea of worthwhile leisure. Though it appeared to be all in good fun and an easy way to get in some light exercise, at the root it was merely a tool used by both sides of society to see and be seen. Naturally, his mother was one of the biggest proponents of the activity, forcing them to parade themselves along the gravel paths and give others no choice but to see them as the idyllic example of a prominent fae family.

Of all the times Wyn had been a part of his mother's puppet show, he'd never taken to the long, winding walkways with someone on his arm before. Of course, he had watched as his siblings all took their turns over the years. He could clearly remember watching Auberon and Rose as they began their courtship: shifting slowly from a stiff, proper stroll to one full of subtle hand touches, shared whispers, and soft eyes.

Wyn stole a glance at Roger as they each played their role in society's most beloved game. If he wasn't mistaken, Roger's hand on his arm was not in place entirely out of obligation. There was a weight to it; a certain comfort that did not come naturally to someone as anxious as Roger Barnes.

Even a strong cup of coffee hadn't been much help after the restless night Wyn had struggled through. As wrung out as he'd been, he still hadn't been able to fall asleep for quite some time after the party ended.

How long had Roger gone on believing that Wyn truly felt the way he'd been told? How many days had he put up a front so they could accomplish their assigned task? And not even for his own sake, but for the sake of others who needed his help. A quick look over the revised notes Barnes had brought him said loud and clear that he had never given up on his goal, even through all of their own personal drama.

Drama that Wyn knew was probably his own fault. That was one thing Sage had been right about: Wyn was a bit of an insufferable jackass. He'd been told as much in gentler words by other people, but it had never bothered him before. If that's what they thought of him, let them think it. What did it matter to him?

Wyn peeked again at the man on his arm.

Maybe it did matter.

Roger's mother laughed in the warm way she always did, and all at once Wyn was reminded of the fact that both of their families were trailing behind them at a reasonable distance, watching their every move, likely gossiping about them and telling embarrassing stories from their youth.

Wyn tilted his chin up to admire the golden leaves on the cluster of sweet chestnut trees they were passing. An excited squirrel was taking its job of collecting nuts very seriously, only scurrying away when they got too close.

"I'm sure I wouldn't know what to do with myself if I had to gather my own food to eat," Wyn said casually. "We have a very nice functional garden in the country in addition to the decorative ones, but I've never learned the first thing about what to do with all of the vegetables and herbs."

"Oh," Roger said thoughtfully. "I suppose a salad would be a simple solution? If you truly meant to make a meal for yourself, that is."

"Do you know how to cook?" Wyn asked.

"Er…well, no," Roger said, almost apologetically. "I've never had a reason to learn. Though I suppose I'm fortunate for it."

Wyn hummed. "Yes. That's probably true." He used the toe of his boot to nudge a chestnut off the path into the grass. "Perhaps," he started, paused, and then tried again, "perhaps we could try to make one."

"One what?" Roger peered up at him with a questioning look.

"A salad," Wyn said, as though it was obvious.

"Oh! Yes, that would be…most interesting."

"It would probably be wise to have some level of supervision, however. I've seen the way our cooks handle knives, and I'm not sure I would be comfortable left to navigate such a responsibility on my own."

"Certainly not," Roger agreed.

Wyn chewed at the inside of his cheek as he struggled to think of what to say next. What was an appropriate conversation to have while strolling? It was quite clear that Roger had very little interest in continuing with the current topic. Maybe he had no interest in talking at all. Wyn thought that would be the easiest solution, but how was he supposed to know if that was what Roger wanted?

A short chuckle was Roger's answer to their extended silence.

"You said you wanted me to be honest with you?" he asked carefully.

"Yes," Wyn told him, arching a brow.

Roger winced. "I detest salad," he whispered.

Wyn felt himself make a face, and then they both laughed.

"Very well," Wyn said, his voice light. "We can make the salad together and then you can watch me eat it."

Roger frowned. "But what if it's terrible?"

"I refuse to think anything we create together would be terrible." Wyn felt Roger's fingers flex slightly against his arm. "You and I are two very intelligent and capable people. It could be that we are the best salad makers in all of London, but nobody is aware of it because we're too spoiled to know how to handle ourselves around fresh produce."

TORQUIL'S TRIBUNE

Greetings, fancy folk and happy humans,

We would like to first declare that if readers do not approve of fae-human marriages, kindly do not send such vulgar opinions to this editor. All messages of the sort will be promptly discarded. We have already disposed of a number of these tedious complaints. If readers have not deduced by now, this paper is decidedly supportive of fae-human marriages. However, we welcome any and all messages praising the union. Do please continue to send those on. We have enjoyed reading every last one.

The Season is off to a remarkable start, with the engagement party of Mr. Wyndham Wrenwhistle and Mr. Roger Barnes. The excellent turnout was unsurprising, drawing in a crowd of well wishers from both sets of society. Mr. Wrenwhistle looked enchanting in a shimmering periwinkle waistcoat. Mr. Barnes is not known for his fashion sense but betrothal looks well on him. He ought to wear bold colors more often. By all accounts, his new outfit suited him.

Reports have come in that the pair disappeared briefly during the party, but not so long as to actually do anything salacious. This writer thinks the happy couple probably deserves a little privacy and is happy they are apparently finding it.

Some readers may recall that this romance likely began when Mr. Wrenwhistle and Mr. Barnes were assigned to work together on Barnes' project to resolve the Hastings score crisis. They are due to appear before the Council today but considering the recent upheaval with their announced engagement, it is uncertain if they will be meeting that deadline.

Reports have come in that although Mr. Ravenwing and Mr. Brooks arrived together at the Wrenwhistles' home, they did not depart together, drawing some disappointment over the potential pairing. Some reports have stated that Mr. Ravenwing left with Mr. Oliver Marigold.

With such developments as these, it is certainly shaping up to be a most eventful Season.

Your esteemed editor,

Torquil Pimpernel-Smith

CHAPTER 41

ROGER

ROGER SAT in the waiting room for the Council. His anxiety was, if possible, higher than usual. He had written out his notes the evening before, trying to itemize what they had accomplished and what they had yet to do. It was, thankfully, similar to the notes he had written for Wyndham, only a more formal version with fewer shorthand references to past conversations. He looked at the doors for what felt like the tenth time in five minutes. Wyndham wasn't there yet and he did not want to go into the chambers without him. It was a strange turn of events, considering the fact that the last time they had been there, they could barely stand to talk to each other, and now Wyndham felt like a necessary grounding force.

He gripped the notes in his hand and then hastily smoothed them out. He was just beginning to think maybe pacing would be a better use of his energy when Wyndham strolled in, looking impossibly cool and calm. He took one look at Roger and gave a small smile.

"Not nervous, are you?"

"I've never had to request an extension on something that I asked to do. It's so embarrassing."

Wyndham frowned a little, walked over to Roger, and gently pried the notes out of his hand. "My grandmother has already assured me it won't be an issue."

"I know. But all the same—"

He smoothed the notes against his leg and Roger found himself distracted by the shape of Wyndham's thigh under the trouser fabric. When Wyndham looked up at him, he quickly averted his gaze. Wyndham straightened and read the notes. "You made us look very efficient."

"It's all true," Roger said.

"I'm not disagreeing with you. I appreciate the way you wrote it. That's all."

"How can you be so calm?" Roger asked.

Wyndham smiled. "Truth be told, this is far too early in the morning for me to be nervous. Who the hell demands an appearance at ten in the morning?"

"It's a reasonable time of day. I've been here earlier than that."

"Be so kind as to never say the word 'reasonable' in regards to anything before noon ever again."

Roger couldn't help his chuckle. "What, no brisk walks around the estate in the morning light?"

"Evening light is just as beautiful and I'm already awake for that."

"I should think you'd enjoy—"

The door opened and an aide beckoned them in. Roger stood and hurried forward, surprised that he had been so caught up in thinking about something else that he momentarily forgot to be nervous. Wyndham followed sedately after, his calm demeanor doing wonders on Roger's anxious state. They approached the stand together and Wyndham placed the first page of notes in front of Roger and laid a light hand on his upper back. Roger straightened a little at the touch and, maybe, leaned into it just a bit.

"Welcome back, gentlemen," Councilmember Williams greeted with a more sober smile than he had offered at the engagement party. "Do you have an update for us?"

Roger cleared his throat. "Yes, sir. I have compiled a list of what we have worked through together so far, and what we have left to do."

He reached for the papers to start passing them out, but Wyndham pulled them out of his reach and held them out in a lofty manner towards a nearby aide. The aide stepped forward, took the papers, and distributed them. Roger hadn't realized that was an option. He waited impatiently for the Council to read through the notes.

"It looks like you two made good progress," Roger's father said. "It would seem pairing you together was the right move. Well done, Iris."

"Yes, in more ways than one," Councilmember Cricket chuckled.

"That actually is another matter that brings us here today," Wyndham replied smoothly. "With all of the social commitments that have come up due to our engagement, not to mention the design of the wedding spell, we would like to ask for an extension."

Councilmember Wrenwhistle's smile was gentle. "Of course. I think that is understandable under the circumstances. Don't you agree, Williams?"

"Most assuredly," he responded.

Councilmember Gibbs made a grumbling sound in his chair.

Councilmember Wrenwhistle arched an eyebrow at him. "Something to share, Gibbs?"

He huffed at the direct question. "I think it's a lot of fuss for a decidedly absurd match."

Councilmember Barnes' jaw dropped.

"Would you care to clarify that statement?" Councilmember Wren-whistle asked coolly.

"It's all well and good to encourage social interactions between our two cultures, but to go so far as *marriage*—it's preposterous."

"There will be challenges, I'm sure," Councilmember Cricket responded. "But that's true of any marriage. I, for one, am curious to see how they plan to—"

"I just think that marriage between fae and humans is going too far," Gibbs went on. "There's a reason it's frowned upon. Although I suppose it isn't quite so bad when they won't have children."

"I take offense to that viewpoint," Roger's father said. "There is no good reason that such marriages are frowned upon. This match is a perfect opportunity to put such outdated views to rest."

"Precisely," Councilmember Wrenwhistle added. "And I should add that this couple has the fae side of the Council's complete support."

Williams gave Gibbs a long look. "They have my support as well," he said gruffly. "And it goes without saying that they have Barnes' support.

Perhaps you ought to take leave from the Council until the wedding has passed, Councilmember Gibbs?"

Gibbs' face reddened and he crossed his arms over his chest. "Not at all," he muttered.

"Very well," Williams said, giving him a beady look. He turned back to Roger and Wyndham. "Now, back to the matter at hand: how much time do you think you will need, gentlemen?"

Roger was struck by how gracious the Council was being, now that they were engaged. "Perhaps another fortnight?" he asked, glancing up at Wyndham.

"That would put you right before the wedding," Councilmember Applewood pointed out. "Are you sure you don't need longer?"

"The wedding will be taking place in the country," Wyndham explained. "As such, we are unsure when we will make it back to town."

A bundle of knowing smiles greeted that answer.

"Well, if you change your mind and need a further extension, do let us know," Councilmember Williams said in a fatherly tone. "You need not appear before us to request it, although I'm sure we would like to hear your progress."

"And congratulations again, gentlemen," Councilmember Applewood put in.

In a daze, Roger followed Wyndham out. As soon as the door closed behind them, he said, "That's it? That's all we needed to do?"

"It would seem so."

"They were far nicer than they've ever been to me."

Wyndham rolled his eyes. "Yes, well, you are now of tangible value to them."

"Oh. Right. Fae and human relations, et cetera."

"Exactly."

Roger let out a breath. "Thank you," he said belatedly. "You were… very good at speaking. I mean," he added quickly, "that you were very calm and it…helped."

"As I said yesterday. Anything we create together is sure to be excellent. Shall we get back to work?"

Roger nodded and they got in the carriage and went to his family's townhouse.

CHAPTER 42

WYN

FOR THE FIRST time in what felt like months, Wyn was feeling confident.

Their meeting with the Council had gone about as smoothly as he'd hoped. They were granted the extension, and it even seemed as though councilmembers from both sides were pleased with Roger's outline on what they'd accomplished. With a little luck and a lot more work, there was no doubt they would be able to deliver a final proposal they could be proud of.

Wyn followed Roger up the stairs toward his room, but then they made an abrupt turn into the drawing room. Wyn felt his confidence falter like a carriage with a broken wheel.

Roger's things had been moved from his room in what Wyn could only assume was an attempt at providing some sort of work-life balance. Unfortunately, it appeared that his belongings had been thrown from that same carriage with the broken wheel, falling into such disorder that Wyn regretted ever thinking Roger's old study was a problem. *This* was a problem.

"Barnes," Wyn wheezed, a look of horror on his face. "What is this?"

Roger turned where he stood in the middle of the room and gave Wyn a bit of a helpless look. "My parents thought it best that we weren't hidden away in my bedroom while we were trying to work," he muttered. "Something about…too many distractions."

Wyn snorted as he stepped into the assemblage of sitting room furniture, empty bookshelves, moving crates, and Roger's massive wooden desk.

"Yes, I suppose they've accomplished their goal. We couldn't fuck in this room even if we wanted to." He bunched his lips to one side and narrowed his eyes. "Although, if we moved some of your boxes off the desk—"

"How about we just start unpacking!" Roger squawked, hurrying toward a crate so he could pry off the lid and see what was hidden inside.

Wyn let out a long-suffering sigh and wandered over to another that was already open. It was full of books. He pulled one out and turned it to see the cover before he cradled the spine in one hand and opened it with the other, flipping through the pages with feigned interest.

"Have you read all of the books you own?"

Roger made a sound of amusement. "Has anyone read all of the books they own?" Wyn caught him peeking over to see which book he was holding. "I have read the majority of them, though some serve as more of a quick reference source than anything else. Others have been given to me as gifts, and a couple of them, well…a couple of them I just thought were beautiful and wanted to display on my shelves."

Wyn hummed but said nothing as he returned the book to its place, stepping around to another crate that was unopened. As Wyn removed the lid, a blast of noxious air rushed out to greet him. His eyes instantly watered, and he tried not to gag as he pulled the lid the rest of the way off and stepped away, fanning at the air with his hand.

"Open the window!" he demanded, and Roger rushed to do as he'd been told. Wyn reached out with his magic and sucked as much fresh air into the room as he could, swirling it around to capture whatever fumes he'd unleashed. The air flowed out as quickly as it had come in, and Wyn took a tentative breath to make sure it was safe.

Roger clambered over his belongings to join Wyn at the box.

"I think I found your small dead creature," Wyn grimaced.

Roger frowned and bent to start carefully digging through the items inside. He inspected some of the jars, checking for cracks and loose lids, before his hand paused over a small cloth bag. He pinched the corner of it and pulled it out, taking another small whiff that made his face twist.

"I thought that might be what it was," he explained as he opened the drawstring of the bag and carefully dumped the contents out into his hand.

The jagged black stone that fell into his palm was split perfectly in half. Both pieces glittered as the light caught each tiny, squared facet.

"You cannot imagine how relieved I am that you did not just dump the corpse of a mouse out of that bag," Wyn said flatly.

Roger gave a pitiful laugh. "Just one of my most rare minerals. Fluorspar has a few very specific uses, but as you can tell, emits a rather foul odor if tampered with. Father warned me I shouldn't keep it in something that left it so vulnerable." He carefully deposited both pieces back into the bag and cinched the top.

Wyn offered a sympathetic look. "Can you still use it?"

"Possibly, but it will never be as strong as it once was."

After spending the better part of two hours sorting through and organizing Roger's magical ingredients, they discovered that almost everything else was still in decent shape. One jar of powdered orange peel had spilled, but fortunately that was something easy to replace.

Wyn hadn't realized how ready he was for a break until Roger called for tea. The two of them sat in matching chairs and sipped at their drinks after Notley had served them without a single comment about the state of the room. Wyn decided that whatever the man earned for being Roger's valet was not nearly enough.

Wyn took a page out of Notley's book of etiquette and decided not to make any mention of how their tea—lavender for both of them—had been served in the set he had gifted to Roger.

"Why does it appear that we've only made things worse?" Roger moaned.

"At least now there's some sort of order to it all. We know where things are. We found your scales and your pencils. I think it's good enough for us to begin working again."

"Yes, I suppose you're right," Roger conceded.

A grin spread across Wyn's mouth. "Mmm, I do like the sound of that."

"What, of being right?"

"Hearing you admit it."

Roger chuckled and shook his head before he sipped from his cup again.

As soon as Wyn finished his tea, he stood and found a safe spot to set the cup down. He gave one final glance around the room.

"This will be a fine starting place in the morning. I need time to prepare for tonight, so I'd best be off. I'll come 'round to collect you the same as last time."

Roger's mouth fell open, but only slightly. "Where are we going?"

"The opera, of course."

CHAPTER 43

ROGER

ROGER STARED at the messy drawing room. He could vaguely see what Wyndham meant about their work improving things. He rang for Notley and instructed him to ready an outfit for the opera. Then he did a little more organizing, putting the books he'd need in a small pile and arranging his most used ingredients on a single shelf for easy access. He tied the curtain back so the open window had less of a barrier. He left the room, feeling more satisfied than when he'd entered.

An hour later, Roger was sitting in the front parlor, dressed and anxious. The last time he had gone to the opera with the Wrenwhistle family, it had felt like generosity. He had been so caught up in the novelty of being invited by an illustrious family that he hadn't considered how his attendance might have looked to the rest of Society. He began to have a niggling understanding of why everyone had been so sure of a romance.

But this visit to the opera would be different. He would be going not only as a guest of the Wrenwhistle family, but as a future member of it. He could anticipate the looks and the whispers. It would not be a novelty this time; it would be an expectation. He adjusted his cuffs nervously, suddenly relieved his father had insisted on new pieces for his wardrobe. He would have hated to make the Wrenwhistles look bad with his usual shabby clothing.

When the carriage arrived, Wyndham came into the house to personally fetch him. The sight of Wyndham in a forest green waistcoat with silver embroidery put Roger in an entirely new spiral of thought. After the wedding, he and Wyndham would be moving to the country together. He'd only encountered the gentleman in London. What was Wyndham like in the country? How did he dress? What did he do for entertainment? Roger realized as he took Wyndham's arm that he knew shockingly little about his future husband, outside of childhood squabbling, adult bickering via the press, and academic work.

He was so caught up in this troubling realization that he could only manage brief and shallow responses to the inquisitive conversation from the rest of the Wrenwhistles. Thankfully, none of them seemed to mind. Roger supposed they were all accustomed to Wyndham's less than chatty nature.

However, when they reached the opera house and Wyndham offered his arm, he leaned down and murmured, "You are in a uniquely somber mood tonight. Are you quite well?"

"Oh, yes," Roger replied hurriedly. "Just a…just in a brown study."

"Hm. Well, please attempt to look like you're enjoying yourself while you ruminate. People are going to think I dragged you here."

Roger couldn't help but chuckle at that. "It might not be entirely incongruous with our image: The socialite and the wooly-headed academic."

"Is that how you see yourself?" Wyndham asked as he nodded to the Cricket family on the stairs.

"I rather think that's how everyone sees me."

Wyndham made a non-committal sound in response.

Roger glanced up at him. "You disagree?"

"I do. Is that what is causing this brown study of yours?"

"N-no. That was something else."

Wyndham raised an eyebrow. "Anything you care to share?"

Roger thought about his concerns that he didn't know Wyndham very well. He wasn't sure if voicing these concerns might be offensive. "No, I don't think so."

"Well, perhaps at supper then," Wyndham said as he led them into the opera box.

Roger took a seat and looked up in surprise. "Are we going to another party afterwards?"

Wyndham sat down beside him. "No. My mother thought it would be nice to have a quiet family supper tonight. With you included, of course," he added, as if Roger hadn't put that together.

Roger swallowed. It was as if his earlier thoughts were being proven. "Quiet family supper," he murmured.

"Do you mind?"

"No, not at all. It's just…" He hesitated and then added quietly, "your family is a little intimidating sometimes."

"They're more bothersome than anything else. You'll find that out eventually. Now," he continued, leaning in a little, "it occurred to me as I was getting ready this evening that if I were really getting married—"

"You are."

"—then I'd be a little more openly affectionate with my fiancé."

Roger blushed. "Er…that is a reasonable assumption."

"So, I thought tonight might be a good opportunity to explore that aspect."

Roger gave a shaky nod. "I see."

Wyndham gave him a long look. "You remember what I said during our engagement party?"

"Complete honesty."

"Yes. I expect it in this regard as well. Understood?"

"Understood," Roger said, although it came out as a whisper.

Then Wyndham picked up Roger's hand, intertwined their fingers, and laid both of their hands in Roger's lap. To his horror, Roger squeaked in alarm.

Wyndham squeezed his hand. "Is this all right?"

"Yes, of course," Roger said.

Wyndham's thumb rubbed over his hand. "Complete honesty, remember?"

"It's all right. It just took me by surprise. I didn't expect it to feel so…*intimate*."

Wyndham chuckled and turned his head so he was whispering in Roger's ear. "Everyone in this theater is watching us. So I daresay your blushing cheeks are causing a great deal of delighted titillation."

"Don't say that," Roger hissed. He fixed his spectacles with this free hand, self-conscious.

"Do you ever go without those things?" Wyndham asked, gesturing to the spectacles.

"Er...no?"

"They don't look very comfortable."

"They aren't. I get headaches from them sometimes. But it's worth it to see properly."

"Couldn't you take them off when you're at home?"

Roger shrugged. "When I'm at home, I'm working. I need to be able to read my work. And I like to be able to see the faces of people I'm talking to. When I'm out, I like to recognize people across the room. And when at the opera, I'd like to be able to see the performers."

"Hm," Wyndham hummed. "It seems to me that something should be done to improve the comfort of them then."

"Don't think I haven't thought of it," Roger replied. He tapped the spectacles up his nose again, overly aware of them after the conversation. Then his hand went to his cravat.

Wyndham reached up to stop the motion, rather like he had done at their previous opera outing. Unlike the previous time, however, he said, "Allow me." He pivoted a little in his seat and tweaked Roger's cravat. Roger couldn't be sure how effective it was, considering he was only using one hand. Then he felt Wyndham's fingers smooth over the fabric before he leaned back in his seat. "There. You look perfect. Now stop fidgeting."

Roger took a deep breath and willed himself to be still. As the lights went down and the curtain went up, his brain caught on Wyndham's words: *You look perfect.* He dared a glance at the gentleman next to him. Wyndham's focus was on the stage but he smiled at Roger's glance, then he lifted their entwined hands, pressed a soft kiss to Roger's knuckles, and then placed them back in Roger's lap. Roger sucked in a breath, his gaze still locked on Wyndham's profile. The music started and he jumped in his seat. Ah, right. The performance had begun.

CHAPTER 44

WYN

EVEN THOUGH WYN's attention was trained dutifully on the performance happening below their seats, the only thing he could focus on was the way Roger's hand felt in his.

Wyn struggled to decide if his hands were exceptionally cold, or if Roger's were just very warm as his thumb continued to rub gently against Roger's. He noted the way his own slender fingers fit between Roger's thicker ones, and how his grip had continued to tighten ever so slightly as time went on, until it felt like Barnes was holding on for his life. Wyn flexed his hand, and Roger seemed to realize how hard he'd been squeezing then, loosening his grip enough that Wyn could regain feeling.

He hadn't been joking when he'd said everyone was watching. Not only could he see others openly staring at them and whispering to their neighbors with their hands covering their mouths, but he could feel it.

Curiosity. Jealousy. Uncertainty. These emotions and more had filled the air the moment they'd walked into the room. Wyn could feel it with his magic, tugging and tingling in his chest as the attention on them grew. In some ways, it was just as bad as how it felt at a party: overwhelming enough to make Wyn want to disappear. At the same time, though, the location offered a layer of protection. Nobody was going to get up and come bother them in their box. Not without an invitation, at least.

Roger shifted in his seat beside him. Wyn's attention fell to their hands on Roger's thigh, and he realized that he'd somehow earned another source of protection in the form of the man sitting at his side.

He'd been wonderful at their engagement party, stepping up when Wyn simply could not. And he'd done it without having any smart remarks to make later on about how Wyn should've been a better host, or how he should've smiled more, or how he could have appeared more grateful for all the well wishes and sacrifices made by everyone who traveled to be in attendance.

His mother had wasted no time in bringing all of those things to his attention. He wasn't sure he could've taken it from Roger, too.

Gratitude swelled in Wyn's chest over the simple kindness he'd been shown. Without thinking, he lifted their hands again and pressed his lips to the bend of Roger's fingers. He allowed his gentle kiss to linger, his eyes sliding shut as his magic pushed.

It pushed away the haze of emotions crowding the air around them. It pushed away the weight of the way his family and everyone else was ogling their every move. It pushed at the cold, hard, unbreakable walls that Wyn had built to protect himself. It pushed away every single thing except for the music and the feel of his lips on Roger's knuckles, and Wyn never wanted that moment to end.

DINNER with his family was mostly miserable until the salad course was served. A small grin tugged at the corner of Wyn's mouth as he studied the way each type of vegetable had been chopped or sliced, before he leaned over toward Roger.

"I think I vastly overestimated my ability to make a salad," he said quietly. Everyone else at the table was talking all at once, and he wasn't sure if Roger had actually heard him at first. But then Roger used his fork to flip some pieces around, offering a little smile.

"I don't know, I think you could probably do this one?" He poked the tines into a piece of spinach and held it up to inspect closer.

Wyn scoffed. "That's quite literally an entire leaf."

"Exactly. All you have to do is wash it and eat it."

"Oh, well do go right ahead," Wyn encouraged with a sly look. Roger grimaced at the leaf and shook his head subtly, wise enough to avoid calling attention to himself at the table. He used the raised edge of the plate to wipe the piece off his fork so he could set it down. Wyn rolled his eyes and used his own utensil to collect Roger's rejected leaf, along with a few other pieces from the plate, and stuck them in his mouth.

"Wyndham," his mother cut in with a brilliant smile. "I couldn't help but notice how much you seemed to enjoy the opera this evening." Wyn managed to look in her direction out of respect, but he continued chewing instead of giving her the answer she wanted. "Or shall I say you enjoyed *attending* the opera this evening?"

"The two of you seemed quite cozy," Emrys added, and Wyn could only imagine what was coming next, but to his surprise his brother had nothing else to add for once. Out of instinct, Wyn's claws came out anyway.

"Jealous?" he purred.

"Absolutely not," Emrys responded, equally as smooth. "I prefer long, slow, *sensual* kisses to be delivered right. On. My. Mouth." He made an obnoxious kissing sound with his lips.

Wyn didn't need to look to know that Roger had turned bright red.

"That would hardly be appropriate in the middle of the opera house," Aveline said primly. "But certainly we could all infer what those back-of-the-hand kisses were leading to." She gave Wyn a wink. "Mother, don't you think you ought to dismiss them from this boring meal so they can get on with their dessert?"

"Aveline Wrenwhistle!" their mother wailed. Wyn's siblings giggled wildly, earning further admonishment until they settled themselves. Roger had shrunk so low in his chair that he was practically under the table, and Wyn announced rather harshly that they were leaving. He helped Roger to his feet and led him away.

The two didn't speak until they were nearly to the Barnes' townhouse.

"Roger," Wyn began, but he was met with a quick hand wave.

"Please, it's my fault. I'm a grown man. I should be able to handle a little innocent joking about…about *that*."

"There's nothing innocent about it. Emrys knows exactly what he's doing when he makes jokes the way he does. He's been that way for as long as I can remember. It might've been funny when we were younger, but it's not anymore." Wyn paused to study Roger in the carriage seat across from him. "Especially when it upsets you so."

"I'm fine," Roger reassured him, even though he clearly was not. Wyn wanted to remind him of their promise, but he also didn't want to push.

When the carriage slowed to a stop, neither one of them moved. The door was opened, and still they remained where they were, looking anywhere but at each other. What Roger said next took Wyn by surprise.

"Do you want to come inside?"

Wyn's brow furrowed as he considered the offer. Come inside?

Did Roger actually want that?

All at once, Roger's eyes flew wide as he seemed to finally realize the implications of what he'd said.

"I mean—I mean do you want to come inside and talk! Or, or do some more work, or have a bit of dessert?" He made a strangled sound. "Cake! Oh good heavens, I meant cake."

Wyn chuckled and reached out for one of the hands Roger had been frantically waving around, effectively calming him back into silence.

"What I want is to go home and go to bed. *Alone*," he emphasized. "And in the morning, I want to wake up at a ridiculous hour, come back here, and eat a piece of cake I've well earned while we get back to work."

Roger nodded, and Wyn made his way out of the carriage to help him down. They said their goodbyes, and Wyn sat heavily on the seat after he'd climbed back inside, his string of lies burning hot on his tongue.

CHAPTER 45

ROGER

ROGER STRUGGLED to fall asleep that night. The feel of Wyndham's hand in his. The feel of Wyndham's *lips* on his hand. The way Wyndham seemed almost relaxed for most of an evening. Wyndham's words: *You look perfect*.

He had been embarrassed at supper. But, in truth, part of his discomfort had surprised him. The Wrenwhistle siblings had teased their youngest brother for being affectionate in public, but they hadn't seen the way Wyndham rubbed his thumb soothingly over Roger's hand for the entire evening. They teased him for the long and lingering kiss placed on Roger's fingers, but Roger had felt, inexplicably, that the kiss hadn't been for show— or at least, not *only* for show.

Roger realized an hour into the performance that he had been gripping the other man's hand with increasing tightness. Instead of extricating his hand and finding another way to touch him, Wyndham had gently asked Roger to ease his grip. It all felt so alarmingly real. Which was why Roger had later wanted to sink into the ground; he didn't like the realness of the moment being mocked so openly.

It was all adding to the puzzle of Wyndham's character. After years of acquaintanceship, Roger was accustomed to Wyndham's snide commentary, his casual insults, his lofty arrogance, and his cool temper. But in the past month he had seen far more gentleness, patience, and kindness than he had ever thought to look for in Wyndham Wrenwhistle. Had the other man truly changed that much? Or had Roger merely known only one version of him? Which was the truth?

He also had a small suspicion that Wyndham's parting speech, as gallant as it was, was not entirely the truth. When Wyndham arrived the following morning, a little bleary eyed, his mouth set in a grim line, and his whole body rigid as if he was holding in his grumpiness, it confirmed Roger's suspicion. It was completely impossible for Wyndham to actually want to be awake, let alone out of bed, at that hour. It made Roger wonder what else Wyndham had been gallantly lying about. Part of him wanted to return Wyndham's own promise back at him: *complete honesty, remember?* But at Wyndham's attempt at a smile, he found he couldn't bring himself to do it.

Instead, he rang for tea and cake while his guest strode to the window and took a deep fortifying breath in. Roger handed over a list he had made that morning. "If memory serves me correctly," he said, "we need three more fae spells. I've written out the human spells I was considering for the remaining three skills."

Wyndham took the paper, covering his yawn with an elegant curl of his hand. "I don't believe I've seen you perform these."

"No, you haven't."

"Are there any you can perform in this…" He looked around the room, clearly debating the right word, "state?"

Roger hid a smile. "Yes, I should think so. Are there any that seem promising?"

Wyndham frowned in concentration. "How is this moving spell different from that floating spell you did?"

"Ah!" Roger said, pleased by the question. "It moves items side to side rather than up and down. So it takes a little less power, and thus, it can be done using different ingredients."

"Show me that one."

Roger got to work. One good thing about working in a complete mess of a room was that there were plenty of crates to move about without ruining any kind of organization. When he was just about ready to cast, the tea and cake arrived.

Wyndham waved at the tea dismissively. "Thank you, Notley. We'll get to it in a moment."

Roger cast the spell and moved a crate across the room.

Wyndham looked thoughtful.

"Would you like to see it again?" Roger asked.

"I thought that you'd said your magic spells cannot be recast."

"This one is still active. So it is more of a case of continuing to cast."

Wyndham nodded. "Then yes. Please do it again."

Roger did, and then he did it again, shuffling the crate across the room in gradual increments. By the time the crate was back in its original spot, Wyndham still looked thoughtful, but hadn't made any suggestions.

"Why don't we have tea while you ponder?" Roger offered.

Wyndham seemed to shake himself mentally. "Yes, of course."

Roger poured out. "I know very little fae magic, but it did occur to me that I have seen you do something similar to the movement spell."

Wyndham took his cup, giving Roger a wary expression. "And that is?"

"Whatever was used to send the oar back to our boat at the garden party," Roger said in as calm a tone as he could muster.

"But that was more of a—" Wyndham started. Then he paused. "I *suppose* it could work."

Roger hid his grin behind a sip of tea, pleased he had gotten that little kernel of truth out at last.

"Yes, yes," Wyndham said. "You're very clever. That's three spells done. I believe I was promised cake."

Roger laughed and cut Wyndham a generous slice.

Wyndham took the plate, eyeing it appreciatively. "Good to know you're not going to be a mean sort of husband."

"I would never deprive you of such simple comforts."

Wyndham cocked an eyebrow and took a sip of tea.

"Oh, you know what I meant," Roger said, flustered. "When it comes to cake," he added, trying to regain his dignity, "I will never be stingy. Spinach, however, has no place on my plate."

"I've heard it has many nutritious qualities," Wyndham said. "There must be some way for us to get you to eat it. I can't have my husband wasting away due to poor nutrition. How would it look?"

Roger pretended a serious moment of contemplation. "Perhaps if we added cream to it?"

Wyndham made a disgusted face. "Why?"

"Everything tastes better with cream," Roger reasoned.

"I'll take your word for it."

Encouraged by their progress, Roger didn't rush the tea and cake. It also seemed like the perfect opportunity to get to know Wyndham a little better, since his weak attempt the previous night had been foiled. "Do you typically eat breakfast?" he asked.

"I take my breakfast at noon like a reasonable person," Wyndham said primly.

"You keep London hours then, when you're in the country?"

Wyndham considered this. "It's a little different in the country. There are fewer social obligations. I'm not arranging my life around other people's calendars. However," he added with a stern look, "do not expect a little jaunt at sunrise from me."

Roger chuckled. "Duly noted."

Wyndham gave a small smile and Roger felt as though another piece of his future husband slotted into place. The sight of Wyndham's smile and the easy companionship of enjoying a leisurely meal together made him feel as though he found a part of himself that he didn't know was missing. He hastily pushed the thought aside and offered Wyndham more tea.

CHAPTER 46
WYN

POWER, focus, control, understanding, and intuition. These five words had effectively buried themselves so deeply into Wyn's thoughts that they were starting to lose meaning.

Wyn stood in the middle of the room with one hand on his hip, the other resting on the side of his face as he struggled to keep his eyes open. Roger had spent nearly half an hour trying to explain the process he wanted to use for demonstrating magical intuition, and Wyn was certain he had no idea how they would be able to align their two forms of magic well enough to accomplish it.

"So, you're saying that you want to apply the same human spell to three objects, with opposite effects but the same outcome?"

"Yes, exactly, because it will prove that the caster can effectively use what they know about the ingredients and sigils and apply them in alternative scenarios."

"But I thought spells have very specific instructions on how they must be executed? Otherwise, wouldn't you fail to get the result you want?" Wyn had never experienced such a thing before. His magic knew what he wanted and carried out the demand, no questions asked.

Roger's face lit up. "That's where the test of skill comes in." Wyn had long since given up trying to follow along with whatever Roger was writing on a piece of paper at the desk. "You see, if someone has the ability to create more freely with their knowledge, then…" he paused, searching. "It's the same as a child learning their letters, or a musician reading notes on sheet music. There are only so many of each, but it's the way you're able to *apply* them that makes something beautiful, like poetry or music."

Wyn allowed Roger his moment of romantic imagery, and then proceeded to crush it. "This seems impossible."

Roger frowned pointedly at him and started collecting materials anyway. "Just have a little trust in me, would you?" Wyn watched him scuttle about and fought off another yawn, moving his hand from his cheek to rub a thumb and finger against his eyelids.

When his gaze landed back on the desktop, Roger had placed three items in a neat row. The first was one of his pencils, used down to a nub. The second was one of the teacups they'd been drinking from with a small sip left. And the third was a deck of playing cards.

Wyn gave Roger a questioning look, and Roger smiled again.

"Move the pencil to the edge of the desk, if you'd be so kind."

"I'm too tired for games, Barnes," Wyn grumbled, but his eyes flicked to the open window as he called on his magic. The fresh air swirled into the room, seeking out the pencil where it sat on the desk, and they both watched as it rolled all the way to the side and fell to the floor.

"I said the edge," Roger chided under his breath, reaching to pick it up. His complaining stopped when he saw the way Wyn was glowering at him. "Do the cards next."

"All of them?" Wyn asked for clarification.

Roger's face showed his surprise. "You can do only one from the stack?"

"I can do whatever I want," Wyn said smoothly. He was satisfied at Roger's nervous adjustment of his spectacles.

"Do all of them," he confirmed.

Wyn felt the flip of his magic as he sent the cards flying, a few of them catching on the nicks and ridges of the work surface while the rest fluttered to the ground. Roger looked as though he wanted to complain again, but Wyn only shrugged as if to say, *I did what you asked.*

Roger sighed and stooped to collect them.

"I can only assume you'll not ask me to fling the teacup to the ground, as well?" Wyn asked, his gaze shifting to where Roger was bent forward.

"Only what's inside!" Roger said quickly, as though he didn't trust Wyn not to send the cup falling to a shattered mess on the floor. When Roger stood upright, Wyn realized that his attention had been lingering on the man's form; specifically the way his trousers had pulled taut over his back-side in a way that was most pleasing, indeed.

Roger tapped the deck of cards against the desk a few times before he placed them back where they'd been. Then, he reached to lift the teacup and carefully poured the remaining liquid out onto the desk. Wyn noted that Roger held onto the cup as he said, "Now the tea."

Wyn took a slow, deep breath, and then released it through his nose just as steadily as the tea carefully traveled toward the edge, holding form as though someone had picked up the corner of the desk to dump it instead. Wyn had the thought to push it all the way off so that Roger might have to bend down to clean that up, too, but he decided against it.

When he'd finished, Wyn's magic still fizzled, excited to do more. Wyn looked at Roger expectantly, but the man's focus seemed to be caught on the little puddle of tea.

"Was that all?" Wyn asked, and Roger seemed to come back to himself in that moment, blinking rapidly.

"Yes." His signature *happy-to-be-talking-about-magic* smile returned. "Yes! Just there, you used your magic with the air to move all three of the materi-als. Tell me, did each time feel the same? What is your process like for each?"

Wyn had to think about it. His process? "I'm not sure I know what you mean. I call for the air, and it comes. I ask it to move the object, and it moves."

Roger's forehead wrinkled as he took a couple steps closer to Wyn.

"Yes, but on that last one, for example, it required more of your energy. I could see how you used your breath to help guide the magic, just here—"

Roger's hand flattened on the middle of Wyn's chest, just below the knot of his cravat, and their eyes met. As quickly as he'd done it, Roger pulled his hand back, as though he'd been burned. He turned and retreated to the far corner of the desk.

"Liquids are not as easy to move," Wyn explained carefully. "Being outside would help, but still it's...one of the areas I fall short in." His biggest failure, in truth, on his own examination. The reason why Emrys was set to inherit and he was not.

"Oh," Roger said quietly. "I wasn't aware."

"Why would you be?" Wyn asked, shrugging one shoulder.

Roger seemed to recover then, to Wyn's relief. "You still did it, though. You moved all three, but each one was slightly different. The pencil rolled. The cards mostly slid, or traveled on the air itself. And the water, you had to push it."

"Yes, that's right," Wyn said, nodding thoughtfully at Roger's assessment.

"Human spells are much the same. You didn't need anything but your magic and the air to accomplish your goal, but the way your magic manipulated the air to meet your needs…that's magical intuition."

"You're able to use the same ingredients and the same markings on your paper, essentially the same spell, but tweak them in such a way that it's most effective for whatever you're trying to accomplish."

Roger's smile was back. "Correct."

"Show me," Wyn challenged. He wanted to watch Roger prove his own point. He wanted to see his meticulous calculations with the ingredients.

He wanted him to come back to Wyn's side, where he'd been standing before he'd scared himself away with a simple touch.

The two of them worked all through lunch and afternoon tea. More than once, they'd had to wipe crumbs from where Roger had been talking over their notes with a mouthful of food. When he managed to drop an entire sweetmeat biscuit—honey and powdered sugar side down—onto the open pages of the book they were referencing, Wyn dropped his head into his hands with a groan of exasperation.

"I'm sorry!" Roger blurted, a bright laugh erupting from him. The sound made Wyn's insides warm in a strange way, and he lifted his gaze back to the man sitting close enough that their knees could touch.

"Please allow me to write out our final proposal for the Council," he begged. "The last thing we need is for them to be unable to read it due to illegibility *and* food residue."

"I will be far too nervous to eat while writing out the final proposal," Roger assured him, while he proceeded to continue munching on the biscuit he'd dropped. "But I would be much appreciative of you writing it out all the same."

Wyn studied him for a moment, a slight grin on his mouth. "I suppose you're not nervous now, then?"

Roger's chewing slowed. "N-no, not currently. Should I be?"

"No. It's just nice to know we've both had time to relax today, what with our plans this evening…" Wyn's voice trailed off as he sat up straight, attention darting to the window first, then to the clock. "Fuck. We'll be late."

Roger's eyes went wide as he stood up, shoving the rest of his biscuit into his mouth and using both hands to wipe powder from his waistcoat. "*Yate hor wha?!*" he asked frantically through his mouthful.

"Another dinner party. Come on, we haven't any time to waste."

CHAPTER 47

ROGER

ROGER LEARNED that *"we haven't any time to waste"* meant that he needed to change into dinner attire immediately, so they could both go to the Wrenwhistle house and Wyndham could change into dinner attire as well—which took significantly longer than it had taken Roger.

By the time Wyndham made his way back downstairs, the rest of the Wrenwhistle family was waiting for him in the drawing room with Roger. It was a little agonizing to put up with Mrs. Wrenwhistle's questions as well as Emrys and Aveline's teasing all by himself.

So Roger was annoyed enough to whisper to Wyndham once they were in the carriage, "You know, I could have finished eating if you'd come here by yourself while I got dressed at home."

"Don't be ridiculous," Wyndham responded. "You lose track of time far too easily. I prefer knowing that you'll be here when I need you."

Roger's annoyance evaporated instantly. "Oh."

"Roger's been telling us what a productive day you two had," Mrs. Wrenwhistle explained.

"Yes," Wyndham replied. "It was most fruitful." Roger noticed his tone was laced with the tension it usually had around his family. It occurred to him suddenly that Wyndham had lost that tone around him.

"I'll bet it was," Emrys leered.

"The door was open," Roger felt compelled to say. He didn't like the way Wyndham's jaw clenched every time his brother spoke to him.

Emrys' eyebrow arched. "Yet, there was a great deal of talk about pencils being shoved around desks and tea being spilled on the floor." He clicked his tongue. "Are you sure the door was open wide enough?"

"When have I ever stooped to innuendo?" Wyndham asked.

Emrys shrugged. "I don't know. Maybe since you started taking up with a proper little human."

"Enough," Mrs. Wrenwhistle chided. "If you don't keep a civil tongue around Mr. Barnes in the future, Emrys, you will no longer be included in our party until their marriage."

"Personally," Aveline remarked into the awkward silence that followed, "I think it's lovely that you two have so many common interests."

Emrys hummed. "True. That will be helpful."

Roger waited uncomfortably for the punchline.

"Especially when you two retire to the country," he continued. "You know our little brother is a dreadful bore most of the time, but it's harder to tell in London. Having some common ground will definitely give you an advantage in terms of conversation."

"*Emrys*," his mother sighed, exasperated. "What a thing to say about your brother. Don't mind him, Mr. Barnes. You two will do very well in the country." Then she pointedly took charge of the conversation.

Emrys gave Roger an ostentatious wink. Roger squirmed under all the attention, but suddenly Wyndham covered Roger's hand with his and gave it a squeeze. *I prefer knowing you'll be here when I need you.* Perhaps suffering through the teasing would be worth it in the end. Roger shifted his hand so he could clasp Wyndham's in return.

As usual, the Wrenwhistles sailed through the crowd, bestowing nods and greetings as though the attention were their due. Mrs. Wrenwhistle took it upon herself to introduce Roger to people he didn't know. Roger noticed, however, that she seemed to be doing it almost as a way to keep Wyndham in her view. He couldn't tell if this was from a motherly concern after the way the other two siblings had behaved, or if there was something more. For his part, Wyndham seemed uncomfortable but resigned, which didn't help Roger piece together what was happening; Wyndham often seemed that way in social situations. Perhaps he was overthinking things.

They were paired together at dinner, which was a relief, as Roger wasn't sure he could handle an entire evening making small talk with a stranger. Another relief came by way of the absence of a salad course. Although Roger felt strangely disappointed that he wouldn't hear any ridiculous commentary from Wyndham about it.

That is, until Wyndham leaned closer to him and murmured, "It would seem you have been spared."

Roger grinned into his wine glass. "Indeed. I should send our hosts a thank you card."

"Please don't."

"Do you have something against thank you cards?"

"I have something against cards thanking someone for anything as ridiculous as no salad course."

"Frankly, I think more thank you cards should be sent out. We should be thankful for all sorts of ridiculous things."

"It sounds like a chaotic sort of correspondence." He paused. "Although I daresay chaotic suits you."

"I have tried to be more organized," Roger protested.

"I've seen you work. I can't honestly say I'm surprised by the chaos anymore. However, dripping tea directly onto the desk might have been a bit much, even for you."

"Nonsense. It got the job done in the end."

"Remind me to increase Notley's wages after we're married."

Roger smiled fondly. "That would be nice."

"Has he been your valet long?"

Roger did not like where this topic was headed. He toyed with his spoon nervously. "Oh, er…well, since I moved out of my parents' house."

Wyndham gave him a sharp look. "That was only a year or so ago, wasn't it?"

Roger nodded.

"What happened to your previous valet, or didn't you have one?"

"I had one," Roger said.

"That wasn't an answer to my first question."

Roger sighed and dropped his spoon back onto the table. "Well, I've always had difficulty keeping a valet. That is, it was difficult finding a valet. Nobody wanted to work for someone like me."

"What do you mean?" Wyndham asked, frowning.

"My Hastings score," Roger explained softly. "It's quite low, you know."

"What does that have to do with a valet's work?"

"Well, no one wanted to work for somebody who wasn't…going anywhere. I was unlikely to marry well and—"

"Why not?"

"No one wants to marry someone with so little talent," Roger answered, hating that he had to spell it out.

Wyndham laid a hand on Roger's arm. "That is absurd. I've seen you work. You are remarkably talented."

"Thank you," Roger said, unwilling to admit how much the compliment meant to him. "But you see, that's why this new rubric is so important. I lack magical power, which is primarily what the Hastings Exam measures. But with a different rubric, I might have made up for it with different strengths and then…"

"And then things might have been different for you, and not just in terms of inheritance," Wyndham finished.

Roger nodded.

"So you were snubbed by a bunch of idiot valets. How did you find Notley?"

"He came recommended to me because…he didn't score well either."

Wyndham's surprise was evident.

"Anyway, my parents told me I couldn't move out of their house unless I found either enough servants to take care of all my needs or a manservant who could act as a valet, cook, and butler. I was struggling to find someone who was willing to do one of those jobs, let alone all three. And I was writing to a friend of mine and she recommended Notley. My mother didn't actually want me to hire him because he had no experience as a butler or a valet, but I hired him anyway because he…"

"He treated you with the respect you deserve."

"Yes," Roger said. "And he is sometimes a little more…er…candid and honest than most servants prefer to be. But he has never made me feel like I'm less than and I value that a great deal more." He paused. "And he puts up with my mess, which is remarkable in and of itself."

"Downright heroic, if you ask me."

"You seem to be putting up with it too," Roger laughed.

"I know. I'm very heroic."

"Speaking of," Roger said, sobering a little. "How are you faring?"

Wyndham took a large sip of wine. "About as well as can be expected."

"Your mother seems to be even more intent on seeing me meet people than she was at our engagement party."

Wyndham grimaced. "Yes. She took some dislike to my disappearance and…overall attitude that night."

"Is she not aware of how these events affect you?"

He shrugged. "It doesn't seem to affect anyone else in the same way. I've learned to cope."

"But that shouldn't be," Roger exclaimed, attempting to keep his vehement tone to a quiet level. "Your needs should be accommodated, not the other way around."

The corner of Wyndham's mouth quirked up. "It really bothers you?"

"Yes! You shouldn't have to put up a front when you don't feel well."

"I've been doing it for as long as I can remember."

"Will it be easier in the country?"

"Decidedly so."

Roger quickly calculated their time left. "So barely another fortnight, and then you can relax?"

Wyndham gave him a long, unreadable look. "Yes," he said slowly. "Barely another fortnight."

"That's good then," Roger said, feeling satisfied. "I'm glad we have that —" He broke off. "Good heavens. Our wedding is in a fortnight."

Wyndham's amused expression returned. "Your days as a bachelor are numbered, Mr. Barnes."

Roger waved a hand dismissively. "Oh, don't be silly. You know no one's thinking about me that way."

"You're not worried then, about married life?"

"Not as such."

Wyndham raised an eyebrow. "But?"

Roger felt his face heat, but he remembered his promise. *Complete honesty.* "Well, it has occurred to me that we…we know so little about each other."

Wyndham shifted in his seat so he was facing Roger more fully. "What is it you would like to know?"

Roger shrugged. "I don't know. I want to know what your favorite book is. What you do to relax. Whether this seemingly endless collection of waist-coats goes with you to the country, and is it, in fact, finite? What makes you happy? Is there anyone you've always looked up to? I know what makes you feel constricted and uncomfortable. What makes you feel free? What do you prefer to be called? Do you have any pets? If not, do you want any? What...er..."

He tapered off as more questions filled his brain. "I-I want to know everything," he finally went on. "I know all of this can't be answered in a single evening, or even a fortnight. And I suppose we have the rest of our lives to discuss these things. But...I feel as though the more I get to know you, the more I want to learn." He gave a self-conscious smile. "Sorry. I'm sure that was all very silly. I did promise you honesty."

CHAPTER 48

WYN

Wʏɴ ᴛʜᴏᴜɢʜᴛ honesty suited Roger well. He liked the way it allowed Roger's thoughts to flow more freely, the same as they did when he was speaking about magic. There was less of his nervous stuttering and more confidence. Wyn thought it was quite the opposite for most people. Honesty could be downright frightening. That is, unless you are most comfortable with whom you are sharing those raw truths.

Before he could respond to any of Roger's questions, another dinner guest said Roger's name across the table and a few seats down, pulling his attention away. They were curious about their progress with the proposal. Roger eagerly jumped at the opportunity to speak about it, and soon there were more faces turning his direction, listening with genuine interest.

Wyn carefully angled his legs forward and used the back of his chair as support so he could settle and listen to his betrothed share his passion with the others. Wyn sipped his wine and decided it was probably something they should start doing more. Getting the support of other prominent members of society would only boost their chances of successfully convincing the Council to implement the new rubric.

By the time the last course was served, Roger had been answering questions and offering explanations to the point of dehydration. When his voice cracked, Wyn set his hand gently on Roger's thigh under the table. He would've settled for Roger's hand instead, but both of them were still caught up in his expressive talking.

Roger's attention whipped around at the touch, and Wyn offered a grin.

"Drink something before your words turn to dust," he said quietly. Roger swallowed hard and seemed to realize only then how thirsty he was. He reached for his glass and took a few generous swallows.

"Thank you," he said on an exhale as he lowered his wine. After inspecting which course was in front of him, his lips pursed a bit. "I didn't realize I'd been speaking for so long."

"You had them well captivated," Wyn agreed. "I think it's wise to start speaking about it all more publicly, now that we have some idea of what the devil we're doing. The more support we have, the better."

"Ah, y-yes, I suppose that's true," Roger said, before popping a roasted hazelnut into his mouth.

As Wyn reached for a slice of pear from his own plate, he realized in a wash of heat that not only was his other hand still on Roger's thigh, but that at some point he'd started moving his fingers ever so slightly. It had been such a subtle comfort for him that he hadn't even noticed.

Wyn withdrew his hand to his own lap and glared at his dessert plate with bewilderment, brows bunched together. Was Roger not going to make any mention for him to stop? Maybe that was his retribution for sending all of the materials to the floor earlier; Roger had decided to let him make a fool of himself at dinner by showing too much public affection.

Very well. If that was the game he wanted to play, then Wyndham Wrenwhistle was prepared to win. He swallowed his bite of sweet pear and leaned far closer than necessary to Roger's ear.

"Dance with me?" he whispered. Wyn leaned back far enough for their eyes to meet, and Roger offered the tiniest nod in response.

Wyn helped Roger from his chair when the meal was over, and the pair found their way to the adjoining room where other couples were already gathering in sets of four.

"Oh, this is one of my favorites," Roger said with a smile. Wyn offered his hand after they bowed to each other, and Roger took it with ease.

After joining hands with the rest of the circle, they fell into step and allowed the music to sweep them up and around. They parted hands when another couple stepped between them, and again when it was their turn to cross the floor and do the same, but Wyn found that he could not look away from his partner for even a moment as they split and came together again.

Roger had asked what makes him happy. Seeing the pure, unadulterated joy on Roger's face as he danced was most assuredly gaining rank on that list.

The music continued to play while they worked through the main figure three more times. As they took their final steps around one another and came to a stop, Roger was the first to start clapping politely.

"You're still an excellent dancer," Roger said breathlessly at his side, the footwork taking more out of them than Wyn realized.

"And you only managed to step on my foot once this time," Wyn teased, though his smirk was more genuine than his words let on. Roger tugged on the bottom of his waistcoat and looked toward the other room.

"I see a couple of open chairs. Shall we go and sit?"

"No," Wyn said, and Roger's mouth opened in what looked like surprise.

"Oh. Well, I…should I go and wait for you there, then?"

"Are you tired of dancing already?" Wyn asked, his head tilting to one side.

Roger blinked. "N-no, but I thought——"

"Then dance with me again." He offered his hand, and Roger looked down at it, before his attention snapped up to Wyn's face. "If you'd like, that is."

The look of uncertainty only lingered on Roger's features for a few seconds, before it turned to something like relief, and he nodded, his smile big enough to crinkle the corners of his eyes. "Yes. Very much," he said.

Wyn kept Roger out on the floor until the man looked as if he might collapse, though his smile never faltered. The dancing had been a wonderful distraction from the crowded room, but Wyn's cravat had become a rope wound tightly around his neck and he needed some air.

They located one of the balconies, a rather large one, and Wyn directed Roger to sit in one of the chairs situated around a small table while he went to fetch them a drink.

As soon as Wyn had secured some water for each of them, the air shifted nearby and his grip tightened on the glasses.

"Worn out from all of your public lovemaking?" Sage asked, his hands immediately finding their way to Wyn's hips from behind. Wyn stepped away from him and turned around, his anger already simmering in his chest.

"Mr. Ravenwing," he greeted coldly. "Good evening. I'm sure I don't know what you mean by that."

Sage laughed, though it was tight. "You've never been subtle when it comes to showing your affections, Wyndham. I would know. They belonged to me for a very long time, until I was replaced." He stepped closer, stroking a hand down Wyn's upper arm as his bottom lip poked out. "Don't you miss me?"

Wyn stared at him. "What is there to miss? All we did was sleep together. Certainly nothing I cannot accomplish by my own hand."

The scandalized look Sage gave him was the smallest taste of victory.

Sage was at least smart enough to keep his voice low as he said, "You cannot convince me that *anything* Roger Barnes can give you in bed is better than what you and I have."

"Had," Wyn corrected firmly. "And I am most certain that *everything* Roger Barnes can give me is better than anything I ever got from you."

With that, Wyn turned and maneuvered his way through the crowd back toward the balcony. His heart was racing from his encounter with the other fae. He regretted not being more direct about how Sage would be wise to never speak to Roger the way he had again. But the blast of fresh air and the sight of Barnes sitting and waiting for him helped to calm him.

Wyn handed Roger his drink and sat in the chair next to him.

"Thank you," Roger said quickly, his mouth already on the lip of the glass.

They sat in silence as Roger drained his water and Wyn took a few sips of his own. Chatter from the party inside and the distant clopping of horse hooves on the street below filled the air around them.

Wyn looked at Roger for a long moment, before his focus settled on nothing in particular off the edge of the balcony. He took a final sip of his water and set it down, crossing one knee over the other, his foot bouncing slightly.

"To name my favorite book would be akin to naming my favorite day of the year, or my favorite type of flower. There are too many to ever pick just one." He felt Roger's gaze on him as he continued. "In my spare time, what precious little I have of it during the Season, I enjoy painting *en plein* with my watercolors. I've worn the same size waistcoat for nearly fifteen years. As such, I've come to own quite a number of them, and they all travel with me wherever I go."

Wyn paused, considering his next answers with more care.

"I look up to my grandmother. She embodies the type of strength and intelligence I have always strived for, while also being kind and generous to everyone she meets."

His teeth found the inside of his cheek briefly before he continued.

"In the country, there is a stream I like to visit. Sometimes I enjoy painting there, but other times I go and simply sit." Wyn decided to save the details of his lack of clothing for later. "We keep horses at the estate. Mother never allowed us to have pets because they're too messy, although I would not be opposed to the idea if it's something you would enjoy."

Wyn thought he saw Roger smile out of the corner of his eye.

"A great many things make me happy, though I am aware I'm not always good at showing it." He huffed out a laugh and looked down at his hands where they were resting on his lap. "In fact, I would venture to say that I do a terrible job of expressing how things truly make me feel."

Wyn met Roger's gaze. "As for what I prefer to be called, I think everyone in my life calls me something different. Wyndham, of course. Wynnie. My grandmother calls me 'darling' most often, and has since I was a boy. *Unimaginable bastard*," he said with emphasis, and they both laughed. "But," he paused again, his smile softening a bit. "I would like it very much if you'd call me Wyn."

CHAPTER 49

ROGER

ROGER COULDN'T THINK of an adequate response. He was sure he was grinning like a fool after Wyndham's—*Wyn's*—speech, but no words came out. He had the uncharacteristic urge to pull the other man into a kiss, which was something he'd never considered doing before, but he didn't feel right doing such a thing.

So before he could talk himself out of it, he did the next best thing he could think of, and took Wyn's hand in his own, giving it a light squeeze. "Thank you," he murmured softly.

He wanted to say more. He wanted to say that he'd always wanted a cat or a dog. He wanted to ask whether Wyn wanted children. He wanted to admit that his favorite of Wyn's waistcoats was the one in robin's egg blue. He wanted to ask to see Wyn's favorite stream sometime. But he looked at Wyn's face, which was relaxed and softly smiling, and decided that maybe he didn't need to say everything all at once. Wyn had given him exactly what he'd asked for, an open and honest look into his soul. Roger also realized that he'd been silently invited into Wyn's necessary social recuperation period. Wyn trusted him. Everything else on his mind could wait.

Wyn rubbed his thumb over Roger's hand. "Any other questions?"

"Only an infinite number," Roger replied. "We'll get to them another night."

Wyn nodded and took another sip of his drink. They sat in companionable silence until Mrs. Wrenwhistle came to collect them.

On the ride home, Mrs. Wrenwhistle complimented them for their time on the dance floor. "Although," she went on, "four dances might have been a bit excessive."

Roger privately thought that she never seemed to be satisfied with her youngest child's behavior.

"And don't forget that we're calling on people for tea tomorrow."

"Pardon?" Roger asked, alarmed.

"Yes, didn't your mother tell you? We thought it would be nice to make our social calls together. Formal events like these are all well and good for establishing connections, but it is regular visits that form real bonds. You two will have a duty to uphold as prominent members of society."

Roger swallowed. *Prominent members of society.* Is that what they were now? Was it because of the Wrenwhistle family name, he wondered, or their fae-human marriage? He glanced at Wyn, who looked weary but unsurprised. Roger took Wyn's hand again, selfishly taking the comfort he needed. When Wyn returned his clasp, he breathed out in relief that the comfort was mutual.

"Of course, Mother," Wyn replied smoothly. "Are we collecting Roger and his mother or are we meeting them somewhere?"

Roger hid the smile that came unbidden at the sound of his name on Wyn's lips.

HE STRUGGLED to sleep that night, his mind filled to overflowing with thoughts of his betrothed—how he moved when he danced, the warmth of his hand on Roger's thigh, how his smile softened when he asked to be called Wyn. The next morning, he was cranky from lack of sleep, as well as the time that was being stolen from their work in order to fulfill social obligations. They still had so much to do. And there was a niggling frustration that Roger couldn't quite name that underlied all of his other irritations.

When he and his mother stepped into the St. Clairs' sitting room, and he saw Wyn sitting alone on a settee, politely answering Mrs. St. Clair's questions, Roger realized what that underlying frustration was—his time alone with the gentleman had been stolen too. He didn't want to have to share Wyn's time with anyone else. This realization was a little alarming, so he put forth a herculean effort to hide it, greeting everyone with more enthusiasm than he felt.

He was grateful that the seat beside Wyn had been left pointedly open for him. Wyn's jaw was tight but he smiled when he greeted Roger. "How are you?" he asked.

Roger returned the smile. "Tired, and regretting the lost time for our project. But it's good to see you. You?"

Wyn's smile widened a little. "About the same."

Then Anthea plopped into the seat opposite and began peppering them both with questions. She was curious about their project, how the engagement had come about, and whether they were going to come back to London after their wedding. "And I'm still mad at you for not telling me about your engagement sooner," she griped.

"It all happened so quickly," Roger explained, in what was now a rote response. "There wasn't time to tell anyone. Even my parents learned about it in the *Tribune*."

He answered all of her questions about their project, but deftly pivoted the topic back to her any time she inquired about their engagement, instead asking her about Lady Fitzhugh and teasing her about how shy she got when talking about the other woman.

When they moved on to their next visit, Roger was thankful that Anthea had been first. Everywhere they went, people asked them the same questions. By the time they were done with their circuit, he was too exhausted by conversation to pretend enthusiasm anymore. As they prepared to return home, his mother bid Mrs. Wrenwhistle goodbye, telling her that they'd see them all shortly.

"What did you mean by that?" Roger asked once they were settled in their own carriage.

"Didn't I tell you?" she answered. "They're coming over for dinner tonight. Nothing formal, but I do want to get to know them all better, considering."

Roger restrained a heavy sigh. "Wyn—Mr. Wrenwhistle and I won't have any time to do our work today."

She gave him a teasing smile. "You both have plenty of time to work on your project later. We don't want either of you to work yourselves to the bone. And besides," she added, patting her hair, "you two can just as easily make swoony eyes at each other in front of your family as you can alone."

Roger wanted to protest but knew it would be a useless effort. At least a small dinner party meant he'd have more opportunities to see Wyn.

CHAPTER 50

WYN

Upon returning home from their string of visits around town, Wyn decided he could not handle one more moment of socialization without relaxing in a bath first. His muscles ached from sitting so stiffly on increasingly uncomfortable sofas and chairs all afternoon. All but two of the drawing rooms had been closed up, with no breeze or even the slightest crack in the window to offer some comfort.

Sitting with Roger had been helpful, but he thought it would've made the man nervous to display any sort of affection in such a setting, so he'd kept his hands to himself.

Wyn bent his long legs and sunk his head underwater for a few seconds. He resurfaced with a steadying sigh and kept his eyes closed, tucking his hair behind the points of his ears as he welcomed the way the warmth of the water eased into his limbs, his lower back, his shoulders.

A knock on the door nearly unraveled him.

"What?" he shouted, his eyes still closed, wishing it was enough to make him disappear for long enough to actually enjoy his time alone.

"Wyndham," his mother called, her voice muffled through the door. The handle jiggled as she tried to let herself in, but it was locked.

"I'm busy," he said, his voice returning to normal volume. That had become his standard response over the years, short, direct, and a clear invitation to leave him alone. He hadn't realized it had picked up any other meaning until she responded.

"Oh! My apologies, I'll leave you to it then. You and your friend just please don't lose track of time or we'll be late."

Wyn's eyes snapped open, and he almost had to take a reassuring glance around the room to verify that he was, in fact, alone.

Could she really think…?

It was no secret Wyn had brought plenty of men to his room over the years, but how could she possibly believe he would do such a thing, given the circumstances? Fool around with someone else a scant hour before they were due for a dinner engagement with his *human* fiancé?

Fae had different ideas of what it meant to be faithful to a spouse. Different views on intimacy altogether. It was not unheard of for fae to marry, but also keep their lovers for entertainment or relaxation. After all, marriage was sometimes nothing more than a business deal. Two families joining to benefit everyone involved.

Imagining the look on Roger's face was enough to make Wyn's stomach go cold. He would be crushed to learn of Wyn doing such a thing, as any human would be. Naturally, Wyn had thought about his lack of bedroom activity over the previous couple of weeks. But, to his surprise, he found he hadn't missed it.

Perhaps he'd been too busy to care. He'd hardly had time for anything aside from his work with Barnes and their social engagements. Spending nearly every waking moment with the man had proven to be *stimulating* enough, in its own way.

Before his water grew any colder, Wyn sat up so he could begin washing with his favorite lavender soap. He smirked to himself as he recalled the look on Roger's face when he'd taken his first sip of lavender tea.

MUCH TO WYN'S SURPRISE, only his mother and father joined him in the carriage as they set out for the Barnes' townhouse.

"Where are Emrys and Aveline?" he asked warily.

"They're staying home this evening," his mother explained. "I've grown weary of the way they have been speaking to you and Roger."

Wyn's eyebrows went up in surprise. "I'm sure Aveline is heartbroken to miss a dinner."

"Yes, well, sometimes there must be consequences for our actions," she said crisply, smoothing her hands over her skirts. Wyn decided not to think too deeply about that response.

When they arrived, the three of them were welcomed with a warmth that Wyn had grown accustomed to. Both of Roger's parents greeted them and guided them toward the dining room with open arms and friendly smiles. Roger was already waiting for them. Nearly as soon as they were seated—Wyn and Roger together, of course—Wyn leaned over to him.

"Lovely to see you again so soon," he began, echoing the forced pleasantries of the conversations from earlier that had exhausted them both. "You've been well, I hope?"

A smile broke across Roger's face so quickly that he brought a hand up to cover it. He pressed his lips together and offered a polite nod, his focus still on the food being plated.

"Oh yes, quite. And yourself?" he said as he accepted a dish and began serving himself, before adding some of the meat to Wyn's plate, as well.

"Much better now," Wyn said smoothly. "Had a bath. Thought of you," he drawled, taking great pleasure in the way Roger's expression changed instantly to that of panic. The serving utensil clattered a bit as he passed the dish to his father. Wyn let him flounder for only a few seconds more before he explained himself. "The soap I prefer is made with lavender. I was only wondering if you feel as strongly about the smell of it as you do the flavor."

"Oh," Roger said on an exhale, visibly relaxing. "I find the smell quite nice."

Wyn wasn't finished. "What type of soap do you use?"

"Th-the kind someone buys for me?" Roger squeaked. Wyn's eyes lit up at the sound, and Roger's cheeks went a satisfying shade of pink.

Fortunately for them, the dinner conversation was carried effortlessly by their parents, allowing them to sit and mostly listen as they chatted about this and that. Only when Roger's father caught them whispering again did he break up their side party with a fond smile.

"What's got you two grinning like thieves over there?" he asked, effectively putting all of the attention on them at once. Wyn decided that Roger had done his fair share of answering questions over tea earlier, so it was his turn to step up.

"We were only discussing the lack of a salad course," he explained. When that was met with much confusion, he sat up a bit in his chair and continued. "It's become a bit of an ongoing discussion between the two of us. We realized that, even with all of the mixing of fae and humans at dinner parties, big or small, whichever side is hosting determines—without fail—if there will be a salad course or not."

Mr. Barnes gave him a curious look. "I suspect fae are serving a salad and humans are not?" They both gave him a nod in return. "A most interesting observation. I'm surprised I've never noticed."

"They attend far more dinner parties than you, dear," Mrs. Barnes said with a little laugh. "Research does require plenty of data to pull from."

"I cannot argue with that," he admitted, waggling his fork in her direction before he poked it down into another bite of food.

"What led you to that conclusion, Mr. Barnes?" Wyn's mother managed to ask this with only the faintest accusation in her voice, taking offense when none was warranted. He finished chewing and swallowed before he gave his reply.

"Well, culturally speaking, humans are more inclined toward cooked food, whereas the fae populace integrates raw food much more frequently."

Wyn watched with mild amusement as his mother tried to follow along with what Mr. Barnes was telling her. "I see," she said demurely.

"I imagine it harkens back to our roots, centuries ago, before fae and humans started to combine societies. And you know how people are, they all tend to cling to their unique tendencies even when it is no longer necessary. Even now, humans favor cooked salads over raw ones, and fae are more likely to use raw ingredients even beyond the salad course.

"But to get back to the origins of this topic, fae magic deals much more closely with nature, as you well know, and as such, fae were able to determine which raw foods were safer to eat, thus avoiding more situations of acute illness than humans could."

"What kind of illness?" Mrs. Wrenwhistle asked, taking a sip of wine. Mr. Barnes opened his mouth, looking a bit uncertain about answering that over dinner.

"Use your imagination, Mother," Wyn said pointedly. After a moment, her face puckered as though she'd smelled something unpleasant, and she nodded her understanding.

"What is it about cooking the food that makes such a change?" Roger asked his father, leaning closer as he waited for his response.

"Well, we're not entirely sure. It could have more to do with the application of heat, or possibly the way the food is broken down when it's cooked." Roger nodded, accepting the answer for what it was, but Wyn's interest was piqued.

"Broken down?" Wyn queried, reaching for his glass.

"Yes," Mr. Barnes said, his eyes sweeping across the table to search for an example to help explain his point. "Ah. The potatoes. Have you ever held one before it's been cooked?"

"I have not," Wyn told him.

"It's very hard, sometimes nearly as hard as a rock. But once you've put it in a pot of boiling water, it becomes softer. And much more enjoyable to eat."

Wyn's eyes narrowed. "I suppose that happens to all foods when they've been cooked?"

"Hmm, yes, I think that's a fair statement. Softer, more palatable, potentially a bit milder in flavor, unless herbs and spices have been added."

Wyn glanced at Roger, who was completely oblivious to how his father was all but proving something Wyn had been wondering about since their project had begun.

"Is heat ever used in the treatment of magical ingredients?"

"Yes, on occasion," Mr. Barnes said easily, taking another bite of his meal. This seemed like an indication that he should slow down with his questions, but his mind continued to whirl.

Wyn sat through three more courses, poised and ready to leap up out of his chair the moment it would be acceptable to do so. As he got to his feet, he put his hand on Roger's shoulder and leaned close again.

"Play along," he murmured. Roger gave him a confused look but quickly hid it away, setting his napkin on his plate as he stood up. "Roger has some notes for me to take home and review, we'll just be a moment," he announced, before swiftly exiting the room. They climbed the steps and fled to the makeshift study.

"Is something the matter?" Roger asked, genuine concern in his voice.

"Quite the opposite," Wyn said, whirling around to face Roger, who stopped short to avoid running into him. He hadn't realized he'd been following so closely.

"I-I haven't got any new notes for you," Roger said, eyes flicking to his desk. Wyn gave him a soft smile and brought his hand to Roger's cheek, stroking it with his thumb.

"Grandmother was right about you," he told him, knowing Roger wouldn't have any idea what it meant, but feeling the need to voice it all the same. Wyn dropped his hand and fisted his knuckles against his hips, moving closer to the open window so he could organize his thoughts.

When he turned back around, Roger was in the same spot, watching him.

"I want to test my theory," Wyn said carefully. "The one about magical ingredients. But I'm going to need your help to do it." He stepped closer and searched Roger's eyes. "Do you trust me?"

CHAPTER 51

ROGER

ROGER DIDN'T HESITATE before answering, "Yes, of course."

Wyn smiled. "Good. Tomorrow, at ten o'clock, meet me in Hyde Park by the duck pond. Can you do that?"

Roger's brow wrinkled in confusion. "Er...yes?"

"Good," he repeated. He turned briefly again towards the open window and took in a deep breath. "It will be nice to do our work outdoors for a change." Then he went back out of the room and Roger hastened to follow.

"Did you say we're going to work outdoors?"

Wyn turned on the stairs so he was facing Roger. A couple steps down, they were at the same height for once. "I'll explain everything tomorrow. I promise. I have a theory but...but I want to show you rather than try to explain it."

Roger had seen the spark in Wyn's expression before, the first time he'd seen Roger perform magic. It meant he was going to get more insight into Wyn's mind and he was never going to pass up that opportunity. "Of course," he said. "I trust you," he added, since it seemed like Wyn enjoyed hearing it. From the smile Wyn gave him, it was evident he did.

THE NEXT MORNING, people were just beginning to trickle into the Park for morning rides as Roger made his way across to the duck pond. When he finally reached it, he found Wyn leaning against a nearby tree, his shoes off and on the ground next to him. When he saw Roger approaching, he smiled and pushed himself off the tree.

"Good morning," Roger greeted. "So, what's this theory?"

"I'm going to show you. Take your shoes off and put them next to mine."

Roger complied, even more confused than when Wyn first mentioned the pond.

Grinning, Wyn took his hand and led him right into the water. Roger gave a small shriek as it came up over his ankles. "It's bloody freezing!"

Wyn guided him further into the water and, surprisingly, into his arms, with his back to the other man's chest.

"What are you doing?" Roger said in a hushed voice.

"Giving you your first lesson in fae magic," Wyndham murmured, snaking an arm around Roger's waist and lacing his free hand through Roger's. Then he crouched into the water, taking Roger with him, until they were both knee-deep in the pond, with their hands plunged under the surface.

"Did you say you're teaching me fae magic?" Roger asked, his voice still hushed.

"Yes."

"Is this to do with that theory of yours?"

"Yes."

"People will talk," Roger muttered.

"I'm just teaching my fiancé what all fae teach their children as soon as they're old enough. If anyone asks, we'll tell them, truthfully, that it's for our project."

"I'm not even sure what it is we're doing," Roger admitted.

"Hush," Wyn whispered, his breath hot on the shell of Roger's ear. "Trust me. Close your eyes. Focus."

Roger complied. "And what am I focusing on exactly?"

He felt Wyn's thumb rub over the palm of his hand and he was so distracted by the sensation that it took him a moment to catch up with what Wyn was saying, "Focus on the water. What do you feel?"

"Cold."

He felt Wyn's chuckle reverberate in his own body. "I know you can do better than that."

Roger sighed and tried to focus. He noted the way the water eddied around his fingers, the way it felt colder further down, and then—he felt something else, a swirling feeling just out of reach, as if by stretching his hand out just a little bit farther, he could capture that feeling. "Oh," he whispered.

"That's it," Wyn breathed. "You can feel it, can't you?"

"What *is* that?"

"There's magic in everything, you know that. When you take the time to experience magic at its source, its power is raw. Wild."

"Incredible."

"Indeed."

The arm around Roger's waist tightened and Wyn straightened them both, keeping Roger steady. "That was your first lesson. Are you ready for your second?"

Roger nodded.

With Roger's hand still clasped in his, Wyn led them back to the bank. He scooped up both of their shoes and walked further into the Park. Roger followed. They stopped at a section full of planted flowers. Wyn dumped the shoes to the side, pulled Roger back against his chest, his arm around Roger's waist again, his fingers lacing with Roger's own, and sank them both to the ground.

"Is there a reason we did the water first?" Roger asked as his knees hit the dirt.

"Water magic is the easiest to feel, even if it isn't the easiest to manipulate. So we always start with that."

"Oh."

Wyn dug their joined hands into the dirt, sinking them both until they were wrist deep. In the confined space, Roger couldn't help but notice the press of Wyn's skin to his, realizing belatedly that they had both neglected to put on their gloves. Wyn's breath ghosted over his ear again, tickling, intimate. Long fingers spread over Roger's stomach. "Breathe. Concentrate."

Roger did as he was told, trying to ignore the feeling of Wyn's hand over his stomach, Wyn's chest pressed against his back, Wyn's legs bracketing his own, Wyn's breath on his cheek, Wyn's long hair draping over his neck, and their hands still clasped under the dirt. He tried very, very hard to focus beyond his fingertips and into the loamy ground. It was more difficult than the water. At first, all he could feel was the resistance, the pressure of his hand intruding where it wasn't meant to be, the coldness of the earth. And then, just out of reach again, *something*. He took a deep breath and sank his hand a little lower. Wyn pulled him a little tighter to his chest, almost imperceptibly, almost encouraging. Roger let out a breath and tried to sink into the sensation, and practically gasped when he realized what the sensation was that he was trying to place. The ground felt *alive*. It felt quiet, like a banked fire which, he supposed, made sense considering the time of year.

Wyn made a pleased sound against him. "You are full of surprises, aren't you, Roger Barnes?"

"What do you mean?"

Wyn's hand shifted under the dirt and Roger felt the other man's thumb slide over his wrist. "I can feel your magic, you know. I can feel it stretching, reaching. It is…unexpected."

"You can feel my magic?"

Wyn gave a hum in answer. "It's so tentative, your magic. It is…unassuming, gentle even. Fascinating."

"You've seen me perform magic before," Roger pointed out. "You never felt it then?"

Wyn pulled their joined hands out of the dirt. Then he extricated his own hand and laid it palm-down against the ground. When his hand came up, the ground looked as if they had never been there, and his hand was totally clean. Then he helped Roger back to standing. "Yes," he said at last. "I've seen you perform magic. But it's harder to feel it when you use your ingredients. Everything is ground up, liquefied, completely divorced from its natural state. It physically pains me and distracts me from getting a good sense of your magic underneath all that noise."

"Oh."

"But that's part of why we're out here. I wanted to see if you could sense wild magic. And I wanted to get a better sense of what your magic feels like." Wyn reached for his hand again. "Come on. Final lesson." Roger bent to reach for the shoes but Wyn said, "Leave them. We're not going far."

The final lesson was, it turned out, a willow tree. Roger was no longer surprised to have Wyn at his back, guiding their hands to the tree trunk. Roger didn't wait for the instructions this time. He closed his eyes and breathed in deeply, surprised by the realization that Wyn's arm around his waist grounded him now rather than unsettled him.

He was also surprised by how different the tree felt to the water and the earth. It felt…unique. There was a hint of temperament, of personality.

"You see?" Wyn asked, low in his ear. "She can feel every branch, every blossom, every leaf. Humans raze these things to the ground and then expect them to surrender their power. Not everything is for the taking."

Roger felt something brush against his face. He turned to see a willow branch dancing against the wind. He looked at Wyn. "Was that you?"

Wyn smiled. "Call it a joint effort. She likes you. Or I should say, she likes your magic. I think the gentleness of it appeals to her."

Roger slid his hand off the trunk and gave the tree a long, contemplative look. "The problem is," he said slowly, "I can feel the magic, but I'm not at all sure I can use it the way you do."

"Perhaps not. But there ought to be a way for humans to tap into these resources without destroying them first. It's like what your father said at dinner last night, how food gets broken down when heat is applied."

"Is that what brought this on?" Roger asked.

"I think the same thing happens to your ingredients when they're treated. Yes, they're easier to manipulate and control, but you lose so much of the power. My theory is that if we could find a way for you—for humans to use raw ingredients, you wouldn't have to treat everything first. Your magic would increase in power and your resources would be kept in better condition. I wanted to bring you out here so I could determine how well your magic communicated with wild magic first, and I wanted to see if I could sense it better."

"And now that you have?"

"I'm even more convinced that this could work."

Roger touched light fingers to the drooping leaves. "You said that not everything is for the taking. How do you recommend we get our resources, even if we use them as raw ingredients? And how would we go about changing human magic? Because that is, essentially, what we'd have to do?"

"I'm not sure," Wyn replied. "I imagine if anyone can come up with a solution, it's us. You know far more about your own magic system than you acknowledge. You have marvelous talent and skill."

The compliments warmed Roger down to his bones. "Thank you," he said softly.

"And as to your first question," Wyn went on as he looked up at the tree, his expression thoughtful. A long, thin willow branch fluttered free and curled around Roger's wrist.

Roger caught it in his hand and stared at Wyn. "Did you——"

Wyn smiled, slow and sultry. "She was ready to lose that one anyway."

Roger held the branch between his hands, his mind whirring. "Perhaps after we finish our rubric project, we can bend our minds to this one?"

"I'd like that," Wyn answered softly.

They put their shoes on and made their way back to the road where Wyndham hailed a hansom. Even though they'd agreed to work on solving the problem later, Roger's mind had already begun forming possibilities.

TORQUIL'S TRIBUNE

Greetings, friendly folk and hearty humans,

After news of their engagement reached the public, Mr. Barnes and Mr. Wrenwhistle officially requested an extension on their joint project to change testing rubrics. They appeared before the Council for Fae & Human Magical Relations on Monday morning. While many are likely disappointed that the much needed solution to the Hastings score problem is postponed, it is hardly blameworthy in this case. The two gentlemen are most likely enjoyably distracted. This writer is a romantic at heart and finds such reasons for an extension perfectly reasonable.

Speaking of the ton's favorite couple, they have been very busy outside of their work as well. Mr. Barnes was a guest in the Wrenwhistle opera box yet again. Several reports have come in that the two were remarkably cozy. This continued throughout the week as the couple attended a dinner party at the Morris family's home. The event was lauded a success, with a good turnout from fae and human invitees alike. According to sources, Mr. Barnes and Mr. Wrenwhistle danced four dances together and then settled properly on a balcony for the rest of the evening. This writer has accused Mr. Wrenwhistle of rakish behavior in the past, but it would seem the former rogue has gone romantic after all.

For those who are not reading this column merely for reports on one particular couple (although we are shocked to learn such people exist), Lady Fitzhugh called on the St. Clair family for tea. Was love in the air?

For those who do only read this column for reports on one particular couple, Mr. Wrenwhistle and Mr. Barnes also called on the St. Clairs for tea, and made a thorough circuit of social calls with their respective mothers. It would seem there are high hopes that these gentlemen will not only be the darlings of society, but leaders of the fashionable world.

Other news of note: Miss Eliza Fairfax eloped with Colonel Atwater earlier this week. Considering the fact that Miss Fairfax is set to inherit and Atwater has been pining for the lady for the past twenty years, and both are of age, no one is remotely shocked or scandalized by this. We are all just relieved they finally figured themselves out. It is true that a special license would have been less dramatic and brought about the same result, but it is also true that drama is far more interesting.

Mr. Ravenwing has not been gracing the arm of any particular gentlemen this week. Some may have been hoping that Mr. Marigold would prove a potential suitor. Alas, Mr. Marigold was last seen calling on Mr. Brooks. Such goings on and the Season has barely begun.

Unmarried hopefuls continue to trickle into our fair city. Many have written to this writer with commentary about the youngest Wrenwhistle getting married before two of his older siblings. To which we say, we were clearly wrong about Mr. Wyndham Wrenwhistle being the least appealing one in his family. Will anyone win another Wrenwhistle heart? Will this be the year Mr. Cyril Thompson and Miss Harriet Thackery realize what everyone else has been seeing for years?

Either way, we can all be sure to be thoroughly entertained.

Your esteemed editor,

Torquil Pimpernel-Smith

CHAPTER 52

WYN

WYN STRUGGLED MIGHTILY to calm his magic on the short ride back to his house. Their joint experience underneath the branches of the willow tree in particular had sent his entire body into a buzz that was overwhelming in all the best ways. He was intensely aware that Roger sitting next to him wasn't helping in the slightest, but as with so many other things that had to do with Roger Barnes, he found that he didn't mind much at all.

Hearing his mother's voice was what finally helped him sober up a bit. Wyn and Roger entered the family sitting room and were inundated with bright flowers, swirling fabrics, dozens of color swatches, decorated and undecorated cakes, and anything else one could ever imagine as a part of the wedding planning process.

"Boys!" Mrs. Wrenwhistle called in a singsong voice as she crossed the room. A brief expression of horror passed over her face as she eyed their dirty clothes, but she quickly recovered with a forced smile. "The latest copy of the *Tribune* has just been delivered. I think you'll be most happy to read what's been printed." She waved the pamphlet around in Wyn's direction. He took it and immediately handed it off to Roger as he peered uneasily around the room.

"What is this?" he asked his mother. He kept his voice low as to not offend any of the people who were working diligently all around the room, smiling at him in that *I'm-so-grateful-to-have-your-business* type of way they always did around his family.

Mrs. Wrenwhistle glanced around as if she had no idea what he was talking about. "They're all here for the wedding preparations, of course. That is the plan we agreed upon for today, is it not?"

"Yes, but I did not realize it meant an entire circus would be set up in our family room," he managed, a tight smile hiding the way he was gritting his teeth.

"Don't be silly, Wynnie," she soothed. "This will help everything go much faster. There's nothing like seeing real examples to make the final decisions that much easier. Come along, let's start with the colors."

Much the same as the last time he'd sat with his mother to talk about wedding details, Wyn slowly melted into a puddle of despair. The only thing holding him together was Roger's presence. And, to his astonishment, Roger actually seemed to find some pleasure in their tasks, all the way up until it was time to be measured for their new wedding attire.

"Oh," he said with great uncertainty, looking up at Wyn in a desperate sort of way. "I was not aware we would be required to purchase new clothes for the occasion. I—that is, my siblings both wore the finest outfits they already owned on their wedding days."

Wyn's mother laughed flippantly. "How adorable."

"Fae traditionally wear something specially made for the ceremony," Wyn explained quietly. "Do not worry about the cost. It will be taken care of."

Screens were erected for modesty as Wyn and Roger were forced to strip to their last layer of clothing in the middle of the chaos, though it did little good since both men stood taller than the height of the panels, one significantly more than the other. Wyn stood with his back turned to Roger, as he thought he might appreciate the gesture.

"I'm thinking we want shades that compliment one another but do not match entirely," Wyn's mother thought aloud as she stood between them, rifling through a basket of fabric samples. "Light colors that complement the season. You know the trees at the estate will be in their full autumn splendor," she gushed.

"Mother, do not even *think* of dressing me or my husband up as a gourd on our wedding day," Wyn warned in all seriousness, watching as a tailor's apprentice measured around his waist. "I would sooner show up nude. And do not think I won't."

"I believe you," she sighed dramatically. "What do you suggest, then?"

Wyn turned as he was directed, and his focus immediately went to where Roger had his arms stretched out, looking miserable.

"Roger, what do you think?" he asked easily.

Roger's head popped up. "What?"

"What colors would you like us to wear?" Their eyes met across the space between them, and then Roger quickly looked away.

"Oh," he mumbled. "P-perhaps we could each pick? For one another? And let it be a surprise?"

Wyn's mother gasped, her hands clasping beneath her chin. "Now *that* is a fantastic idea, my dear."

As soon as the measurements were finished and they'd dressed again in their own clothes, all of which Mrs. Wrenwhistle had sent off to be treated with cleaning spells, it was time for them to taste the cake. Plate after plate of various flavors had been laid out for them to try, but Wyn was certain that nothing was as delicious as watching Roger take each bite, savoring it as though it were the last piece he'd ever be allowed to eat.

"Any favorites?" Wyn asked with a grin, handing away his plate and fork to prepare for the next.

"All of them," Roger said with confidence. Wyn chuckled.

"Unfortunately, I think we're expected to narrow it down a bit more than that. Although, I suppose it is our special day. If you really want all of them, I'll see that you get them."

"I'm only joking," Roger assured him, though the look in his eye said otherwise. "I don't know how I could possibly decide, though. Even the flavors I wouldn't normally pick are toothsome."

Wyn reached for his tea, which had conveniently been served as they'd sat down for their tasting. He took a slow sip and considered their options.

"What flavors did Frederica and Bernard have?"

"I've never seen a wedding cake that wasn't mashed full of fruit and alcohol," he said with a grimace. "That's what they both had."

Wyn hummed. "Do you think it would be important to your family and our other human guests that we serve fruitcake, as well?"

Roger took a sip of his own tea and tipped his head side to side as he gave it some thought, before he shrugged. "As you said, it's our day. I think we're allowed to pick and everyone else has to be all right with it."

Wyn smirked. "My, Mr. Barnes, look at you thinking of yourself for once."

Roger snorted and set his tea down, ready for another piece of cake. "I cannot deny that food is very important to me. If you're saying I'm allowed whichever flavor I want, then I am prepared to take full advantage. And it most decidedly will not be fruitcake."

By the time both of them had consumed enough sweets to make their hands shake, they were tasked with one final decision: the flowers. Every prominent florist in London had set up a display for them to scrutinize, each of them presenting their best work in hopes of being selected for an elaborate fae wedding that would no doubt be talked about for years to come.

As much as Wyn disliked seeing all of the cut flowers, he would never be able to ignore the beauty of them. He took his time looking at each bouquet, each bundle, his magic reaching toward the blooms as though they were long lost friends reunited once again.

Wyn brought his hand up to some of the delicate petals, his fingertips barely touching them. The tingling in his chest intensified as he reached a peony the color of a sunset. He plucked the flower out of the bunch with care and brought it to his nose.

"A fine choice, Mr. Wrenwhistle," the florist said, smiling brightly. "Those are a favorite of mine for weddings."

"Yes, I can see why," he mused, turning to where Roger was lingering near some roses. "Do you like this color?"

He adjusted his spectacles and came closer.

"Most striking, indeed," Roger observed. Wyn recognized the tone as one he used when he was genuinely interested in something; soft and open and curious. "Quite like a peach."

Without warning, something sharp twisted in Wyn's chest, and then faded in a warm way down to his stomach. He recovered quickly, but he found that he could do nothing to ease the grin that threatened to hurt his cheeks. With a step, he closed the distance between them and used the flower to tap Roger gently on the nose, fighting every muscle in his body to keep himself from following the gesture with a kiss—a curious and somewhat alarming notion.

"These will be fine," Wyn said to nobody in particular. As everyone else around them started into action, packing up and clearing out as though they were being timed, Wyn simply stood and stared at Roger, and Roger stared back, and Wyn was certain that something terrible was happening to him.

"Do you feel quite well?" Roger asked finally, barely above a whisper.

"I think I've had too much cake," he whispered back. "My stomach is… doing strange things."

Roger's face pinched in concern. "Are you going to be sick? Perhaps you should lie down."

Wyn swallowed thickly, coming back to himself as he blinked and finally managed to look away from the warm, comforting brown of Roger's eyes. "Yes," he said, still whispering. "If you'll excuse me."

Wyn's heart raced as he took the steps to his room two at a time, shutting the door behind him and locking it securely. He nearly stumbled to his sofa by the double doors and collapsed onto it on his back, eyes fixed on the ceiling overhead. When he realized there was something in his hand, he lifted it to find that he was still holding the peony.

Wyn brought the flower up, brushing the petals gently over his lips. With his other hand resting on his stomach, a desperate attempt to settle all the fluttering going on, he decided it wasn't something terrible happening to him, but something terrifying.

He was falling helplessly in love with Roger Barnes.

CHAPTER 53

ROGER

Roger stood awkwardly in the middle of the rapidly emptying room, winded from everything that had happened that day. The fae magic lessons had been unexpectedly exhausting. He'd enjoyed the sensation of being held by Wyn a little more than he probably should. He'd liked the way Wyn's long fingers felt spread over his stomach and the warmth of Wyn's breath on his cheek. Then, for the wedding planning, there had been so many moments of *something*—something he was too scared to delve into because he wanted it a little too much.

When Wyn had lightly tapped him on the nose with the flower, Roger could have sworn the man was about to close the distance between them with a kiss. That was surprising in and of itself, but doubly surprising was that Roger really wished Wyn had done it. As much as Roger admired the beauty of others, he had never *desired* before. That is, until Wyn. Wyn describing his favorite stream in the country, Wyn crouching as he watched Roger place a fire spell, Wyn laughing during a particularly energetic dance progression, and Wyn kissing his knuckles in the opera box had unlocked a yearning in him that he'd never before felt.

He was a little frightened by the new sensation—mostly because he was completely sure he would never have the courage to do anything about it. After all, how could he be sure Wyn felt anything other than friendliness toward him? How could he be sure it wasn't simply the effects of being thrown together in such a way, working together for long hours, and learning to trust each other as they had? The truth was, he couldn't be sure. So although he knew his own admiration for Wyn's beauty and grudging fascination with his intelligence had both grown into something brighter, warmer, and gentler, it felt too bold to assume Wyn felt the same.

It was strange, really, to wonder if his future husband had anything more than fond regard for him. Then again, it was about the best situation he would have ever thought possible. So even if playful affection with flowers never turned into something deeper, perhaps it would still be enough.

As Roger bid Mrs. Wrenwhistle farewell, collected his coat, and left to walk back home, he allowed himself to turn the matter over and over in his mind. By the time he reached his parents' house, it had occurred to him that while he might never have the courage to express his feelings for Wyn in the typical ways, there were other ways too.

He thought back to Wyn's soft *I'd like that* in response to Roger's sugges-tion that they work together on a second project. He walked up to his study and gently pulled the willow branch out of his coat pocket and placed it on his desk. The wedding planning had disrupted the thoughts that had begun percolating, but now that he was back in the quiet of his own space, those thoughts bubbled back to life.

For once, they had no evening plans, so he took advantage of the oppor-tunity to start working. He began pulling out books, marking pages, and scribbling down notes and ideas. He made a running list of spells that could be done with only willow leaf or willow bark. He went to bed late and woke up early to continue his work. He stopped only when his father came in and told him to eat some breakfast.

After breakfast, he finally landed on a good spell to try. Breeze spells were tricky as they had to be tightly controlled, but they were typically less powerful than wind spells. Even with a raw ingredient, he hoped the gentler spell would cause little disruption in the drawing room. He placed the willow branch on a large sheet of spellpaper. He had a few more hours before Wyn was due to arrive, so he kept writing down notes. He tweaked the branch so it was laying horizontally along the paper, and researched that. Then he changed it so it was in a spiral with the tip of the branch in the center and the thickest part of the branch on the outside. That looked better. Slowly and carefully, he began writing formulas, calculations, and sigils.

He was so caught up in his work that he didn't even hear Wyn enter the room.

"What's this?"

Roger jolted in alarm and then breathed a sigh of relief that the jolt hadn't caused him to ruin his work. He sat back on his heels and turned to Wyn. "I know we said we'd work on it later, but I couldn't get your theory out of my mind."

Wyn looked at the spell that was in mid-preparation. "You want to experiment with the willow branch?"

"Yes."

Wyn stepped around the paper. "How do you intend to accommodate the increase in power?"

Roger took a deep breath. "Well...that's where you come in."

Wyn tilted his head slightly, a silent invitation for Roger to continue.

"I'm thinking that you can feel the magic I'm using and tell me if I need to do anything differently."

"But I won't know what you need to do."

"You can tell me if it's unbalanced or too powerful."

"And you'll be able to correct it as you go?"

Roger nodded. "I think so."

"You *think* so," Wyn repeated. He rubbed the space between his eyebrows. "I'm very appreciative of your enthusiasm, Roger, but I had rather expected there to be more...I don't know, research or something beforehand. How will you know how much more power you're working with?"

Roger stood and retrieved the jar of powdered willow bark. He pulled out his handkerchief and said, "Hold out your hand, please." Wyn did, looking very wary. Roger placed the handkerchief on his hand and then dumped some of the bark powder into the handkerchief. "How does that feel in comparison to the branch?"

Wyn heaved a sigh. "It's difficult to tell. My magic can't feel this as easily."

Roger poured half the jar into the handkerchief.

Wyn closed his eyes in concentration. "I can feel it, but it definitely feels weaker."

Roger poured the entire contents of the jar. "Now?"

"Still weaker, but a little closer." He opened his eyes and gave a sound of exasperation. "What the devil are you going to do with this mess?"

Roger carefully folded the corners of the handkerchief together and picked it up out of Wyn's hand. "I'm going to weigh it." He was feeling excited as he weighed it and then adjusted his calculations and formulas accordingly.

Wyn squatted beside him, intent. "What is the spell?" he asked in a low tone.

"Breeze spell," Roger answered, bending over the paper. "It's like a wind spell but…er…gentler."

"Gentler when you use powder."

"Yes."

Wyn was silent for a long moment. "I think it might be wise to wait until your father returns—"

Roger sat up. "No! We can—" He broke off and took a breath. "I think we can do this. Together. You can feel my magic. You can feel this branch's magic. And if anything goes wrong, you can just flip the paper."

Wyn blinked at him. "Flip the paper. That's it?"

"Yes! It will disrupt the spell if I haven't already canceled it."

Wyn sighed and looked at the paper intently. "You've done a lot of work in preparing for this. You really think it will work?"

"I really want it to."

"That is not remotely the same thing." He hesitated. "Very well. But I'm flipping the paper at the first sign of danger."

"Wonderful," Roger said. "Ready?"

Wyn settled on the floor.

Then Roger cast the spell.

CHAPTER 54

WYN

THE MOMENT the spell was cast, mayhem struck. Every book, piece of paper, and other assorted magical item Roger had piled onto his desk was shoved to the floor with an unbridled gust of air. Wyn's arms shot up to cover his head protectively as Roger screamed beside him.

Footsteps running down the hall ended in a most startled address from Notley. "Sirs!" he panted. "Is everything all right?"

Wyn uncovered his face and looked over at Roger, who had fallen nearly flat on his back, both hands clamped over his mouth in surprise.

"Yes," Wyn managed, scooting over on his knees to help Roger. "Apologies, Notley, everything is fine." The valet said nothing else, so Wyn proceeded to wrap one arm behind Roger's shoulders and guide him up to a sitting position. When he was sure Roger wasn't going to topple back over, Wyn grabbed his chin and made sure Roger was looking him in the face. "Too powerful," he said sternly.

Roger nodded and Wyn let him go. He got to his feet and proceeded to pick up the scattered papers and tumbled books. When Roger joined him, Wyn stuck his hand out in caution.

"Be careful of the broken glass," he warned gently. "Allow me to handle this. You go back and fix your calculations."

"Y-you want us to try again?" Roger asked incredulously. "After that?"

"How else will we learn?"

As Roger began fiddling with the markings on his paper, Wyn rolled his sleeves up to his elbows and crouched over the mess, using two pieces of double-folded paper to sweep up the shards of glass. He pulled his handkerchief out of his pocket and began sopping up whatever it was that had spilled from the broken jar, careful not to get any of the mystery liquid on his fingers.

Wyn stole a careful glance at Roger. He hid his grin when Roger quickly averted his eyes. *Caught you*, Wyn thought, even though he was just as guilty.

After tucking away as many loose items as he could into the open packing crates around the room, Wyn sank to his knees next to Roger again and studied the spellpaper. He hadn't the slightest idea what was different from before, as it had already looked senseless when he arrived, but all the pencil scratching he'd heard as he cleaned must've been for something.

"So my first calculations were a bit off," Roger started, and Wyn had no chance of stopping the snort of laughter that escaped him. Roger gave him the most pitiful frown. Wyn shook his head and bit his lip hard to make himself stop.

"I'm sorry," he said, forcing his expression into something more outwardly neutral. "Go on."

Roger gave a heavy sigh before he looked down at the paper again. "I've adjusted what I can without rendering the spell basically useless. It should allow us to encourage the strength of the magic to grow, rather than needing to be, er…" Roger paused.

"Restrained?" Wyn offered.

"Yes," Roger agreed, still sounding disappointed with himself over the first failed attempt.

Wyn took a deep breath and squared his shoulders a bit. "All right. Let's have it, then."

Roger sat up straighter beside him, cleared his throat, and cast the spell.

At first, there was nothing. Both men sat perfectly still, their eyes darting around the room looking for a fluttering curtain or whirl of dust motes in the afternoon sun, anything to indicate a breeze.

Wyn closed his eyes and tried to seek it out with his magic. Perhaps he had to find it first before he could help give it more life. He felt the tug in his chest toward the willow branch where it was curled up on the paper. He felt the whisper of life in the rest of the magical ingredients tucked inside the crates. He felt Roger's magic; the richness of his hope, the tang of his lingering embarrassment, and something else that was sweet and light and invigorating enough to tilt Wyn's focus away from their experiment.

Roger gasped when the air finally swirled around them, ruffling their hair and caressing their faces. Wyn opened his eyes and it stopped.

"Could you feel it?" There was an excitement in Roger's voice that he so badly did not want to crush.

Wyn winced a bit as he looked up at the open window nearby. "I think that was mine."

"Oh," Roger said, crestfallen.

Wyn stood gracefully and went to the window, pulling it shut. "I couldn't feel anything other than the willow branch itself," he explained. "And I could feel your magic, but nothing you'd cast out."

"It was too weak, then."

"I think you should try writing it out on a new spellpaper," Wyn said, sitting down with his legs crossed this time, matching Roger. "No extra scribbles or markings to distract from the exact result you're aiming for. Make it just a bit stronger and we'll see what happens."

Roger laid out a new paper, just as large as the other had been, and arranged the willow branch in another spiral. As Roger began to copy his work from the previous setup, Wyn leaned forward to adjust one of the long, slender leaves that was tucked under the others at an awkward angle.

"There," Roger said as he completed the sigil in the corner closest to him.

"Much better," Wyn told him with a gentle smile. "Nature appreciates when things are simple."

Roger gave him a weak grin in return and shuffled up onto his knees. Wyn leaned his weight back on his hands to watch Roger cast a third time. His breathing was heavy with anticipation. Wyn wanted to reach out to him with a supportive touch or an encouraging word. Anything to reassure him.

Roger cast the spell.

The air was still.

Then he could have sworn he heard the faintest sound of leaves rustling, before a gentle breeze passed between them.

Roger turned his head to meet Wyn's gaze, his eyes wide.

"Was that—"

"No," Wyn breathed, his smile growing. "That's you."

Wyn's magic fizzled brightly as he reached out as carefully as he could, feeling Roger's cast magic as it wound its way around the cluttered space, weaving through the furniture and boxes.

"Give it more," Wyn instructed. Roger picked up his pencil and immediately started drawing new lines on the spellpaper. The magic responded beautifully, gaining strength as it had been told to do. Roger leaned even closer to the paper then, making more changes until the entire room was caught up in the breeze spell.

When he started to write something else, Wyn reached for his wrist and pulled Roger up with him. They stood facing each other, hair and cravats blowing like a storm was rolling in. Then Roger smiled his magic smile.

"We did it," Roger said, and Wyn heard the wet emotion in his voice.

The sound struck Wyn in a big way. Before he could stop himself, he wrapped his arm around Roger's shoulders and brought his other hand to the back of his head. He pulled Roger close and set his cheek against the man's hair.

"Well done, Mr. Barnes," he whispered, allowing himself a small pleasure as he closed his eyes and nuzzled ever so slightly into their embrace.

The touch lit Wyn up inside, but he only allowed it to last for a moment longer before he stepped back and realized that the air had gone still again. That was the last thing he needed. He took another step back and then went to open the window again.

Wyn braced his hands on the sill and breathed deeply in an attempt to clear away the emotions clouding his mind. Heat crept up his neck as he realized what he'd just done.

No, he'd made that choice.

It was something else making his whole body warm.

It was the way Roger had returned his embrace, without hesitation.

It was the way Roger's magic had felt mixed with his own.

It was Roger.

CHAPTER 55

ROGER

ROGER COULDN'T TAKE his eyes off Wyn, standing with his hands against the window sill and his face turned up toward the sky. In truth, he would have liked the embrace to have lasted longer. He would never have expected that being pulled into Wyn's arms would feel so *right*. And yet, when he'd felt Wyn rest his cheek against his head and Roger had breathed in deeply enough to catch a hint of lavender soap, it had felt like home.

Strangely, Roger would have supposed that the feeling of home would have felt more safe and familiar like his family's country estate, or dark and snug like his old flat. But Wyn, who opened every window he found, who brightened a room with his waistcoats alone, and who had just encouraged Roger to recast a spell that had been proven to be difficult, was hardly safe, familiar, dark, or snug.

Roger's brain snagged a bit on that last thought. "We recast the spell," he murmured.

Wyn shifted a little so he could look at Roger over his shoulder. "What?"

Roger bent down to look at his spell again. "Human spells can't be recast," he explained. "The magic gets used up too completely."

"In treated ingredients, you mean," Wyn said. He pivoted so he was leaning against the window frame, one ankle elegantly crossing over the other.

"Yes," Roger replied slowly. "I suppose treating them takes a lot of their magical power."

"I imagine so, considering how difficult it is for me to feel them."

Roger touched a fingertip to the willow branch. "Can you still feel anything in this?"

"Oh, yes."

Roger looked up at the light tone. "You mean it still feels strong?"

Wyn frowned a little in concentration. "Perhaps…not quite as strong as it had been on the tree, or when we first started. But I'd say there's still a considerable amount of power left."

"More than the entire jar of powdered willow bark?" he pressed.

"Decidedly more."

Roger couldn't hold back the laugh that escaped.

The corner of Wyn's mouth lifted.

"I'm sorry," Roger said. "I just—do you realize what this means?"

"Tell me," Wyn said, his smile widening a little.

"This changes human magic as we know it." Roger stood and paced, too excited to stay still. "This means that we can not only use our materials more ethically, but more efficiently too. We can reuse the same items multiple times. And yes, I know we have a great deal more research and experimentation before we get too excited—before *I* get too excited but…"

He paused in front of Wyn and put his hands on the other man's chest. "I was worried that no one else would be interested in this new project. I thought this might only be a change I make for my own magic. But recastability changes everything. It means we might be able to get more humans to move away from treated ingredients too. We could revolutionize the way humans do magic all over the world!"

He realized his hands were still on Wyn's chest and he quickly pulled them away, clasping them together to keep himself from touching Wyn or gesticulating overmuch. "I'm sorry. I tend to get carried away when I get excited. It's just that I'm usually doing this sort of thing alone. This is the first time I've ever experimented alongside another person. So my excitement is usually experienced in private."

Wyn reached out and wrapped his hand gently around Roger's wrist. "You don't need to apologize for being excited. But, did you say you had planned to change the way you do magic?"

"Well, yes."

"Even if this recastability hadn't been part of it?"

"Yes?" Roger was confused. Was Wyn upset by that?

Wyn stared at him for a moment. "So you were planning to change the way you do magic, even though it might have limited you?"

"Well, yes, of course."

"Why?"

Roger blinked. He'd thought that would be obvious. "You said it physically pains you sometimes when I do magic. I have no desire to cause my husband pain every time I do a spell. That-that sounds dreadful."

Wyn gave a soft smile and his thumb rubbed lightly over the inside of Roger's wrist. "I would never have asked you to do that."

Roger shrugged. "Quite frankly, that was the part I was least worried about in terms of this whole project. I've been thinking about it since the Park yesterday and I was committed to testing your theory, but I wasn't sure if we could do anything substantial with that information. I mean, I expected some people to be open to making the attempt—my family, for instance, are all very academically minded when it comes to magic, so persuading them to try a new way of magic for the sake of science and protecting nature would have been easy. But—"

Wyn squeezed Roger's wrist slightly. "Thank you," he said, his voice hushed.

"Don't mention it," Roger whispered. It hadn't felt like the correct thing to say, but Wyn didn't seem to mind.

Then a knock at the door made them both jump. The door swung open and Roger's mother poked her head in. She smiled at them. "Sorry to intrude. Are you staying for dinner, dear? We'll be eating a little early tonight so we can arrive at the ball on time."

Wyn glanced at the clock. "*Fuck*," he breathed, so only Roger could hear. He added, louder, "Very kind of you, Mrs. Barnes. But I ought to be going. We were invited to the dinner beforehand."

Roger's mother seemed unsurprised. "Will Roger be joining you or should he come with us?"

"We'll come collect Roger on our way," Wyn answered.

"Wonderful." With that, his mother left.

Wyn straightened and dropped his hand from his grip on Roger's wrist. "I'll see you in an hour."

"With the way you dress? I doubt it."

ALTHOUGH HE COULDN'T PUT his finger on how, Roger felt as though something important had changed when Wyn helped him into the carriage two hours later. He might have attributed it to his own feeling of giddiness at the prospect of another evening of dancing with his betrothed. Or he might have blamed it on the embrace they'd shared, or the way Wyn had held his wrist, or the way Wyn had whispered *Well done, Mr. Barnes*. But when he sat down beside Wyn in the carriage and they shared a glance as the carriage rattled down the street, he knew that Wyn felt it too, whatever it was.

Dinner was an elegant affair, filled with gentle clinking of silverware against china and polite murmurs of conversation. Roger and Wyn sat together and whispered jokes about Roger's relief at the lack of salad, whether Wyn's coral waistcoat was, in fact, superior to his salmon one (Roger said he couldn't discern a difference between the two, but Wyn was adamant that not only was there a difference, but that one was decidedly better), and whether they ought to exceed their record of dances for the evening. Wyn was apparently taking the idea as a personal challenge.

Roger had always felt out of place in the upper echelons of society. With his father's position on the Council, they were invited more often than their modest wealth would normally permit. But with Wyn at his side, lifting his aristocratic nose at Roger's commentary on cabbage, arching an eyebrow as he described the virtues of navy-colored embroidery, and grinning cheekily at Roger's flustered response to the idea of five dances, the evening felt bizarrely normal. He could do this. Wyn had helped him do what most humans considered the unthinkable: using a raw, untreated ingredient. Perhaps with Wyn he could do anything? *They* could do anything together.

As such, when dinner was finally at an end and the rest of the guests trickled in for the ball, Roger was feeling peculiarly buoyant. The sight of Harriet dashing across the room to greet him, with Anthea and Cyril at her heels, only added to his happy mood.

"You two have been outrageously evasive since your engagement was announced," Harriet commented.

"We've been very busy—" Roger began.

"It's incredible," Cyril added. "You two are the most talked about people in London."

"Yes," Harriet said. "I'm out of breath from reminding everyone that I've known you for years. The promise of secrets has gotten me three invitations already."

"What secrets?" Roger asked warily.

Harriet only gave a sly grin.

Anthea rolled her eyes. "She still thinks it's impressive that she saw you sleep walking at that house party three years ago. As if that's anything exciting—"

Harriet hushed her, looking around as if they'd been overheard.

Roger laughed. "I'm not sure anyone cares about that, Harriet."

"Do you sleep walk?" Wyn inquired quietly.

Roger shrugged. "Occasionally. I've tried tonics for it but—oh! Is that going to be an issue? Goodness, it never even occurred to me. I *am* sorry. It doesn't happen very often. But perhaps we can—"

"Perhaps you can keep a tight hold on him, Mr. Wrenwhistle," Anthea teased. "You know, for safety."

Roger felt himself blush. "Perhaps we should dance."

"Absolutely not," Harriet said, stepping between them and tucking her hands around each of their arms. "I have declared this an emergency situation. We've barely seen you at all," she added to Roger. "And *you* are practically a stranger," she said to Wyn. "You must stay and entertain us for the whole of the night."

"Good gracious, Harriet," Cyril murmured. "They can still dance."

"You want them to add to the mystique, don't you?" Anthea asked.

Harriet looked conflicted. "Oh, all right. Dancing will be permitted."

"Very generous," Roger muttered.

They settled into a corner of the room, as they usually did when they were all together. Although Roger kept glancing nervously at Wyn. Was he enjoying himself? Was he getting overwhelmed? Were Roger's friends, perhaps, a bit too much? At one point, Wyn saw one of his anxious glances, and put a hand on Roger's back. Roger felt immediately calmer and then he began wondering when a single touch from Wyndham Wrenwhiste caused his entire body to relax. All in all, he was most distracted.

Once the next set ended, Wyn raised his voice a little and said, "I'm going to dance with my fiancé now, with your permission," he added to Harriet.

She giggled. "Well, when you ask so nicely."

They took up their places for the next dance.

"I don't seem to recall you being this nervous around your friends at the garden party," Wyn observed.

"Well, I-I wasn't," Roger admitted.

Wyn raised an eyebrow. "Complete honesty, remember?"

Roger gave a small huff as he circled behind his neighbor. "It's just," he began when he was facing Wyn again, "that I would like you to be enjoying yourself too. I don't want you to feel like you need to be with us...if you're uncomfortable." Wyn frowned a little. "I mean," Roger hastened to add, "if you need to step away, I want you to know that you can. Or if you want me to come with you, I can. Or—"

"Roger," Wyn said quietly as he took his hand for the next step. "Stop fretting. I'll tell you if I need some fresh air."

"You will? Oh good. Promise?" He had no idea why he was belaboring the point.

Wyn looked amused. "If you like."

"Good," Roger replied.

After the set was over, they returned to Roger's friends.

"You two look impossibly romantic," Cyril commented.

"Perhaps you can tell us all about how you fell in love when we go out on Sunday," Harriet said.

"What?" Roger asked.

"Oh, that's *right*," Harriet drawled. "I forgot I haven't seen you in years at this point."

"I'm pretty sure I saw you last week," Roger pointed out.

"We're going to Vauxhall Gardens on Sunday and you must come with us. I'll brook no argument." She looked militant in the manner she always did when she was about to get her way.

"Oh," Roger said. "Er...I'm not sure. We have a number of engagements and I have a devil of a time keeping up with them." He looked up at Wyn.

"But you must come," she pressed, taking his hands. "My Uncle Felix will be there. You've met Felix. He's such a dear. And so much fun! He's going to play chaperone. He's promised we can rent a supper box, and we're going to take the boats, and then you two can dance even *more* if you really feel the need. Just think how exciting it will be!"

"Romantic," Cyril hissed. "You should be telling them it's romantic. Roger will never go if he thinks it will be exciting."

"Good lord," Anthea groaned. "Sometimes you act like you don't know old Rodge at all." She laid a hand on Roger's arm, even though Harriet was still gripping his hands. "It will be a very lovely evening and we're going to behave ourselves like civilized people," she went on with a glare at Harriet, "and I promise to make sure Harriet only drinks one glass of Arrack Punch. You two can dance under the lanterns while pretending you don't know us because Harriet and Cyril will be singing along to the orchestra."

It *did* sound fun, and just a little bit romantic, but Roger really didn't know what social engagements they'd committed to. He was worried about what Mrs. Wrenwhistle might say to her son if they canceled an invitation that they'd already accepted, let alone what *his* parents would say about an outing with only Harriet's Uncle Felix as chaperone.

But then Wyn's hand was on Roger's back again. "We'd be delighted to join," he said.

CHAPTER 56

WYN

ROGER LOOKED up at Wyn in surprise. "We would?"

Without even needing to ask, Wyn knew why Roger's reaction was laced with hesitation. He clearly wanted to spend the time with his friends. After all, Wyn had plucked Roger from his own social calendar without so much as an apology, and there must've been things he'd missed out on. He'd never once made any mention of it, which made Wyn think that the only reason he was sounding so torn over it was because of how badly he wanted to go.

"Of course," Wyn offered with a smile he hoped conveyed his sincerity.

Before Roger could even direct his attention back to his friends, Harriet was already bouncing excitedly; her firm grip on Roger's hands meant his arms joined in the celebration, as well. It felt like a good time to step away for a moment.

With his hand still on Roger's back, Wyn leaned down close to his ear and whispered that he would be back shortly, before he excused himself from the group and went searching for a quiet place.

He found what he was looking for in the form of a low bench in the back garden. A trellis covered in vines shielded him from the house, so he felt it was safe enough to remove his shoes and let his feet settle into the grass.

The past few days had been thoroughly overwhelming. Wyn could hardly recall what had happened on which day or where he had been at what time. All he knew for certain was that he'd spent more time with Roger in a couple of weeks than he'd spent with another person in his entire life, and somehow, he still wanted more.

Wyn eased himself off the bench and sat on the ground, moving so that he could lie down with his hands clasped behind his head, ankles crossed. He took a deep breath and let it out slowly as he stared up at the night sky.

How could he know for sure that what he was feeling for Roger was real?

Was it even possible to go from knowing a quiet yet somehow frustratingly annoying, know-it-all human boy to loving him as a quiet yet somehow frustratingly passionate, intelligent man? Was it possible for Roger to look past a lifetime of anger, jealousy, and hateful behavior and somehow come out on the other side not only as friends, but as something more?

And there was something more, Wyn was certain. Even with his own thoughts and emotions clouding his every waking moment, he knew by the way Roger showed more concern for him than any one person deserved. He knew by the way he'd felt that sweet undercurrent in Roger's magic that morning. He knew by the way that Roger never shied away from his touch, but often seemed to lean into it instead.

Could it be that he was in love with the man he was going to marry and was lucky enough to have that man love him back?

Wyn brought his hands from behind his head to cover his face.

Maybe a visit to Vauxhall Gardens was exactly what they needed.

Roger wanted to spend time with his friends. Wyn wanted to spend time with Roger. They had earned a break from their work, if their success earlier in the day meant anything at all.

His mother would be furious, of course. She had very little tolerance for changed plans, and though it usually didn't bother Wyn to refuse her at least a couple times during the Season, it felt entirely different knowing that Roger was a part of it now. He would never subject Roger to her venom if he could avoid it.

One of Wyn's hands slid up into his hair as he brought the other down to tug at the fashionable knot at his throat. He couldn't wait to be back in the country. Limited social engagements and no close neighbors meant far less ridiculous clothing to wear. As much as he enjoyed his selection of waistcoats—the coral was most *definitely* superior to the salmon—he found nothing quite as enjoyable as relaxing with his feet bare, his shirt untucked, and as little restriction from his wardrobe as possible.

Without permission, his trail of thoughts wandered back to Roger.

What did he like to wear when nobody of note was looking?

A little smirk tugged at his lips as he thought of the nightshirt Roger had been wearing the morning he'd delivered the news of their engagement.

Would he expect Wyn to wear something similar?

As he thought of what Roger had said amongst his friends, his smile grew even more. Would it be an issue if he was sleep walking? Wyn supposed the implications of that had been lost on him. Or perhaps it was more common for humans to always share a bed after they were married. Regardless, the fact that Roger's concerns had immediately gone to such a thing was telling.

"You sweet, innocent man," Wyn muttered to himself.

"Wyn?" came a harsh whisper, followed by the sound of a door being shut. "Are you out here?" Wyn tilted his head a bit to see Roger coming down the path toward him.

"Yes, I'm here," he said back. When Roger finally spotted him, he picked up a little speed.

"Why are you on the ground?" Roger asked with concern. "Are you hurt?"

"I needed to think for a bit," Wyn told him. He moved his hand from his cravat to his chest and simply gazed up at Roger, fighting the urge to invite him to lie down at his side. Roger sat on the bench instead.

"That seems uncomfortable," Roger mumbled.

"I quite enjoy it," Wyn said, uncrossing his ankles and pulling one leg up at the knee. Something almost playful crossed Roger's face in the low light.

"You get a lot of thinking done on your back, do you?"

Without missing a beat, Wyn chuckled and gave Roger a sly grin.

"Mr. Barnes, I daresay that's a question for *after* we're married."

Roger's mouth fell open and then shut again, his hands tightening on his knees. Wyn knew it was cruel to tease him so, but his reactions were irresistible.

"I came to see if you need anything," Roger said, changing the subject entirely. "A drink, perhaps?"

"I'm feeling better now," Wyn told him, sitting up. "Shall we try for another dance before the evening is over?" He brushed off the seat of his trousers once he'd put on his shoes and made it to his feet. Roger took his arm when he offered it. "We do have all of London here to impress tonight, after all."

CHAPTER 57

ROGER

IN THE END, they only danced three dances together. Mrs. Wrenwhistle seemed to approve of their restraint and his friends approved of the spectacle. When it was time to leave, Wyn helped Roger into his parents' carriage and reminded him that they were due to promenade in the Park the following day. Roger went to bed feeling satisfied with the day's events.

The next morning, Roger woke up and spent his breakfast and late morning doing more research for their new project. He listed out different spell options for the willow branch, trying to keep his handwriting tidy. Although after the second time he spilled honey-covered crumbs on his list, he gave up the notion of tidiness altogether.

He made a tentative list of items he might have around the house that could be used for spellwork. Then he made a list of items that would likely be easy to acquire. He was in the process of making a third list of items that would be fun to use *if* they could get them, when his mother told him it was time to meet up with the Wrenwhistles. He folded his lists and followed her out the door.

It was the kind of afternoon that hinted of autumn, with a crispness to the breeze and a promise of cooler weather. Roger couldn't help his grin when he saw Wyn standing under an oak tree with his mother, wearing a waistcoat in salmon-or-coral. Wyn bowed when they approached.

"Coral," he said with a pointed look.

Roger stifled a laugh. "It's very lovely," he said in a serious tone.

"I know. That's because it is the superior color."

Roger daringly traced a fingertip over the navy embroidery. "You were right about this part. The embroidery is stunning." He glanced up to see Wyn giving him that soft smile. "So I daresay I can concede the rest," he muttered, pulling his hand away.

Wyn caught his hand and looped it around his arm as he turned to lead them down the gravel path. "Good," he said. "I'm relieved to know my future husband can, in fact, be reasoned with."

They walked in silence for a few minutes. It was odd how quickly they had become accustomed to each other's company. So many things had become second nature: the feel of his hand around Wyn's arm, matching his steps to Wyn's, picking up conversations where they'd left off, and even the companionable silence they so often shared. He allowed himself some time to revel in that comfort.

Then he said, "I've been doing more research on our project."

Wyn's eyebrows lifted. "Do you ever relax?"

"Not when I'm excited about things."

"Duly noted. Tell me about your research then."

Roger pulled the bundle of notes out of his breast pocket and handed them over. "The first is a list of spells we can do with the willow branch, and the rest are ingredients I'd like to experiment with. I thought we could decide on the ingredients together and then I'd work on a list of spells for each."

"How thorough," Wyn muttered. He squinted and lifted one page up to his nose.

"Sorry," Roger muttered. "Honey."

Wyn gave him a sidelong glance. "I think I shall have to make a rule of food only being permitted at the table. You are a menace."

"Oh, hush," Roger laughed. "My working notes are always messy. I promise I'm more put-together when I present things."

Wyn gave a small smile.

"So what do you think of the lists, other than the honey?"

"I think it is a good start. I like the idea of trying different ingredients.

We might be able to gauge whether some of them are stronger than others, and so on."

"Yes, I was thinking that too," Roger said, excited.

"And I like the idea of trying different spells with the item we already have. It might also be worth noting how long it retains a usable source of magical power."

Roger nodded, wishing he could take notes.

"And I think it would be good to observe how the spells change based on your mood."

That took Roger by surprise. "My mood? Why should that signify?"

"Well, yesterday, you were nervous, especially after that first attempt. I imagine that had an impact. So I think it would be good to try it when you're feeling confident, happy, and so on." He looked thoughtful. "It would be good to know how your anger impacts it as well, but I don't think we should attempt anything when you're in that mood until we have a better handle on what we're doing."

"Hold on," Roger said. "Are you saying my mood impacted my ability to do magic?"

"Of course," Wyn replied. "Haven't you ever noticed that?"

Roger shook his head. "Does it impact yours?"

"In a very noticeable way, yes."

"Oh. And you've seen this with anger, nervousness, a-and—"

"Confidence, happiness, sadness…" He gave a sly grin. "Pleasure can impact it as well, of course. You know, of the *carnal* variety."

Roger sputtered and glanced around to see if anyone was listening. "You're having me on."

Wyn laughed. "I'm really not. But there are other conditions too. If I'm hungry or tired. If I'm feeling discouraged or overwhelmed. Our magic is a part of us. I'm not just talking fae magic. Your magic is a part of you. It stands to reason that how you feel changes how your magic comes out."

Roger could see what he meant. "I'll have to experiment…"

"Well, I would certainly enjoy being a part of that." He gave a smug smile. "Although perhaps some of those experiments ought to wait until after we're married."

Roger tugged at his cravat self-consciously. "Sometimes I think you say these things just to—Anyway, why don't you tell me how your emotions impact your magic? Although I wish I had a way to write all this down."

CHAPTER 58

WYN

WYN FOLDED Roger's notes and tucked them neatly into his pocket before he laid his hand over the one Roger had on his arm.

"If you want a thorough explanation, then I have to admit I'm fine with none of it being written down," Wyn said with a chuckle.

"Oh?" Roger looked up at him, and Wyn chewed on the inside of his lip as he considered where to start.

"It has taken me a very long time to get where I am today with my magic," he started. He kept his voice low so only Roger could hear, though he was aware that many people within earshot—namely his own family—were aware of Wyn's past when it came to such a topic. "My progress is something I've come to be proud of, but unfortunately my past is a bit of a different story."

Roger brought his free hand up to adjust his spectacles. "I remember, I think," he said quietly. "At least, I remember hearing what other people said about you."

Wyn hummed thoughtfully. "Yes, I know I had quite the reputation. My mother still loves to remind me of it."

This pulled a heavy sigh from Roger.

"That's very unfair," he grumbled. Wyn's mouth twitched into a little grin, and he stroked his fingers against Roger's on his arm.

"I probably deserve it. *Unimaginable bastard*, remember?" Wyn hoped the reference would make him laugh, but it didn't, so he continued. It was as good a time as any to give Roger some of his own honesty. "I hate London. I've always hated it. Being here makes me feel like a caged bird, desperate to escape but unable to fly, even when the door is open. My family's obligations to be here are so crushing to me, and for a long time all I knew how to do was take that out on everyone else."

"I had no idea," Roger said.

"My parents have never understood it, even when I've tried time and time again to explain it. Even my grandmother cannot offer her support, though it isn't for lack of trying. I'm just…different," Wyn said with a small shrug.

"Different how?" Roger's tone was so encouraging that Wyn felt his final protective walls starting to crumble.

Wyn thought for a moment as they continued down the gravel path. From the outside, it probably looked as though they were discussing something as simple as the weather. But Wyn wanted Roger to understand. He wanted, as he had never wanted before, for someone else to know what it felt like to hold such power with no way to let it free.

"When you cast your magic, what does it feel like?" Wyn asked finally.

"Feel like?" Roger frowned a bit. "I suppose I feel happy, usually…"

"No, I mean what do you *feel*? Inside."

Roger looked at him as though he were speaking another language, and Wyn sighed. That was the same reaction he always got. Wyn set his jaw and took in their surroundings. Certainly there was a way for him to make someone as empathetic as Roger Barnes understand. When his gaze settled on the sky, he had an idea.

"You've been outside in a storm before, haven't you?" Wyn asked.

"Well, not if I can help it, no," Roger said uneasily.

Wyn resisted rolling his eyes. "But you've at least watched out the window?"

"I don't particularly care for storms," Roger told him. Wyn made a sound of exasperation and pinched the bridge of his nose with his free hand.

"Roger, please tell me you have seen one thunderstorm in your life."

"I've seen one, yes," he agreed.

"Great. Then you've seen the clouds. The way that they differ from regular clouds? How they grow dark and heavy, full of rain and unspent energy?" Roger nodded, so Wyn went on. "And when the storm finally breaks, it's a rush of everything being released at the same time. The rain, the thunder, the lightning. The power of it all."

"Yes, it's very frightening," Roger said, and Wyn gave him a rueful grin.

"That is what my magic feels like, all day, every day." Wyn placed his hand on his chest, where he often felt it the most. "I am tasked with holding it inside so as to not disturb anyone while we're in London. But it speaks to me constantly. It knows what I want, what I'm thinking, sometimes even more clearly than I know myself." He paused then. "And it knows what I'm feeling."

Wyn took a deep breath and let it out slowly. The air changed around them, picking up the fallen leaves by their feet and swirling them around Roger in a pattern so neat they could've been tied on a string. Wyn let them fall away except for one, making it dance a bit before landing gently on Roger's arm.

Wyn couldn't decide what to make of Roger's expression, so he went on before he had to face the same confusion and uncertainty that everyone gave him when he tried to explain himself.

"When I was eight, I broke a very expensive vase on our first day back in London because I was so upset. It was entirely by accident. All I remember is yelling at my mother, bursting into tears, and then the hideous thing was shattered across the floor. I've broken doors off hinges. I've ripped important papers to shreds." Wyn's gaze fell as he thought of his next words. "I've played cruel tricks on innocent people because I was hurting."

He knew he did not deserve it, but Roger's hand squeezed supportively on his arm, and Wyn's chest swelled with warmth. He took a steadying breath so he could continue.

"Managing my emotions is something that I will likely have to work on for the rest of my life. I cannot explain how difficult it is sometimes to hold back a wave of anger or frustration *and* a wave of magic all at once. However, I must admit that certain changes in my life of late seem to be helping with this endeavor. And for that, I am grateful."

Roger was quiet for an impossibly long time as their stroll continued. Wyn could only imagine what was going through the man's head. Had he been *too* honest? Was Roger second-guessing their agreement to protect their reputations and follow through with the engagement? Was he deciding that Wyn wasn't worth the trouble, after all?

Just as Wyn was considering excusing himself from their promenade altogether, Roger peered over his shoulder to check how closely they were being followed. He must've been satisfied with what he saw, because the next thing Wyn knew, Roger was sliding his hand down Wyn's arm and lacing their fingers together.

"You are a magnificent creature, Wyndham Wrenwhistle," he said softly. "And I cannot wait to learn everything about you."

That sharp something twisted inside Wyn's chest again. He didn't care if the whole world was watching as he brought their joined hands up to press his lips to the back of Roger's fingers, slow and purposeful and full of meaning that Wyn wished so badly to put into words, but he wasn't sure how.

"Wyndham!" his mother called from behind them. "We'll be leaving soon!"

Wyn squeezed his eyes shut and placed a second short kiss to Roger's knuckles before he let their hands fall between them again. Reluctantly, he reached into his pocket to grab Roger's notes so he could return them.

Roger seemed equally as resistant to take the folded papers, but he took them and stuffed them away. This was the first evening all week that they wouldn't be spending together, and Wyn wasn't looking forward to sitting through dinner with his family without Roger to help him.

"Come home with me," Roger blurted, as if he'd known what Wyn was thinking. Wyn gave him a look of surprise, and Roger's face went pink. "I-I mean, if you haven't got other plans for tonight, we could do some more work?"

Wyn chuckled and pretended to give it some thought.

"Will you feed me dinner, as well?" he asked. "As I said before, nothing makes my magic go wild like an empty stomach."

Roger grinned up at him and nodded. "I'll ask Mother to have another place set for you."

"Very well," Wyn said on an exhale, feigning a great sacrifice. "Take me home, Mr. Barnes."

CHAPTER 59

ROGER

ROGER WAS FAIRLY sure an innocent statement such as *Take me home, Mr. Barnes* should not produce such a strong reaction in him. Then again, the twinkle in Wyn's eye suggested it might not be so innocent a statement and maybe the fluttering in his stomach was warranted. All he had really known was that he didn't want the conversation to end, he didn't want to walk away from Wyn—especially after he bared his soul so vulnerably—knowing he wouldn't see him again until the following day. And he was still eager to work on their new project.

When they walked into Roger's study, he opened the window and turned back to the room. Looking at the tangle of projects strewn across the desk and the floor struck him with a pang of guilt.

"Is something the matter?" Wyn asked. He looked around the room. "Is it worse than when you left it?"

That made Roger laugh. "No, I was just thinking about how I'm neglecting our other project. Is that—is that selfish of me?"

"I have a hard time imagining the word applying to you in any context."

Roger tugged at his waistcoat, feeling self-conscious from the compliment. "That's very kind of you to say. All the same, perhaps we *ought* to—"

Wyn laid a hand on his shoulder. "Roger, you have been working your-self to the bone for weeks, if not months, on a project that isn't even going to benefit you. Not to mention you have been trying to solve a problem that is actually other people's responsibility to solve. We will finish the rubric. It might not be done before the wedding, but the Council has already intimated that they will be willing to give us another extension if we need it." The hand on his shoulder moved to cup his cheek. "You are one of the kindest people I've ever met. It is not selfish of you to want to work on something you enjoy for a little while."

Roger swallowed. "Thank you," he whispered.

Wyn stroked Roger's cheek once with his thumb and then dropped his hand. "Now, where would you like to begin?"

Roger pulled out the bundle of notes from his pocket and looked through them. "Perhaps for today, we ought to continue with the willow branch. We can decide on our next ingredient later. That will give me time to research potential spells."

"Very good. What spell are we doing next then?"

"I made a list of spells that only require willow bark or willow leaf. Would you like to pick the next one?"

Wyn took the list and read through it. "This calming spell looks interesting. I'd be curious to see that. Or perhaps this shade spell. What does that one entail?"

"Oh, the shade spell can be done with any type of bark. It's meant to replicate the shadiness of a tree."

"That sounds intriguing. Do that one."

Roger breathed out in relief. "Good. I'm not sure I ought to do the calming spell until we have a better handle on this. For all I know, I might render us both unconscious."

Wyn laughed.

Roger laid out a fresh sheet of spellpaper and placed the branch on it in the same spiral placement he'd used the previous day. He pulled out the books he thought he might need, turning first to a list of common sigils. He knelt in front of the paper and bent over to scribble on it. He noticed that Wyn leaned against the desk behind him to watch.

"Can you explain what each marking is for?" Wyn asked.

"Y-yes," Roger stammered as he finished the one he was writing. He sat back on his heels. "This one is the primary sigil for the spell. It's the one telling the magic to cast shade." He shuffled a little to the side to write the next piece. "This one will take a moment." Wyn was patient as Roger carefully copied his work from the previous day. Then he leaned back and pointed. "This is the sigil and calculation I used yesterday that worked the best. They will essentially tell the magic how much power we need from it. So I'm using the last one we did."

"Is it exactly the same? Will it matter that some of the power is already gone?"

"It shouldn't," Roger replied as he reached for another book to double check. He spent a few minutes looking it up and then, satisfied, confirmed, "No, it won't make a difference. It is not a sum of the magic in the item, but a sum of the magic needed."

Wyn nodded. "I see."

Roger put the book down and then cast a speculative eye around the room. Then he leaned over and penciled in his measurements. "These are the dimensions I intend to cast for."

"What happens if you don't write that? Will it attempt to cast everywhere?"

"Thankfully not," Roger answered, shuddering a little at the thought. "It will just be confined to the paper. You remember the fire spell I showed you?"

Wyn nodded.

"I don't need to write dimensions for that one because the magic will stay confined to the paper."

"You wrote dimensions for the breeze spell then?"

"Yes. That's...er...probably why the entire house wasn't leveled or something," Roger said, feeling his face get hot.

"These buildings have loads of protection spells on them for just that purpose," Wyn said. "That wouldn't have happened."

"They do?" Roger asked, looking around with surprise. "Can you feel them?"

"It's like a vague feeling. Nothing too strong. But most places in London have them."

"Like the press building?"

"That one was...different."

Roger was intrigued, but there were more important things to worry about. "Right," he said. "This next one is the longest and the trickiest." He moved around to the opposite side of the paper and wrote it out carefully. "This sigil and corresponding calculation are more or less intended to mute whatever is left, so we don't get what happened with that first breeze spell. That's where I went wrong the first time. It was too strong because I didn't mute out enough of the branch's magic." He pointed to the first calculation he'd written. "That's where I went wrong the second time. I didn't request sufficient power because I was too nervous."

Wyn squatted beside the paper and studied the sigils with interest. "You often burn your other papers when you're done. Is there a reason you didn't burn yesterday's?"

Roger shrugged. "I wanted to keep track of what worked and what didn't. Burning the paper is mostly a way to tidy things up. As you've experienced, magic ingredients can go rather rancid, especially after they've been used. People used to believe that the magic would eat through the paper and into the surface beneath it but…well, that *can* happen, but we've learned enough to safeguard against that sort of thing. That's what things like the muting sigil and calculation are for. They will keep the magic from getting out of hand."

"Fascinating," Wyn murmured.

"I think that will do it," Roger pronounced. "Shall we?"

They both settled into sitting positions. Roger glanced at Wyn to make sure he was ready. At his nod, Roger cast the spell. They were blanketed in shadow. He was glad he had written the dimensions he had as there was light all around the edge of the room, so they weren't in total darkness.

Roger sighed. "I overdid it again."

Wyn chuckled. "Perhaps shade is not the right spell to use when you're needing to write corrections."

Roger jumped to his feet. "It will be if I get a candle." He ran to the door and opened it, unsurprised to find Notley nearby. "Fetch us a lit candle, will you?" Notley did so and Roger closed the door and carefully carried the candle to the center of the room. Then he bent over and began writing out adjustments to the calculations.

"It's easing up a little," Wyn reported.

Roger did one more adjustment, just to be safe. Then he glanced up at Wyn.

"Much better," he said. He looked around with curiosity. "It does feel a bit unbalanced. I'm not sure how but it's heavier to that side of the room."

Roger studied his paper critically. "It might be the way I have the branch laid out. The spiral seemed like the most even way to put it but it might not be entirely...let me try something." He picked up a book and hastily searched for the right formula. Then he bent over and wrote out a formula, taking care to write it in its smallest increment. "How is that?"

Wyn looked thoughtful. "A bit better. Can you do it more?"

Roger added to it.

"Better."

Roger sat up. "That took...well, I suppose it took as long as the first one but it felt less chaotic."

Wyn gave a hum and leaned back against his hands. "I imagine the nature of the spell we're doing helped."

Roger tried to ignore the fizz in his chest at the casual use of *we*. "Is there anything else that needs adjusting?"

"I don't think so."

Roger took down the spell. They blinked a little in the light. Wyn blew out the candle.

"Well done," he murmured.

"Thank you. I couldn't do it without you, you know."

"That doesn't make it any less impressive."

Roger fidgeted. The intensity of Wyn's expression mixed with the gentleness of his tone did things to his heart that he didn't know what to do with. It brought to mind their earlier conversation in the Park. Wyn had been so beautifully honest with him. But Roger felt as though he was still hiding parts of himself from his future husband, despite Wyn's honesty.

He bit his lip. "Do you remember our conversation earlier? I mean about emotions a-and other things?"

"I do."

"You mentioned something that...well, I feel I ought to tell you..."

Wyn straightened from his semi-reclined position. "Yes?"

"It's about what you said in terms of...um...p-pleasure?" he stammered, annoyed by how breathy his voice got at the word.

"Yes?" Wyn asked again, although now his voice was laced with amusement.

"Well, the thing is...I'm not sure I've...that is...well, you do know I have...erm...no experience with intimacy, yes?"

"You're human. I assumed as much."

Roger gave a small huff. "There are plenty of humans who have intimacy before marriage. It's just...it's usually done secretly because it's frowned upon."

"I see. But *you* haven't."

"N-no." He took a deep breath. This was something he'd never told anyone, not even his friends. He had always felt shy around the discussion of intimacy, in part due to human culture and his parents' preference for propriety, and in part due to a personal awkwardness about the subject. He knew there were people in the world who did not enjoy intimacy at all, or who never craved it. For years, he had supposed himself to be one of them, but there had been enough occasional fancies to make him doubt that assessment. Now with Wyn, he had no idea how to categorize himself.

He was worried about what Wyn might say in response but they were going to be married soon. It would be his business. It was time to bare a little more of his own soul. "Do you remember when I told you I find people of every gender attractive?"

Wyn nodded.

"Well, that was true. But...but when I say I find them attractive, what I really mean is that I think they are beautiful."

Wyn frowned a little. "Is there another meaning for the word?"

Roger twisted his hands together, uncomfortable with how poorly he was doing this. "I find people beautiful but my attraction is not...t-tangible. Not usually."

Wyn's eyes widened in understanding. "Oh. I see. This worries you?"

"Well, in terms of our previous conversation, I'm not sure how well I'll be able to experiment on that particular...erm...mindset."

Wyn gave a small smile. "Ah. Don't worry about that. Did you say it's not *usually* tangible?"

Roger felt his face get impossibly hotter. "It's happened a couple times over the years, with people I knew very well. I've long suspected that would be the extent of it. But I have noticed it happening more often...recently."

Wyn's smile grew. "Oh? Anything I should know about?"

Roger groaned and covered his face with his hands. "Why is this so difficult?"

Wyn chuckled and Roger heard him moving and then suddenly Wyn's fingers were circling Roger's wrists and gently pulling his hands away from his face. "Roger. I appreciate you telling me all of that. Truly. You don't need to be embarrassed by it. It doesn't change anything."

"I don't want you to be disappointed."

"Why would I be disappointed? If intimacy is not something you're interested in, I will understand. I'm perfectly capable of taking care of myself in that regard."

"I *am* interested," Roger muttered quietly, steadfastly looking at the floor. "And I only recently started feeling…anything. Which I probably shouldn't even tell you. But I did want you to know that I won't know…that is, I won't have any…"

Wyn lightly squeezed his wrists and Roger met his gaze. "I didn't expect you to have any experience. When the time comes, if you are interested, I'll take care of you."

Roger didn't have an appropriate response. He was sure he was staring at Wyn with his mouth open (again), but no words came out. No intelligible thoughts came through. Finally, he whispered, "Thank you."

Wyn smiled. "What are husbands for?"

A knock at the door made them both jump. "Mr. Barnes," Notley's voice came through the door. "Mrs. Barnes wishes you to know that dinner is almost ready and she'd like you both to come to the sitting room."

Roger let out a shaky breath as Wyn stood gracefully. Then he leaned down and helped Roger to his feet.

"They don't know about this…experiment yet," Roger said, gesturing at their work.

Wyn nodded. "I understand." He leaned forward and whispered, "It'll be our little secret."

CHAPTER 60

WYN

ROGER WAS ODDLY quiet through their short stint in the sitting room, and remained that way as they were called and seated for dinner. Wyn hoped it had more to do with all of the emotional unloading they'd done that afternoon rather than something he had done to change Roger's mood.

Had he said the right thing after Roger's confession? It had clearly been difficult for him to say, and somehow he'd seemed even more embarrassed after he let the words out.

Wyn supposed it would be a bit unsettling to have such concerns, considering the expectations of their rapidly approaching wedding day, which would naturally lead into their wedding night. That had been the last thing on Wyn's mind when their engagement was announced in the *Tribune*, but he couldn't deny that he'd since let the thoughts trickle in on occasion.

He glanced at Roger out of the corner of his eye as he accepted the dish of food being passed to him. Wyn couldn't relate to what Roger had described in the slightest. In some ways, his own experience had been quite the opposite. While he had no problem recognizing if he found someone attractive or not, it had rarely ever influenced his desire to be intimate with them. He desired the pleasure over the person, and if he happened to think they were beautiful, then all the better.

A small grin tugged the corner of Wyn's lips as he considered more of what Roger had said. Of course he'd hardly been thinking of himself as he admitted that he was worried Wyn would be disappointed. From the little Wyn knew about human marriages, it seemed that Roger should be the one disappointed being stuck with a rake of a man who had spent more than a decade giving in to his insatiable state of lust.

"Wyndham?"

Wyn looked up and realized everyone was staring at him. Before he could put any thought behind the fact that he'd been too distracted thinking about fucking her son to hear her question, Wyn cleared his throat and reached for his wine.

"Sorry, what was that?" he asked Mrs. Barnes, offering her a smile.

She returned the gesture with a quiet laugh. "I was only curious if you're looking forward to being back in the country so soon. It's early yet in the Season for a wedding."

"Oh, yes," he told her honestly. "If I could pack Roger up tonight and steal him away to hurry things along, I would." Roger looked at him in surprise. "Unfortunately, my mother would disown me if I ruined her planning in such a way, so I'm afraid we'll have to wait a little longer."

Roger's parents exchanged a knowing look that was laced with something soft and comfortable. Mr. Barnes reached out to rest his hand atop his wife's.

"It seems like only yesterday we were having the same trouble waiting," Mr. Barnes said fondly.

"I still have all of the letters we wrote back and forth during our engagement," Mrs. Barnes added. "There were so many. Some were no more than a few words in length, but oh how I looked forward to them."

"We simply could not get enough of one another." Roger's father bounced his eyebrows a few times. "But it was all worth the wait, in the end."

"Father, *please*," Roger scolded quietly.

Mr. Barnes laughed warmly and turned his attention back to Wyn.

"Speaking of being back in the country, why don't you tell us more about where it is you'll be *stealing* our son away to?"

Roger seemed ready to slide out of his chair and disappear under the table. Wyn started to reach out a supportive touch, hesitated a bit in fear of embarrassing Roger even more, and then decided to do it anyway, resting his hand on Roger's thigh. They exchanged a look, and Roger gave him a miserable little smile that caused Wyn's attention to linger on his mouth a second longer than he'd meant for it to.

"It's only a simple country house," Wyn started, returning his focus to his hosts. "A few outbuildings and some land. Near to my family's estate, but thankfully far enough away that it's not convenient for any of them to show up unannounced."

"You are far too humble for your own good, Mr. Wrenwhistle," Roger's mother tutted. "With nearly £3,000 a year, the property must be lovely."

Wyn felt Roger's leg jolt under his hand as he sputtered, coughing hard around a bite of his meal. Wyn's brow furrowed as he turned to make sure Roger was all right. Roger reached for his glass and drained the rest of his wine in a few strong swallows, panting after the last.

"Apologies," he managed, his voice a bit strained.

"Is it workable land?" Mr. Barnes continued like nothing had happened.

"Not currently, though there is potential. I would be satisfied to see it remain as it is. I've also already promised a portion of it to Roger's interest in keeping companion animals," he said, his faint grin returning. "I'm not entirely sure what the space requirements are for such a thing, but if it's anything like horses, then we could keep quite a few of them very comfortably."

"How wonderful," Mrs. Barnes said, directing it at Roger. "You've always said how much you'd enjoy that when you got married." She gave a little frown. "Sadly, both Roger's father and I experience severe reactions when we're around cats and dogs."

"Reactions?" Wyn asked cautiously.

"One step too close and it's itchy eyes, sneezing, the whole lot," Mr. Barnes explained. Roger must've noticed the growing concern on Wyn's face.

"That doesn't happen to everyone," he reassured him.

"I should hope not," Wyn said primly. "Otherwise I might have to reconsider my offer."

The four of them shared a laugh and lapsed into a comfortable silence as they ate. Wyn kept his hand on Roger's thigh, moving his fingers absently from time to time.

Eventually, the conversation picked up again with questions about the wedding, including who had been invited and Roger's final decision about the cake—lemon, of course. Roger's father almost avoided being Councilmember Barnes for the evening, but his curiosity seemed to get the best of him when he asked about how their project was coming along.

"We've only two spells left to sort out," Roger said. Wyn was glad to hear a hint of pride in his voice, rather than the heavier feelings he'd had about it earlier.

"Excellent," his father said with genuine enthusiasm. "What a productive time you've had since we arrived back in London. You've nearly secured yourself an accepted proposal *and* a spouse!"

"We're so proud of you," Mrs. Barnes added, her eyes a bit wet.

"I daresay one would've been impossible without the other," Roger said, his gaze falling to Wyn's hand.

"Improbable," Wyn corrected. When Roger looked at him, he grinned. Roger grinned back.

When the meal couldn't possibly be stretched any longer, Roger led Wyn to the foyer. Roger fidgeted while Wyn put on his coat and hat.

"My friends are calling on me in the morning for tea," he said quickly. "I don't think we'll have any time to work before our trip to Vauxhall. I... er...do you want to have tea with us?" Roger only paused for a breath before he continued. "If it's too much, I understand—"

Wyn crooked a finger under Roger's chin and angled his face up, closing his mouth in the process. The way Roger's eyes went wide made him laugh softly.

"Have a good time with your friends. I will be sleeping." Wyn brushed the pad of his thumb beneath Roger's bottom lip before he let his hand fall to his side. "Good night, Roger," he murmured before he slipped out the door.

CHAPTER 61

ROGER

ROGER FELT sure he used to be better at sleeping. There was always something keeping him up these days. He tossed and turned, thinking about Wyn, trapped in a city he didn't like, struggling to keep his emotions and his magic under control, and then scolded and teased when he failed. For all the Wrenwhistles' wealth and resources, it seemed odd they would use none of them to help their youngest be happier or more comfortable. He thought of how Mrs. Wrenwhistle always seemed to have a strict expectation of what was acceptable behavior—perhaps it was more about keeping up appearances than anything else. Roger felt a pang in his chest at the idea of Wyn being so neglected by his own family. He curled a fist around his sheets, promising he would rectify the situation as soon as they were married. Wyn would never have to come to London again if he didn't want to, not if Roger had anything to say about it.

Roger turned over, wondering what Wyn would be like in the country. Would he be more relaxed? What was a completely relaxed Wyn like? Had Roger ever seen it? He supposed he'd seen glimpses—Wyn lying on his back in the garden during a ball, Wyn leaning over to blow out a candle after a successful experiment.

He flipped onto his back, thinking about how understanding Wyn had been when Roger had admitted his lack of experience and even his lack of attraction. Roger knew a little about the fae attitude towards intimacy and relationships. He had even seen that attitude in action—he felt his face get hot at the memory of Wyn in the pergola with Sage Ravenwing. It had been reasonable to suppose Wyn might be less than enthused to learn that his future husband wouldn't be able to keep up with his appetite. But he hadn't. He had applied no pressure whatsoever to the prospect of Roger sharing that level of intimacy.

Roger bit his lip thinking about it. He really *did* want to experience that with Wyn. *When the time comes, if you're interested, I'll take care of you.* He found himself deeply curious about what that would be like. He knew the weight of Wyn's hand on his thigh, on his stomach, on his cheek. He'd enjoyed that one brief embrace they'd shared. He wanted more. He'd never wanted more before.

There had been brief instances—when he'd believed himself to be in love with Cyril, and when he'd fancied his dance instructor—but those had faded away. This time felt different. He was coming to know Wyn better than he'd ever known anybody and that changed things. It changed the shape of his desire and the keenness of his yearning.

As he finally drifted to sleep, he found himself imagining what Vauxhall Gardens would be like with Wyn. Would it be as romantic as his friends had promised? He rather hoped it would.

THE NEXT MORNING, Cyril, Anthea, Harriet, and Harriet's Uncle Felix invaded the sitting room for tea.

"Now," Anthea began, "it's not that I don't find Mr. Wrenwhistle perfectly charming, but now that he's not here, can you *finally* tell us what happened? One minute we're gossiping about him and you are denying any interest whatsoever, the next minute you're engaged. And not only engaged, completely besotted!"

"I'm not besotted," Roger murmured.

Cyril raised an eyebrow. "Have you seen yourself around the man?"

"Oh, how I adore young love," Uncle Felix said with relish as he took a sip of tea.

Uncle Felix was the youngest of Harriet's mother's siblings by a good number of years. He had been born a scant few years before Harriet, and they'd always shared a friendship more akin to cousins than uncle and niece. Roger gave him a quizzical look. "Aren't you in your mid thirties?"

Felix waggled a finger. "Very disrespectful to ask your elders for their age, darling."

Anthea gave a snort.

Roger decided not to press the matter. "How is married life treating you then, *sir?*"

Felix gave him a radiant smile. "Oh, it's divine. My spouse spoils me rotten. I don't deserve it. But I do enjoy it. You'll enjoy it too, I assure you. I cannot wait to meet this fiancé of yours. I've heard he's very attractive."

"He…is."

Harriet waved her hand impatiently. "Yes, but how did it happen?"

"Well, you know we've been working on that project for the Council."

Felix gave a solemn nod. "I do admire responsibility in the youth."

Roger refrained from rolling his eyes and turned his attention back to his friends. "Well, it happened somewhat naturally, really. We didn't get along at first but he…he liked seeing me perform magic. And I liked seeing the way his mind worked when he asked me questions. A-and then I got to see some of his magic and it was marvelous. And…I don't know. I suppose working long hours together toward a mutual goal did what everyone said it would." He shrugged.

Anthea pursed her lips. "I confess I was unsure of how a man like Wyndham Wrenwhistle could have captured your affections so completely. But I've seen the way he is with you. So I guess I understand it now."

"How he is with me?" Roger asked.

Cyril heaved a sigh. "Oh my goodness. Is he as oblivious as you are? He can't keep his eyes off you. And every time he touches so much as a fingertip to you, you immediately melt." He turned to Felix. "It would be disgusting if it weren't so sweet."

"Adorable," Felix drawled.

"And," Harriet added, bouncing in her seat, "he accepted the invitation to Vauxhall. And you know what that means."

"What…what does that mean?"

Harriet rolled her eyes. "Oh, Roger, *really*. There will be all sorts of romantic corners for you two to escape to."

Roger glanced at Felix, who gave him a wink. "I was young and in love too once," he explained. "I'm happy to lend my aid."

Roger felt his face get hot. "Is that what this whole evening is really about?"

"It's not all about you, Roger," Harriet sniffed. "*I'm* hoping to see Anthea get drunk."

"And Anthea's secretly hoping Lady Fitzhugh will be there," Cyril said in an exaggerated whisper.

"Oh?" Roger asked, turning excitedly to his friend. "She will? That is exciting."

Anthea tossed her head. "I don't know what you're talking about. We aren't courting."

"The *Tribune* suggests otherwise," Harriet said in a singsong voice.

"And *I* am going," Felix said, "to enjoy a nice supper with my favorite niece and her darling friends. Just think of me as your doting mother hen or kindly shepherd." He glanced at the door and then lowered his voice. "But I won't say a word if you and your beau wander off together."

"Right," Roger muttered under his breath.

"However," Harriet said. "I insist on dancing with each of you. We can make that the beginning of the night so everyone else can be all romantic elsewhere."

"And who exactly am I supposed to be romantic with?" Cyril asked.

Harriet gave his hand a patronizing pat. "Don't worry. I'll keep you company if no one else will."

Cyril's face went pink. "How generous of you."

Felix gurgled a laugh into his tea. "We shall have such a lark together. It will be like old times, won't it? Being around you all will allow me to relive my own misspent youth."

Anthea quickly changed the subject to ask about Roger's project and they chatted amiably for another hour or so, with everyone teasingly chiming in to comment on how romantic an aspect of the project was.

When they finally left, Roger escaped up to his room. He leaned against the door and closed his eyes. Should he tell Wyn about the true nature of the evening? Did Wyn already know? Had he known when he accepted the invitation? Roger sat down on his bed. Now that he knew, he didn't know what to do with the information. Did he want Wyn to pull him into a dark corner of Vauxhall Gardens? He thought of all the times he'd wished Wyn would kiss him, or wished Wyn's arms had stayed around him just a little longer. He put his hands on his knees and pushed himself to his feet.

Whatever happened, Wyn would take care of him. If Roger trusted anything, he knew he could trust that. With a strange feeling of excitement that could have almost been described as giddiness, he rang for Notley and set about planning what he would wear.

HIS FRIENDS CAME to pick him up first. Roger was grateful his parents had never met Felix as he was tolerably certain they would have insisted on coming too. As it was, the carriage was already nearly full when he climbed in next Anthea.

Cyril cast a critical eye over his outfit. "Don't you look dashing? Hoping to woo your gentleman friend?"

Roger rolled his eyes. "We're already engaged."

"Mmhmm," Felix hummed, drawing out the sound in an exaggerated manner. "But it never hurts to keep them interested."

Roger prepared himself for a night of embarrassment. When they picked up Wyn, he was quick to slide inside.

He gave an interested glance around the carriage. "Cozy," he murmured.

"It is a bit tight," Roger admitted.

"I'm not complaining."

"Was your mother angry?"

"Oh, yes," he said in a light tone. "How are you?"

Anxious. Excited. He didn't know what he was.

Wyn must have seen something in his expression for he laid a light hand on his thigh and whispered, "Relax."

"Oh, you must be the dashing young man everyone has been talking about," Felix enthused. "Yes, yes, you're just as lovely as everyone said. Roger, you lucky little thing. I'm not a bit surprised that you two are eager for some time alone."

Wyn raised an eyebrow. "Lovely to meet you," he said in his most elegant voice.

Felix grinned. "The pleasure is all mine, darling, I assure you."

Wyn squeezed back into his corner and turned to whisper in Roger's ear, "I had no idea our chaperone was going to be our age."

"Harriet's Uncle Felix."

Wyn looked amused. "Yes, I can see the resemblance. And I can see why you were already blushing before I got in the carriage."

"You two will have all evening to whisper in each other's ears," Harriet said. "Pray do not start now."

"But, my dear niece, it's so romantic of them."

Wyn squeezed Roger's thigh and said to the carriage at large, "I hear we are taking the boats this evening."

"Yes!" Harriet shouted, successfully distracted. "It is *the* best way to arrive. Don't you agree? You can see the lanterns from the river and it adds such an exciting element to the whole affair."

"I've reserved us a supper box," Felix announced. "My treat. It's not every day I get to spoil my favorite niece and her lovely little friends."

Wyn gave a quiet snort and drummed his fingers on Roger's thigh as the conversation continued. Roger was torn between the comfort of the gesture and the thrill of it, particularly after the conversations of the past couple of days. But all he knew was that he didn't want Wyn to stop.

Arriving by boat was, indeed, romantic. Well, it would have been more romantic if Harriet hadn't insisted on leaning far out to get a good glimpse, requiring Cyril to tug her back, which caused them to topple onto each other, which caused Felix to tsk and comment on the *frivolity of youth.*

Roger had never been to Vauxhall Gardens before. His parents had been uninterested in paying the toll to get in, on top of the expense of a supper box and the food and drink to go with it. So he marveled at the spectacle of the lanterns strung over the dance floor, the orchestra, and all of the alcoves of tables. As they walked to their box, with his hand on Wyn's arm, Roger glimpsed trails leading into the gardens themselves and he felt a small thrill at the possibilities. He glanced up at Wyn to gauge his reaction. Wyn smiled down at him and stroked gentle fingers over Roger's hand.

"I'm glad we came," Roger admitted. "Thank you for...for making it happen."

Wyn's smile broadened. "Your open mouthed awe was definitely worth it."

Roger snapped his mouth shut, embarrassed. But Wyn chuckled and moved his free hand to tap a finger under Roger's chin. If Roger didn't know better, he would have almost described the gesture as *affectionate*.

They all squeezed into a box. Harriet loudly pointed out that Lady Fitzhugh was present and Anthea quickly demanded a bowl of punch. Roger was nervous as they ate supper and chatted amiably. He wasn't sure what to do in the circumstances. Wyn wasn't even aware that Roger was willing to do anything, let alone before their marriage. He drank his punch distractedly, until Wyn slid his glass away.

Roger looked up at him, confused.

Wyn leaned over and whispered, "Arrack Punch is notoriously strong."

"Oh!"

Felix picked up Roger's discarded glass and drained it. "I've heard you two are likely to dance the night away. Is that true?"

"Yes," Wyn replied. "I think we'll start now. Shall we?"

"Y-yes," Roger said, following him out of the box.

"Ah, young love," Felix sighed as they walked to the dance floor.

CHAPTER 62

WYN

DESPITE ROGER'S indulgence in the potent drink and his friends surrounding him with their comfortable conversation all evening, Wyn couldn't help but notice the other man was thoroughly distracted by his own thoughts. They struggled through two dances together. One of them was a favorite of Roger's, if Wyn remembered correctly, but even that wasn't enough to keep his focus.

When the second dance was nearing its end, Roger lost his place completely and knocked into the young woman beside him. He apologized profusely and gave Wyn a look that screamed *help me*. Wyn guided him through the last of the music so as to not embarrass Roger even more by dragging him away from a public dance, and then they left the floor together.

"Roger," Wyn began gently, and that was all it took.

"I am sorry," Roger said in a rush, bringing one hand to slap against his forehead. "I cannot even say what happened. I know that dance so well, and the steps are second-nature, but for some reason my feet turned me the wrong way, and—and—"

"Roger, listen to me," Wyn continued, cutting him off before he could spiral. "Everything is all right. You offered your apology, and she accepted it. There's nothing more to it."

Roger's face twisted in a mix of emotion. "It's you I'm trying to apologize to! How embarrassing to be paired with a man who cannot even follow the steps to a dance small children can master."

Wyn was glad Roger's hand had found his arm so easily upon their departure from the crowd. It made it that much easier to steer him down one of the paths so he could regain some of his composure in a more private place.

"I hear what you are telling me, but this isn't why you're really upset," Wyn said after a while. "Something has been bothering you all evening."

Roger let out a small, wavering grumble. He seemed to consider if he wanted to admit it or not, before his shoulders drooped. "Yes."

"Is it something I can help with?" Wyn felt Roger's fingers shift against his arm. "I had hoped you would enjoy this evening out with your friends, but quite honestly you seem miserable."

"I've had a lovely time," Roger protested. "I hadn't realized how much I've missed them until this morning when they came 'round for tea." Wyn felt a pang of guilt over Roger's admission. He'd kept him away from his friends unintentionally, but clearly it had affected him.

"But…" Wyn encouraged gently when Roger stopped for longer than he should have. There was more. Wyn could feel it. Roger was tense and nervous, and he'd barely even smiled while they danced.

Roger let out a long breath and stared up at the lanterns in the trees overhead, the lights reflecting in his spectacles. It made Wyn think of their first time at the opera together. That seemed like a lifetime ago. Wyn tried not to smile in the seriousness of the moment they were having, but then Roger looked at him, and the grin broke across his mouth anyway.

"When Harriet offered the invitation to join them here tonight, I did not…that is, I was unaware of the *implications* attached." Roger's attention fell to his feet as they walked. "They so kindly informed me of those implications this morning, and I suppose that I've just been worried that you thought…well, that you thought…"

Wyn swallowed down the laugh that bubbled up his throat.

"Vauxhall is one of the few names in London with a reputation more scandalous than my own," Wyn teased. "You've never heard the reason behind these being the *pleasure* gardens?"

"No!" Roger cried beside him. "Obviously *not.*"

"Otherwise you wouldn't have accepted the invitation?" Wyn pressed, his tone genuinely curious but laced with a grin. Roger opened his mouth to respond, but his words seemed to catch in his throat. Wyn arched an eyebrow at Roger's hesitation. When no answer came at all, Wyn's smile turned sly. He decided to let Roger ruminate rather than poke at him any more.

Roger's voice finally broke the silence a few minutes later, though it was barely above a whisper. "Have you ever…" he trailed off.

"Here?" Wyn asked. When Roger nodded, Wyn narrowed his eyes a bit. "Do you truly want to know the answer to that question?"

Roger shook his head tightly. "That's answer enough," he managed. Roger let go of Wyn's arm and tugged on the bottom of his waistcoat a few times. Wyn brought his arm up behind his back to grasp his opposite elbow, keeping pace with Roger, trying desperately to figure out the best way to help the poor man through the crisis he was having.

Wyn knew there was no point in regretting his past. Even if he did wish he'd done things differently, which he did not, he found himself wondering for the first time what Roger thought of his past. Wondering if, perhaps, that was the root cause of Roger's worries. He'd said he didn't want Wyn to be disappointed. Did he mean Roger's lack of desire when it came to intimacy? Or in Roger's overall experience with such things?

"I'm sorry if that bothers you," Wyn offered quietly. "I'm afraid I cannot change the things I've done."

"It doesn't bother me," Roger said just as quietly, and in a very unconvincing way. Wyn frowned as he peered down at Roger, who had put a bit of space between them on the path. The longer they strolled, the more it felt like Wyn was being accompanied by some sort of wild animal that was ready to lash out at any moment. The air around them had grown tight and uncomfortable.

When Wyn was about to break the silence for fear of his magic bursting out of him from all of the tension, Roger threw his hands up before they came down and smacked against his legs.

"It's just—" Roger started, his voice high and anxious. "It's just that I cannot stop thinking about it. About you, and well…everything," he mumbled, losing steam quickly.

Wyn considered his response very carefully. "You cannot stop worrying about it? Or *thinking* about it?"

"Thinking about it?" Roger responded. Wyn gave him a stern look.

"Now is not the time to answer a question with another question."

Roger's eyes met his, and somehow, Wyn understood.

Roger was feeling things he did not know how to put into words. He was experiencing something so new that it was indescribable. It wasn't that he did not want to express his emotions, but he simply couldn't. They were so jumbled in his mind that there was no hope of picking one out of the mix, let alone sharing it with someone else.

Wyn understood because he was living it just as Roger was.

He knew what Roger needed.

Wyn reached out and took Roger's hand, slotting a couple of his fingers with Roger's as he pulled him along toward one of his favorite parts of the garden.

The section was practically buzzing with plant life. It was evident that fae were responsible for looking after the flowers and greenery, for it was lush and full of vivid color, even at night. The winding path curved through layer after layer of meticulously plotted beds of short blooms, which spread into taller flowers, and eventually into the shaped hedgerows that created a feeling of escaping the real world entirely. Only a few lanterns lit the way, giving an ambiance of wild magic that Wyn was certain even a human could appreciate.

Wyn continued to hold Roger's hand, in part because he wanted to, but mostly to keep him from walking too quickly. He just needed to breathe. He needed to focus on something else.

"Relax," Wyn said, echoing his own words from earlier in the evening.

"It's so beautiful here." Roger quickly lost himself in observing the plants along the trail.

Wyn felt his magic mellowing in his chest. He took a deep breath and sighed it out slowly. The patch of daisies Roger had been admiring suddenly awoke from their slumber, turning toward Roger as though he was the morning sun. For the first time all evening, Roger's smile was genuine, and Wyn thought that the flowers might've been onto something. He truly was bright and warm and wonderful.

"There's more," Wyn said, tugging on Roger's hand again.

Trickling water was the first indication that they'd come the right direction. A small stream worked its way over smooth rocks, which were visible thanks to the fairy lights floating lazily just above the surface of the water. Roger gasped softly when he saw them.

They stopped in the middle of the arched bridge that spanned the gap from one side of the bank to the other, and Roger bent down to reach his hand toward a couple of the lights. As Wyn knew they would, they moved away just fast enough to avoid being touched.

"It seems unfair that something so pretty cannot be held," Roger said as he stood up again. Wyn chuckled and led Roger off the bridge.

"What would you do with one if you could hold it?" he asked.

"Well, I would like to say that I'd just appreciate it from up close. But I think we both know I would really like to tuck it into my pocket and take it home to study it," Roger admitted with a sheepish grin.

"Yes, that sounds more like you," Wyn agreed.

A little farther down the trail, the lantern light had given way to the light of the moon. It helped to cast interesting shadows on the ground as a slight breeze picked up. Roger stepped closer to his side, and Wyn was a bit upset he hadn't thought of that himself.

The faint rustling of leaves filled the air, and Roger's attention caught on something. Wyn looked up to see what it was.

A massive willow tree stood sentry at a bend in the path, branches swaying.

Wyn and Roger exchanged a look, and then Roger's forehead wrinkled as his eyebrows pinched together.

"Could we feel the magic again?" he whispered.

Wyn couldn't have denied him if he'd tried.

The two of them abandoned the trail and made quick work of removing their shoes and stockings. Wyn used his arm to brush the branches aside so they could get closer to the trunk. Roger reached for it with both hands, eager as ever when it came to magic, and Wyn laughed.

"Easy," he said as he let the branches fall back into place. Two steps and he was close enough to slide his hand around Roger's waist to his stomach. It was almost effortless as he moved to press himself against Roger's back, holding him perhaps a little closer than he really needed to. Wyn placed his other hand over the one Roger still had braced against the tree.

Roger gasped in a breath, and Wyn was confused at first. Certainly he couldn't feel something already? But then he realized what he'd done. He realized the way he had put the side of his face against Roger's. He realized just how close they were in almost every way that they could be.

"Breathe," Wyn whispered, closing his eyes. He followed his own directions and took a breath so deep that his lungs ached, and when he blew it out, he felt Roger do the same.

Wyn's magic erupted in his chest, washing through the rest of his body in an intoxicating wave as it felt the magic of the tree, felt the life of it. And there in between them was Roger, and Wyn could feel him, too. He could feel the lingering tension from earlier in the night. He could feel the same sweetness he'd felt during their experiments with the willow branch.

But there was something else. Something new that Wyn had felt hints of from others in the past, but never anything so strong as what he felt in that moment from Roger. Wyn had the strangest urge to claim whatever it was for himself and never let it go.

"Roger?" he tried, realizing he'd gone silent.

"Wyn," Roger breathed, his head leaning back into the support of Wyn's jaw and shoulder. "I want you to show me," he added shakily.

"Show you what?" Wyn had to tighten his grip as Roger relaxed into him.

"Show me what you said. A-about how it can impact your magic?"

Wyn smirked against Roger's ear.

"About how *what* can impact your magic?" he asked slowly. Wyn rubbed his thumb against Roger's stomach, though his hand remained in place. Roger swallowed hard before he could continue.

"Pleasure," he peeped, and Wyn felt a flicker of heat in his gut. He hummed and nuzzled his nose against Roger's cheek.

"Are you certain that's what you want?" he asked.

"Y-yes," Roger said weakly.

"Can you feel the magic from the tree?"

"Yes," he repeated with more confidence.

"Can you feel my magic?"

"Yes." His answer was unsteady again.

"Can you really?" Wyn breathed out again, reaching more for Roger instead of the willow that time. Could Roger feel his magic the same way he felt Roger's? The shiver that went through Roger's entire body was answer enough.

"I enjoy it very much when you ask me questions, Wyn, but please do not make me think right now," Roger begged, his hand squeezing on the arm Wyn had wrapped around his waist. Wyn supposed he'd accomplished his goal of helping Roger's mind relax, then. Unfortunately, it was not a request he could honor if he wanted to do things the right way.

As Wyn's fingers began to stroke gently against Roger's stomach, he closed his eyes so he could cling to the shreds of his own focus.

"What do you like?" Wyn asked against Roger's neck.

Roger whimpered softly. "What do you mean?"

"I mean what do you enjoy when you're alone?" Wyn's hand shifted a bit lower, two fingertips teasing under the hem of his waistcoat. When Roger didn't answer, Wyn tried to form the question another way. "Is there something you do that you'd like for me to try?" He'd found over the years that most men had similar preferences when it came to such things, but there were always a few exceptions.

"I—" Roger said. "I don't."

"You don't have anything you'd like me to try?"

"I don't...*do* anything," Roger emphasized.

Wyn's eyes opened. He blinked a few times in the dark, his fingers slowing.

He suddenly felt like the most unworthy person alive to be holding a man like Roger Barnes underneath a willow tree in the middle of a romantic garden.

"I see," Wyn choked out, before his surprise became obvious. *Fuck*.

Wyn dropped his hand from Roger's stomach. He wrapped his fingers around Roger's wrist and pulled him out from under the tree toward where they'd abandoned their shoes. Wyn scooped them up and directed his attention toward where he knew might provide them with a bit more privacy.

It was a hurried affair, locating one of the many secluded alcoves that Wyn knew were tucked all throughout the gardens. Without so much as a glance around, Wyn practically yanked Roger inside. He never broke contact as he adjusted his grip on Roger so that he was embracing him from behind again, but this time with a vine coated stone wall to support his own back.

"As you have promised me honesty, Roger Barnes, I expect nothing else in this moment," Wyn murmured against the shell of Roger's ear. With one hand settled just beneath Roger's cravat knot, Wyn let his other hand slide smoothly down the buttons of his waistcoat, ending in a gentle flourish over the front of his trousers.

Wyn took a breath and released it, allowing his magic to envelop Roger in the way he'd done under the tree. He hoped it was enough to count as what Roger had actually asked for as he closed his eyes again, sliding his fingertips down across the inside of Roger's thigh.

Roger was already breathing heavily, his hands gripped tightly on Wyn's arms. Wyn focused on that grip with everything he had to spare, waiting for the slightest indication that Roger was pulling him away. Wyn bumped his nose against Roger's ear.

"Yes?" Wyn asked.

Roger bobbed his head once.

"I cannot see you in the dark," Wyn teased.

"Yes," Roger panted.

Wyn dragged his delicate touch up from Roger's thigh and pressed what he hoped was a reassuring squeeze to Roger's chest as he curved his hand over the front of Roger's trousers, cupping him gently at first. Roger's full-body reaction was enough to make him pause, but then Roger nodded again, almost desperately.

"Yes," he repeated, and Wyn moved his hand, hiding his smile in Roger's dark hair. He continued until he was satisfied with the way Roger felt against his fingers, hard and wanting.

"Do you want me to continue?" Wyn asked. Roger gave his nod. "Like I am now? Or more?" Roger's hips shifted and he let out a small moan.

"I don't know what more means," he admitted.

"Underneath your clothes," Wyn explained.

"Y-yes," Roger fumbled. "That."

With great care, Wyn unfastened Roger's trousers so he could slip his hand in the front of them. Roger's whole body jerked again when Wyn touched him. Wyn couldn't help but notice how hot Roger's skin was as he took him in his hand, working him in the familiar way he used on himself. Best to stick with what he knew, he decided.

Wyn felt the way Roger relaxed into him after being so tense at first. He felt the way the air changed around them as Roger's heart raced, beating furiously under the hand Wyn still had on his chest. Roger's hands still never pushed him away, or asked him to slow down.

Just as Wyn's urge to press his lips to Roger's neck almost overwhelmed him to the point of giving in, Roger cried out, squeezing Wyn's arms as he came. Wyn's eyes went a bit wide as he felt what Roger had spent—or rather, how much—and he gave considerable thought to the best way to handle the situation. It might've been wise to think of the light colored trousers Roger had worn. There was still plenty of the night left to enjoy.

"Stay still," Wyn cautioned him, even though Roger had become dead weight, pressing him back against the wall. Wyn did the best he could with his one handkerchief and then chuckled when Roger really did not move at all. "Are you all right?" he asked against Roger's ear.

CHAPTER 63

ROGER

Wʏɴ's ǫᴜᴇsᴛɪᴏɴ was gentle and Roger dragged his sluggish brain into action enough to say, "Y-yes, I—I mean, that was…that was…"

Wyn chuckled. "You enjoyed it?"

"*Yes.*" Wyn had needed to hear that word throughout the experience. Roger hoped it would be sufficient now.

Wyn nuzzled his cheek again. "I'm glad."

"Can I—that is, would you like—"

"No."

Roger felt his stomach sink with the quick denial.

Wyn rubbed his thumb a little on Roger's chest. "This was about you. We'll worry about me another time. Right now, I'm primarily worried about getting you sufficiently cleaned up."

Roger stirred enough to look down and let out a small squeak of horror. Then he clamped a hand over his mouth. "S-sorry," he stammered. "I know you hate the squeaking."

Wyn's hand pulled him infinitesimally closer. "I don't hate it," he murmured softly.

Roger pulled out his own handkerchief, and Wyn smoothly plucked it from his hands and made quick work of the clean up. He gently spun Roger around and gave him a careful onceover. Roger tried not to fidget under his gaze.

But then Wyn smiled at him. "There. I think that will do."

Roger buttoned his trousers before Wyn could offer to do it and they both put their shoes and stockings back on. "What should we do with the handkerchiefs?"

"I'll take care of them later," Wyn reassured him. He folded both up together and tucked them into his pocket. "Do try not to get food on your-self for the rest of the evening, however, as I'm certain we will be discovered if I were to pull one of these out now. They'll be stiffer than you were soon enough."

Roger had an overwhelming sense of—something he couldn't entirely name. It was a mixture of gratitude, and fondness, and perhaps something a bit more intense than fondness. He dearly wanted to pull Wyn closer and kiss him. Thank him for taking care of him so well, let him know how much he enjoyed and appreciated it. He wanted to ensure Wyn knew how much it meant to have a soon-to-be-husband who understood him so well. But, strangely, the prospect of kissing Wyn felt almost more intimate than what they had just done together. So, instead, he smiled up at the other man and said, "Thank you. For everything."

Wyn returned the smile with a soft one of his own. "Do you wish to return now or wait? I have a feeling our companions—particularly our chaperone—will be in no rush to see us again."

Roger puffed out an embarrassed laugh. "You're probably right. Can we stay here a minute?"

"Of course." Wyn leaned back against the alcove wall, as if he truly had nowhere else to be.

Roger settled next to him and tried not to show his delight when Wyn slid an arm around his shoulders and pulled him closer. They stood in silence together, with the distant music from the dance floor lilting through the air. Roger wondered how it would be to rest his head against Wyn's chest, but didn't quite dare.

Wyn rubbed a thumb idly over the curve of his shoulder and said, "I haven't yet mentioned how well you look tonight. This color is lovely on you."

Roger looked up and met his gaze. "Thank you," he whispered.

Wyn chuckled and slid a hand down the front of Roger's waistcoat. "I'll be pleased if this marriage results in you becoming fashionable. A worthy cause for a marriage, in my mind."

Roger rolled his eyes. "Oh yes, far more important than what it means to society, or our families."

"Decidedly more important."

"Cyril thinks I'm trying to woo you," Roger said without thinking.

"Hm. Well, you're certainly going the right way about it." Before Roger could make sense of that, Wyn continued, "Would you like something to drink?"

Roger nodded and they stepped out of the alcove to go back to the supper box but Roger froze midstep. Sage Ravenwing was sitting on a stone bench with one heel hitched against the seat, and the other kicking idly in the air as he sipped wine. He turned to look at them and his smirk told Roger all he needed to know. Ravenwing *knew*. Either he'd heard or simply guessed. Roger felt the cold weight of dread fill his stomach as he realized his reputation was now in tatters.

Wyn looped Roger's hand around his arm and led him up the path, not even acknowledging the other fae.

As soon as they were out of earshot, Roger tugged on Wyn's arm. "He knows."

Wyn gave a little sigh. "Yes, I'm afraid he might. Goodness knows why he was sitting around listening though."

"He's going to do something or—or tell someone. I suppose," Roger went on before Wyn could speak, "that it's just as well we're engaged. I mean my parents can't force us to get married now. We're already getting married. They'll never trust us alone together. Oh, Lord, our projects— what a mess. Maybe they'll just send Notley to watch us. That wouldn't be too bad. But it *is* a wrench. Maybe—"

"Roger," Wyn cut him off, turning and framing his hands around Roger's shoulders. "I'm sorry we were caught. I'm sure it will be all right. As you pointed out, we're already engaged. I know my family will have expected this. Your parents may be shocked, but I'm sure they'll get over it."

Roger wasn't so sure of that. He bit his lip.

Wyn's thumbs rubbed gently over his shoulders. "Do you regret it?"

Roger looked up in surprise. "What? No! Of course not!"

Wyn gave a small smile. "Good. Why don't we have a little more punch —we'll share a glass this time—and then we can dance some more?"

Roger nodded and took Wyn's proffered arm. "Y-yes. That will be nice."

Wyn sighed. "Wouldn't it figure the one time I get you to truly relax."

Roger squeezed his arm. "Wyn?"

"Hm?"

"It was wonderful. Thank you."

Wyn chuckled. "You're very welcome."

They took a seat at the supper table, blithely ignoring Uncle Felix's wink. They couldn't ignore his direct question: "Having a nice time, darlings?"

"Oh, yes," Wyn replied. "I was showing Roger the gardens. He is quite enamored of fairy lights."

"Oh, I'm *sure* he is," Felix drawled. He gave a happy sigh. "I'm going to wander around for a bit. Don't want to break up the romantic mood, you know."

Wyn watched him go and remarked, "You know, he lacks subtlety but he really is surprisingly thoughtful."

"Well, that's Harriet for you too."

"Ah. I wonder where she is."

"Probably with Cyril," Roger said as he ladled out some punch. "They've been dancing around each other since their debuts. It'd be absurd if it wasn't so amusing."

He managed one sip before Wyn plucked the glass out of his hands. "Are you entirely sure you don't regret it? You seem almost as miserable now as you did at the start of the night."

Roger grabbed Wyn's free hand. "I promise you, I don't regret it. It…it was disconcerting to come out of a moment where I felt—" He broke off, unsure of the right word. *Safe? Happy?* "Relaxed and then bump into someone who hates me and wouldn't hesitate to ruin my reputation."

Wyn gave him a long look. "It's really worrying you, isn't it?"

Roger boldly took the glass back and took a small fortifying sip. "I suppose I'm not worried about any real consequences. We are engaged and our wedding is in less than a week. But…but I do worry about losing my parents' trust. Although I suppose I—"

"Don't you dare say you deserve it," Wyn said with more heat than

Roger expected. "You are appallingly respectable and incredibly responsible. If you can make a proposal to solve a crisis that the Council has been struggling with, you deserve to enjoy yourself. Besides, you're of age."

"That's true," Roger replied, feeling a little encouraged about that. "I'm sorry. I don't want to seem ungrateful. It was...it was truly—well, I don't know if I can provide adequate words. But I did enjoy it and I'm very grateful."

Wyn smiled. "Good." He took the glass again and leaned back in the seat. "And how did the experiment part of it go?"

It took Roger an embarrassingly long moment to understand what Wyn was hinting at. "Oh!" he said as Wyn smirked. "Oh, I...well, I must admit I got a little distracted. It wasn't the most scientific of...erm...but I did notice your magic got...I don't know, sharper?"

Wyn's smile broadened. "Yes," he said quietly. "We shall have to talk more about how you can feel my magic." He tilted the glass in his hand. "Perhaps another time when we're not drinking a notoriously strong beverage."

"It isn't all that remarkable," Roger admitted. "I can't say I felt it very well. More of a vague...well it was stronger than the tree. But it's nothing like what you experience."

"All the same. It's worth looking into."

Roger nodded.

Anthea plopped into the seat opposite.

Roger stared at her. "What are you doing back so early?"

She slumped in her seat. "I cannot talk to Imogen knowing that everyone is watching me."

Roger kindly did not comment on her referring to Lady Fitzhugh by her first name. "I'm sorry," he said.

She sighed. "I should have expected it. I suppose I imagined us walking in the gardens together—and we did—but...it feels noticeable. And I know Cyril and Harriet will be giggling over it. I just—I couldn't."

Roger nodded sympathetically.

Wyn shifted beside him and set the glass on the table. "Don't leave," he muttered as he stood. "I'll be back shortly."

It occurred to Roger that it was the longest time Wyn had gone through an event without needing a break, so he was not entirely surprised. "Are you all right?" he asked, just to be sure.

Wyn smiled and squeezed his shoulder. "Yes."

It was strange how such a small word had come to carry so much weight.

CHAPTER 64

WYN

WYN SLIPPED AWAY from the crowd, which had grown considerably more raucous in their absence. There was something about the place that was inherently *free*. Wyn guessed it was the result of a number of things, including the encouragement of overindulgence when it came to the food and drinks, as well as the fae in charge of overseeing that guests got their money's worth to keep them coming back.

Without subtlety, Wyn retraced his steps along the trail through the gardens. He did not pause to look at the flowers or linger on the bridge as he and Roger had done. He cut across the grass rather than taking the bend around the willow tree.

Wyn was fairly certain he would find Ravenwing still lurking about where they'd left him. He always had a propensity for lingering in Wyn's wake. The bench was empty, but an uneasy feeling told him to check their abandoned alcove.

Sage's laugh revealed his level of intoxication before he spoke.

"Well," Sage started, dragging the word out. "If the guilty look on Barnes' face wasn't enough to give you away, the stench certainly is." He took a strong sniff of the air, as though to prove his own point. "You must've drained the poor man dry."

Wyn's jaw worked as he stared at Sage in the moonlight. Anger flaring, he thought of Roger; his supportive touch, his encouraging words, his gentleness.

"What is it you want from me?" Wyn asked finally. "There must be something because no matter where I go, you always seem to find me and you *always* have something to say." He took a step closer, his hands fists at his sides.

Sage let out a scoff of a laugh and drained the rest of his wine. Rather than setting it down on the table nearby, he threw it and the glass shattered on the ground. Wyn's brows bunched. He'd seen Sage drunk many times, but this seemed to be something more. Wyn waited for him to yell or make another smart remark like he was famous for doing.

"You are so *fucking* stupid," is what came out of Sage's mouth, a whisper thick with hate, and something else Wyn couldn't quite name. Sage's feet shuffled against the ground as he moved to support his weight against the stone wall.

"Roger is concerned that you're going to talk about what you saw this evening," Wyn told him. "I came to ask that you respect our privacy and keep your gossip to yourself for once. We are to be married. Nothing untoward has happened here tonight, at least not between him and myself."

Sage let out a hiss through his clenched teeth. His head fell back against the stones and Wyn watched his throat work a swallow above his cravat.

"Why should I, Wyndham?" he asked weakly. "Why should I care what a human like Roger Barnes is worried about?"

"Because he's a man who cares deeply about his family and wants to protect them," Wyn challenged. "You and I have both done marvelous work at dragging our family names through the mud over the years, but he is not that way. And I'll be damned if I'm going to see that change just because his name is associated with mine now."

Sage picked his head up to offer Wyn a drunken snicker.

"The same way your mouth was associated with his prick just now?"

Wyn snapped.

He let out a growl of frustration as his magic lashed out, sending a blast of wind sweeping hard enough to shove Sage back against the wall.

"What is wrong with you?!" Wyn shouted.

"Me?" Sage demanded. "What is wrong with me? I'll tell you what's wrong with me. The same thing that's been wrong with the countless other lovers you've used up and tossed aside."

Wyn's magic recoiled as his confusion grew. Sage let out a heavy breath and stood up off the wall, crossing his arms over his chest in a way Wyn had never seen him do.

"I don't understand," Wyn said.

Sage stared at him for a long time, the movement of his eyes catching in the moonlight overhead. They were more wet than they should've been.

"You really do not see it, do you?" Sage asked finally. Wyn made a vague shrug, lost on how to respond. Sage let out a pitiful little laugh and shook his head. "You've no idea how your coquettish behavior has stirred the hopes of many over the years, then. No idea of the utter confusion you've caused."

"Enough with the poetry, Sage. Just say whatever it is you need to say."

"I cannot stand to see the way you look at him." Sage stared down at his feet. "The way you smile when you dance with him. The way your hand always seems to find its way to him." He met Wyn's gaze again. "You are in love with Roger Barnes as I have been in love with you for over half of my life," he said, his voice breaking on the last word. "And the pain of watching you give him what I have always wanted is more than I can take."

The words hit Wyn like a gunshot, so completely unexpected that it was startling. Sage loved him? And there were others who had felt the same? It couldn't be true.

"Why did you never tell me?" Wyn asked, though it was guarded.

Sage scoffed again. "Because it has always been painfully obvious that my feelings were unrequited. Why would I tell you and scare you away, when keeping my secret meant that I could still be close to you? I suppose in some way I always hoped your parents would force you to marry, and that you would choose me because we had been fr—" Sage cut himself off. "Because we had known each other for so long."

"You know I never wanted to get married," Wyn said quietly.

"So imagine my surprise when I read of your engagement in the *Tribune*," Sage told him bitterly.

A silence stretched between them and Sage scraped his boot against the ground, arms still wrapped tightly around himself. "I know I owe you an apology," he started, but did not continue.

"You owe me nothing." Wyn was unaffected by the sad look Sage gave him. "But you would do well to apologize to Roger. He told me what you said to him."

Sage's expression went blank. "I—"

"I do not want to hear it. You will apologize to Roger. If he accepts, then I will consider things settled between you and me."

After a moment, Sage nodded his understanding. Wyn turned to leave, but Sage spoke up again.

"Can you just tell me why?" Sage took a step closer. "Why was I never what you wanted?"

Wyn gave him a long look as he thought of the best way to answer. It seemed too crushing to tell him the truth, that he simply never felt anything toward the man other than a sense of familiarity. Instead, he decided to angle it in a way that would perhaps speak to his own emotions.

"If what you say about your feelings for me is true, then you already know why. It has nothing to do with you and everything to do with him. I'm not sure I can explain it beyond that." Wyn paused to let out a small sigh. "I am sorry I've hurt you. Quite obviously that was never my intent."

Sage grumbled. "That doesn't make it hurt any less."

"No, I would imagine not. But something I've learned recently is that feelings can change faster than you thought possible. And though it can be thoroughly overwhelming to allow yourself to open your mind to it, you might discover that it's the best decision you've ever made."

When Wyn returned to their box, Anthea was still sitting where she'd been before, but Roger was missing.

"Harriet pulled him away for more dancing," Anthea explained before he could ask. As he sat, he turned casually to look for them on the dance floor. He found Roger instantly, his smile big and indicative of the alcohol lubricating his inhibitions. Wyn peered down at their shared glass of punch where it sat empty. A grin tugged at the corner of his mouth.

"I suppose they'll be fun trying to get back across the water," Wyn mused.

"We can only hope they'll be passed out by then," Anthea said dryly.

Wyn looked at her with amusement and they shared a quiet laugh. A squeal of delight drew their attention back to the floor. Harriet was nearly doubled over with laughter as she and Cyril and Roger twirled around with each other, completely ignoring the steps to the dance they were supposed to be following.

"You are all welcome to visit us in the country whenever you'd like," Wyn said, extending the offer in case Roger had not already. "It certainly will not be as lively as this, but I see how important you all are to him, and I want to make up for the time I've stolen away."

"Stolen away?" Anthea asked, her face pinching in confusion. "Are you mad? I've never seen Roger happier in all the years I've known him. Whatever it is you two have been doing together, it's done wonders for him."

Wyn's eyes followed Roger around the floor until the music stopped and the three of them finished stumbling over one another. The sight of Roger holding his stomach from laughing so hard warmed Wyn from the inside.

It's done wonders for both of us, Wyn thought to himself.

TORQUIL'S TRIBUNE

Greetings, festive folk and honorable humans,

The Wentworths' ball on Friday night was a smashing success, according to all reports. The couple of the Season, Mr. Wrenwhistle and Mr. Barnes, danced three dances. Lady Fitzhugh and Miss St. Clair danced a respectable two, and Mr. Thompson and Miss Thackery danced a disappointingly single time. This writer fervently wishes for more romance to happen amongst the ton. Otherwise this article will start appearing overly obsessed with the pair that most frequently graces the column.

Speaking of the happy couple, they were seen promenading with their families. According to sources, the gentlemen appear to be quite cozy and still very much in love. No one knows what they were talking about, but they never seem to run out of conversation. If others could follow their example, that would be most appreciated.

They were also seen at Vauxhall Gardens last night. However, they were accompanied most properly by a chaperone and a collection of Mr. Barnes' friends. There is nothing to report, despite multiple accounts to the contrary. This writer requests that people stop trying to besmirch good names.

Other noteworthy appearances at Vauxhall included:

Miss St. Clair, who again danced twice with Lady Fitzhugh—a promising development.

Mr. Thompson and Miss Thackery continue to elude us, however, by being more raucous than romantic. More's the pity.

Mr. Ravenwing was also present, although reports suggest he was lacking a partner, despite many who might have been pleased by his attention. This writer humbly recommends the gentleman turn his attention to more promising possibilities.

In other news, Mr. Marigold and Mr. Brooks were seen at a dinner party last evening. The two seem to have been inseparable. Could there be more to their friendship than a mere overlap of social circles? Also at the dinner party was the Wrenwhistle family. Miss Wrenwhistle looked stunning in mint green gossamer. The lady has only to find a good match to be a leader of the fashionable world.

Invitations are reportedly being received for the much anticipated Wrenwhistle-Barnes wedding. Many humans will be experiencing the day-long festivities of a fae wedding for the first time. If this writer could receive an invitation, much of London society would likely be very grateful for the opportunity to live vicariously through their favorite society papers.

Your esteemed editor,

Torquil Pimpernel-Smith

CHAPTER 65

ROGER

Roger had little experience with overindulging. As a rule, he did not drink very much when socializing, and he barely drank at all when alone. He was glad Wyn had stopped him from drinking too much earlier in the evening but, God, why had Roger not shown more restraint towards the end of it?

"Damn Arrack Punch," he muttered as he leaned his pounding forehead against his palm. He was hunched over his desk, trying desperately to concentrate on his work. They didn't have time to waste on his own foolhardiness.

When Wyn arrived, Roger was both relieved—because, most shockingly, he missed him when he wasn't present—and a little dismayed to be seen in such a state.

Wyn gave him one look and then smiled. "How are we feeling today?"

"Extremely foolish," Roger replied, and then winced at how loud his voice was.

Wyn chuckled, reached into his breast pocket, and pulled out a small crystal bottle. He placed the bottle with a soft thump on the desk. "Drink this. It will help."

"What is it?" Roger asked, academic curiosity briefly masking the intensity of his pain.

"A tonic to help with the pain in your head. I'll tell you more about it later."

Roger took the tonic, pleasantly surprised it was not foul-tasting like the medicine he was accustomed to. "Thank you," he said. He clasped his hands together on the desk. "And…er…sorry."

Wyn pocketed the vial. "Whatever for? We went so you could have an enjoyable evening with your friends. I was under the impression you had one."

"Well, you warned me about the punch and then I—"

"If I'd been truly worried, I wouldn't have given you another glass. Now," he went on, taking a seat. "What are we working on today?"

There was something in Wyn's tone that made Roger pause before answering. "Did you have something in mind?"

Wyn seemed to hesitate and then replied, "Well, I would like to further investigate you feeling my magic. That was…unexpected."

Roger blinked as the pain in his head started to dissipate. "That stuff works remarkably fast."

Wyn's smile was smug.

"Anyway," Roger said. "Yes, we can…er…we can explore that. Although I-I'm not sure it was all that impressive. It's nothing like what you experience. And you were the one who taught me to feel magic during our lesson in Hyde Park."

Wyn leaned back in his seat, looking thoughtful. "Yes," he said slowly. "I did. But that was a slightly different situation. There were fewer distractions. We were both focused on the lesson at hand. And, truth to tell, I wasn't entirely sure you'd feel the magic at all. I *hoped* you would. But wild magic is…well, as you've experienced it's quite strong, so your feeling it was a very good sign. But your feeling *my* magic, that's rather different."

Roger considered this. He folded his hands together on the desk again. "Would this be an additional project then?" His mind was already scrambling to organize their work and a viable to-do list to accomplish each project.

"I was rather thinking we could try it in conjunction with our second one."

Roger stared, furiously trying to figure out the connection.

Wyn laughed, stood, leaned over the desk, and curled a finger under

Roger's chin to gently close his mouth. Surprisingly, he didn't pull back afterwards, but cupped Roger's chin and said softly, "I have a hunch. And I'd like to see if it's correct, if you'll indulge me."

Roger was fairly sure he would indulge Wyn anything at this point. He was reluctant to speak and lose Wyn's touch under his chin, so he nodded.

Wyn smiled. "Thank you."

He pulled his hand back and Roger found his voice again. "You know I could never deny an exploration for academic curiosity."

"Yes, and it seems to be rubbing off," Wyn remarked. "Speaking of which." He reached into his waistcoat again and passed over a handkerchief. "I burned the other ones but this can replace the one you lost."

Roger took it, at a loss for words again. The handkerchief was soft and made of very fine fabric. Roger had never bothered with embroidered handkerchiefs; they were always more expensive and were going to be dirtied anyway so what was the point? And he had never gained sufficient expertise in needlework himself to pursue it as a pastime. But the handkerchief Wyn handed him was delicately embroidered with violets. Roger ran a thumb over one of the flowers.

"This is lovely," he murmured. "Thank you. It's so beautiful, I'd be afraid to use it."

Wyn snorted. "Pray don't. I'd much prefer honey and jam on that than on your papers. If it makes you feel better, I'll get you a whole collection of them."

Roger didn't want to admit that a collection of beautiful handkerchiefs from Wyn would mean an entire collection of beautiful handkerchiefs that he'd be loath to ruin with food. So instead he tucked it into his pocket and said, "Right. So what did you have in mind for this experiment?"

"I'd like to start from the beginning with that breeze spell. You said last night that you needed more scientific conditions to feel my magic—" Roger blushed at what Wyn was referencing. "—and I think these are suitable conditions."

Roger stood and began collecting his notes from the breeze spell. "And what are we doing differently?"

"I want you to cast the spell. I'll tweak it and I want you to see what you can feel."

Roger paused in the act of selecting a fresh sheet of spellpaper. "Tweak it?"

"Indulge me," Wyn replied, his tone almost plaintive.

Roger felt a little weak in the knees at the tone and he quickly focused on getting the spell prepared in an attempt to hide his reaction. "Right," he said, laying down the fresh sheet and unfolding the spellpaper from their final breeze spell attempt. "The last one worked best, yes?"

"Yes," Wyn answered. "Although, you can make it a mite stronger and we can correct as we go. Like you did with that shade spell."

Roger blinked at him. "You want me to make it stronger?"

"Yes."

The single word brought back a rush of memories from the night before, and along with it a wave of heat between his thighs that took his breath away. Roger didn't ask any further questions. When the spell was ready, Wyn sat across from him on the floor, his legs folded neatly in front of him.

"Are you ready?" Roger asked. "It will be stronger than last time."

Wyn nodded. "I'm ready."

Roger cast the spell and braced himself for another gust, but it didn't come. At first he'd worried that he'd completely miscalculated and made it too weak, like his second casting. Then he noticed that Wyn's face was tight with concentration and Roger tentatively felt for his magic. As it had been with the willow tree the night before, Wyn's magic was winding around him, as gentle and sure as Wyn's touch so often was. Last night, Roger had been so taken up with his multitude of conflicting emotions that he had given little thought to Wyn's magic other than the novelty of feeling it at all. Now, sitting in his makeshift study, performing a magical experiment at Wyn's particular request, Roger focused a little harder on how Wyn's magic felt.

His magic was winding around Roger but he realized it was filling the whole space that he had cast for. It felt like a heavy blanket enveloping the room. Then he felt the breeze gently trickle past, ruffling the curtains and assorted papers. Roger stared at Wyn.

"Are you *controlling* the spell?"

Wyn nodded, his jaw tense. "That's the idea. Can you make it weaker?"

Roger hastily bent over the paper and made adjustments to his calculations. He heard Wyn let out a small sigh.

"That's better." Wyn seemed to hesitate. "You felt it then?"

"Yes," Roger replied quietly.

"What did it feel like?"

"Like a...a blanket or something, all over the room."

The corner of Wyn's mouth ticked up. "Excellent." He paused. "Mind if I try something else?"

"Are you joking?" Roger asked. "This is the most extraordinary thing we've ever done—" He broke off. "Well, magically speaking, of course."

Wyn let out a bark of laughter. "Here, hand me your handkerchief for a moment."

Roger passed it over and Wyn tossed it in the air. The breeze that was still circling the room picked it up and soon it was floating in a circuit around them. Roger stared. "Are you doing that?"

"Mm," Wyn hummed. "Our magics blend more seamlessly than I expected."

"You *expected* this?"

"Let's say I had a theory. Can you feel them blending together?"

For all of their lessons and experiments on feeling magic, Roger had yet to actually try and feel his own magic. He took a few moments to register the shock of that. Then he gathered his wits and focused.

He felt Wyn's magic first—the careful restraint of it. And yet there was something else, a playfulness he hadn't expected. And then underneath was his own magic. He reeled a little at the steadiness and strength he found. Then, he noticed that the two were intertwining, following the pattern of the handkerchief as it wove through the air. Their two magics danced around each other—steady, playful, strong, wild, yet controlled. Roger's gaze met Wyn's. He opened his mouth to comment but nothing came out.

CHAPTER 66

WYN

"Splendid, is it not?" Wyn asked, giving Roger a wink. That snapped Roger's mouth shut faster than anything else he could've tried.

Wyn filled his lungs and pushed the air out, watching as the breeze spell made one impressive final lap around the room. It curled tightly and then whipped up toward the ceiling directly above where they sat.

As Wyn let it go, the handkerchief fluttered down and landed on the floor between them. Wyn was glad Roger stared at the embroidered cloth long enough for him to subtly shift the way he was sitting. He kept his weight back on his hands as he stretched his legs out in front of him, crossing one over the other to carefully conceal the bulge at the front of his trousers.

His heart was racing with such fervor that his breath wavered each time he exhaled. He swallowed hard and closed his eyes for a moment, a weak attempt to calm the emotions coursing through his body.

Never had he become so stimulated by the use of his own magic. Even when something similar had happened in a bed he was sharing, magic spiraling and brushing with that of another, it was *nothing* like that.

Of course, he had never done it with another human.

Only Roger.

But he had a sneaking suspicion that there was more to it.

"Did you overexert yourself?" Roger asked, his voice cutting into the fog that had formed in Wyn's brain.

Wyn opened his eyes and let his head loll onto his shoulder as he peered at the man sitting next to him.

"Not a bit," he said smoothly, ignoring the heat pooled beneath his cravat and his weakening lust. "Should we try something else?"

Roger got to his feet and collected more spellpaper and a couple of the books Wyn recognized as Roger's favorites for references. The two of them sat on the floor for several hours as they played around with their notes, their ideas, and their combined magic.

When Notley brought in their tea, Wyn helped Roger up and settled him into one of the chairs before he claimed his own, opting to sit with a bit of distance between them so he could collect himself more thoroughly.

"I feel that there is something we need to discuss," Wyn said finally, after they'd had a moment to settle with their tea.

Roger's eyebrows went up as he turned his full focus in Wyn's direction, making Wyn proud by continuing to chew, rather than trying to speak and spraying crumbs across the floor.

"There is one small part of the wedding planning my mother has no control over, and I believe it would behoove us to take full advantage of that." Wyn gave a small laugh. "Well, perhaps it would be for my benefit alone, but I'd be much obliged if you could help me with it."

Roger took a swig of his tea to wash down his biscuit before he nodded enthusiastically. "Yes, of course." But then he paused warily. "What is it?"

"An important part of fae wedding traditions is the wedding spell. Traditionally, it's a simple act performed between the two getting married to demonstrate that their magics are compatible. Or at the very least, that they will not tear one another apart after the wedding bliss is over and the reality of married life sets in."

"How romantic," Roger mumbled.

"It isn't always, but then again, marriage isn't always romantic, either," Wyn reminded him.

"I suppose that's true," Roger agreed.

"As there have historically been very few fae-human weddings—*very* few —I've been doing a bit of research on what it could potentially look like for us to perform this spell together."

"I'm surprised you've had the time," Roger marveled. "I've been going straight to bed every night after all of our social obligations. Although, that doesn't necessarily mean I've been sleeping well…"

Wyn frowned a bit at this information.

"I'll have to share my favorite sleeping tonic with you. It works even better than what I gave you earlier." Wyn smirked at the way Roger's eyes went wide at that.

"Have you been able to learn anything useful? A-about the wedding spell, I mean?" Roger encouraged.

Wyn gave a bit of an uncertain sound in response, tilting his head from side to side a few times as he considered if what he'd found truly counted as reliable information.

"Well…" he hedged, forming his response carefully before he said it. "The books I've been reading have not been entirely based on research and facts alone."

Roger stared at him blankly for a moment, and then he gasped as Wyn had really hoped he wouldn't. "Wyndham Wrenwhistle, have you been reading romance novels before bed?!" The joy in his voice made Wyn smile, despite himself.

"Please, do shout it for absolutely everyone to hear," he grumbled. Roger cackled so wildly that he brought a hand up to cover his mouth, and Wyn rolled his eyes as he felt his cheeks go warm. "*Anyway*," he pressed, "I still have not been able to find very much. The authors seem to glaze over that part when the time comes. They're all naturally eager to charge forward to what happens after the ceremony, as I'm sure you could imagine."

It was Roger's turn to blush.

"So you're saying that basically we will be doing what nobody else has ever done before? And we have to do it in front of everyone we know?"

"And some we do not know," Wyn added helpfully.

Roger groaned and leaned forward to set his tea down before burying his face in his hands. "I really did not need something else to be nervous about."

Wyn chuckled softly. "Well, it could always be worse. At least fae tradition doesn't include something as ridiculous as your human bedding ceremonies."

"I do not even want to know what that is," Roger said miserably from behind his palms.

"Oh, it's when the newly married couple is forced to consummate their marriage in front of an audience."

Roger made a strangled noise and glared at Wyn. "I said I did *not* want to know!"

Wyn's smile grew even more. "But it's so enjoyable to see you blush."

Roger sighed heavily and flopped against the back of his chair. "So what are we going to do, then? Have you any ideas? Because I think I am nearly at my limit."

Wyn looked at Roger for a long moment until the silence finally made Roger pick up his head and return the attention.

"I think we should use what we've done today. It's like nothing I've ever seen before, Roger, and I'm certain no one else will have seen it, either. If my mother wants this to be the most memorable wedding of the Season, then I think we should give it to her."

Roger's eyes searched his across the distance between them.

"On one condition," he said finally.

"What is your condition?" Wyn asked, one eyebrow arching.

"This will not be for your mother. This will not be for anyone else. This will be for us."

CHAPTER 67

ROGER

Wᴙɴ's ᴀɴsᴡᴇʀɪɴɢ smile was slow and beautiful. "Very well."

Roger nodded once and then clapped his hands to his knees. "Right then. Shall we get to it?"

They settled back in front of the spellpaper. Roger stared at his work for a moment. "Frankly I'm still shocked I can reuse all this."

"I'm frankly shocked that this is the most extraordinary part for you."

Roger rolled his eyes. "I didn't say it was the most extraordinary. But it really is remarkable. Are we doing the spell exactly as we did it before?"

"I thought that would be as good a start as any."

Roger paused in the act of picking up his pencil. "As good a *start*?"

Wyn shrugged. "I think we're onto something truly…different. I haven't worked out exactly what we've stumbled upon, but this seems to only be the beginning."

Roger picked up the pencil and twiddled it in his fingers. He thought about their magic weaving around each other. He thought about the handkerchief, carried by two different forms of magic, working together and—he sucked in a breath—*complementing* each other.

Wyn chuckled at Roger's expression. "When you're done thinking over your latest discovery, do share."

"Our magics work together," Roger murmured slowly.

"Yes. I think we established that."

Roger frowned and got to his feet, hastening to his bookcase and pulling out several books before hurrying back to where Wyn sat. "Human magic doesn't normally work like that. Even when humans do magic together, we do separate pieces. Each person has their own spell, their own spellpaper, and we cast spells that will work in conjunction. But…but what we did wasn't like that at all."

Wyn looked pensive. "This is not an uncommon aspect of fae relationships. As I mentioned, the general purpose of the wedding spell is to demonstrate magical compatibility. It proves that the match is a good one."

"But it wasn't merely compatible," Roger went on. He opened a book and flipped through the pages. He found the page he was looking for and leaned over to write down the sigil. "This is an extension of the breeze spell," he explained as he scrawled the sigil and the coinciding formula. "It will give it a specific direction to go in."

"Was it not in a specific direction before?"

"Not really. It usually goes in a specific way, particularly when it's cast in a small space, there's only so much space for it to go. But you recall when I first cast and everything fell into chaos?"

"I recall," Wyn chuckled.

"I hadn't bothered to give it a direction because, well, I didn't expect it to be that strong and I didn't expect it to be an issue. But…" He finished the formula and sat back. "But I want to try something. I'm going to cast it and it will be the same level it was when we finished last time. I want to see if you can alter the spell as we go." He carefully laid his reference books with the pages he needed facing up. "I can go along behind and adjust to match. Just…er…just tell me what it is you're doing, if you would."

"So, you want me to intentionally disrupt your spell—"

"Yes."

"And you'll adjust it to match what I'm doing?"

"Yes."

Wyn considered. "And what about any elements that I add in?"

"Like the handkerchief?"

"Yes."

"I think...I think that will be interesting too. Honestly, let's throw whatever we want at this and see where it goes."

"Right." He picked up the handkerchief that was still on the floor where he had let it fall. "Ready when you are."

Roger cast the spell and then sat back, focusing furiously on the magic. As before, it took him a few moments to sort out what he was feeling—Wyn's magic, his own magic, he even thought he was beginning to sense the underlying raw power of the willow branch.

Wyn tossed the handkerchief in the air and it caught in the breeze as it had earlier, making a slow and lazy path around the room. "I'm going to reverse its course," Wyn murmured.

Roger felt Wyn's magic loop and weave backwards around his own. It was slower, like a trout swimming upstream. He hastily bent over and wrote out the reverse spell. He felt the change before he had time to look up and see it—their magics weaving back together, synchronized despite their differences—like two instruments playing a corresponding melody.

"Are you ready for the next trick?" Wyn asked.

Roger looked in time to see Wyn give him a mischievous grin before he tossed a second handkerchief in the air, sending it bobbing in the opposite direction to the first.

Roger swore, but he had never been more excited in his life as he scrambled to find a good sigil to try next. "Can you keep your handkerchief going while I focus on mine?"

Wyn leaned back, the picture of relaxation. "Of course."

Roger added a sigil to his sheet: a slight bump in power. The handkerchief buffeted a little in the briskness of the wind. Roger looked up, feeling for the magic. They were blending even more now, better than they had the first time. If he were keeping with the instrument metaphor, his own magic was the melody and Wyn's the playful counterpoint, both working with and around the main spell. Roger felt goosebumps over his skin.

"Why is yours going faster?" Wyn mused.

"I gave it a little bump in power."

"Hmph." Wyn's handkerchief picked up speed, while Roger's magic slowed a little.

Roger couldn't help the laugh that escaped him. "You bastard!" He leaned over and added more power to the spell. Without even looking up, he felt Wyn reverse the course of his own handkerchief and tug at Roger's speed spell to slow it down. He added to the calculations. Wyn added a boost to the breeze. On and on they went until the spellpaper was completely full of scribbles. Roger laughed as he sat back. "I've run out of space," he admitted. "I suppose I shall have to concede this one."

Wyn's smile was bright as the two handkerchiefs drifted back down towards the ground. He reached up and snatched them out of the air. He handed Roger's back to him. "You wrote like a man possessed. I had no idea your writing could be even harder to decipher. But I can't exactly complain. That was—"

"Magnificent," Roger breathed. He knew he was smiling as wide and free as Wyn. "Do you know what this means?"

"I think so but do tell me anyway."

"Our magics—they don't just correspond. They complement each other. They improve each other. Your magic gave my own a boost, even when you were racing me. It—that—that was the most powerful my magic has ever been, I think."

Wyn's expression sobered into one of thoughtfulness. "My control was…" He frowned. "After that little bout of magic, I would have expected to be exhausted, but instead I feel—"

Roger leaned up on his knees. "I feel invigorated."

"As do I."

Roger laughed again and clapped a hand over his mouth. "*Wyn*," he whispered. "Do you think this is true of all fae and humans or just us?"

"I couldn't say. But I can tell you're already putting things together. What global problem are we solving now?"

Roger had the sudden and inexplicable urge to haul Wyn closer and kiss him, he was that excited. Or perhaps it was the way Wyn accepted that Roger was always trying to solve things and, furthermore, had the ability to do so. He hastily squashed both thoughts and clasped his hands together.

"What if fae magic and human magic have been compatible all along? We've spent decades—no!—centuries fighting and squabbling and debating over whose magic is superior and whose magic is too wild and whose magic is too rigid. What if they were always meant to be done in tandem? Just think what we could accomplish together? I-I mean humans and fae working together instead of against each other?"

"It could mean a whole new way of doing magic," Wyn said quietly.

Roger sank back down from where he'd been kneeling. "Oh my," he said. He framed his head with his hands. "How is it that we keep making such massive discoveries together?"

"I'm not sure but let's set the world-changing solutions for tomorrow, all right? One thing at a time."

"Yes, you're probably right." He straightened his waistcoat. "Shall we try again?"

IN THE END, they worked until dinnertime, at which point Wyn looked at the clock, swore under his breath, and left to return to his family. Roger continued making notes, lists of ideas for spells and tricks they could try together. The next morning, he started a new list for their wedding spell.

When Wyn arrived, they worked on the breeze spell more. And though they agreed to not solve all of the world's problems at once, they continued to experiment with their collaborative magic, racing handkerchiefs then pencils. In one mildly terrifying episode, Wyn elevated two lit candles for them to try in the breeze. With each new experiment, their magics seemed to understand each other better, move more synchronously, the music fine-tuning to an elegant harmony.

Roger had never had so much fun in his life and it was with unmitigated disappointment that he learned their next social engagement was another fae wedding one.

"A garden party," Wyn explained.

Roger thought back to the last garden party they'd been to and how Wyn had seemed even more isolated than usual. "Will you be all right?"

"Oh, I'm sure I will survive," he said in a light tone. "See you tomorrow."

Roger went to bed disappointed by the loss of their time alone together. Not for the first time, he began looking ahead with some anticipation to their marriage. Would Wyn want to continue such experiments in the country? The idea of spending the rest of his life with someone who enjoyed studying, learning, and experimenting with magic filled him with such astounding joy, Roger had to force himself to calm down and be realistic. Wyn was likely indulging him in the same way he had indulged Wyn's own curiosity. He tugged his blankets up to his chest, fisting the fabric. *But what a heavenly life that could be*, he thought as he drifted off to sleep.

CHAPTER 68

WYN

THE MORNING of their second engagement party started with a flood of rain. If anyone else in London had been hosting, there would've been a good chance they'd have to postpone. Unfortunately for Wyn, his grandmother's home was built up so heavily with charms and wild magic that the rain had not touched the garden, the house, or anything else nearby.

As he expected, the garden hardly showed the season at all. The space inside the stone walls was caught in an early spring for the occasion, with fresh blooms and singing birds at the ready. Wyn had always thought he would like for his own garden to be similar someday.

This thought was interrupted when Wyn spotted Roger arriving with his parents. Wyn brought his drink up to fake a sip, rim of the glass pressed delicately against his bottom lip, hopeful it disguised the way he grinned like a fool at seeing how nicely Roger was dressed.

Wyn grabbed another drink from the table nearby and followed the smooth stones of the path toward the Barnes family.

"Mr. Barnes," Wyn greeted coolly, knowing it would make the man smile. He was right. Roger smiled and accepted the glass Wyn offered him.

"Mr. Wrenwhistle," he said back with a nod. "I'm not entirely sure what I was expecting, but it wasn't this."

"Impressive, isn't it?" he asked, eyeing Roger's outfit again. "You look very nice. I daresay I should've worn a flashier waistcoat. Next to you I practically blend in with the common folk."

"Oh, hush," Roger said, waving a dismissive hand at him. "You could never."

Wyn played his part and greeted Roger's parents, followed by the other guests as they started to arrive. They all made mention of the rotten weather in some way or another, making sure to compliment the Wrenwhistle family magic and how outstanding it was. Wyn nodded politely and agreed when it was necessary, thanking everyone for coming and directing them to the refreshments when asked.

After what felt like quite a long time of making small talk, Wyn realized that perhaps this did not feel as taxing as it always had before. He glanced at Roger standing nearby, close enough to touch, but enjoying his own conversation with some of the guests his family knew.

Was it possible that simply knowing Roger was around could calm him so?

When Iris Wrenwhistle finally made her appearance, she was dressed as though she was the one being celebrated. As always, her silver hair was done up in soft curls pulled away from her face, a bejeweled flower comb tucked into the style. When the attention of the crowd shifted to her, Wyn let out a slow sigh of relief.

"Now the rest of us can stop worrying about who is best dressed," Roger's voice came beside him. Wyn hummed and nodded.

"I would be happier if I could stop having the same boring conversation with everyone," Wyn said quietly. "I would much rather be back in your study working on more important things."

His words pulled a small smile across Roger's lips.

The crowd parted as Iris stepped closer to Wyn and Roger, giving them a bright smile that they both returned.

"You look lovely, Grandmother," Wyn told her.

"I could say the same about the pair of you," she said with a hint of a knowing smile. "The right clothes can do a lot of good, but there is little that could match the way you two are glowing."

"Yes, well, let's try and not embarrass my fiancé to death before the big day arrives, shall we?" Wyn said, stepping closer to Roger and placing a gentle hand on his back. "Walk with me?"

Despite the first smooth escape, they were continually pulled aside as Wyn attempted to guide Roger to a less crowded part of the garden.

"Gentlemen!"

Wyn swallowed back his groan.

"Councilmember Cricket," Roger greeted as he turned around on the path. "So lovely you could make it."

"Yes, thankfully the weather decided to cooperate after all," she said with a wink. "I do hope it will be this nice for your wedding. Will it be held outside?"

"Mother decided that was one of the fae traditions we could not compromise on," Wyn said, his voice a little tighter than he'd intended.

"I would imagine the large guest list lends itself to making use of an outdoor space, as well."

"Indeed," Wyn nodded, his focus wandering.

"After attending both of your siblings' weddings, I will be most interested to see how you make this day your own." That caught Wyn's attention. He blinked down at her, and she continued before either of them could respond. "I know I am not alone in wondering how your ceremony will end," she said, her eyebrows jutting up toward her hairline, heavy with implication.

Wyn decided to play along. Perhaps it would help build the anticipation.

"Ah, you must be talking about the wedding spell," he said casually.

"Well yes, of course," Councilmember Cricket said, her eyes going big as she turned her attention to Roger. "It's only the most important part of the day."

Wyn watched a little color drain from Roger's face.

"Oh," Roger said weakly, risking a peek up at him. "I-I was under the impression that it was just something of an expectation. Another tradition."

Councilmember Cricket laughed loudly.

"Dear boy, you've been misled. I know little about human traditions when it comes to matrimony, but there simply cannot *be* a fae wedding without the wedding spell!" Her eyes narrowed somewhat critically. "I daresay we're all immeasurably curious to see how you'll manage it, what with only one of you having the natural ability to call on magic." She leaned in and lowered her voice, hungry for gossip. "How will you do it?

Must there be an utterance of words? A coupling of thoughts? A physical connection of some sort?"

Wyn felt his stomach twist uneasily. This was the last thing Roger needed to be hearing. Yes, the wedding spell was important, but she was turning it into something far more than what Wyn had told Roger about. Maybe he'd made a mistake by not explaining what the rest of fae society would be expecting to see.

When neither of them spoke, she stepped back into her own space with a huff of annoyance, turning up her nose at their refusal to share any details. "You would both do well to remember that this is important. Not something to be indelicate with just because you are wading in unprecedented waters."

"It's always seemed like entertainment to me," Wyn said with as much indifference as he could manage, trying to stop her before things got worse. "To give the guests something to talk about for the rest of the evening."

"That's probably true," she agreed, her displeasure over being slighted fading as her grin returned. "But all the same, there's nothing more romantic than when it actually *works*."

The emphasis on that final word was all it took.

Roger gave her a puzzled look. "W-works?"

Councilmember Cricket looked between them a few times, her smile growing uncertain, as though she could tell she'd done something bad. Maybe it was the way Wyn was looking at her like he wished she would disappear.

"Everyone knows that the wedding spell can only truly work if the two people who perform it are in love," she said, the joy in her voice from before falling a little flat.

CHAPTER 69

ROGER

ROGER OPENED HIS MOUTH, but immediately closed it again. *The wedding spell can only truly work if the two people who perform it are in love.* In love? No one had mentioned they had to be in love. He dared a glance at Wyn whose polite expression barely masked a strong emotion underneath, although Roger couldn't determine what emotion Wyn was masking. All he could tell was that Wyn's jaw was tight and his lips were thin as he glared at Councilmember Cricket. They were supposed to be in love? How the devil were they going to get away with that?

Roger felt a little sick. He knew he had been falling in love with Wyn gradually in the past few weeks (although he briefly wondered if a few weeks *could* be considered gradual). But he wasn't at all sure Wyn loved him back. Considering the way he was looking at Cricket, Roger felt it might be safe to assume he didn't. He felt they could accurately describe themselves as friends, right? Friends seemed reasonable. They had bared their souls, they had been appallingly honest, they had been *intimate*. He knew he felt better when Wyn was around, happier, and more at ease. But did Wyn feel the same? Was Wyn looking forward to married life as much as Roger was beginning to? What would happen if the love was only one-sided? Would friendship be enough?

Feeling their gazes still on him, Roger opened his mouth to respond but only managed a faint little croak. He cleared his throat. "I...see," he replied. "I, er...I was under the impression it was common for fae marriages to be... you know...er...more like business contracts."

Councilmember Cricket glanced at Wyn. "Well, yes, of course, that does happen on both sides of society."

"So what happens then?" Roger pressed. He needed to know this rather desperately.

She gave a fragile laugh. "It's...it lacks spectacle. But everyone usually anticipates that with those sorts of marriages. Your marriage is sure to be different."

Wyn's hand slid from Roger's back to tuck around his arm as he said, "Yes, well, we've been hard at work in designing our spell. I'm sure you won't be disappointed."

Her smile brightened. "I was sure that would be the case." She looked between the two of them and finally seemed to decide it was time to bow out of the conversation. "I'm certainly looking forward to it. I daresay all of London is." She gave another laugh.

Roger felt his nausea worsen. Wyn's hand tightened on his arm. As soon as Councilmember Cricket strode away, Wyn practically hauled Roger to a section of the garden that was mercifully empty.

"I can see you panicking," he began, bringing his hands to rest on Roger's shoulders. "It will be all right."

Roger put a hand to his chest. "Did you know that we had to be in love for it to work?"

Wyn looked conflicted. "That is the general belief, yes. But, Roger, we've practiced. You said it yourself only the other day. Together, our magic is marvelous. We will amaze everyone. I'm sure of it."

"But they'll *know*."

Wyn's expression tightened almost imperceptibly. "They'll know what?"

Roger wrung his hands. He couldn't say *We aren't in love* because that was false. One of them was. He wasn't at all sure of Wyn's feelings but he had no desire to lie about his own. He finally managed, "Do you really think our breeze spell will be enough?"

Wyn seemed to relax a little. His thumbs gently rubbed over Roger's shoulders. "I'm certain it will. If we can replicate the joy on your face when we raced our handkerchiefs around the room, no one will be talking about anything else. I promise."

Roger let out a shaky breath. "All right. I trust you. B-but, Wyn?"

Wyn smiled a little at Roger's words. "Yes?"

"Can we please practice as much as possible tomorrow?"

Wyn's smile widened. "I'd like nothing better."

Roger *did* trust Wyn, but that didn't stop him from continuing to worry. He worried as he laid in bed, thinking about Councilmember Cricket's words, about the unreadable expression as Wyn asked *They'll know what?* He felt sick at the thought of performing in front of everyone. He'd been trying not to think about that aspect of the wedding. Having it mentioned by someone else had disrupted the blissful little haze that surrounded his magic work with Wyn. Everyone would be watching. Everyone knew Roger's Hastings score had been embarrassingly low. What would they say about him performing for an audience? What would they say about his own meager abilities paired with the awe-inspiring magic that Wyn could summon?

Alone in his room, he tried to remember how steady and strong his own magic had felt. Had that just been the excitement of the moment? His magic had never seemed strong before. It had wobbled most miserably during his examination. What if he failed again? What if he failed Wyn? What if everyone saw him fail and came to the dreadful conclusion that Roger didn't care for his husband? They would be the talk of London in the worst possible way.

By the time Wyn showed up after breakfast, Roger had worked himself back into a state of complete terror. Wyn stepped into the room, took one look at Roger and sighed. Then he leaned back out of the room and asked Notley to bring in some tea.

"Why are you sending for tea?" Roger asked, his voice more high-pitched than he would have liked. "We have so much work to do."

"Because you look like you're going to keel over and I would like to mitigate that particular catastrophe."

"I'm not going to *keel over*," Roger muttered, but he took the seat Wyn gestured to anyway.

Wyn gave him a long look. "Roger," he said in a low voice. "Talk to me."

Roger sighed. "It's just—I just—I couldn't stop thinking about it. I know what we're doing is marvelous and I really think it might be groundbreaking but—well, Wyn, you do recall how poorly I did on my Hastings Exam."

Wyn frowned. "What does that have to do with this?"

Roger flapped his hands expressively and then quickly clasped them together in his lap. "You *know*. What if I do just as horrible a job at our wedding? What if I fail? What if I ruin everything? What if—"

Wyn reached over and slid his hand around one of Roger's. "You are not going to fail. Isn't this exactly what you've been working towards? Proving to everyone that magic is not a single skill, but a multitude of strengths? Yes, you did poorly on your Hastings Exam." He paused. "You may recall that I am not the heir to my family's fortune either. The whole reason we were thrown together was to demonstrate the nuance of magical talent. And what better way to demonstrate that than with our breeze spell? Roger, you've *felt* it. You are not going to fail. I would never let that happen."

Roger met Wyn's gaze.

"You trust me not to let that happen, don't you?"

Roger took a deep breath. "Yes," he whispered.

Wyn smiled. "Good."

Notley rapped on the door and then brought in the tea set. Wyn squeezed Roger's hand once and then released him as Notley poured them both tea. After he left, they sat in silence as they drank. Roger noted that he could smell the lavender buds in Wyn's teapot from his seat and, surprisingly, the smell was comforting now. He took a deep breath in and out.

Wyn looked up from his own teacup. "Better?"

Roger nodded. "Thank you."

Wyn smiled again. "We're in this together, Mr. Barnes."

Roger returned the smile. Perhaps what they had—whatever it was— would be enough after all.

After they finished their tea, they got to work. They worked for hours. They worked through lunch—although Wyn protested at the sight of food being brought into the workspace. They worked through teatime. Roger used sheet upon sheet of spellpaper. They made the breeze spell carry handkerchiefs, they raced bundles of pencils around the room, they let the power ebb and flow, switching from one direction to the other.

But as the sun began to set, they knew their time to experiment was quickly drawing to a close. Dinner would be called soon and reality would come rushing back into the sacred little space they'd carved out together. Roger cast the spell. Wyn increased the power, sending papers flying off of desks. As their cravats began to pick up the breeze, Roger was brought back to the first day they'd practiced the breeze spell. Wyn uncapped the tube of powdered willow bark Roger had pulled out after lunch and tossed it in the air. Roger bent over his paper and added two separate sigils—one for one direction, one for the other. Then he looked up to see his work and drew in a gasp. The powder was spinning around them in the two different breezes, with Wyn adding currents to give the breeze even more motion, causing the powder to trickle up and down as it spun around them. His gaze met Wyn's.

"Do you think this would work?" he asked, his voice no more than a whisper.

Wyn smiled and took Roger's hand in his, gently pulling them both to their feet. "I think this would do very well. Perhaps some flowers instead of the powder." He looked around them at the powder still spinning around their little space. "Everyone will see that we're in our own little world. It's perfect."

Perhaps it was the exhaustion from working for so long. Perhaps it was the relief after such acute anxiety. Perhaps it was the soft smile that Wyn was giving him. Perhaps it was the magical way the spell was making him feel as if they were, in fact, in their own little world. Perhaps it was the final culmination of feelings he'd been trying to make sense of ever since he'd first shown Wyn his fire spell. Whatever the reason, Roger clasped his free hand around Wyn's embroidered lapel, tugged him forward, and kissed him.

CHAPTER 70

WYN

THE KISS WAS SO FAST that Wyn had no time to react before it was over. Roger pulled away with a sharp gasp, his hands flying up to cover his mouth.

"I'm sorry," he squeaked behind his fingers. "I'm so sorry!"

All at once, the willow bark rained down on them as their combined magic crashed to a halt, littering their hair and clothes. Wyn barely noticed.

"Wyn, please forgive me!" Roger continued, his voice getting thinner and shakier. Wyn reached up to hold the back of Roger's head as he closed the space between them. Roger's hands curled into fists under his chin in reaction, and Wyn grabbed both of them with his free hand and pulled them against his own chest. "I-I don't know what I was thinking, I just got swept up in the moment, I didn't mean to——"

"Stop talking," Wyn breathed harshly and pressed their mouths together. He kissed Roger through a second of resistance, through the moment he felt him relax, all the way to when he relented and leaned in. He kissed Roger until the man's knees threatened to give out, and they had to break apart so Wyn could steady him on his feet.

Roger pressed his hands to his cheeks as they changed color. The two of them stood staring at each other in the middle of their mess, breathless.

"Oh," Roger whispered, and Wyn could have sworn he was trembling.

"Roger," he tried, as gently as he could. He'd seen that same look on a wild hare just before it darted away, never to be seen again.

"You kissed me," Roger said, his voice wobbly.

"You kissed me first," Wyn said back, feeling nearly as uncertain himself.

"I did?" Roger swallowed hard. "Oh, good heavens, I did." Roger's legs really did give out then, and luckily he was close enough to one of the chairs that Wyn was able to guide him to a gentle landing. "I've gone and kissed Wyndham Wrenwhistle. Oh, how the boys at school would be jealous," he murmured, his fingertips coming up to his lips again.

Wyn laughed quietly and smoothed a hand down the front of his waistcoat before he tucked his hair back behind the points of his ears. He could feel how warm they were.

"I'm happy to help you realize any schoolboy fantasies, Mr. Barnes, but usually you save the gushing about it for when I'm no longer in the room."

"I—" Roger started, his face twisting in horror, and Wyn smirked.

There was a knock on the door, and it was Notley announcing dinner. They were quiet for a moment, giving time for the valet to escape to wherever he went when he wasn't standing outside the door, and then Roger puffed out a sigh.

"I understand if you want to go home now," he said.

Wyn's brows bunched together. "You force me to work through lunch and then dare to deny me dinner?" Their eyes met. "What kind of cruel husband are you going to be?"

Wyn's words seemed to break some of the tension in the room, but he still kept himself from helping Roger up out of the chair. He didn't want to do too much.

No, that was a lie.

He wanted to do too much. He wanted everything. He wanted to skip another meal and drag Roger up to his bedroom and kiss him until it was morning. He wanted to give in to every urging of temptation he'd shoved away for fear of pushing Roger beyond where he was comfortable.

Had he done the right thing by kissing Roger back?

Perhaps Roger had pulled away because he really had felt like it was a mistake, and Wyn had gone after him anyway.

Wyn reached out for Roger's wrist and pulled him back as he started for the door. Roger gave him a confused look and a million words flooded

Wyn's brain as he tried to think of what he wanted to say. *I'm sorry too? Did you want me to kiss you back? Are you glad that I did?* When he finally decided on something, he opened his mouth and simply asked:

"Yes?"

Roger stared up at him, and Wyn stared back, until finally there was the tiniest nod.

"Yes," Roger whispered back.

TORQUIL'S TRIBUNE

Greetings, fresh-faced folk and hospitable humans,

The second engagement party held in honor of Mr. Wrenwhistle and Mr. Barnes was another successful event. Humans and fae of distinction and status flocked to a garden party hosted by Councilmember Iris Wrenwhistle. Though the skies were grey, the party was full of life. Sources say Mrs. Wrenwhistle's garden is a horticultural and magical feat.

Mr. Barnes was among the best dressed, according to reports. This writer suggests that romance suits the gentleman. Sources also say that Mr. Wrenwhistle appeared smitten with his fiancé. All of London is happy in the knowledge that these two seem ready for a lifetime of love together.

The Ravenwings were notably not present at the party. But all of the Council was there, along with their families.

Sadly, that was the only time our favorite couple was seen this week. According to reports, the two have been holed up together working on their project for the Council. In their absence, London has turned its attention to Lady Fitzhugh, who called on Miss St. Clair twice during the week. The Thompson and Thackery families dined together—although sources suggest this is not an uncommon occurrence—still, hope springs eternal within the bosom of this writer.

The fae set was sadly lacking in gossip this week. We request that they do better next time.

As a small warning, the next column will be a little delayed as we will be breathlessly awaiting the verdict of the proposal Mr. Barnes and Mr. Wrenwhistle intend to present to the Council.

Until then, gentle readers,

Your esteemed editor,

Torquil Pimpernel-Smith

CHAPTER 71

WYN

WYN WASN'T sure what to expect on his way to the Barnes' townhouse Friday morning. There had been considerable awkwardness between them at dinner the previous night as they ate with Roger's parents and Wyn couldn't decide if it was more his fault or Roger's.

The truth was, he'd made a point of *not* kissing. It felt terribly intimate and much more emotionally charged than the other things he did with men between the sheets. Sage Ravenwing was the one exception, only because they had known each other for so long. Otherwise, on the rare occasion he had been kissed by someone, he'd bid them a good night and never seen them again.

But there he was, trundling along after leaving the florist on Bond Street, minutes away from seeing Roger. It was the same place they'd selected to arrange the flowers for their wedding, so Wyn had told his mother he was going to pay them a visit to check on how everything was coming together.

Wyn looked at the large bouquet resting across his legs. Not sunset peonies, but they would serve their purpose well enough.

At least, Wyn hoped they would.

After pulling a handful of the blooms out and instructing that they be put in water for Mrs. Barnes, Wyn carried the rest of his flowers up the steps to the study, where he found Roger already hard at work.

When Roger looked up at him, Wyn was satisfied with the way his mouth fell open in surprise.

"Good morning," Wyn said with his most dashing smile.

"G-good morning," Roger said, coming around from behind his desk. "What've you got there?"

Wyn looked down at the bundle of red roses tucked into the crook of his arm, eyebrows going up as though he wasn't sure how they'd gotten there.

"Oh, these?" he asked, lifting the bouquet and turning it this way and that. "These are for our work today."

Roger approached him slowly, adjusting his spectacles on his nose.

"You don't mean for us to use all of these in our experimenting," Roger said with a frown. "They're far too beautiful for that."

"Of course not," Wyn said, scandalized. He brought his free hand up to glide the faintest touch of his fingertips over the deep red petals before he plucked one rose, handing it to Roger. "This one is for you."

Wyn wasn't sure if it was on purpose or not, but Roger gave him a coy grin as he accepted the rose. "Thank you," he said quietly.

Wyn pretended not to notice as Roger brought it up to his nose. The act was so simple, but it warmed Wyn all the way through. He stepped past Roger to set the rest of the flowers on his desk.

"What are you working on?" Wyn asked, peering at the scribbles on the papers Roger had laid out. Some of them looked vaguely familiar, but none stood out as something Wyn could easily identify. He supposed he had plenty of time for that yet.

"Just trying to fine tune some things we've been working on. I hate to admit it, but I'm starting to think that perhaps my handwriting actually does have an impact on the way the magic works."

Wyn hummed thoughtfully. "Perhaps this is something else we need to include in our presentation to the Council?"

Roger let out a small laugh. "One thing at a time," he said.

To Wyn's immense relief, the two of them fell into their usual routine without any residual discomfort from what had happened between them the night before. Everything felt the same as it had before their kiss.

Wyn watched carefully as Roger set up for their breeze spell, narrowing his eyes slightly at the roses. "Do you think we should start with petals first, rather than the whole flowers as they are?" Roger gave a look that Wyn took as an invitation to continue. "It may be easier for you to learn the magic of them that way."

"Oh, yes, I suppose that makes sense," Roger agreed. Then his expression turned playful. "Though I'm not sure I like you saying it's for *my* benefit. We are both learning, are we not?"

A slow smirk spread across Wyn's mouth, and this time he made a point of noticing the way Roger's gaze lingered.

"If there is one thing my magic knows, it's flowers," he purred.

Roger's attention snapped away from Wyn's lips then, and he nodded quickly before returning to whatever it was he had been writing. Wyn pulled a few of the roses out of the bundle and, though he didn't enjoy it one bit, began pulling the petals off until there was a pile of them on the desk.

"Should we move to the floor as we have been doing?" Roger asked.

"We will likely be standing when we perform the wedding spell, so it might be wise for us to practice that way."

"Oh," Roger said, nodding again. "Ready when you are, then."

Wyn nodded as well, and Roger cast his spell.

That part of the magic was nearly flawless after so much careful work. Wyn's magic swooped up to join Roger's as it bent at the corner of the room, making its familiar curve behind the bookshelves. Oddly, Wyn recognized a new sort of resistance in the way his magic felt in the space as it moved. He focused harder. It was still there, almost teasing.

Wyn spun to find Roger scribbling furiously on his spellpaper.

"Is that you?" he demanded. "Are you pushing my magic out of the way?"

Roger chuckled. "Perhaps."

"Oh, absolutely *not*," Wyn challenged. He grabbed a fistful of petals and underhand tossed them into the air as their magic raced overhead. They were immediately swept up the way Wyn knew they would be, and he urged his magic to carry them faster.

Roger laughed and returned to the spellpaper, his magic temporarily losing the strength he'd been pushing into it. Wyn took his moment of distraction as an opportunity to send his magic looping directly into the side of Roger's face, pelting him with the rose petals in the process.

Roger gasped in surprise, and Wyn's own laughter faltered as he realized he had knocked Roger's spectacles off by accident.

"I'm sorry," Wyn said, fighting a grin. "Let me get them." He came around the desk and bent to retrieve them from the floor. When he stood up, Roger was right there, looking up at him with brown eyes and long lashes and Wyn's heart stumbled a little. Had he always been so winsome?

In an act that was entirely unnecessary, Wyn decided to slip Roger's spectacles back over his ears for him, settling the thin frame of them onto his nose. Anything to stay close to him. Any excuse to let his fingers brush Roger's cheeks, to tuck his short hair behind his ears.

Wyn gave him a little smile. "There. Much better."

"You won't think it's so funny when you're the one buying the replacements when you break them," Roger reprimanded, though it was half-hearted.

"I think we'll manage," Wyn reassured him.

With no more excuses to stand so closely, Wyn moved back to his side of the desk. Now that the petals were also scattered across the floor, Wyn turned his attention to the rest of the flowers.

"Well, I think that went better than expected. Do you feel ready for more?"

"And why should I trust you not to throw them into the side of my face, too?" Roger asked, hands moving into fists on his hips. "Those will have thorns!"

Wyn rolled his eyes playfully. "Roger, really. You think the best florist in London would sell roses with *thorns*?"

Wyn had never planned to keep the long stems for their experiments, so they worked together to remove them. After they tucked the stems away for peace of mind, Roger cast his breeze spell again.

By the time they let the spell fade away for what had to be the twentieth time that day, Wyn and Roger were on their backs on the floor, flower remnants scattered everywhere, laughing so hard they could scarcely breathe.

"Can—can you imagine if that happens at the wedding?" Roger wheezed, his hands finding their way up to wipe tears from his eyes. Wyn cackled and pushed a hand into his hair, the other resting on his stomach, willing himself to stop laughing.

With a slick twist of his magic, Wyn had changed the direction half of the flowers had been going. When they slammed into the ones Roger's spell had been carrying, they had burst apart into a thousand little pieces, creating a sort of natural confetti.

"I don't know," Wyn managed, his laughter finally mellowing. "It was actually quite impressive, if you ask me."

They settled into silence as they both worked to breathe normally again. When the only thing Wyn could hear was his own heartbeat, he turned his head to look at Roger. He was smiling up at the ceiling, eyes closed.

"Roger," Wyn said.

"Hm?" Roger asked.

Wyn felt his honest words come out faster than he could stop them.

"I'm glad it's you."

Roger's eyes popped open and he turned to look at Wyn with bewilderment at first, though it quickly faded to something softer.

"Do you mean that?" Roger asked on a whisper.

Wyn moved his hand off his stomach and laid it on the floor between them, palm up, fingers relaxed. Tentatively, Roger brought his hand down to place his palm against Wyn's, their fingers lacing together.

Neither of them said anything else, but for Wyn, it was enough.

CHAPTER 72

ROGER

Roger did not know how a person could feel so happy. *I'm glad it's you.* After Wyn had left the previous night, he hadn't been able to get the moment out of his head. Nor did he want to. It had taken everything in him not to pull Wyn into another kiss, but he didn't feel his side of things had gone particularly well the last time he'd tried that. It seemed best to let Wyn handle such things for the time being.

He still struggled to sleep, but at least the reason was a blissful one this time. He relived how it felt to lie on the floor next to Wyn, hands clasped together. The experience in Vauxhall Gardens had been extraordinary, but *this*—this had felt marvelous in a whole new way. It had felt soft, yet vital, tender and yet somehow solid. It felt like a foundation—but not a new one. It felt like a foundation they had been building together over weeks of trust, honesty, and understanding.

An anxious part of him worried that something bad would happen to mar all of the lovely feelings bubbling inside him. However, when he walked into his study the following morning, he felt too inspired to let anxiety cloud his thoughts. On and off the previous day, an idea had tickled the edges of his brain. He sat down and wrote another list.

When Wyn arrived, Roger had finished the list, but was busy adding notes and addendums to it.

"I think, just once, I'd like to see you take a leisurely morning," Wyn said as he entered the room.

Roger looked up and smiled at him in greeting. "I had an idea."

"Of course you did. I'm beginning to think your ideas are as endless as my waistcoat collection."

Roger chuckled. "I wouldn't go so far as to say that." He bit his lip before continuing. "What if we each used a breeze spell for the proposal on Monday?"

"Which skill are you thinking it would work for?"

"Control."

Wyn looked thoughtful as he sat in a chair. "We've definitely exhibited a mastery of that recently."

"Exactly. And…and I'm thinking if we present it last, we can tell them what we've been working on."

"For the wedding spell?"

Roger nodded. "I'm not suggesting we show them that, of course. We can present our rubric. And then we can…we can tell them what we've learned about raw magic and what we've learned about casting spells together."

"And tell them they'll see our theory in action at the wedding."

"Exactly!"

Wyn seemed to hesitate. "I think it's an excellent idea, but you do realize that's going to put added pressure on the wedding spell itself? Are you sure you're comfortable with that?"

Roger had considered that but he gave the question due thought. "I'm not sure to be honest. I-I know I'll be nervous no matter what. And regardless of what we say to the Council, we'll be showing everyone a new way to perform magic. That isn't changing."

"That's true," Wyn replied. "And what happens if the Council comes up to us at the wedding and says that it's a very nice idea but they don't think it would work on a larger scale?"

Roger took a moment to mull over the question before responding. "I don't think it would change that you and I…that you and I enjoy casting spells that way."

"No," Wyn said, smiling. "It definitely wouldn't change that."

"Then I think we should do it. The worst that will happen is…is that they won't adopt our rubric."

"Very good," Wyn said. "I like it. So that's four spells down, is it?"

"Yes. And that leaves us with only one. I've made a list of possible ideas for it. It got a bit messy though."

"That is shocking to hear," Wyn commented as he picked up the sheet. He read over it, turning the sheet this way and that to read all of Roger's slapdash notes. Then he tapped a spot on the page. "I think we should go with your fire spell for knowledge. You know I've always liked that one."

Roger couldn't help the grin that came over his face. "Wonderful."

Wyn stood and handed the sheet back. "Why don't you cast it for me again and I'll start thinking of something comparable?"

Just like that, they were back to work. It was remarkable how easy it was to work together. As Roger knelt in front of the fireplace, he was struck by the parallel moment from the beginning of their time together. The rapt expression on Wyn's face had been the first thing to give Roger hope in their partnership, and the first thing to make him want to know the man more. Now, with Wyn kneeling beside him, the rapt expression back on his face, Roger spared a moment to study his profile. It was so familiar now. Not just familiar, it was dear too.

Wyn caught him looking and gave him a sly grin. "A bit distracted, are we?" he teased.

"You could say that."

"Anything you care to share?"

Roger opened his mouth but, once again, words failed him. Finally, he settled on giving Wyn's own words back to him. "I'm glad it's you too," he whispered.

Wyn's smile broadened and he reached for Roger's hand, laced their fingers together, and brought Roger's knuckles up to his lips.

CHAPTER 73

WYN

FOR ONCE, Wyn wished he was sitting in his own library rather than Roger's study. He needed to put eyes on his own reference books or flip through the pages of information his family had compiled over the years. After practically forcing Roger to perform his fire spell again, Wyn sighed and sat back on his heels.

"What is it?" Roger asked.

Wyn rubbed a thumb and finger against his eyelids, working away at the strain he felt building there.

"I…" Wyn paused, the weight of failure pressing down on him before he could even form the words. "I do not have any idea how to match your spell."

He stared at Roger's fire on the hearth. He watched the way the flames flickered and bit the inside of his cheek hard, trying to smooth out the jumble of thoughts that had made a mess of his mind. Eventually, all he could manage was tossing his hand toward the fire in frustration.

"I cannot do something like this. Your human magic created it. Fae magic does not *create* things. It only manipulates what is already there." To prove his point, Wyn pulled at the air around them, feeding the flames so that they danced higher and brighter before them. "My magic thrives on air, and water, and life." He finally felt brave enough to look at Roger. "My magic *is* life."

"Yes," Roger said slowly. Thoughtfully. When a slight frown formed on his mouth, Wyn got to his feet and stepped away, his back turned to Roger.

It was unacceptable for them to make it as far as they had just to have his lack of an answer be the reason Roger's proposal failed. The man would never forgive him.

"I know that answer is not good enough," Wyn muttered. He heard Roger shuffling around behind him, and then there was a hand on his arm, and Wyn turned to look down at him.

"Perhaps it's the perfect answer," Roger said with a little smile. "Nothing says that each skill has to be performed exactly the same way, only that we want to see it demonstrated to the best of a person's ability." Wyn gave in as Roger tugged on his arm, guiding him toward the chair that had become his somewhere along the way. "Despite everything we have learned to prove how our magics can work together, there is no denying that human and fae magic are still entirely unique." Roger sat on the edge of his own seat, leaning toward Wyn as he continued. "If you have determined that the answer to the skill is something other than what I've come up with, then I trust you."

Wyn stared at Roger as he allowed the words to settle.

"You have worked so hard on this," Wyn said softly. "And I know how important it is to you. How important it is for so many. I only want every-thing to be exactly the way you want it to be."

Roger's forehead wrinkled before he let out a quiet laugh.

"Rarely have things ever been exactly as I've wanted them to be. But I am closer now than I can ever remember being." Roger reached out and put his hand on Wyn's knee. "I couldn't have done this without you."

How the moment had become so emotional, Wyn wasn't sure, but he placed his hand on top of Roger's and tilted his head a bit.

"Of course you could have." The corner of his mouth twitched. "It might've taken you thirty more years, but you would've found a way."

Roger made a face, but chuckled through it.

"Thank you, I think?" he said, sliding his hand out from underneath Wyn's so he could lean back in his chair.

Wyn looked at the clock before turning his attention back to Roger.

"Does Notley have anything against adding a little something extra to tea for us, or will I have to do it myself?" Wyn asked lightly, even though he was only half joking. Roger laughed again.

"Has today taken that much out of you? I do apologize if that's the case."

"I'm only getting my stress and worry out now so I can help take care of yours until Monday," Wyn told him. "We both know it's coming."

Roger's eyes went big for a moment as he forced out a sigh. "Yes. I'm trying not to think about it." Wyn watched Roger drum his fingers against his knees.

"You know," Wyn started, drawing the second word out thoughtfully. "I would suggest that we try another type of stress relief, but I know how you feel about that sort of thing when your parents are around."

Roger cut his eyes at Wyn, giving him a disapproving look.

Wyn's eyebrows went up in surprise.

"What's this? Not even the slightest hint of a blush? Are you starting to become unaffected by my charms already, Mr. Barnes?" Wyn lifted his chin with a bit of a frown. "I suppose I'll just have to try harder."

"I wish you wouldn't," Roger grumbled, which made Wyn chuckle.

"Promise me something?" Wyn asked.

"Yes?"

"I know you'll never agree to it for tomorrow, as we have quite a bit of preparations to make yet. But promise me you won't do any work before we meet with the Council on Monday?"

"How am I supposed to do that?" Roger asked, looking over his shoulder at all of the things scattered across his desk. "If I am here, then I will be working."

"Then I will make sure you are not here," Wyn told him.

"Where will you take me?"

Wyn smiled. "I'll come up with something."

WYN WORKED HARDER than he thought he could as he helped Roger prepare for their presentation. Armed with copious amounts of tea and biscuits, they'd spent every moment they had left making final notes, talking through their most important points, and deciding the order of everything. Wyn brought a stack of his finest paper so he could write out all of the final copies, keeping them far away from Roger's snacking.

Even though Wyn triple-checked that there was absolutely nothing left for them to do, he found Roger pacing frantically when he arrived to collect him on Monday morning,

Wyn fisted his hands on his hips with a pout.

"You promised," he said, following Roger with his eyes.

"I'm not working," Roger said quickly. "I'm panicking."

Wyn's expression turned more serious as he realized what Roger was wearing. "Is that the same outfit you had on yesterday?"

"I'm afraid so," Roger confirmed.

"I thought we decided what we were wearing today?" Wyn looked down at his own waistcoat. He'd picked a bright yellow to go with the gold one Roger had said he was going to put on. "Why did you put this back on instead?"

"I never took it off," Roger said shortly.

"Roger," Wyn sighed, striding forward to stop him before he could make another lap. He wrapped an arm around Roger's shoulders and guided him out of the room and up the stairs. Wyn waited patiently outside the door while Notley wrangled him into his clothes.

After collecting the papers Wyn tied up with twine the night before, he swept Roger out to the waiting carriage.

"Where are you taking me?" Roger asked miserably.

Wyn scoffed. "Away from your torture chamber, you poor man."

When the carriage stopped, Wyn got out to help Roger down. Roger gave a critical scan of their surroundings when his shoes reached the ground.

"I thought a stroll around the Park would do us both some good," Wyn explained. He was relieved when Roger took his arm without an argument.

They walked in silence for some time, only broken up by Roger's heavy sighs and whispers that Wyn did not ask him to elaborate on. He simply stroked Roger's fingers where they were gripped tightly on his arm and kept them moving. The longer they went, the less tension Wyn felt pouring from Roger, until Roger finally looked up at him.

"The worst they can do is say no," Wyn said.

"Right," Roger agreed tightly.

They had repeated the same conversation no less than ten times the night before, but Wyn knew Roger needed to hear it again.

"And if they say no?" Wyn prompted.

Roger took a steadying breath. "Then we try again."

"Very good."

"But—" Roger tried, and Wyn shot him a look, cutting him off.

"We try again. That's the end of that sentence."

Roger made a face like he was going to be sick.

"I think I would like one of those strong drinks you were talking about before," Roger said weakly.

"Absolutely not. My hand still hurts from writing out all of those copies. I daresay it'll be sore for a week. You will not be eating or drinking anything near those papers."

Roger nodded. "After, then?"

Wyn offered him a grin. "Well, naturally. We're going to have to celebrate somehow." He patted Roger's hand a few times as they rounded a curve in the path.

The lack of chattering behind them brought on a new wave of reality that Wyn wasn't sure Roger needed to hear at the moment. In a couple of days, there would be no more room for concern over an unchaperoned walk together like the one they were having. No more lingering as they told each other good night so that Wyn could return home. No more worrying about anything except for making sure they both got what they wanted.

Wyn had thought for so long that he knew what he wanted.

A life in the country with nothing to restrict his magic, no social obligations, and all the time he wanted to paint or read or do whatever else he saw fit to fill his time with.

Wyn peered down at the man on his arm.

How had he ever imagined a future without Roger Barnes in it?

CHAPTER 74

ROGER

ROGER COULD FEEL Wyn's gaze on him. He felt as though he was letting the man down by letting his panic take over. He hated that. Although he couldn't deny that the quiet walk in the Park, the singing of birds overhead, and the crunch of the gravel underfoot, was helping. So was the gentle stroking of Wyn's fingers over Roger's own. The arm under his grip, keeping him steady as they walked.

When had Wyndham Wrenwhistle become so necessary to his wellbeing? He used to think of himself as an independent individual. Yet here he was, needing the gentleman's calm like he needed tea. It was amusing to remember how horrified they'd both been when Wyn had been assigned to the project. Now he could no longer imagine doing this proposal alone.

They finally made their way to the Council's chambers. Wyn retained possession of the Council copies, which was just as well, since Roger did not trust himself not to crumple them. He took out his own notes and started to read through them again, his hands visibly shaking.

Wyn laid a hand over Roger's wrist. "It's going to be all right," he murmured. "We've been over what we're going to say. We're prepared for the worst-case scenario." Then he gently pulled the paper out of Roger's hands and added it to his stack. "Let's talk about what ingredient we're going to practice with next, after the wedding spell is no longer looming ahead of us."

Roger's mouth went dry at the reminder of the wedding spell, but he attempted to rally his mind in response to Wyn's suggestion. "Well," he said, his voice distressingly wobbly. He cleared his throat. "I'm quite partial to the idea of…er…of herbs or produce of some kind."

"Hmm," Wyn hummed. "Why is that?"

"Well, our pantries are likely to already have them, which means we won't be needing to cut anything unnecessarily. And it means we won't need to buy anything especially for the purpose."

"Frugal and ethical. I like it. Any particular herbs or produce in mind?"

Roger took a deep breath and let it out slowly. He clamped his hands together in his lap. "I was thinking berries might be nice. Although that does put us at the mercy of the seasons."

"Not necessarily," Wyn mused. "You will be married to a fae, remember."

Roger smiled at the reminder. "True. That will make things more convenient, won't it?" he asked, turning to meet Wyn's gaze.

Wyn returned the smile. The door opened into the chambers but Wyn caught Roger's chin with a light grip. "Whatever happens in there, remember that what we have put together is remarkable. We should be very proud of ourselves." He licked his lips. "I'm very proud of you and you should be too."

"Thank you," he whispered.

Then Wyn stood and offered Roger his arm. They walked in, side-by-side.

The councilmembers smiled down at them, which was a good sign. Wyn placed Roger's notes on the stand and handed off the copies to an aide. Then he slid one hand against Roger's.

Roger took a deep breath and began, "We have completed the rubric, as requested."

"Excellent work, gentlemen," Councilmember Wrenwhistle commended. "Would you be so kind as to walk us through it?"

Wyn gave his hand a squeeze. They'd expected this. In fact, they'd hoped for it.

"Yes, ma'am. Shall we start with the first skill? Power?" His voice went up at the end, so he cleared his throat. "We have identified a shrinking spell as a good choice to exemplify this skill for humans. It takes a significant amount of power to do this effectively and multiple times, so we think this will be an effective way to determine an individual's magical power."

"And for the fae equivalent," Wyn went on, smoothly sliding into presentation mode, "we have identified that the encouragement of growth in nature would showcase power. This is not altogether different from the current fae testing."

The fae side of the Council nodded approvingly.

"Next," Roger said, "for focus, we decided on a glowing spell for the human side. This will determine an individual's spell scope."

"Fairy lights seem like a natural equivalent to this," Wyn said. "Not only because of the nature of the magic being cast, but by the range for the lights themselves."

"Intuition will be tested with similarly parallel spellwork," Roger said. "The human spell for movement and the fae spells to manipulate air and water. This skill is unique as it will require several spells done in succession to verify the individual can apply the same logic and talent to multiple spells."

"For understanding," Wyn explained, "fire works well to test human magic. It is a basic spell and, when done correctly, destroys itself." He took a deep breath of his own before continuing. Roger squeezed his hand for encouragement and Wyn's mouth tipped up at the corners in response. "For the fae side, we discussed our options at length. Unlike human magic, fae magic is less reliant on bookish knowledge. There are no sigils to learn, no calculations to apply. In the end, we determined that a fae should have a thorough understanding of the nature they are able to manipulate. We would do well to ensure all fae children know what their powers are and can demonstrate that knowledge. It will differ from the other spells in that fae children will be expected to verbalize what their power can manipulate and then demonstrate it."

The fae nodded again. Councilmember Wrenwhistle smiled at her grandson. "A creative solution, darling. I'm sure we can all appreciate that."

"Finally," Roger said, "for control." He shared a look with Wyn before he went on. "For human magic, we recommend a breeze spell and for fae magic, we recommend a similar manipulation of air and wind." Wyn adjusted his hold on Roger's hand so their fingers were laced together. "However, we have an added observation."

The councilmembers looked up from their notes with interest.

"We learned, through much experimentation, that while fae and human magic are very different, there are some interesting similarities." Roger's gaze fell to his father, who gave him an encouraging smile. "Not only are there similarities, we discovered that the two magics are…compatible."

There was a small rustling across the Council at these words. "I take it," Councilmember Cricket said, "that you learned this while designing your wedding spell?"

"Yes, ma'am," Roger answered. "Although it started with a slightly different project in mind. Mr. Wrenwhistle and I were discussing the ingredients humans use for their spells. They are always treated before use, which compromises their magical integrity." He glanced at his father again. "They are broken down, much like they are when cooked."

His father's smile widened.

Wyn took over, just as they had rehearsed. "We agreed that using raw ingredients was kinder to the wild magic and we began experimenting with an untreated willow branch to see how it would interact with human spells."

"But that was highly dangerous!" Councilmember Gibbs said. "You could have injured yourselves severely."

"Clearly they did not," Roger's father commented in a mild tone. "Please continue, Mr. Wrenwhistle."

"It took some trial and error to get the sigils and calculations correct," Wyn went on. "I should like to add that it took far less time than it might have. Mr. Barnes has an excellent understanding of his own magic system. We had a workable spell within a single afternoon."

Warmth blossomed in Roger's chest at the words. He knew he was looking at Wyn like a lovelorn puppy. Wyn's thumb rubbed over the back of Roger's hand.

"After we found success with the initial part of the project," Wyn continued, "we started incorporating my magic as well. It is true that we did this, in part, with the wedding spell in mind. However, we were both struck by how well the two magics worked together."

"Which brings us to a new proposal," Roger said. "A separate one from our rubric. We learned that casting spells together gave us both added power and control. Moreover, we were not drained from the casting, even after hours of rigorous work. Our magics are unique and remarkable on their own. But together, we can expand the limits of what we know to be possible."

"As you are all invited to our wedding this week," Wyn added, "we would like you all to take note of our wedding spell when it is performed. It will be a display of magic unlike anything you've ever seen."

Roger's father chuckled. "I'm already impressed. We gave you one task and you came back having completed several. Regardless of the decision we make on your new proposal, you two have accomplished a great deal in a short space of time."

"Indeed," Councilmember Wrenwhistle said. "What a team you two make. I would also like to hear more about your work with raw materials. That would change a great deal for human magic, would it not?"

Roger nodded. "And it has recastability." More murmurings met this statement. "We've been using the same willow branch for over a week."

"And there is still a significant amount of magic left in it," Wyn added.

"However," Roger went on. "We need to do more experimentation on different ingredients and different spells."

"Well," Councilmember Wrenwhistle said. "We have much to think about. I believe your rubric will do quite nicely. Are we in agreement on that point?"

Councilmember Williams nodded. "It seems very well thought out."

Councilmember Wrenwhistle glanced at the rest of the Council, apparently taking note of the nods in agreement. She smiled. "Then I think it's safe to say your proposal has been accepted. Congratulations, gentlemen."

Roger felt as though he would faint with relief. Wyn's grip on his hand suggested he knew it and was determined to keep Roger conscious.

"I think we would all like to see more information regarding your other two findings. However," she added with a grin, "that can wait until after you have been married."

"And we most certainly look forward to seeing the wedding spell in action," Councilmember Cricket said.

"Indeed," Councilmember Applewood agreed. "That will be most interesting."

"Thank you, Mr. Barnes, Mr. Wrenwhistle," Councilmember Williams said.

Wyn scooped up Roger's notes with his free hand and practically hauled him out of the room. As soon as the doors closed behind him, Wyn dropped Roger's hand and his arms came around Roger's waist. Their foreheads met and they shared a breath for a beat before Wyn whispered, "We did it, Roger."

"We really did it," Roger whispered back. "I can't believe it."

Wyn chuckled. "You should. We worked damn hard."

Roger smiled, tasting Wyn's laughter as it swept over his face. "Thank you. I couldn't have done it without you."

"We already covered this," Wyn said, one hand sliding up from Roger's waist to cup the back of his neck. "You are a marvel, Roger Barnes. The world is lucky to have you and your glorious mind in it."

Before he could think better of it, Roger went up on his toes and kissed him.

TORQUIL'S TRIBUNE

Greetings, fearless folk and heroic humans,

It is indeed a momentous day. The Council for Fae & Human Magical Relations has accepted the Barnes-Wrenwhistle Rubric. This writer hopes that is what it will be called, as it has a very nice ring to it. Any letters arguing this point will be summarily thrown in the fire. The Council has not yet announced when this new rubric will be adopted although it was made clear they will be working to implement this change as soon as possible.

The rubric was not the only item of note in the presentation made to the Council. According to sources directly from the Council, Mr. Barnes and Mr. Wrenwhistle made two additional proposals alongside their rubric. Or, rather, in conjunction with it. The details were scarce, but it was inferred that more will be revealed at the wedding of the two gentlemen in question.

And on that note, this writer has most happily accepted an invitation to said wedding. We hope it will not be the event of the Season, but a glorious harbinger of more joyous occasions to come. Readers can expect an early morning edition detailing the events of the wedding on Thursday morning.

Your esteemed editor,
Torquil Pimpernel-Smith

CHAPTER 75

WYN

THE FIRST KISS from Roger Barnes had been a fluke. Wyn was certain of it. They'd been muddled with stress and exhaustion at the time, and Roger's reaction had been less than ideal. Wyn could hardly remember it, aside from the way Roger had scrambled away from him and apologized over and over again.

The second kiss from Roger Barnes had been irrefutably, shockingly *real*, and Wyn was still reeling from it as he crept down the front steps of his family's townhouse. It was late enough that he was certain the rest of the house was asleep, but he still wasn't taking any chances.

He had to make use of what little time he had left. The last thing he needed was one of his nosy siblings, or worse yet his mother, interrupting him.

Wyn pulled his greatcoat tighter around himself as he walked at a brisk pace. Though there was little to indicate it just yet, Wyn could feel a storm brewing in the thick air. He thought absently about what a miserable day for travel it would make if the rain stretched on into the morning. His family was set to leave for the country at a ridiculously early hour as it was; poor weather would only extend the misery of being cooped up in the carriage with them.

As he approached the Barnes' home, Wyn chewed the inside of his cheek. After all of the time he and Roger had spent together over the previous weeks, and considering that their wedding was in less than two days, he knew it was not altogether odd for him to show up unannounced. The late hour, however, was the reason that he'd come up with a story to explain, just in case.

Wyn politely declined handing over his hat and greatcoat after he was welcomed inside. He took care to make his boots quiet on the stairs, and paused outside the door to Roger's temporary study where he'd been directed to go.

The door was partially open, allowing Wyn a glimpse into the madness that had unfurled since he'd seen the room last. With no light coming in from the windows, and only a pair of candles to see by, Wyn was instantly reminded of the first time he'd visited Roger at his flat. It was dark and cluttered with random stacks of things piled everywhere. In the middle of it all was Roger, bent over the edge of a crate as he rifled through whatever was inside.

Wyn smiled fondly and tapped his knuckles against the doorframe a few times.

"I'm afraid I'm not going to be finished with this anytime soon, Notley," Roger said in a hushed tone without looking up. "I won't need you for the rest of the night."

"What about me?" Wyn asked playfully, his voice equally as quiet. Roger gasped and stood up, his hand flying to his chest.

"You startled me," he scolded, expression softening. "What are you doing here? It's the middle of the night." Roger glanced at the clock as though he was second guessing his assessment of the time.

Wyn reached into the deep pocket of his greatcoat and pulled out a bottle.

"I thought now was a good time to have that celebratory drink," Wyn said, a smirk tugging at his lips. Roger looked at him like he'd gone completely mad, but then snorted out a tiny laugh as he smiled.

"I'll go find some glasses," he said, shuffling out from behind the box he'd been packing.

"See if you can find some cake, as well," Wyn whispered.

"How many hands do you think I've got?" Roger demanded as he slid past Wyn into the hallway. "Come and help me."

After stumbling around the kitchen for a ridiculously long time, they returned to Roger's study with the wine glasses, half a cake, and two forks. Wyn poured the wine as Roger shook his head at their late night snack.

"Mother would be furious if she knew we were eating this way. It's so... it's so *improper*," Roger said.

Wyn narrowed an eye at Roger as he handed him his glass.

"Has your mother actually ever been furious about anything?"

Roger pursed his lips. "Well, no. Not that I can recall."

Wyn hummed thoughtfully and took a sip of his own wine. They'd moved everything off the sofa and settled the cake on the cushion between them. Wyn watched as Roger scraped the tiniest bite off the edge of it with his fork and stuck it in his mouth.

"I know you can do better than that," Wyn said flatly. "We're supposed to be celebrating." He picked up the second fork and poked it down into the cake with some force. The piece he brought away was misshapen and much heavier on one side, which caused it to fall apart just as Wyn got it to his mouth. The pieces tumbled down the front of his waistcoat, leaving a trail of crumbs.

They barely had time to look at each other before they fell apart with laughter.

"*Shhh*," Wyn admonished as he wiped at the mess he'd made on his clothes. He found the biggest pieces where they'd landed in his lap and ate them.

"You are a menace," Roger whispered loudly, still giggling.

"You cannot possibly believe I am the only contributor to the crumbs on this sofa," Wyn told him. "Or in this entire room, for that matter."

Roger gave him a sheepish grin, and Wyn's stomach fizzled, warm and happy. They sat in silence, eating and drinking and listening to the rain that had arrived. The candles flickered in the light breeze coming from the open window.

Wyn bounced his foot, staring at his wine glass where it rested on his knee that was crossed over the other. Evidently the one glass wasn't enough to bolster his confidence, so he poured another.

"You're going to be miserable in the morning," Roger observed after looking at the clock again. "Aren't you leaving early?"

"It will be worth it to have spent more time with you," Wyn said. He blinked at his own words. Ah, there was the wine.

"Oh," Roger said quietly, watching his own glass as he swirled it slowly in the dim light. "Yes, I was thinking it will be rather strange to not see you at all tomorrow."

"Quite," Wyn agreed. "I'm starting to question what I even did with my time before our project began."

Roger huffed out a laugh. "Enough to always give Torquil something to write about." He took another bite of cake and swallowed it. "I have to admit, I always wondered how much of it was actually true. The things they wrote about you, I mean."

Wyn considered his answer before he gave it.

"There has usually been some accuracy to what's been said," Wyn admitted. "Though exactly how much, I'll never tell." Roger's grin was enough to keep his words coming. "However, I happen to know first-hand that what's printed is not always the truth. What with the unreliable sources and all."

Roger's expression faded, and they exchanged a long look.

Wyn broke the heavy moment by draining his wine. No better time than the present. He stood up and set down the empty glass on his way to where he'd placed his greatcoat over the back of a chair.

"I've something to give you," he said as he reached into one of the inside pockets. Roger got up as well, but Wyn shook his head. "Sit, sit," he instructed as he joined him on the sofa again, moving what was left of the cake to the low table nearby. Wyn turned so he was facing Roger more fully, tucking one leg under the other. Roger did the same.

"What is it?" Roger asked, sounding suspicious.

Wyn took a steadying breath and held out the box for Roger. It was flat and rectangular, tied neatly with a thin silk ribbon. Wyn was glad his hands weren't shaking enough for Roger to notice as he took it. Roger set the little box against his thigh as he used both hands to untie the ribbon. After removing the top and unfolding some thin layers of parchment, Roger found what was inside and held it up between them.

"A…key?" Roger asked. He turned it to look at the other side, as though it held any more answers than the first. It did not.

Wyn pushed a hand into his hair, propping his elbow on the back of the sofa as he watched Roger's mind start to work over the simple gift. Watching Roger think had quickly become one of his favorite things.

When Roger finally gave him a helpless look, Wyn dropped his hand and sat up again, reaching for Roger's wrists. He gave them both a gentle squeeze.

"It's the key to your new study," Wyn said softly. "I've had one of the bedrooms completely redone with everything you'll need." He peered over his shoulder at all of Roger's belongings scattered around the room before he held his gaze again. "New bookshelves. New furniture. A new desk. I found someone to make it custom for you. It even has a neat little contraption that holds an entire roll of spellpaper, so that you won't have to keep loose sheets of it lying around all the time. You can simply pick however big you want the piece to be and tear it off."

Wyn felt himself starting to ramble, so he stuck the tip of his tongue between his teeth, breathing through his racing heartbeat.

"The morning our engagement was announced in the *Tribune*, I had never felt more terrified in my life. It seemed as though everything I had been working toward was swept away in a single moment. And I was powerless to stop it."

Wyn squeezed Roger's wrists again, his gaze falling to their hands.

"I wish I could tell you that my biggest regret is sitting down to write those letters to the gossip paper. Or all of the terrible things I've said directly to you." Wyn's face pinched with remorse. "I've said and done so many unforgivable things, Roger, and I am so very sorry for all of it. But my biggest regret is that it's taken me so long to treat you the way you deserve to be treated. The way you've *always* deserved to be treated."

Wyn slid to the edge of the sofa and carefully moved onto the floor, one knee bent, never letting go of Roger's hands.

"If you'll allow me to, I'm going to start this very moment and never, ever stop. Roger Barnes, will you marry me?"

Roger's jaw went slack, his eyes went wide, and Wyn let him go when he pulled his hands away to cover his mouth and nose. Wyn prepared for the worst. He braced himself for rejection.

"Yes," Roger whispered, and Wyn's magic burst. Wyn felt Roger's arms come around his neck. The air in the room swirled wildly, the candles went out, and Wyn got to kiss Roger first for once.

They didn't pull apart until they were breathless, hair mussed and faces flushed. At some point, Roger had hauled Wyn back up onto the sofa, and Wyn was painfully aware of how much of him was pressed firmly against Roger. With nowhere to go, he started placing gentle kisses on Roger's neck, just below his ear. The sound Roger made in response was far too enjoyable.

"Do you want me to stop?" Wyn breathed. "I can help you pack. Or I can pack while you finish the cake?"

Roger shook his head. "Yes. I-I mean no." He paused. "What did you say?"

Wyn chuckled and sat up enough to see Roger's face, but it was too dark. He snapped his fingers and a small cluster of fairy lights blinked to life overhead. Roger gasped quietly and stared up, the same as he'd done the first time he'd seen them, and the second. It warmed something in Wyn's chest.

Just as Wyn was about to repeat his questions, Roger lost a valiant battle with a yawn that he tried to cover with his hand. Wyn grinned down at him affectionately and shifted off his knees, moving to stand.

"Come on," he said, holding out his hand for Roger to take. "Let's get you to bed."

CHAPTER 76

ROGER

ROGER ALLOWED Wyn to lead him into his bedroom, too tired to be embarrassed about having the man in his private space. Although when Wyn started to help him undress, he woke up enough to be a little embarrassed by it.

I shouldn't have sent Notley to bed so early, he thought.

Wyn chuckled as he slid Roger's spectacles off and set them on the dresser. "That was me, remember?"

Roger gasped. "Did I say that out loud?" Then at Wyn's amused expression, he frowned, trying to remember. "Er...was it you?" Then Wyn started unbuttoning his shirt. "I can...I can manage."

"Would you like me to leave?"

Roger didn't, although he knew it to be ridiculous. They were only going one day without seeing each other. "No," he said, laying a hand on Wyn's wrist. "But could you turn around for a moment?"

He made quick work of changing out of his clothes and into his nightshirt. When Wyn turned back around, Roger realized he hadn't thought very far ahead. He flopped his hands at his sides. "I suppose it makes sense for you to go, after all, doesn't it? It's not like you can stay here when I'm going to bed."

Wyn cocked his head. "Can't I?"

Roger stared at him. "Do you...want to?"

Wyn plucked at the nightshirt Roger was wearing. "Do you have an extra one of these?"

Roger quickly pulled one out and then got into bed, averting his eyes to give Wyn some privacy. He heard Wyn chuckle again.

"I don't mind you peeking, you know."

Roger grumbled as he steadfastly kept his eyes on his lap. Then Wyn was sliding under the covers and gently pulling him into his arms.

"I know it's silly," Roger said as he tucked his head against Wyn's shoulder. "I'm going to see you the day after tomorrow."

He felt fingertips combing through his hair. "I'm not looking forward to going a full day without seeing you either."

Roger immediately felt better and relaxed. "We should probably think of an escape plan for you."

"Don't worry about it. We'll figure something out. If anything I'll climb out your window."

"You wouldn't!" Roger said, louder than he intended, as he looked up at Wyn.

Wyn smiled. "You mean you wouldn't like it?"

Roger settled himself back on Wyn's shoulder. "I didn't say *that*." Carefully, he let one hand slide down Wyn's chest and around his waist. It felt daring and intimate, despite the fact that they were both wearing nightshirts. "Thank you for staying with me," he whispered. "And thank you...for taking care of me today."

"You're always taking such good care of me," Wyn whispered back. "It was nice to return the favor."

"Well, soon, I'll be able to take care of you forever," Roger went on happily, although a voice at the back of his drowsy brain told him he was being a bit *too* honest. He yawned and rubbed his hand idly up and down Wyn's side. "You'll never have to go to London again, or suffer through social engagements or—" He yawned again and brought his hand up in front of his mouth before folding it between their chests. "Or anything. Just us in the country with our magic and our pets." *Fairy lights in the evening*, he thought. *Lavender tea in the afternoon. Breakfast at ridiculously late hours.* He nuzzled into Wyn's chest, still ruminating sleepily. *No silly columns to report on how much I love you.*

He thought he felt Wyn pull him just a tiny bit closer before he fell asleep.

IT TOOK Roger a few moments to realize why he felt so happy when he woke up. But then he felt a hand comb through his hair and he bolted up and away. "You stayed!" he whispered.

"I did."

Roger blinked at the early morning light shining through the curtains. "It's morning."

"It is."

"Someone will find out."

"Notley already did. He came in just now to fill your basin. I imagine that's why you woke up."

Roger contemplated this. "Did he…mind?"

Wyn laughed. "No, he didn't seem too fussed about it. Nor surprised either, actually."

"We really do need to increase his wages," Roger muttered.

Wyn hummed in agreement and then slid out of bed, tossing off the nightshirt and reaching for his trousers. Roger didn't look away fast enough. Wyn seemed to notice as he glanced over his shoulder and winked. Roger blushed and got up, pulling out his most comfortable clothes to travel in. Before he could take off his own nightshirt, Wyn was turning him around and pulling him back into his embrace, resting his chin on the top of Roger's head.

"We seem to have solved the potential sleepwalking problem," he teased. "Although I wasn't aware you talked in your sleep too."

"Oh, dear," Roger said, circling his arms around Wyn's back. "I do? I didn't keep you up, did I?"

"No," Wyn murmured softly. "You didn't keep me up."

"What did I say?"

"Lovely things. Lavender tea and fairy lights." He pulled back a little and when Roger looked up at him, he kissed him softly. "Travel safely, all right? My mother will be adamant about us not seeing each other until the ceremony. Another fae tradition. The gatehouse will be ready for you and your family. If there's one thing about my mother, it's that she's startlingly efficient."

Notley knocked on the door and then slid inside. "Mr. and Mrs. Barnes are in the breakfast room," he reported quietly. "I thought Mr. Wrenwhistle might like to make use of the servants' stairs."

"Thank you, Notley," Wyn responded. He turned back to Roger and kissed him again. "See you tomorrow."

Then he followed Notley out the door. Roger got dressed, too distracted to pay much attention to how well he was buttoning his shirt and his waistcoat. Then he asked for breakfast to be brought up to his study so he could continue packing, only to have his parents insist on him spending his last morning in London with them.

It was a frenzied day, full of packing and organizing, casting more shrinking spells than he remembered casting on his last move. He didn't even realize he'd missed a button on his waistcoat until Notley helped him into his traveling cloak. As they settled into one carriage with the servants in another, all his worldly belongings piled on top of the two carriages, Roger realized what had kept his head so firmly in the clouds for hours. Wyn told him what he had said in his sleep: fairy lights and lavender tea. But Roger had a niggling feeling his thoughts had continued beyond that. The carriage lurched into motion and Roger leaned against the side, staring out the window. He couldn't help but think that he *might* have told Wyn he loved him without realizing it.

They made their way out of London and onto country roads, picking up speed with the lack of hindering traffic. Bits of the previous night floated in and out of his memory: Wyn's proposal, soft kisses against his neck, his hand sliding down Wyn's chest. And then: *No silly columns to report on how much I love you.* He had told Wyn he loved him. And Wyn had stayed.

CHAPTER 77

WYN

LEAVING the cityscape behind always gave Wyn such a sense of relief. Watching the world transform outside the carriage, the buildings and walls fading into trees and grass, usually left him awash with calm and peaceful thoughts. Typically, there would be nothing waiting for him at the end of the journey except for warm summer weather and endless days of lazing about, painting and reading and napping in the sun.

This time was different.

This time, he would arrive in the country and step into a future he'd scarcely had time to process, let alone accept as his new reality. Wyn knew the warmth welcoming him home would come in the form of one simple, extraordinary man who had captured his heart so wholly that it felt like a dream.

A dream like the one Roger had talked through as Wyn held him the night before, unknowingly sharing some of his desires and secrets.

A small grin tugged at the corners of Wyn's mouth.

There was no doubt in his mind that Roger would've turned as red as the roses he liked so much if he'd known what he was mumbling under his breath in the dark. But Wyn could hardly deny that hearing Roger's words was everything he'd needed to know and more.

Roger loved him. *Him.* And not just vaguely, but in an amount that

Roger had deemed quantifiable. As Wyn's smile became irrepressible, he turned his face more toward the window in an attempt to hide it.

"Aren't Roger's prudish parents going to be disappointed when they find out their precious little boy has been deflowered before his wedding night?" Emrys teased loudly, extending his leg across the carriage to prod Wyn's shin with the toe of his shoe. "Or is there some other reason you were out all night and cannot keep that smile off your face?"

"Emrys, *really*," Mrs. Wrenwhistle scolded under her breath, sounding equal parts annoyed and too exhausted to actually care what he had said. She didn't look frazzled, exactly, but something close to it.

Wyn turned his attention to his brother, smile fading only slightly.

"At least I had someone to sneak out for," he said smoothly. "Isn't it odd that, even as the Wrenwhistle heir, nobody can seem to stand you? Come to think of it, your name hardly even comes up in the *Tribune*. I daresay that's quite an accomplishment, all things considered."

The smug look on Emrys' face slid into something darker. Wyn braced for the sort of wicked response that his brother was always so ready to give, but Emrys just leaned back in his seat and crossed his arms over his chest.

"I think it's terribly romantic," Aveline chimed in. "A few stolen moments to savor until you are both reunited for the ceremony." She sighed wistfully. "Is he a good kisser? I always thought his lips looked particularly soft."

Wyn snorted out a small laugh and caught their mother's exasperation out of the corner of his eye.

"I'm most certain that he would not want me talking about that sort of thing with anyone," Wyn told her. Aveline gave an indifferent shrug, and mercifully the carriage settled into silence for the rest of the journey.

As much as Wyn wanted to make a stop to check on the house he and Roger would be claiming as their own, it wasn't exactly on the way to the family estate. His mother had promised that everything had been taken care of. A new staff had been assigned to the house, she'd told him, and they'd been working for nearly two weeks to make sure it was ready.

Wyn managed to push away the thoughts of having his own steward and servants reporting to him as the carriage arrived outside the estate. He didn't care what his mother had planned for the rest of the day. His only goal was to escape to his bedroom one last time and sleep for as long as he possibly could.

FOR ONCE, Wyn was already awake when the pounding on his door started.

Reluctantly, he'd opened it to accept the large breakfast his mother had sent up. It was possibly the most thoughtful thing she'd ever done for him, considering how uninterested he was in facing whoever else had already arrived far too early for the festivities.

As Wyn ate, he thought of Roger.

He wondered if he'd been able to sleep restfully, if his trip to the country had been uneventful, if he was too nervous to eat his own breakfast.

Wyn checked the time. He guessed a human wedding would've already been over and done with. Meanwhile, theirs had not even started. He could already hear guests from Roger's side complaining about how late in the day the event was set to take place, while the fae side complained that humans made such a fuss over rushing to get things done. Had his mother planned anything at all with the humans in mind? Would there be a salad course to fight over?

Wyn closed his eyes and let out a slow sigh.

This day was not about any of those people.

This day was about Roger and himself.

After only a few bites, Wyn was hurried away from his breakfast, stripped down to nothing, dunked into a scalding hot bath that required not one, not two, but three servants for some horrific reason, and dressed.

Wyn turned around to look at himself in the full length mirror when he'd finally been released. His gaze trailed all the way down to his shoes and back up again. A small part of him had worried about what Roger picked for him to wear. After all, the man had zero fashion sense.

He grabbed the lapels of his gray coat and tugged gently, turning his shoulders to the side a bit. The waistcoat was a shimmery robin's egg blue with intricate silver embroidery and beading to tie everything together.

"Well done, Mr. Barnes," Wyn muttered with a grin.

Perhaps there was hope for the man yet.

The early afternoon was a whirlwind of greeting family and friends, accepting well wishes, and eating just enough to balance out the drinks Wyn was handed left and right.

Somewhere nearby, Wyn knew Roger was living through his own version of this party with his family, and he'd never wanted so badly to sneak *into* an event as he did that one. Even if he wasn't able to stay with him, or even talk to him, he thought a simple glimpse of Roger would be enough to reassure him that everything was going to be all right.

The sight of Auberon approaching him through the crowd was the next best thing. His brother offered his calm smile and stopped an arm's length away to take him in.

"Looking sharp as always," he said. "I expected nothing less."

"Roger picked it out," Wyn explained.

"You've trained him well, then." Auberon chuckled and reached up to squeeze Wyn's shoulder. "Happy wedding day, baby brother."

Wyn studied Auberon's face for a moment, let out a breath, and stepped forward to wrap his arms around him in a tight embrace.

"It's good to see you," Wyn said quietly before he let go.

Auberon's brow arched as he inspected Wyn a bit more carefully.

"Are you the same Wyndham I left in London?" he teased.

Wyn finally allowed himself a tiny grin. "Hardly," he admitted.

"Well, whatever it is that's happened to you, I approve." Auberon glanced toward the hallway and then gave Wyn an encouraging nod. "It's time."

Wyn followed his brother back up to his bedroom, trying to hide his sigh of relief when the door was closed behind them, shutting out the noise.

"Darling," his grandmother greeted, stepping closer to place her hands on Wyn's cheeks. She peered up at him with a twinkle in her eye and a satisfied smile that spoke volumes. *Yes*, he wanted to tell her, *you were right all along.* She seemed to know it and gave him a cheeky wink as she let his face go.

"Grandmother, I do not want to hear one single word about how fortuitous tonight's happenings seem to be," Wyn warned, though he couldn't stop himself from grinning back at her. "Take as much credit as you see fit, but do not pretend you've had no part in how this has turned out."

"I haven't the slightest idea what you're talking about," she said primly as she accepted a bundle of fabric from one of the servants. Iris laid it out on Wyn's writing desk and gently started to unroll it, revealing what was inside.

A mixture of curiosity and nerves started to burble in Wyn's chest as he glanced at the items. He knew what each one symbolized quite well, as he'd presented them to Auberon before his own wedding over the summer. Wyn had taken his duty very seriously, honored to have been asked to stand with him for the ceremony. He thought knowing exactly what was about to happen would help ease his own nerves. However, watching his brother accept them and accepting them himself were two entirely different things.

Iris took the time to arrange each item with care before she gestured to Auberon and stepped back, clasping her hands in front of her. Auberon moved to stand in front of Wyn and cleared his throat. Wyn knew all the words he was about to hear, and he wasn't sure if that made him more or less anxious.

Auberon picked up the peachy pink peony and laid it neatly against Wyn's lapel before he collected the small pin and secured it in place. "A single bloom of your choosing," he began carefully, "to represent the beauty and growth your union will bring."

Next, he reached for the small glass vial full of oil. He opened it slowly and held it out for Wyn to take. Wyn accepted it and held the tip of his middle finger over the opening, tilting it just enough so he could feel a drop of it collect there. "A blend of the fauna from your new home," Auberon continued, "to welcome you into the next steps of your life together." Wyn swallowed and tucked his fingers underneath the curls of his hair so he could dab the oil behind his ear. He repeated the process on the other side, his heart fluttering at the thought of Roger doing the same with the other half of the oil that had been mixed specifically for them.

Auberon capped the vial and set it back down. He grabbed the nondescript sachet next and held that out for Wyn, too. "Rosemary," he said, "to encourage love and happiness into your relationship." Wyn brought the little bundle up to his nose and breathed in the scent of the dried herbs, closing his eyes for a moment before he tucked the sachet into his pocket.

There was only one item left, and it was arguably the most important. It would serve as the reminder for everyone who saw it that this was real.

Wyn held his hand out, palm up, and accepted the thin band he would place onto Roger's finger. "And the ring," Auberon said finally. "This one is self explanatory," he added under his breath. Iris cleared her throat in a disapproving way, and Auberon gave her a guilty look before he voiced his conclusion properly. "And the ring, an endless reminder of your commitment and dedication to Roger, and his to you."

Wyn pocketed the ring and pressed his lips together, offering his brother a tight nod. "Thank you," he managed.

A knock on the door pulled their attention. Mrs. Wrenwhistle poked her head inside before she opened it all the way. She had picked a dress the color of their flowers, and Wyn would've expected nothing less.

"Oh, Wynnie, everything looks just perfect in the garden," she gushed, both hands landing over her heart. "I know you're going to love it." His mother wrapped her hand around his arm and beckoned him toward the door. "Everyone is waiting."

Wyn nodded again, not trusting himself to speak. He allowed her to drag him out of the room, down the stairs, and to the set of double doors that led to the main patio of the garden. Auberon and Iris slipped out ahead of them to take their places. Wyn took a steadying breath and turned as he felt another hand on his shoulder. His father was there, silent and supportive as he always was.

When the doors opened and the music started to play, Wyn felt a thousand eyes on him like sparks from a flame, burning tiny holes into his clothes and face. He tried to take everything in and appreciate all of the work his mother had put into this, but he could hardly focus on anything aside from walking down the narrow path and taking his place at the end like he knew he was supposed to.

Wyn shrugged away from his parents' hands as quickly as he could and locked eyes with Auberon, seeking some kind of reassurance that the pain he'd just lived through was worth it. He found what he needed in his brother's gentle smile and encouraging nod.

With a deep breath in and out, Wyn moved to stand where Auberon gestured. Slowly, he turned to face the crowd of people staring back at him. When it had been promised that all of London would turn out for the event, Wyn thought it'd been an exaggeration. It was not.

His magic stirred in his chest with uncertainty as he processed the reality of the situation. He and Roger were about to stand in front of all these people and not only promise their love to one another, but *prove* it. The wedding spell would reveal all of their hard work and truths all at once. Wyn's jaw worked as he forced himself to focus on calming things. The magnificent displays of their sunset peonies. The fairy lights. The gentle music.

The sound of the doors opening again made Wyn snap to attention.

There was his calm. His balance. His person.

CHAPTER 78

ROGER

ROGER HAD FELT off-kilter all day. From waking up in a strange bed, to greeting friends and family who traveled for the occasion, to finally being pulled away to a quiet room for what turned out to be the beginning of the ceremony. His father brought forth a bundle of items, wrapped in fine fabric. Included was a small script that his father read from as he handed each item to Roger. Each item had weighty meaning to it, causing Roger to sweat a little with every added symbolic gift.

Although, the effect was marred somewhat by his father's commentary punctuating the proceedings. "*I wonder what they do to create this oil. Is there a magic used in the making of it?*" Or "*Rosemary holds a great deal of significance to the fae culture, you know. Although I really ought to ask Iris why this is the herb used for weddings, instead of, say—oh, sorry, Roger. Getting distracted. Where was I?*"

It all drove home the great social significance of this wedding. He and Wyn had, thankfully, gotten so carried away in their own little world that he had forgotten why they'd been pressured into the union in the first place. People were counting on them to represent the union of two halves of society, two squabbling factions finding peace.

Would he be able to tuck Wyn safely away in the country and still uphold that promise? It was strange how quickly he'd gone from begrudgingly marrying the man for the sake of society to being outrageously protective of him, prioritizing him even higher than the good of society. He took a deep breath as his father led him out of the room and to where his mother was sitting. Such worries could wait. They had a wedding to get through. A wedding, a party, and a wedding spell they had promised would be magic the likes of which had never been seen before. *Why had that seemed like such a good idea?*

He was grateful that the fae tradition did encourage both of his parents to lead him to the ceremony. He found he needed two arms to grip as he made his way through the building and to the garden.

The doors opened and the first thing Roger saw was the crowd of people turning to look at him. The attention was enough to make him tremble. But then he caught the color of the peonies he and Wyn had picked out. There were lavish bouquets all over the garden. The same blooms that Wyn had tapped him on the nose with in his mother's parlor were now spilling out of vases and tied together with ribbons. Then, above the crowd of spectators and the sea of flowers, stood Wyn on the other side of the garden.

They strode slowly down the aisle and Roger couldn't keep his eyes off the man waiting for him. Everything else fell away. Wyn looked utterly beautiful in the robin's egg blue Roger had picked out. The silver embroidery had turned out even better than he'd imagined. A part of him had worried that Wyn would scoff at his choice of gray for the suit. But it looked so lovely and stately with the blue that he couldn't resist a small feeling of pride in his choices.

When he had seen the waistcoat Wyn chose for him, he'd clapped his hand over his mouth at the burst of laughter that tumbled out. He still could not have described the difference but he *knew* it was coral. The dark blue of the suit to go with it had given him a small fluttering in his chest—they had both chosen blue for each other—surely that meant something.

Soon, he was standing in front of Wyn, who reached out to take his hands. Roger's mother kissed his cheek before moving to her seat, while his father took up his place beside Roger, opposite Auberon Wrenwhistle. Roger realized that he had absolutely no idea what to do. In all the talk about the wedding, there had been precious little discussion about what was expected of them during the ceremony. But Wyn squeezed his hands and gave him a soft smile. Roger smiled back up at him. They could do this. They had pushed the bounds of magic together, they had redefined skill together, they had done things that would change people's lives. Together, they could do anything.

The ceremony was something of a blur. They sipped wine from a glass as they recited promises of sharing joy and trouble. They exchanged the rings they'd been handed before. They clasped hands as ribbons were wound around their wrists. Crowns made of flowers, woven vines, and little bells were brought forth and placed on their heads. And finally, *finally* they were told to kiss. Roger privately felt that the kiss was the best part of the situation. Their hands were still wound with ribbon so Wyn was unable to cup his neck or his cheek but Roger liked the way the ribbons tightened as Wyn clasped his hands and pulled him close.

As they broke apart from the kiss, Wyn rested his forehead against Roger's and whispered, "If you get nervous, just keep your eyes on me, all right? You can even send the flowers directly into my face if it helps."

Roger laughed in surprise and Wyn's answering smile made him feel lightheaded. The ribbons were carefully untied and unwound. From what Roger could determine, it was tradition to keep all of the little items from the wedding. Then a small table was brought forth, along with all the things they'd listed as necessary for their spell. A hush fell over the crowd, which immediately caused Roger's nerves to flare. He remembered Wyn's words and met his gaze. Wyn reached up and cupped his cheek, stroking his thumb over Roger's temple. Then he nodded.

Roger nodded back and turned to the items before him. They had managed to get a lovely willow branch—not *their* willow branch as it had wilted somewhat after over a week's worth of use. Roger set it in the familiar spiral and picked up his pencil. His hands were shaking. He looked up at Wyn and then got to work.

As planned, he cast the breeze spell first. He heard the murmur of the crowd as the spell began its circuit of the garden—Wyn had given him the approximate dimensions when they'd started planning. Then he felt Wyn's magic scooping up flower petals and twining them into Roger's breeze spell. Roger smiled at the familiarity of it all. It didn't feel exactly like it had in his study—it felt bigger, grander, with more power behind it. He remembered their conversation in Hyde Park. He had worried that his nerves would negatively impact the casting. But while he certainly felt nervous, he also felt light and giddy. It was terrifying to show people what they'd worked so hard on, but it was thrilling too. He bent over his paper and added another sigil, sending the spell in the opposite direction. Wyn brought up another bundle of petals to slide into the second breeze.

This time, there was no race, no laughing on the floor until their stomachs hurt. But there was still the lingering feeling of Wyn's hushed words in the darkening room, *I'm glad it's you.* He felt their magic twining in and around each other. He added more power to his spell and felt Wyn do the same.

Wyn's hand closed over his wrist and he allowed himself to be pulled away from his paper. They stood in the center of the two spells—although Roger was certain that Wyn was keeping them both going at this point. Then, Wyn snapped his fingers, adding his fairy lights to the mixture, bobbing in between flowers. Murmurings of awe and approval rippled through the onlookers. Like their first day doing it, their cravats whipped in the breeze, their hair ruffled by passing petals.

Fairy lights in the evening, Roger thought. *And I don't even care if the* Tribune *reports how much I love you.* Then Wyn pulled him closer and without ribbons to keep their hands restricted, Wyn's fingers were in his hair, cupping his neck and Wyn kissed him deeply and tenderly. Wyn, who had asked him to marry him when no one else was around, who told him he was clever, and who held him when he slept. Roger smiled against his lips and kissed his husband back.

CHAPTER 79

WYN

WITH THE CEREMONY COMPLETE, Wyn and Roger had no other wedding obligations to fulfill. They'd played their part as they'd been told. They'd performed the wedding spell flawlessly. They'd proven to everyone in attendance that while Torquil Pimpernel-Smith may sometimes rely on highly questionable sources for their gossip paper, ultimately they'd been more insightful about Wyn and Roger's relationship from the very beginning than perhaps anyone else—aside from Iris Wrenwhistle, of course.

If it had been up to Wyn alone, he would've ended their kiss and scooped Roger up into his arms that instant so that he could finally make good on his promise and steal him away. Wyn knew exactly where their carriage was waiting.

Unfortunately, he knew it could not be so simple.

His mother had already warned him that they would be expected to stay and partake in the drunken merriment that would unfold as the party stretched into the morning. Their wedding spell was history in the making, as was their marriage. It only made sense for them to linger at the party. They needed to celebrate their role in changing the way society viewed human and fae relationships—be it magical or romantic.

Wyn decided to acquiesce under one condition: he and Roger would be allowed a few minutes alone after the ceremony.

It only occurred to him that he'd failed to tell Roger this little detail until he was all but dragging him away from the ceremony space. Roger went willingly, but the look of confusion on his face grew with every twist and turn through the empty part of the garden.

"Where are we going?" Roger asked in a loud whisper.

"Somewhere quiet," Wyn whispered back.

They ended up in a spot that was dark and private, far enough away that the sounds of the party were nothing but a distant hum. Wyn guided Roger to the little bench he'd known was waiting there for them. It had seemed so big when he was a child, but when they sat, there was hardly enough room for both of them. Wyn didn't mind the way it forced them to sit so closely, pressed together from shoulder to hip to knee.

Wyn crossed his knees so he could close the space between them even more as he pulled Roger's hands onto his lap and held them. He closed his eyes and pulled in a slow, steady breath. He had many things he wanted to say to Roger, but all of them felt too small. *Lovely to see you*, he thought to himself, rather than saying it aloud. *I missed you.*

When Roger pulled his hands out from underneath Wyn's, he worried he was being ridiculous. Given the circumstances, he knew what everyone at the party would likely think when they stumbled back into the spotlight together after disappearing into the night for a short while. But that wasn't what he wanted. He just wanted a moment with Roger; a moment to escape.

Wyn opened his eyes and began to offer an apology, or at least an explanation. His words were cut short as he felt Roger's arms wrapping around his middle. Roger's cheek landed against his chest, and then he squeezed just enough to convey his quiet support. Just enough to give Wyn exactly what he needed, even though he hadn't known it himself.

The back of Wyn's throat burned with emotion as he wrapped Roger in an equally supportive embrace, resting his chin against Roger's dark hair.

Upon returning to the ceremony space, they found it had been entirely transformed. Wyn thought it looked impressively similar to the dance floor at Vauxhall. Roger's face lit up with a quiet gasp when he saw it. Wyn tucked away a mental note to thank his mother for everything later as he and Roger took to the floor for their first dance.

The two of them were inseparable until Roger made a comment that he was in desperate need of a refreshment. Wyn left Roger to talk with his parents as he searched for a couple of drinks. The process was slowed considerably by the number of people who stopped him to offer more congratulations, most of which had something to do with their wedding spell. He'd been correct that nobody had ever seen anything quite like it. They all wanted to know more. How did it feel when their magics combined? What had their process been like, using a raw ingredient with human magic? Had it been at all dangerous?

Wyn tried his best to offer some succinct answers so he could move on, but secretly he didn't want to be giving away any information without Roger. It felt wrong to speak about their experience without sharing both sides.

After successfully evading the praise Councilmember Cricket tried to give him, Wyn made his way to the table lined with rows of flutes that bubbled with sparkling wine. Wyn inspected them briefly, a small frown forming on his lips, before he asked one of the servants for water instead. As they rushed to fetch two glasses, Wyn turned around to watch the party happening all around him.

He wasn't entirely surprised to find Sage slinking toward him. Wyn eyed him carefully where he stopped a short distance away.

"Mr. Ravenwing," he greeted. "Enjoying your evening, I hope?"

"Mr. Wrenwhistle," Sage returned. "Your mother always did know how to throw an impressive party."

Wyn let out a tart laugh as he turned his focus back to all of the chattering and laughter and dancing. "Yes, she's outdone herself this time."

Unease grew between them until Sage broke the silence.

"I only wanted to offer my congratulations," he said. "The wedding spell was remarkable. Undeniable."

"That was the intent," Wyn told him. He had little interest in conversing with the man until he knew for sure that he'd apologized to Roger. The servant returned with his water then, and he accepted the glasses before giving Sage a dismissive glance.

"He's lucky to have you," Sage called after him.

Wyn kept walking. "I'm the lucky one," he said under his breath.

Roger accepted his drink readily when Wyn found him again. Even though their dance had been over for some time, Roger appeared flushed. Wyn's brows pinched together.

"Are you well?" he asked softly.

"Y-yes," Roger said, nodding. "It's only...er...well, Emrys was just saying something about you and me being gone for a while. You know, before."

Wyn rolled his eyes and scanned the crowd for his brother.

"You'll do well to ignore everything he says, Roger," came another voice. Wyn and Roger both turned to find Auberon giving them a playful grin. "It's what the rest of us have done for as long as I can remember."

"Oh," Roger said quietly, looking uncertain. Wyn placed his hand on Roger's back and gave Auberon a grateful smirk.

"The two of you looked wonderful performing your wedding spell. I think you've managed to put Rose and me to shame," Auberon said with a quiet laugh.

It was a compliment all on its own, but Wyn knew to look deeper. He and Rose were madly in love long before their wedding day arrived. Their own wedding spell had been nothing short of beautiful, a clear expression of their feelings for one another. Wyn felt heat creep in underneath his cravat at the thought of what he and Roger had done being even half of what Auberon and Rose had shown off for all of their family and friends.

Somehow, everyone knowing how intense Wyn's feelings were for Roger was twice as embarrassing as them thinking they'd snuck off for a quick romp behind the hedges.

"Was it because of the fairy lights?" Roger asked earnestly, grinning up at Wyn. "I do enjoy that, no matter how many times I see it."

Auberon and Wyn exchanged a glance. His brother's expression softened into something telling, and Wyn's nerves prickled as he tried to decide what Auberon was about to say.

"I meant the kiss," Auberon said. "But I must admit, the more I hear you speak, the more I understand why Wyn has fallen completely in love."

Wyn's eyes went wide as his face burned hot. Roger's nervous laughter only made the situation worse. Wyn gulped down the rest of his water and excused both of them from Auberon's ridiculous, eldest-brother antics.

Before Wyn could even begin to collect himself and form a coherent thought, they were intercepted by another annoyingly satisfied smile as

Torquil Pimpernel-Smith took a long sidestep into their path, hands in their pockets.

"Ah," they sighed. "There are my lovebirds."

"*Your* lovebirds?" Roger asked.

"Well yes, of course. I take full credit for this evening. I told you you'd be thanking me soon enough."

Wyn tried to find it in himself to be angry with the gossip writer who had gone so far out of their way to twist their story for society's entertainment. He tried to think of a way to express the frustration and shock he and Roger felt after being smeared across the *Tribune* week after week.

In the end, Wyn could only let out a sigh and gesture vaguely to the party.

"And have we given you what you hoped for?"

Torquil's eyes sparkled as their smile grew impossibly wider.

"Most certainly. In more ways than one. But of course, you already know that." Torquil breathed in noisily and let out a satisfied sigh.

Wyn narrowed his eyes. "I only ask one thing of you." Torquil's eyebrows went up expectantly. "Make sure that this wedding gets the recognition it well deserves. It's the only hope I have for my mother letting me move on with my life in peace."

Torquil laughed and dipped their head in an understanding nod.

"That's an easy one. The real challenge will be waiting to see what the two of you give me next. The possibilities are endless, gentlemen."

CHAPTER 80

ROGER

TORQUIL WINKED AND SAUNTERED AWAY. Despite their playful attitude, Roger thought he detected a tightness in the writer's shoulders and a paleness to their complexion that reminded him of Wyn when he was uncomfortable. He wondered if the writer's ease was an act.

"I do so hate to say it," Roger murmured, "but we really might owe them our thanks."

Wyn sighed. "Perhaps. I imagine they have a good enough impression after our wedding spell."

Roger thought back to Wyn's oldest brother's comments on the spell. He'd said Wyn was in love and Wyn's eyes had gotten wide at the statement. Roger had been too nervous to say anything other than laugh gamely. He didn't know if Wyn was truly in love with him. He had proposed, and he had kissed him so spectacularly during the spell, and the spell had gone *so well* that Roger was beginning to hope Wyn felt the same way he did. But Wyn hadn't said the words yet and Roger was determined to not expect it of him. What they had was enough, whatever it was. He looked at the wake Torquil made as they strode through the crowd.

"I suppose we can always send them a letter when their ego is a little less…um…"

"Most decidedly," Wyn said. He offered Roger his arm and Roger took it.

"How long is this party going to last?" Roger asked.

"They tend to last into the morning."

Roger stared at him in horror. "Not really?"

"The fae do love a good celebration."

"Heavens," Roger muttered. "In that case we probably shouldn't dance anymore. It wouldn't do for me to fall asleep in the middle of my own wedding party."

Wyn chuckled. "Duly noted."

They continued their way through the crowd, stopping to receive compliments and congratulations. Roger couldn't help the pride that kept leaking into his voice every time he got to talk about the wedding spell. When his siblings approached, he was thoroughly unsurprised by the spell being the first topic of conversation from Bernard, while Frederica wanted to discuss the beautiful ceremony.

"We picked out the flowers together," Roger explained to his sister. "And I'm glad you liked it. We worked very hard on it."

"I can imagine," Bernard replied, stuffing his hands into his pockets. "Father hasn't stopped talking about it. He said you two promised the Council they'd see magic they'd never seen before and you certainly delivered."

Wyn's hand came over Roger's where it still rested on his arm. As was his wont, Wyn stroked fingertips over Roger's knuckles. "Thank you, Mr. Barnes."

Bernard grinned and leaned closer. "I have a multitude of questions for you, you know. I need to know how you practiced with the raw ingredients, which ones you have attempted so far, and what your plans are for future attempts. I need to know if Roger did anything foolish in the practice because he does tend to get a little overenthusiastic when it comes to magic. And I need to know how the two magic systems worked so well together."

Wyn's fingers stopped their stroking and he straightened a little. "Roger did not do anything foolish." This was, of course, thoroughly untrue, although Roger couldn't deny it made him happy to hear Wyn say it. He went on, "He conducted a significant amount of research. We went about everything very cautiously. We worked our way up to the power of the spell you saw today." He paused. "If you wish to know more, I suggest a letter. Then Roger can be as detailed as he likes to be."

Frederica put a hand on Bernard's arm when he opened his mouth—most likely to ask more questions. "He's right. Let them enjoy their wedding."

Bernard glanced between them and chuckled. "Oh, all right. I'll write so you can respond when you're feeling bored and listless in the country."

"Thank you," Roger said quietly after they'd walked away. "It was very kind of you to say that."

"It was the truth," Wyn muttered in an irritable tone.

Roger peeked up at him. "I'm not sure I'd consider our first attempt particularly cautious."

Wyn resumed stroking Roger's hand. "Academics who inherit their family's wealth do all sorts of experiments that are far more dangerous than what we attempted. And they are permitted that luxury because society thinks their scores denote more intelligence or entitlement." He started to pull Roger back into the crowd. "Yes, our first attempt was less than perfect. But you selected a spell that was less violent in nature. No true damage was ever actually done. *And* you didn't do it alone. Does your brother always talk to you like that?"

"Oh, we both took after our father in that regard," Roger answered. "We go about it in different ways, of course. Bernard likes to write essays on the subject. He's always being published in journals and things. So I'm not surprised he had so many questions."

Wyn's lips pinched together. "That wasn't exactly what I meant."

Before Roger could ask what he did mean, Harriet's shout interrupted them. She didn't wait for Roger to drop his hand from Wyn's arm before she threw her arms around his neck in a hug.

"Good Lord!" she shouted. "That was marvelous!" Then she pulled Wyn into a hug, which seemed to take him by surprise.

"You probably ought to ask if he minds that," Anthea commented. "We've had a devil of a time finding you two," she added to Roger. "I give you some leave for being elusive as you are the center of the party, but you didn't need to be this difficult to locate."

"It was completely unacceptable," Harriet agreed, attempting to look annoyed. Although she kept ruining the effect by giving them both calf eyes.

"But that spell was so divine. You two should perform in public more often."

"Really Harriet," Cyril said in an exasperated tone. "Must you make such a suggestion sound so tawdry?" He turned an appreciative eye to Roger's outfit. "Thank God marriage seems to be improving your wardrobe. Color suits you."

"Wyn picked it out," Roger said.

Cyril grinned at Wyn. "Well, that explains everything."

"Roger picked out mine," Wyn added, with a hint of pride.

Cyril blinked in surprise. "Good heavens," he breathed. "Where was this little talent hiding?"

Harriet clasped her hands together. "Love brought it out."

Roger felt his face heat. He stuck a finger under his cravat and tugged a little, self conscious. "Must you, Harriet?"

Anthea laughed. "Still shy about discussing romance, even on your wedding day. You are impossible." She kissed his cheek. "But I forgive you. Congratulations."

"Thank you," he said. He leaned closer to her and whispered, "Are we going to be attending your celebration soon? I noticed you dancing with Lady Fitzhugh earlier."

Anthea glared at him. "Do not get Harriet started," she said through gritted teeth. Then she gave him a sly smile. "And if all goes according to my plans, yes."

"I think it is highly impolite for you to whisper to anyone other than your husband," Harriet commented loudly.

"Oh, go on with you," Anthea laughed, flapping her hands at him.

He bid them all goodbye, giving each a promise to write before Wyn led him away.

"You could have invited them to stay with us," Wyn said. "I'm sure you'd like that."

"Well," Roger admitted. "I wasn't sure when we'd want visitors. And I wasn't entirely sure *you* would like that."

Wyn smiled at him. "We'll discuss it later. The house is big enough for you to have visitors and for me to escape when I need privacy."

Roger had not actually made it so far as to imagine day-to-day married life. He had some vague ideas about Wyn painting while he read, or experimenting with magic together, or curled up in bed together—but his brain always seemed to stop thinking of anything after that.

They accepted congratulations from distinguished guests, more family and friends. Roger did notice, however, that throughout the evening, no one from the Council had approached them with anything other than general compliments and well wishes. He was trying very hard not to be concerned about it. After all, the wedding spell had gone beautifully. Did it really matter if the Council took it as an opportunity to change the way magic was practiced, studied, and discussed? He knew it shouldn't matter. He knew marrying Wyn was the true importance behind the event. But he couldn't help the small worry at the back of his mind that, perhaps, it hadn't been good enough after all.

At one point, Wyn pulled him into a corner and leaned in close to whisper, "Your grip on my arm is getting progressively more tight. I'm not complaining but I do need you to know that tonight isn't going to be any different than Vauxhall Gardens. I won't do anything you don't like."

It took Roger several moments to catch up to what Wyn was talking about. "I wasn't thinking about *that!*" he said. Although, of course, *now* he was.

Wyn cupped his chin and tilted his face up, giving him a long look. "Then what's worrying you?"

Roger wrung his hands a little. "Do you think the Council liked the spell?" he asked in a whisper.

Wyn frowned. "What are you talking about? Of course they liked it. I think most of them have expressed their most adamant praise of it." He paused. "You think they don't mean to adopt it?"

Roger nodded. "And I know it doesn't matter. I know it still went well and I know *we* both plan to continue so it hardly signifies if—"

"Roger," Wyn said gently. "If it's going to worry you for the evening, it matters. We can go ask my grandmother or your father about it if you'd like."

"It's so silly," Roger muttered.

Wyn stroked a thumb over his cheek. "It's not silly," he whispered. "Come on, let's go find your father. I imagine he'd be the easiest one to ask."

It took them some time to locate him, since people continued to stop them. They finally found him sitting next to Councilmember Williams.

"Maybe I can just write to him," Roger said, edging back away.

Wyn sighed. "Come along." And then he practically dragged Roger to the pair of men.

Roger's father beamed up at them. "Looking for me, son? Are you leaving?"

"Not for a while yet," Wyn replied. "But we were wondering if the Council had reached a decision in terms of what we said in our proposal earlier this week."

"Ah," Roger's father said, exchanging a smile with Williams. "We have, actually, but perhaps we ought to get the rest of the members together before we talk about it. Will you excuse me?" he asked of Williams.

Then he slipped away.

Williams gave them both an amused look. "We were going to write to you both about it," he explained. "So as not to take focus away from the wedding."

"I can appreciate that," Wyn said smoothly. "But, of course, you probably know how much this means to us."

Councilmembers began drifting over, having been sent by Roger's father. The chit chat continued in the inane way it had all evening. How nice the flowers were, how well they looked together, weren't Mrs. Wrenwhistle's parties so elegant, did you hear that Pimpernel-Smith person was present and what would they say about the evening's events. No one would give either of them any hint as to what they thought of their other proposals. It made Roger want to scream.

Finally, Roger's father returned with Councilmember Wrenwhistle. She smiled at both of them and then exchanged a look with Councilmember Williams.

"You both did a remarkable job on the spell. We were all very impressed," she began.

"Haven't been able to stop talking about it," Councilmember Cricket piped in.

Councilmember Williams stood. "We think your proposals—all three of them—have a great deal of merit. Your first proposal was already accepted of course. But we'd like to explore your ideas about raw materials and combined magic."

Roger's father stepped forward and placed a hand on his shoulder. "And we think you two are a force to be reckoned with when it comes to magic and magical innovation. We've discussed the matter and we're in agreement that your combined talents can and should continue to make an impact."

Councilmember Wrenwhistle put her hand on Wyn's arm. "We'd like to offer you both positions on the Council," she announced. "You can continue your work with our resources to assist you. And the process to have your proposals heard and accepted will be significantly less arduous."

Roger could hardly believe what he was hearing. Their proposals had been accepted. All of them! And a position on the Council? That was usually reserved for people with high scores. Heirs or those who had come in second. Who was Roger to receive such an honor?

But the idea of having a more willing audience for solutions and ideas made him giddy. This could change everything. They could have an additional income. They could experiment and research with more funds and the opinions of experts. He glanced up at Wyn to gauge his reaction and then his thoughts screeched to a halt. They couldn't take the position. Wyn couldn't stay in London. Roger had no desire to keep his husband trapped in a city he hated, merely for his own gain.

"That's really very kind of you," he began.

Wyn's hand covered his own. "Indeed. We are honored. Can we think about it and discuss before giving our answer?"

Wyn's grandmother smiled. "Of course, darling."

Roger's father squeezed his shoulder. "Enjoy the evening and think about it at your leisure. Our offer won't change."

Wyn turned to lead Roger away but Roger paused. "Can I make one suggestion?"

Councilmember Williams laughed. "Do you ever run out of them, young man?"

Roger blushed. "It wouldn't change our answer either way. But have you ever considered adding an uneven number of members to the Council? Someone to aid in the case of ties?" He hesitated. "Someone, perhaps, who is not represented currently, and who could stand to gain much by having their voice heard?"

Councilmember Williams frowned. "What do you mean?"

Wyn squeezed Roger's hand in encouragement.

"Someone of half-fae and half-human descent," Roger explained. "They experience so much prejudice and unkindness. And they would offer a suitable neutral party at the center of the Council. Even one would be sufficient, although I think several would be advisable."

His father looked thoughtful.

Wyn leaned forward. "And if you're unsure, you might consider talking to Pimpernel-Smith. They're present at the party, after all. I'm sure they would offer a strong opinion." He smiled at Roger. "I might even suggest them as a viable candidate." Then he led Roger away before he could make any more suggestions.

CHAPTER 81

WYN

AFTER LEAVING the councilmembers with something to ponder, Wyn took Roger past the drink table to collect some champagne for himself. He couldn't get the look on Roger's face out of his mind. Or the one on his grandmother's, for that matter. A position on the Council? For both of them? Since when did anyone think Wyn was an appropriate choice for a role with such great responsibility?

In theory, the idea was not entirely preposterous. The gap between him and Emrys was so thin one could hardly slide in a few sheets of spellpaper when it came to their ranking. But the fact remained that Wyn had been fighting to *leave* London for more years than he could remember. The responsibility fell to Emrys, not him.

The bubbles of his drink tickled his nose as he took a delicate sip, before peering down at Roger on his arm.

He realized it was time to change that course of thinking.

Wyn would be responsible for their new home. He would be responsible for deciding what happened to the land around it and the people he employed.

Wyn's chest squeezed as Roger laughed at something someone said.

He would be responsible for taking care of this precious man, giving him everything he desired to the best of his ability. Family wealth would help a great deal in that regard, but Wyn had come to learn that sometimes money was not the only requirement in making someone happy.

His mind flashed to some of the most seemingly insignificant moments he and Roger had shared during their time together. Wyn kissing Roger's fingers in the opera box. Their strolls through the Park. Sharing copious amounts of tea and sweets. Lying on the floor and laughing until their stomachs ached. Plucking little bits of flower confetti out of Roger's hair while he smiled at him.

Wyn knew what their answer to the Council would be. He could already feel the quill pen in his hand, ready to write out their acceptance so that Roger wouldn't have to worry about his handwriting in such an important moment. They would sign their names at the bottom, together, and seal the letter with their new stamp in the wax.

There was plenty of time for that, though.

Nobody would expect to hear from them for at least a week, if not more.

Wyn finished his drink and handed the glass away, before he leaned down to gently press his nose to the soft spot just below Roger's ear.

"I'd like to take you home now," he whispered.

A GRIN TUGGED at Wyn's lips as their carriage turned through a high gate. His magic buzzed in his chest, longing to be set free in a place it already knew it would be welcomed.

Wyn turned his attention to where Roger was tucked into his side, head lolling against his shoulder with each dip in the road. He'd fallen asleep almost instantly as they'd left the estate. Wyn had been more than willing to keep an arm around his waist and allow him his rest.

"Roger," Wyn murmured, rubbing his free hand on Roger's thigh.

Roger drew in a breath and sat up, blinking at his surroundings.

"Oh, *drat*," he said groggily, tugging at his coat. "Did I fall asleep? I was hoping to pay attention to the road so I could become familiar with where we are."

Wyn held back on his smile. "It's dark out. You'll learn it soon enough."

The carriage eased to a stop and Wyn peered at the house as the door was opened. He got out and filled his lungs with the fresh, crisp air, before he offered Roger his hand.

It turned out he needed both hands as Roger nearly tumbled out onto the ground. Wyn reached to catch him before he could fall as Roger gave a yelp of surprise.

"Watch it," Wyn said with a chuckle as Roger regained his balance. "I didn't see you drinking enough tonight for all of that." Wyn could still feel the bubbles from his last drink working on his system, mild but pleasant.

"I-I wasn't," Roger managed, his mouth hanging open. Wyn followed Roger's gaze over his own shoulder to the house. He arched a brow and turned back to Roger.

"Do you like it?" he asked, releasing his steadying grip in favor of taking one of Roger's hands and lacing their fingers together. Wyn expected a bit of Roger's familiar sputtering and stuttering, but all he got was silence. Wyn's expression turned more serious as he worried that perhaps Roger didn't like it at all.

"It's *massive!*" Roger finally blurted.

"It's only seven bedrooms," Wyn said, almost defensively. "Or well, I suppose it's six now."

Roger gave him an incredulous look. "I see what you meant when you said you'd have room to escape. You could have guests and not even be able to find them for days!"

Wyn laughed at that and tugged gently on Roger's hand. "Let's have a look at what sort of mess Mother has made of the inside."

Their arrival had been expected, of course, so the staff was waiting to greet them. Wyn and Roger listened dutifully as introductions were made, and then Wyn promptly dismissed them all until it was time for a late—*very* late—breakfast come morning.

As Wyn had become accustomed to, nearly every room smelled of fresh paint and furniture oil. The pillows on the beds and sofas were fluffed to perfection. The mirrors and shelves hadn't one speck of dust on them. It felt as though they had stepped into the backdrop of a painting, with each space designed so carefully that it must've been done with an artist's touch.

Eventually, they came to one of the few doors that hadn't been propped open. Wyn squeezed Roger's hand.

"Have you got your key?" he asked.

"Oh!" Roger said excitedly as he reached for his pocket. "Yes, it's… somewhere…" Roger patted his hand over another pocket, then another, and finally let go of Wyn's hand so he could dig into another. When he pulled it out and held it up for Wyn to see, he felt his insides warm at the sight of what was attached to it. It was the thin silk ribbon he'd tied around the box he'd wrapped the key in. His *real* engagement gift.

It took Roger a couple of tries to fit the key into the lock in the low light of the hallway. When the latch gave, the two of them exchanged a look, and Roger turned the handle and pushed the door open.

Roger took the candle Wyn had been carrying and began touching the flame to the candles scattered about the room. Wyn wandered to one of the windows and pushed it open, satisfied with what he could see of the view in the moonlight. When he turned back around, he was pleased to find that everything looked exactly as he'd wanted it to.

"Are these my books?" Roger asked as he stepped closer to one of the bookshelves that stretched all the way to the ceiling.

"They should be," Wyn said, making his way to Roger's side so they could inspect them together. "Their instructions were to put all of your things where they belonged, except for the old furniture."

Wyn watched as Roger's head tilted to the right, his fingertips walking gently along the spines as he read the titles on them. Then he took a step back and looked at the rest of the shelves, many of which sat empty.

"There's so much space," Roger marveled.

"I had to take into consideration all of the new books you'll be needing," Wyn said easily. "I have my books to add, as well, if you'd like them to be all in one place."

Roger grinned up at him. "I'd like that very much."

The nap Roger had taken seemed to give him all the energy he needed to start making the space his own. Wyn settled comfortably on the chaise lounge he'd selfishly picked out for himself and watched as Roger scuttled about the room. It took no time at all for him to tear off a piece of spellpaper, find his ingredients, and cast a fire spell in the generously-sized hearth.

Wyn caught Roger's wrist as he started back for his desk. He crossed one ankle over the other to give Roger more room to sit down with him. Roger wrung his hands in his lap as he watched the guttering flames he'd made.

"This all feels like a dream," he admitted quietly. Wyn smirked.

"Not a bad one, I hope?" He'd meant for it to be lighthearted, but even he could hear the honesty in his words as he spoke them.

Roger's lips twitched into a grin.

"The best kind of dream," Roger told him. "The kind you never think will actually happen, no matter how badly you want it to."

Wyn's expression softened. "Is this truly what you want?"

Roger turned to look at him then, their eyes meeting. Roger's mouth bunched up to one side and then he nodded. "Yes."

Wyn's heart fluttered in his chest as he sat up off his cloud of pillows. He brought his hands to either side of Roger's face and closed his eyes, pressing their mouths together for a soft, slow kiss. He felt Roger lean into it, which was what he'd been hoping for, but the surprise came when Roger shifted to angle his body more, one hand gripping Wyn's lapel as the other found its way to the back of his neck. Heat coursed through Wyn's body as Roger made a pleading little sound.

They were already breathing hard when they pulled apart, and Wyn was quickly losing all hope of making this moment at least somewhat romantic for Roger. He wasn't one to kiss and tell, but he could already hear Harriet and Anthea and Cyril begging Roger for all the details. That was his place to decide how much he wanted to share; all he hoped was that it would make him turn pink in a good way, not from the embarrassment of it being over too quickly.

With as much restraint as he could muster, Wyn moved his hands from Roger's face and tucked his thumbs under the fabric of Roger's coat lapels so he could push it off Roger's shoulders. Roger wriggled a bit to help with the process, and Wyn kissed him again as he tossed the coat aside.

Roger broke their kiss to protest. "Wyn, that's brand new!"

"I'll buy you a thousand just like it," Wyn promised him as he toed his shoes off so he could move up on his knees. Roger bent to remove his own shoes as Wyn stripped off his coat and began to unfasten the buttons of his waistcoat. He grinned as he watched Roger start on his own.

Wyn encouraged Roger to take his place against the pillows as he got to his feet, stepping over their discarded clothes so he could reach for a drawer on one of the side tables nearby. He pulled out the small vial and brought it back with him, feeling Roger's heavy gaze the entire time.

"What've you got?" Roger asked warily as Wyn settled back onto the chaise on bent knees, his legs on either side of Roger's.

"You'll see." He set the bottle aside and tugged at the knot of his cravat. The silky fabric slithered to the floor as he dropped it and undid the top few buttons of his shirt, before he pulled it off over his head and tossed it away.

Roger stared up at him as though he'd just performed a human spell all on his own. Wyn curled a finger under Roger's chin and gently closed his mouth. He leaned down to give him another soft peck on the lips before he untied the knot of Roger's cravat, as well.

"Wyndham," Roger panted.

"Hm?" Wyn asked, sitting back on his heels.

"Do I have to…that is, I mean, must I take *all* of my clothes off?"

Wyn's brows went up a bit at the question. "Of course not," he said easily. A layer of guilt coated his stomach as he realized that maybe he really was going too fast. "You don't have to do anything you don't want to do. And you can change your mind."

The force of Roger's swallow was audible, and Wyn placed his hand on Roger's cheek, stroking his thumb there.

"Is this more than you wanted? Should I put my shirt back on?"

"No!" Roger squeaked, before covering his mouth with his fingers.

"I see." Wyn paused for a moment. "How about this? I'll do what makes me most comfortable, and you'll tell me the same for yourself, whatever it may be."

"All right," Roger whispered shakily.

Wyn pressed a kiss to Roger's forehead.

"Shirt?" he asked, plucking at the fabric of it. Roger shook his head, and Wyn sat back a bit more. "Trousers?" he tried. After a long pause, Roger gave the tiniest nod. Wyn hummed his understanding and shuffled down Roger's legs toward the end of the chaise and began unfastening them. He was surprised at what he found underneath.

"Of all the nights to wear drawers," he chuckled, giving Roger an amused smile. Roger brought his hands up to cover his face. The new band on his finger flashed in the firelight and caught Wyn's attention.

Sliding it over his knuckles during the ceremony with all of London watching had felt like little more than tradition, but looking at it now in this moment made for just the two of them, a warmth spread through him.

He remembered his brother's words. It was more than a ring. It was a promise.

"I read that it's...supposed to build intrigue for the wedding night," Roger explained miserably. Wyn curled his fingers around Roger's wrists so he could move his hands away from his face. His lips brushed over the band on Roger's left hand before he placed a lingering kiss to it.

"Every single thing about you intrigues me," he said gently. "But I do appreciate the effort." Wyn stood up and undid his own trousers so he could push them down off his hips. "Unfortunately, I was not aware that under-things were a part of wedding tradition." Watching Roger struggle to decide if he should look or not was painfully entertaining, but Wyn ended his suffering as fast as he could manage as he pulled his trousers the rest of the way off, along with his stockings, and sank to his knees at the edge of the chaise.

Roger stared at him. Wyn stared back.

When Roger didn't say or do anything else, Wyn stuck the tip of his tongue out to wet his lips and pulled the bottom one between his teeth. In past experiences, having a man just lie there and watch him hadn't been a particularly good sign. But Wyn could clearly see that Roger was aroused by what they were doing. He seemed like he wanted to continue.

Wyn stopped chewing on his lip. He realized that it had nothing to do with how much Roger wanted this. He'd simply never done anything like it before.

That heavy feeling of new responsibility washed over Wyn as he tugged at Roger's trousers. "Lift your hips a bit?" he asked, and Roger did.

Wyn continued until Roger was left in his stockings and shirt, looking flushed and mussed and deliciously inviting. "Is it all right if I continue?" Wyn asked, and Roger nodded. Wyn wondered if Roger had lost his ability to speak altogether as he leaned up to kiss him, his hand sliding flat over the thin fabric covering Roger's soft stomach. He let that hand wander as their kisses got slower, until Wyn's fingers found Roger's erection and he gripped him confidently.

Roger whimpered against Wyn's mouth as his hand started to move.

The heat from the fire at Wyn's back grew more intense, and it was only then that he realized his magic had crept free, pulling air from the window and feeding the flames.

As Wyn abandoned Roger's kisses and leaned down to take him in his mouth, there was a *whoosh* of life from the hearth. The precious little brain power Wyn had left to spare told him that the situation was edging toward hazard. He pulled off of Roger—which caused the most scrumptious moan to escape the man—and sent a rush of wind toward the fire, putting it out along with all of the candles in the room.

"That's better," Wyn muttered under his breath as he worked Roger with his hand again. He remembered the little vial and reached for where he'd tucked it in between the cushions. The scent of rose oil was strong as he uncapped it and poured a generous amount into his hand.

"Pull your shirt up some?" Wyn asked, partially because both of his hands were coated with the viscous liquid now as he rubbed them together, but also to make sure Roger was holding up all right. Roger did as he asked as Wyn kissed his neck, nuzzling the spot after with his nose as he gripped Roger's length again.

Wyn's other hand found its way between his own legs, and for a time they both dissolved into nothing but heavy breaths and soft noises.

"Wyn—" Roger moaned tightly, his hips jerking a bit.

"Yes," Wyn breathed, moving up off the floor and settling himself over Roger. He supported his weight on one arm by Roger's head against the pillows and kissed him deeply as he collected both of them in his other hand, working them together. Wyn broke their kiss before his lungs screamed, resting his forehead against Roger's, and suddenly something lit up in his brain.

Roger's hands had finally come to life, but not in the way Wyn ever would've expected. He'd grown so used to the rough-groping, back-scratching, hair-pulling encounters of his past that he almost couldn't process what was happening.

One of Roger's hands had come to rest on Wyn's lower back. But with the other, he was stroking Wyn's upper arm in the most heartachingly gentle way. And Wyn realized, there in the new study, with Roger tucked neatly beneath him, that he was doing something he'd never done before, either.

He and his husband were making love.

Wyn let out a shaky groan as this realization filled him up.

He moved his hand from between them and continued rocking their hips together as he brought his palm to the side of Roger's face so he could kiss him. Roger kissed him back, and Wyn pushed his fingers through Roger's hair as tenderly as he could manage before he pulled his hand away to snap his fingers.

Fairy lights flooded the air above their heads, floating and pulsing and making a spectacle of themselves as Wyn knew they would.

Roger gasped loudly in delight, and then his breath caught as Wyn's hand came between them again. Wyn felt the pressure grow where Roger was holding his hip and shoulder, fingertips pressing into his sweat dampened skin. Wyn leaned hard into the thickness of the air as their emotions and his magic swirled, stirring the fairy lights much the same as they had done during their wedding spell. He kissed Roger's neck when he came with a breathy moan, and pressed his mouth to Roger's as he found his own release soon after.

Discovering their bedroom would have to wait one more night.

CHAPTER 82

ROGER

AFTER WYN'S RELEASE, he collapsed onto the chaise lounge, practically on top of Roger, although Roger was certain he had tried to avoid putting all of his weight on him. He found he didn't mind. Their breathing was heavy and labored as they both came down from the experience.

Then Wyn nuzzled into the crook of Roger's neck. "I'll get something to clean us up."

Roger tightened the hand on Wyn's arm. "Not yet," he whispered. "Stay here." He swallowed. "Please."

Wyn shifted so he was wedged against the back of the chaise lounge, taking more of his weight off of Roger. He felt a kiss on his jaw. "Hmm. We'll need to be washed later. I suppose we'll have to have a bath together then." Wyn's kisses returned to Roger's neck. "What a pity."

Roger smiled at the sarcasm lacing Wyn's voice. His smile grew when Wyn's hand drifted down his chest and over his stomach. Gentle fingers slid under Roger's shirt, coming to rest on his waist. Wyn tucked his head against Roger's shoulder and Roger found his own hand coming up to twine in Wyn's hair.

Roger glanced at the banked fire, thinking about how it had blazed when Wyn had dropped to his knees and brought Roger's erection into his mouth, and then how Wyn had gotten rid of all of the flames completely with the wind that flew through the window. Even in the heat of the moment, Wyn was thinking about their safety.

Roger looked up at the ceiling. The fairy lights had vanished shortly after their release. He was sure it was absurd to be thinking about magic at a time like that but he had finally understood what Wyn had been talking about in Hyde Park. The lights had been brighter, sharper, and even more mesmerizing the closer Wyn had gotten to climax. Roger found himself eager to see them that way again. He liked having a visible indication of Wyn's emotions by way of his magic. He wondered idly what else Wyn would show him, now that they were safely in the country.

The moon cast a faint glow in the room, and as Roger's eyes adjusted to the darkness, he was able to make out the bookshelves and the desk. He ran a hand through Wyn's hair. Wyn had given him so much. He might have worried if he deserved it. From anyone else, he surely would have counted that fear at the top of his list. But Wyn had settled onto the chaise lounge so naturally that Roger had a feeling it had been installed in the room for that very purpose. He couldn't put into words what that meant. Not only did Wyn feel he deserved this marvelous space, but he wanted to see him use it.

Roger had never had a space that he could truly take up. The little rooms he'd rented with his parents' money had been close. But he had always known it was temporary and it had been hard to feel fully at home with the clatter of neighbors on all sides. And of course, the makeshift study in his parents' home was never intended to be his. But *this*—this was different. The desk had been designed with him in mind. The shelves had been installed with room for growth. Everything had been placed in such a way that he would have all the space he needed to work, and Wyn had carved a space for himself in there as well. As if any place where Roger felt most comfortable was where Wyn belonged too.

Wyn's weight settled more heavily on him as his breathing slowed. Roger tilted his head to kiss Wyn's forehead.

"I love it here," he whispered. "I love…" He took a deep breath. "I love *you*. I'm sure it's very cowardly for me to wait until you're sleeping to admit it, but well, I'm not always good with words, you know. I'll have to try and find a more capable way of showing you that I love you. I've never admitted it," he went on, "but I've fancied you for years. Of course, back then I fancied you because you were so beautiful and refined. So impossibly elegant. But now—God, you're so much more than any of that. You're so kind and clever. You make me a better person. You give me courage I've never possessed and you make my dreams seem possible. I don't know how I ever got by without you, truly I don't."

He pressed another soft kiss to Wyn's forehead. "I know you're the one responsible for the finances and everything, so I imagine you expect to be the one to take care of us. And Lord knows you take care of me far better than I'd ever dreamed. But...but I hope you know I intend to take care of you too, in my own way. We'll discuss it when you're awake, of course, but I think we ought to decline the Council's offer. Yes, it's a wonderful opportunity. But I refuse to force you into another cage. London will get by just fine without us." He took a shaky breath.

"Thank you for tonight. For everything. I would never have guessed that our project would turn into everything I never dared to hope for. It bears repeating—probably when you're conscious, to be frank—but...I love you. I love you more than I've loved anyone in my entire life. I count myself impossibly fortunate to have gained your friendship. I promise to never take that for granted, Wyndham Wrenwhistle."

Then as the wind curled through the window, ruffling the curtains and skimming over their skin, Roger settled himself under Wyn's weight and fell asleep.

TORQUIL'S TRIBUNE

Greetings, fantastic folk and heavenly humans,

Well, the event of the Season has come to an end, and what an event it was. Mrs. Wrenwhistle is surely to be congratulated for what can only be described as a triumph. Everyone is talking about how beautiful the wedding was. The flowers, the lighting, even the hostess' clothing added to the splendor. This marriage has been heralded as a promising start to better fae and human relations and the wedding most certainly reflected that. Guests from both sets mingled and celebrated together. While many have bemoaned the timing of this event so early in the Season, this writer hopes it will set the tone for a more harmonious social period.

The two grooms were beautifully dressed, each with a distinct style but with corresponding shades of blue. A lovely nod to the union as a whole. Their wedding spell had been much anticipated as Mr. Wrenwhistle promised the Council for Fae & Human Magical Relations that it would be like nothing they had ever seen. While many have been wary of such a promise, it cannot be denied that the gentlemen delivered. The spell was a marvelous blending of magic, showing outsiders a glimpse into a love both pure and complex, as all love should be.

The spell was the topic of much conversation in the celebration afterwards as Mr. Roger Wrenwhistle (*née* Barnes) used a whole and untreated willow branch for his portion. As many know, human magic does not use raw materials as it can be dangerous and always impacts the power of the spell. That alone is worth noting.

To see the two distinct magics blend together seamlessly in a spell will undoubtedly cause the Council much debate. What does it mean for the future of magic? Were humans and fae always meant to cast together? This writer hopes that the two gentlemen have uncovered a secret that will change the shape of magic for centuries to come.

As this column will likely receive a tirade of complaints about the lack of attention to any of the other guests, here are some additional observations to pacify those readers:

Miss Aveline Wrenwhistle looked lovely in a cream-colored gown. She had no shortage of dance partners throughout the whole of the evening.

Miss Anthea St. Clair was seen dancing twice with Lady Fitzhugh. Sources say that a proposal is likely any day now.

Mr. Thompson and Miss Thakery were inseparable, as they usually are. Upon personal inspection, this writer hazards a guess that romance may not be the best description for the pair. However, platonic love is not to be dismissed. A union may yet come to pass and the pair might indeed become one of the happiest couples in England.

Mr. Auberon Wrenwhistle and Mrs. Rose Wrenwhistle were also present and many were pleased to see that romance has certainly not lessened in their time together. They continue to be one of the most beautiful couples.

A final bit of news for our gentle readers. This humble writer has been offered a unique and exceptional honor: to join the Council for Fae & Human Magical Relations. This offer has, of course, been accepted. Other offers were also extended, apparently, over the course of the evening. Although we will refrain from announcing them until official acceptance has been sent, as it inevitably will. Readers can continue to expect the best gossip in town from this modest column. That was a stipulation upon acceptance.

After such a magnificent start to the Season, many wonder what could possibly come next. This writer thinks the rest of the single people of

London should consider relaxing for once, and simply enjoy themselves this year. The most recently married couple have already taken care of enough drama and excitement to satisfy the throng for a little while yet.

Your esteemed editor,

Torquil Pimpernel-Smith

EPILOGUE

WYN

THE LIGHT PATTERING of rain against the slanted glass roof of the sunroom was wonderfully conducive to the lazy morning Wyn had been hoping for. It wasn't quite as nice as if they'd been able to take their breakfast in the garden, but they'd already done that a couple of times, so he wasn't about to complain. After such a rare stretch of perfect weather, it was no surprise to anyone when the storms had finally rolled in overnight.

Four days. Four days of sunshine, of fresh air, of doing absolutely nothing aside from eating and sleeping and making zero attempt to spend one second away from one another.

Wyn couldn't remember a time when he'd felt happier.

When Notley and two other servants strolled in with their trays, Wyn waved a hand toward the table and chairs he and Roger had abandoned in favor of their position on the floor.

"You can leave everything," Wyn instructed them. "But I'll take the cream and saucer here." He accepted both items, placing the small dish on the ground between them so he could carefully pour in the cream.

"There we are," Roger cooed, sliding it closer to the bundle of fur huddling close to him. Wyn watched with great interest as the small ginger cat stuck its nose out to inspect the offering before it made quick work of its own breakfast.

The storms had proven to be frightening to more than just Roger. Wyn had heard strange cries coming from somewhere outside, and they'd taken the soaked animal in before they could even get a good look at it.

Judging by the adoration painted on Roger's face ever since, Wyn could only assume that they'd found themselves the companion Roger had been wanting. It was a scrawny little thing, and evidently very hungry. It lapped at the cream so readily that specks of it flew up and stuck to its whiskers.

Wyn chuckled and arched a brow at Roger.

"Yet another family member to get morsels of food all over the place while they eat, it seems," he said playfully. "Perhaps my mother was right all along."

Roger feigned being hurt with a scoff as he reached out to stroke the cat behind its ears. "If you're willing to know this about me and still keep me around, then certainly you'll allow us to take care of the poor thing, as well."

"Yes, very well," Wyn sighed out. "I suppose it will be worth the sacrifice." Roger gave him a cheeky grin and Wyn returned it with a wink.

Four days of sunshine, and fresh air, and moments like these when his heart swelled so much that Wyn thought it would burst right out of his chest. Wyn sat up from where he was reclined on his side and moved to sit beside Roger. This was apparently unacceptable, as the cat darted away from them and disappeared behind some of the potted plants near the windows. Wyn stared after it, perplexed.

"What happened? I didn't even touch it."

Roger laughed and moved closer to Wyn's side.

"Cats can be quite nervous little things," he explained. Wyn hummed and placed a kiss on Roger's temple as he settled his weight back against his hands.

"Scared of thunderstorms, messy eater, generally anxious. Are you also a cat?" Wyn asked. Roger laughed lightly and shrugged.

"Perhaps," Roger said, shifting more so he and Wyn ended up lying on the floor together. Wyn put one arm behind his head as he wrapped the other around Roger's shoulders. It already felt so natural for Roger's head to settle against the curve of his neck. A smirk played across Wyn's lips as Roger tucked a leg over in between his own.

"You are also very soft and adorable," Wyn reasoned. "It's all becoming so clear."

Roger's laughter turned more self-conscious as he buried his face against Wyn's neck, and Wyn held him tighter.

"I suppose it makes sense," Roger mumbled, and Wyn was almost certain that his pause was marked with a gentle kiss to the skin just above the collar of his shirt. They'd both taken to wearing only shirts and trousers around the house, if anything at all. "For why we disliked each other so."

"Why is that?" Wyn asked mildly.

"Well, if I am a cat, and you are a bird…" Roger trailed off. This time, Wyn knew the press of Roger's lips to his throat. He swallowed and considered Roger's words. A bird?

"Wrenwhistle," Wyn finally realized. He brought his hand up from Roger's back to thread his fingers through his hair. "You are clever, aren't you?"

Wyn's magic tingled in his chest, a match to the way his heart started to beat a little faster thanks to Roger's teasing, and Wyn made no attempt to stop it.

As Wyn used his fingers under Roger's chin to tilt his face up for a kiss, he felt his magic stretch and swirl, searching for a place to land. He didn't have to open his eyes to know that the plants all around them grew more vibrant all at once. The blooms opened wider, gaping at Wyn and Roger there on the ground. The small crack in the open window was all Wyn needed to draw the air in, and when they finally broke apart, it was as though the entire room was *alive*.

Flowers bobbed, leaves swayed, hanging ferns stretched all the way to the floor. Even the rivulets of rainwater seemed desperate to join them, dancing across the glass in patterns that made no sense at all.

As Roger watched the spectacle unfold around them, Wyn could see nothing but him. Wyn brushed his knuckles against Roger's cheek, finally drawing his attention back.

"I cannot promise you that we will never argue again," Wyn started, speaking a little louder than he'd had to before to be heard over the swishing greenery. "And I cannot promise you that we will never disagree. But I think, perhaps, that may be useful when it comes time to settle issues with our fellow councilmembers."

Roger's smile faded instantly, replaced with confusion and surprise. Wyn cupped his cheek, his thumb tracing slowly back and forth under his eye. Some of the rustling leaves quieted, though the rain continued to come down harder.

"I know what I've said about wanting to leave London for good," Wyn went on. "But if the last several days are any indication, then I feel most certain that no matter where we go, as long as we go together, I will be just fine."

"Wyn," Roger breathed out, shaking his head. "I could not possibly—"

"We will keep the house here in the country," Wyn cut him off gently. "And we will have a place in town. We will arrive not one hour sooner than we must, and we will return here the moment we are allowed to leave. We will continue in the role that has been built for us, serving as an example of what humans and fae are truly capable of when they put all other issues aside."

Wyn took a steadying breath and gave Roger a soft look of hope.

"As badly as I want to keep you here all to myself, I would be doing the rest of the world a disservice if I did not allow your beautiful mind the freedom it deserves. To continue solving problems. To make things better where nobody else has even thought to try."

Wyn swallowed at the lump that formed in the back of his throat, emotion prickling there and at the backs of his eyes.

"I love you, Roger," he said. "And I want to give you more than the life you and I can build together. I want you to have everything. And if that means I get to spend six months of the year in London, attending one ridiculous event after another, then I will do it. Because I will have you on my arm, and in my heart, and I could never ask for anything more."

Wyn blinked and felt hot tears roll down his cheeks. He moved to quickly wipe them away, but Roger was faster, grabbing his face with both hands and kissing him softly.

When they pulled apart, Wyn huffed out an embarrassed little laugh.

"Does that sound most agreeable?" he tried, his voice weak.

Roger's chin wobbled as he smiled so big that it crinkled his eyes. "Yes."

The End

NOTE FROM THE AUTHORS

Greetings, Radiant Readers,

This story started when Sarah posted a tweet in her Instagram story. The tweet was simply a historical romance story prompt. But when Shannon replied to the story with the suggestion that they should write the story together, Sarah immediately jumped on the opportunity.

What passed afterwards was six weeks of feverish writing. We were like two people possessed. From the get-go, the collaboration has been nothing short of magical. We were both completely obsessed with the story, the characters, and the world. Brainstorming had never been more exciting. Phone calls got longer and longer. Writing this story felt like the ultimate treat: to write something we each enjoyed, while simultaneously reading a new story that felt tailor-made to our interests.

When we finished the rough draft, it felt like emerging back into the real world again. The lack of conversation and writing felt like withdrawal. It wasn't long before we started talking about sequels.

We hope you enjoyed this story. A lot of heart and passion went into it. And we hope you'll stick around for the next installment of the *Fae & Human Relations* series because there's even more magic to come.

Your winsome writers,
Sarah & Shannon

ACKNOWLEDGMENTS

This book wouldn't be possible without our network of support. Thank you to our alpha readers, Ashley, Alexis, Katie, and Lellie. Thank you to our beta readers, Kayla, Anna, and Meg. Thank you to our amazing editor, Mackenzie! Thank you to our wonderful proofreader, Ashley. Thank you to our fantastic narrator, Matt. Thank you to all of our cheerleaders who encouraged us throughout the process, especially John and Ashley.

And thank you to fran @galacticidiots, who wrote the tweet that started this entire story.

Thank you to Shannon for having the courage to suggest a collaboration. And thank you to Sarah for agreeing to it.

Cover art: Caras Alexandra
Editor: Mackenzie Walton
Proofreader: Ashley Scout

ALSO BY...

ALSO BY SARAH WALLACE

Letters to Half Moon Street

One Good Turn

The Education of Pip

Dear Bartleby

The Glamour Spell of Rose Talbot - Free to all newsletter subscribers!

ALSO BY S.O. CALLAHAN

Fella Enchanted

Fella Ever After

ABOUT SARAH WALLACE

Sarah Wallace lives in Florida with their cat, more books than she has time to read, a large collection of classic movies, and an apartment full of plants that are surviving against all odds. They only read books that end happily.

ABOUT S.O. CALLAHAN

S.O. Callahan has always been fond of sweet things, namely chocolate and love stories. When she's not writing or reading, she enjoys baking, visiting National Parks and Historic Sites, and traveling with her husband. They live in Georgia and have two very spoiled cats named Ozzy and Beau.

Milton Keynes UK
Ingram Content Group UK Ltd.
UKHW040914230124
436466UK00024B/574